3/09 10⁰⁰

ID1008565

ABANDON

ABANDON

A Romance

PICO IYER

Alfred A. Knopf  *New York 2003*

THIS IS A BORZOI BOOK
PUBLISHED BY ALFRED A. KNOPF

Copyright © 2003 by Pico Iyer
All rights reserved under International and Pan-American
Copyright Conventions. Published in the United States by Alfred
A. Knopf, a division of Random House, Inc., New York, and
simultaneously in Canada by Random House of Canada Limited,
Toronto. Distributed by Random House, Inc., New York.
www.aaknopf.com

Owing to limitations of space, all acknowledgments for permission to reprint
previously published material may be found following "A Note of Thanks."

Knopf, Borzoi Books, and the colophon are registered trademarks
of Random House, Inc.

Library of Congress Cataloging-in-Publication Data
Iyer, Pico.
Abandon / Pico Iyer — 1st ed.
p.   cm.
ISBN 0-375-41505-X
1. British—California—Fiction.   2. California—Fiction.   3. Actresses—
Fiction.   4. Sufism—Fiction.   I. Title.

PS3559. Y47 A64 2003
813'.54—dc21   2002070059

Manufactured in the United States of America
First Edition

All the events and characters in this book are made up. The
author—to pick examples at random—has never been to Iran,
never attended a Sufi conference or seminar, never even met
a Sufi. All lectures, articles, and newspaper clippings—and most
poems—included in the text are peculiar to this book.
It is, in short, a work of complete and utter fiction.

Fire is the most tolerable third party.

—Thoreau

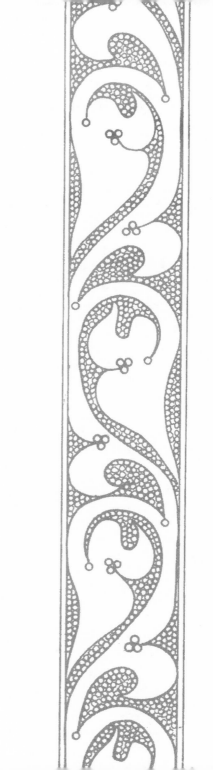

I

He reached for his alarm clock in the dark, and then realized that the sound was coming from somewhere else. All across the city the long, slow, heart-torn cry of love—*"La ilaha illa 'Llah"* (There is no god but God)—rose up, as if from a widow in her grief alone. Pulling back the curtains, he saw the high-rises with their rickety antennae in the brownish light, pictures of Assad the size of six-story buildings, green-lit minarets standing sentinel across the town. Nearby, on the hill, a scatter of lights, and then the desert began.

He went down, as was now his custom, to the lobby—two women slumped enigmatically in chairs—and saw a pair of taxis idling under the line of trees. He walked up to the first, tapped at the window, and the man, startled from his sleep, reached back a lazy arm to open the door. Then they drove through the hushed, still-darkened streets to where the suq began, inside what looked to be a Crusader castle.

Even now the smell of cardamom and spices, as if, he always thought, he were walking into a curry. The store where they'd shown him a manuscript, two days before, that came, they said, from Isfahan; the other stall, where the owner, it was rumored, was a member of the secret orders. Everywhere, thin alleyways trailing off into silence, and then, five minutes later, out again into the faint light to see a few huddled figures slipping into the great mosque through its northern entrance. He followed them in, and a huge flock of pigeons took sudden flight, lit up against the blue-black sky, and settled around the minarets like guards.

Inside the prayer hall, everything was hushed. But everywhere, across the red-carpeted space, was a sense of murmurous chant, as if the building itself were muttering prayers under its breath. Mullahs sat here and there, thirty or forty before them, and delivered soft talks on the faithful's duties. A woman sat on a raised platform at the center of the hall, reading her Quran while her son banged his legs impatiently on the step. Under the great dome, tall students from the desert countries paced back and forth, reciting their holy verses in a quiet singsong.

He'd been told that someone might approach him here, in the safety of the sacred place at dawn. No one knew who the Sufis were, of course—not even their partners or their children—but if anyone were to make contact, his adviser had told him, it would most likely be here, under cover, as it were. He watched a gang of elders walk across the carpets, clapping rough hands on familiar shoulders, telling their beads. Not far away, a young man was sitting in front of a mihrab, so motionless and alone it looked as if he had taken flight himself, and lost himself in the silence all around.

The visitor watched and watched, but no one showed any sign of acknowledging him. Defeated, he got up and slipped out, through the southern entrance this time, into the riddle of lanes that snake around the Old City, this way and that, like a theological argument. Passageways so narrow that opposing houses seem to touch on their second floors; alleyways that lead to alleyways, and then under archways too low for a man to walk through without bowing. Colorful checkerboard doors in the low walls, and, now and then, in the distance, the outline of a fruit tree, a minaret.

The streets were always deserted at this hour, no sound to keep him company but the fall of his own footsteps. Following a dusty alleyway—a woman in black emerged from a door, and looked at him—he turned a corner, and found himself amidst a blaze of lights and stalls and shouts: children running under carts, men calling out prices, a press of women, all in black, pushing their way across a marble floor into a courtyard guarded by a golden dome. He followed them in—the marble cold on his bare feet—and stepped into Iran. Ten years before, after Khomeini's triumph, his followers had built two mosques here in Damascus, white and gold and blue, to house two Shia saints.

Across the marble space there was a small door, and when he went through it he found himself inside a space as hectic and overlit as a casino in the desert. Like walking into a kaleidoscope as it was being shaken, the low chandeliers, the tilework and glinting mirrors, the pieces of colored glass in the windows throwing off an ecstasy of reflections. Everywhere, people were sitting or standing, tears streaming down their faces, or hunched over (even the roughest men) as if they'd lost everything they cared for in the world.

Grown men came up to other men, and patted them on the shoulder, then began to cry, to cry again. Younger men, in light black jackets, as if they'd just stepped out of a restaurant in Los Angeles, sobbed and sobbed, wiping away their tears and then collapsing once again. Around the grille of the shrine, where the great-granddaughter of the Prophet lay, women were running their fingers along the bars and then running the same fingers along their faces, as if to pass on the sympathetic magic. Men sat with heads buried in their hands, and at the center of a great group on the floor, fifty or sixty perhaps, a young man, lightly bearded, with an elegant rosy face—the kind of man you might expect to see emerging from a nightclub—was singing, in a beautiful, high, and quavering voice, as if he'd lost his sweetheart yesterday.

The scholar's habit is to take down everything as it happens, before the moment flies away. But this time, the weeping men bent over beside him, the women running their frenzied hands along the bars, as if to pull back a two-year-old now thirteen hundred years dead, the young couples reading from their Qurans, he reached for his notebook, and held back. A few hours later, the people around him would be merchants and housewives and butchers once again; now, for a few moments, they could let their real selves out.

As soon as the sun was fully up, he returned to his hotel room and packed his few things in his case. He'd hoped Khalil would call him in response to his letter, but the long days had passed and his small room had remained silent. Now, with only a few hours before his departure, he realized he would have to take the initiative himself.

The phone didn't work, of course, and in any case he remembered what Sefadhi had told him about the old professor's need for privacy. Since Fatima had died, the rumor had it, he scarcely left his apartment, and stayed inside the circle of his books like a medieval hermit. Besides, a scholar of Sufi poets must always be circumspect in Assad's Damascus. "Go and visit him one day on a whim," his adviser had said. "Make nothing of it; don't even make a plan. If you don't know when you're going, they can't, either."

He went out into the street, the sun already high and hot, and walked around the square, stopping in at the bookshop, and looking around the lounge of the Umayyad Hotel, as for a friend. Then, consulting a map he didn't need, he walked deliberately in the wrong direction, doubled back, and then crossed over into one of the quieter streets, all doctors' signs and dusty Plymouths. Scanning the map, as if a lost tourist, he walked past the house he had scouted out before. Then, as if suddenly struck by a question, he went back and walked up to the door and rang the bell.

The professor opened up a few seconds later—he moved slowly, but clearly there was not much space to move through—and the visitor said quickly, "Professor Sefadhi," and was ushered in. In the low, dark hall the man looked him over to see what he had brought in, dust clinging to his own dark clothes, as he patted his thinning white hair.

"John Macmillan," he said, extending a hand. "I hope you got my letter."

"Of course," said the man, inclining his head a little, but not returning the handshake. "Come." And led him through the corridor into a small room which obviously hadn't been cleaned in a very long time. Now and then, he had heard, Khalil visited his daughter and son-in-law in a distant quarter of the city; otherwise he stayed at home alone with his research. There were three black-and-white photographs in silver frames beside a cabinet. Where another man might have kept bottles, he kept books.

"Professor Sefadhi told me that if I was in Damascus I should come and see you," he said, feeling he'd said this already, but needing somehow to fill the silence. The old man, without a word, disappeared into a tiny kitchen and returned a few minutes later with two glasses of tea and a sad-looking plate of biscuits.

"You're old friends, he told me."

"Yes," said the man. "We have known each other many years."

A silence fell again, and the man showed no signs of responding to it. "Professor Sefadhi said, actually, you might be able to help me with the poets I'm working on. It's an honor to meet you, after reading you for so long."

This was the local form, he knew, but the man seemed indifferent to it.

"You study with Javad now? In Santa Monica?"

"Barbara, yes. I learned Farsi at SOAS under Professor Willingdon and then—well, I moved to California to study with Professor Sefadhi."

"I see," said the man, who looked as if he was waiting to be back with his books. "And Javad, he is well?"

"Very well. He has quite a following in Santa Barbara. They say he may get a chair."

"Of course," said Khalil, as if this were news from another planet, and he knew it in any case. "Javad has always had friends."

It was hard to know what exactly lay behind the comment, so he returned to his theme as before. "He said, actually, you might have some suggestions about where I could go for more information. I'm working on the Sufis—lesser-known works of Rumi—and he said you might know of resources not widely available in the West."

"The Shiraz Manuscript, you're speaking of?" said the man, sharply, quickly, as if they were haggling over something in the suq. "We are the last to know about that."

"The 'Shiraz Manuscript'?" The term was new to him. "That would be . . ."

"Nothing," said Khalil. "Rumors. In Tehran you will hear one hundred people tell you that the Imam is alive and in hiding. And two hundred people will tell you that the Shah is coming back. It's only rumors."

"But it was one of the manuscripts that came out in '79?"

"Whispers," said the man, as if to brush off a persistent fly. "To keep the people busy while they wait for the Twelfth Imam. You are studying Hafez, Saadi in Santa Monica?"

"Barbara, yes. All of them. But my main interest is . . ."

"You know Kristina Jensen? A friend of mine."

A friend of a Syrian professor in Santa Barbara? He'd been told to keep on alert around Khalil—"He knows how to play poker even if he isn't holding any cards," Sefadhi had said. "Life's not easy in Damascus"—but already he felt that the conversation was being taken away from him.

"I don't think so. She lives in Santa Barbara?"

"Yes. California. I met her at the Islamic Symposium in Oslo, four years ago. You can take a small gift for her?"

"Of course." It was all happening so quickly, as he'd been warned it would; he'd come here in search of information and now, somehow, he was being used as a courier for the old man, taking who knows what around the world.

He was in no position to say no, though, and already the professor was in the next room, loudly rummaging through what the visitor assumed to be boxes and old papers. Looking around him in the small room, he saw nothing but loneliness and devotion: the biscuits spoke of how few people ever came here, and the black-and-white photographs in the frames had not been dusted for a long time. Above them, on the wall, much larger, was a whole array of photographs of President Assad and his two sons.

"Here, this only," said the man, coming back into the room with a small package the shape of a box, wrapped in a page of the previous day's *Al Baath*.

"You have her address?"

"Address?" said the man, looking suddenly put out. "No. No address. But her telephone number is 00-1-805-964-3271. Please call her and you can find the address. She is close to Javad, I think." Socially? Geographically? The man claimed only to have met her at a conference, and yet he knew her phone number by heart? "Go into the field," Mowbray had told him years before, "and you'll find yourself moving from darkness into deeper darkness."

"She probably knows Professor Sefadhi?" he tried. "If she's interested in Islam."

"Perhaps," said Khalil, but now that his chore had been taken care of, he seemed to have lost all interest in their talk. He placed his small hands on his large thighs as if to suggest that the interview was over.

"You don't know anything about Rumi that might be helpful to my project, then?"

"A great poet," said the man, in what might have been his public voice. "Even we do not know all that he has written."

The "we" was a way of putting him in his place—reminding him he was a trespasser here—and he realized he would get nothing more from the old man.

He followed him down the unlit corridor, and when his host pulled open the door, he heard, "My regards to Javad, please. And Miss Jensen. A safe trip to Santa Monica."

"Barbara," he said.

"Of course," and the door closed in his face.

That night he couldn't get to sleep—the way, if someone just mentions a name she thinks you know, you search and search until you lose all focus. When, after what felt like hours, he fell away at last, he was in a desert somewhere, a dusty and abandoned place, and Martine was by his side, though it didn't look like her. She was working on a puzzle of some kind, and then an alarm went off, and there were voices, lights, a man who looked like Khalil walking past.

"There's just room for one more letter," she was saying.

He woke up and realized he'd had the answer to whatever it was she was looking for, but hadn't managed to bring it out in time. Strange tears were pricking at his eyes.

By the time he got to London, and Nigel and Arabella's house, he was still feeling displaced somehow, as if the love song in the airport taxi in Damascus, slow and plangent, was still going through him in some way. He made up an excuse, said he had to do something before he came back for dinner, and Nigel looked at him strangely, more than ever convinced, no doubt, that California was robbing him of his reason. But there was nothing his friend could say to stop him, and soon he was out again, in the streets, joining the crowds as they pushed towards the river. The center of London was always jam-packed in the summer, every language audible but English, and as he made his way to Westminster—not at all where he'd expected to be going—he felt like a foreigner at home. The light was just beginning to fade as he slipped into the back of the great drafty space.

The choristers were taking their places in their stalls as he sat down, surpliced and translated out of their schoolboy selves; the red lamps above the scores in front of them threw a strange and ancient light up into their faces. Outside, it was getting dark—he could tell by the smudged light through the stained-glass windows—and as he sat on a bare pew in the back, suddenly the young voices began to rise up around him, high and unfallen, as if angels were summoning every creature to their presence. The voices rose and echoed through the huge space as if to pull the whole building up into the air, and for a moment he thought back, for no reason he could fathom, to the great mosque in Damascus, the men on the floor, their hands upturned on either side of them.

Do with me what you will, their cupped palms said. I am nothing; you are all.

When the hymn was over, a somewhat older boy went up to a lectern and practiced the lesson, and then the choirmaster led them all in a small, massed chanting of the Lord's Prayer—*"Adveniat regnum tuum. Fiat voluntas tua sicut in cœlo et in terra"*—before letting the sweet unbroken voices rise again, sanctifying everything before them, and making it clean.

"There's something different about you," Nigel said after dinner, as they started clearing away the dishes. "Something strange. I can't put my finger on it, but, I don't know, you're different."

"It must be California."

"Must be," said his friend, who didn't sound delighted by the change. "You seem more serious in a way. More—how can I put it?—hungry."

"It doesn't sound like a good thing, the way you put it."

"Probably isn't, no. Are you going to call Martine while you're here?" He slipped it in so casually, it was clearly what he'd been leading up to all along.

"I think she's probably glad of a break from me."

"Yes. That part hasn't changed." And Nigel was off again, to collect the salt and pepper shakers, while he went on with the drying. When he went out, the rites complete, his friend said, "Sleep well. If we don't see you in the morning, give us a call sometime when you're back home."

In the morning, however, they were both waiting for him in the kitchen, bleary over mugs of Nescafé, and Nigel left him with "Don't lose your sense of humor, will you?"

"I don't think I can, if I'm studying religion."

"No, suppose you're right. Anyway, it's good to see you, even if you do seem half mad."

At the airport, in the departure lounge, he picked up a receiver and put in his card, then held the instrument in place and put it down again. Whatever he said at this point could only come out wrong: if he sounded happy, if he sounded bereft—all of it could only be an insult.

"So the prodigal returns," Alejandro said in his ironic way, three days later, outside the lecture hall, as they bumped into each other in the corridor, on their way to Ryan McCarthy.

"And the fatted calf awaits him."

"How was it?"

"Amazing; really amazing. It sounds stupid, I know, but it really puts you in your place."

"I can imagine. Hafez Assad has that effect, I've heard."

Though Alex had been in California for three years or more, he'd never lost the raised eyebrow of Buenos Aires.

"And you? What have I missed?"

"Everything. Nothing. I toil in the pastures of the heartbroken. Becoming a doctor who can't heal when I wish only to be a bachelor once more." He spoke a strange, overflowery English, fluent, but sounding, often, as if it had passed through Spanish first.

"And so our investigation into the death of God proceeds," his friend went on as they passed through the open doors and claimed some seats a few rows in from the back. " 'Can you tell us where you were on the night of May 17? We have reason to believe that it was then that this person with whom you were involved—the "Higher Power," as He is sometimes called—first went missing. Unless you can shed some light on when you saw Him last, we will have to presume Him dead.' " He'd come to this New World to make a new life for himself, everyone assumed; but he'd never lost his habit of masking his intentions in the devices of the Old.

Around them the same faces as usual were taking the same seats as usual, some near the back, with a view to a rapid escape, others near the front, in the hopes of a rapid ascent. Religious Studies was in permanent danger of following the gods it studied into oblivion; though the number of its students was ever on the rise, that was mostly because it presented itself now as a science, and offered classes on "Rage" and "Men's Wildness." A researcher from MIT—so the persistent rumor ran—had actually been called in to conduct experiments on how laboratory mice responded to an image of the Virgin Mary.

Sefadhi still fought a rearguard action, however, and he was a seasoned and determined fighter, "from a culture where faith is not such a dirty word," as he was fond of saying, glossing over some of the finer points of Persian history. He'd made it his mission to bring in wandering speakers, like prophets from the desert, to remind the rabble of "primordial fire," as he called it. Now, standing at the podium, he shuffled through his notes and motioned for a lowering of the lights, a return to sacred silence.

"Fortune, the ancients held, favored those who paid homage to it in secret," he began, speaking with the forgotten courtesies of his native Isfahan. "Much as a woman might drop a handkerchief to lure a passing knight's gaze towards her window. Just so, we in Religious Studies must have been burning offerings in private to merit the visit of one such as Ryan McCarthy."

There were a few uncertain snickers, the inevitable rolled eyes. The ornamental phrases rolled on and on—treasures scattered out of a jeweled box—and their object, a man with tufts of reddish hair around his ears, and an aging herringbone jacket with huge patches on its sleeves, stood up to take the stand.

"Many of you, I know, are familiar," Sefadhi continued, bald head glinting in the lights (and the visiting dignitary sitting down again), "with Professor McCarthy's ground-breaking work on scriptures in a secular world, *Sensuous Seducers,* with its elegant subtitle, *Lures and Gambits in the Bible.* All of you, I know, are acquainted with his exchange with Huston Smith in the *Journal of Religious Studies.* But none of that, I think, can prepare us for what he will be sharing with us today. It is with something more than honor, and with a feeling much deeper than pride, that I give you Professor Ryan McCarthy."

The applause was scattered, and then the promised savior got up again and trudged over to the podium, looking around all the while as if he'd blown his cue again. When he faced them, they could see, even if he could not, that his blue-striped shirt was misbuttoned and his shoelaces were loose. He looked like a passerby dragged by mistake into a frat-house party.

He cleared his throat, straightened the papers before him, and, looking down, began to flick, half desperately, through them.

"Another step forward in the long march of the soul," muttered Alejandro, who had the schoolboy's way of defining himself by what he could see through.

"The subject of my address to you today," McCarthy began, speaking faster as he picked up the thread of his talk, "though hardly worthy of the praise that Professor Sefadhi has lavished on it, with such characteristic generosity" (he glowed down at the front row), "is what I have called the 'Higher Temptations.' The devices by which we are pulled towards the good. By this, of course, I refer not to those common wiles and stratagems that seem to take us farther from our destinies, but to those that return us to our original mission, if I may put it in those words."

Bodies slumped lower in their seats, and all around was a faint scattering of whispers exchanged, and notes passed back and forth.

"It is commonly supposed, even—I dare say, especially—by us Catholics" (there was a ripple of laughter, as if to acknowledge that he was trying to be human), "that the Devil has been given all the best lines. Iago is a wordsmith, Othello professes inarticulacy. Satan makes off with the poet's verses. Yet why, I wonder, should Satan's master and maker—his evident superior—not have as many words at His disposal? Are we to surmise that words themselves are a part of the fallen Creation? All life, after all, is a constant, agitated battle between those who see this world as the only one that matters— earthly patriots, as we might call them—and those who remain true to another order. Are words the instruments only of the mortal?"

Every now and then someone laughed, but it was in the nervous, uncertain fashion of someone laughing at a foreign film as if in happy surprise that these people were just like us.

"Scholars might assert, in fact, that Satan's greatest temptation to Jesus is to imagine himself beyond the temptation of a Satan. 'Tell us you're the son of God,' he says, like a master logician, 'tell us you can never die.' His offer, in effect, is to make Jesus a lord of infinite riches in a world that doesn't exist."

This was more, perhaps, than any of those in attendance had expected, and the audience had not yet given up on him entirely.

"Here, perhaps," he went on, putting down his typescript and picking up a large book, "I can give you an example of a higher calling.

"'Like an apple tree among the trees of the forest, so is my beloved among young men.'" His voice was high and shaky, and the words got lost or smothered, yet something of their tingle still came through. "'To sit in his shadow is my delight, and his fruit is sweet to my taste. He has taken me into the wine-garden and given me loving glances. Sustain me with raisins, revive me with apples; for I am faint with love. His left arm pillows my head, his right arm is around me.'"

He put the book down again, and faced his startled audience once more. "Thus can we see how some scholars maintain that 'Eve' comes not from the Hebrew word for 'life,' but from the Aramaic for 'serpent.' Which of us, after all, would be proof against such lines?

"And yet, of course, to the believer this is as it should be. The sensuous words are a call not to pleasure but, if anything, its repudiation—

or, at least, transcendence. They mark a summons to what we might call, without undue exaggeration, the highest and the truest in us." He beamed over at them from his place onstage. "All religious verse, we may say—and here I refer not only to the poetry of our own tradition, but to the love songs of the Sixth Dalai Lama, the Zen verses of Ikkyu, the riddles of the Sufis—all religious verse is written in a kind of code. It is administering a test to us. That could, in fact, be adduced as one of the signs of religious verse: that it moves as if inside a veil."

Here, as he rose towards his climax, the papers on the podium began to form new patterns of disarray, and it seemed as if he would as easily move from omega to alpha as the other way round. He fumbled for a moment over a word he couldn't read, then realized he'd lost his place.

"The sensuous seducer claims another conquest," murmured Alejandro, sinking deeper into his seat.

"Thus," the visitor continued, trying to regain his momentum, "all religious verse speaks to us in a language we can understand. To those with eyes and ears the poems are a kind of holy come-on; to those without, they appear as love songs, emblems of profanity. These ceremonial seductions, if so I may denote them, are a way of defining our relations to the world around us. A good man sees a man in rags, sitting in the street, and recognizes him as an angel traveling incognito; another man sees the same creature, and writes him off as a homeless beggar. We are no greater than the height of our perceptions."

Again, he put down his text and broke into an antique, mock-poetic voice.

" 'May I find your breasts like clusters of grapes on the vine, your breath sweet-scented like apples, your mouth like fragrant wine flowing smoothly to meet my caresses, gliding over my lips and teeth.' "

"Where is Joni Mitchell when we need her?" asked Alejandro from his place, slumped down towards the ground.

"Who you are, in short, what you believe, and where you stand on the cosmic battlefield—everything is in its way revealed, perhaps defined, by how you respond to these verses. Do you see a sensual incitation or an epithalamion in the realm of the invisible? All that separates one from the other is a curtain of assumptions. And no argument or preaching or scholarly discourse can raise the curtain for those who see it, or lower the curtain for those who don't. The religious transaction is—it has to be—a love affair conducted in the inner chambers of the heart. Those not party to it"—he cleared his throat here, for his crescendo—"can do no more than turn away in embarrassed silence, or cling to their own quite different loves."

A round of surprisingly enthusiastic applause greeted the end of the talk, and not only because it was the end: if nothing else, the man himself had seemed what Debra Saperstein habitually called a "performative statement"—his very being brought home the point of his lecture more forcibly than his words could. To those with the right kind of ears, he could seem a luminous messenger; to everyone else, just a vague figure staring over his stand at the scattering of claps, and squinting without much pleasure as someone said something about the Song of Songs as the only book in the Bible that failed to mention God and someone else said something about the second-century rabbi who, in spite of that (because of that?), had called it the "Holy of Holies."

Faced with their challenges, he peered over the lectern like an uncle who suddenly realizes that he was supposed to bring the Christmas presents.

"Of course there is much virtue in what you say," he said, in answer to a question about the sovereignty of the subjective. "The death of the author is a way of talking about the death of God. The world itself becomes a poem whose author disappeared long ago. Like, in fact, the Song of Songs. Yet for me—born, perhaps, into a different world, and a different generation, from your own—every comma is, in a way, a fragment of God. I stand, so to speak, on the far side of the invisible veil."

He'd put himself out of harm's way, though for most of the beings in the room his admission merely underlined his irrelevance.

"What better note on which to end?" said Sefadhi, abruptly rising to his feet, and bringing the confrontation to a close. Averting bloodshed was his strength. "Or, should I say, on which to begin? For what

Professor McCarthy has given us today is not just the fruit of decades of deep scholarship; it is, no less, the stimulus for decades of serious thought to come. Thank you, Professor McCarthy; and thank you, one and all."

A few bodies began to get up, and then Sefadhi went on. "I am reminded of the ancient Sufi tale in which a seeker, knocking at his master's door, hears the sheikh call out, 'Who is it?' 'It is I, sir, me,' he responds, and the teacher's voice calls back, 'Go away! Where there is an "I," there can be no true instruction. Come back when you are no one.'"

More bodies got up now, as if to force him to be quiet, and, with some claps of relieved applause, they all began making for the refreshments next door.

"So God, we learn, is an Irish mystic," said Alejandro, gathering his books and standing up.

"I liked it. He didn't make distinctions between religions; only around them."

"He knows his audience," said Alex dryly, and led him into the room where plastic bottles of Diet Coke and 7-Up sat sentinel above paper plates filled with unpromising wedges of cheese. He cast a quick glance around the room to see who might be worthy of his attention and then said, "That girl over there? You know her?"

He followed his friend's eyes to a wall where a young woman was sitting on a folding chair, by herself, balancing a paper plate on her knees, and concentrating on her drink as if not to advertise her loneliness.

"She was at the back of the hall, I think. With someone else."

Not missing a moment, Alex began walking across the room to see where this new adventure might lead. As they went over, slipping between bodies, they heard someone say something about Eliade, and the "erasure of the Other"—"apocalyptic pressures" and the "abolition of Eternity"—and then they found themselves in front of the stranger, as she looked in startled shyness up.

"You are," said Alejandro, "a spy, perhaps, here to inspect us lesser mortals? Or eager to see what happens to those of us who make raids upon the unknowable?"

The woman looked up at him, bewildered by his extravagance. "I'm here with my friend," she said. "She's—somewhere over there." She pointed towards the crowds, and Alex turned around for no more than a second. "Are you from England?"

"Buenos Aires," he said, "but it comes to the same thing. I studied with the nuns in Hurlingham."

"Great," she said, uncertainly, going back to her cheese. "That sounds really exotic."

"And you," he continued, pantomiming some Latin charmer, "you are a supporter of Professor McCarthy? Or just a passing admirer?"

"It's my friend," she said, unhelpfully. "She's into this stuff—or at least her sister is. I just came to keep her company."

"A surrogate spy, then. You are forgiven."

She looked up at him with a smile that said she still didn't know what was going on, and he, with all the gallantry he could muster, looked around the room. "I'm sorry to say I must return to my labors," he said, "but I wish you sweet dreams, and good data to take back to the sister," and then turned towards the exit. "The passage from the spirit to the senses," he whispered back over his shoulder, as they left, "may be less direct than the good professor would have us believe."

He'd got in the habit, on summer evenings, of riding his bike along the path above the cliffs, past the mattresses that stood on terraces, the shopping carts left out on the street, everything that spoke of this as a society in transit, in flux. All student communities have this air of having just been thrown together to be disassembled with the next season, but here in California, the air of improvisation never ended. "It's like a whole society of students," he'd written to Martine soon after he arrived. "I mean, everything's permanently in motion and everyone's about to find the love or secret of his life. I think that's what really makes it feel most like a desert. The sense of every day being founded on shifting sands." What he hadn't bothered to say, though she knew him well enough to guess at it, was that it was therefore a perfect place for someone who wanted to live alone; you can't fall in love in a place that lacks all mystery.

His other habit, in the summer, was of pouring himself a drink when he got home, usually around nine-thirty, and taking it out to the terrace, as he called it to himself. Though walled and covered, the room he used for a study had once been an open veranda facing onto the sea, and even now, despite the windows and the way in which it had been made to look like an extra room, it had the feeling of the outdoors, the long views and closeness to wind that had brought him to the West. On quiet evenings he sat at his desk, the sea foaming and receding before him, the moon sending patterns across the darkness, and imagined he was in a different century, and the rolling swells before him were sand.

This time, he sat down at the desk, and thought back on what McCarthy had just said. Indirectly, it seemed another way of describing what he had encountered in Damascus: the impermeable wall that separates those inside the community from those outside. Not just because they see things differently—he'd made it his vocation to see the world in a Sufi light—but because their very sense of north and south was different. He'd come all the way here to live differently: but what use was any of it if he changed only his circumstances, not his eyes?

When he woke up the next morning, it was to find the light on his machine blinking with its customary ferocity: a call from London, he assumed. He pushed the button and heard a voice almost, but not quite, the one he'd been dreading and hungrily awaiting. "Johno, it's Dominique. Chancellor. I find I'm going to be in L.A. a few weeks from now. On business. Any chance you might be free for a day of sightseeing in Santa Barbara? I'd love to come up and look in on you." "Look in" meant "look at," he knew, and "I'd love" meant "I will": he hadn't forgotten England in his time here. Clearly Martine was sending her older sister to check up on him.

"Anyway, when you get this, could you call my office, please, to confirm? It'd be wonderful to come over and make sure you're up to no good, as it were."

He flipped through his address book to find her number, and when he did, he saw her sister's, with the "June 10, 1967" scrawled above it in a handwriting that still had the capacity to touch him: the night of Hugh's party, in the dead of winter, when she'd come down to his room on the pretext of looking up some Richard and Linda Thompson record and, during the long night that followed, in the innocence of youth, he'd written down her birthday, with all the plans he could weave around it already beginning to form in his head. As he went on, dialing Nicki's number almost absently, he suddenly remembered: he'd gone to all the trouble of buying Martine a present in Aleppo, and now, somehow, he'd forgotten to unpack it. Everything she'd said about him borne out—"So lost in those bloody poets of yours that you hardly notice whether I'm in the room or out of it."

He told the emissary he'd be glad to see her, and went over to the closet to search for the present. It must be in the suitcase, he thought, sifting through the clothes still neatly stacked and folded, maps of Palmyra, and hard-to-acquire copies of Sufi texts he'd brought back. At the very bottom of the case, in the shopping bag he'd taken pains to put them in, were the two boxes he'd brought home, one of them containing the bracelet that the Armenian had packed for him so carefully, the other whatever it was Khalil was sending to his "friend." At the time, he'd written "P" on one, for "present," but now, of course, he couldn't remember whether this referred to his present for Martine or Khalil's for his acquaintance. Why did every shop in Syria have to wrap its booty in the same copy of the party newspaper?

He felt the boxes in his hand, peered around the covering for marks, and then gave up: he'd have to open one up, as carefully as he could, and then reseal it later. He picked the fresher of the two offerings, gently pulled against a flap—tearing the whole thing in the process, of course—and then just ripped it apart to see what was lying inside. A small black-and-white box, one of those geometrical puzzles and talismans that make the suqs of the Middle East seem to spin. The visual equivalent of a mantra, he sometimes felt: a pattern so dizzying that just to look at it was to step outside your daily self. He opened its top—it groaned a little, the mother-of-pearl glinted—and saw a small blue perfume bottle, with verses from the Quran in gold around its sides; next to it, a tiny envelope on which someone had written, with an equal sense of ceremony, "Kristina." He started to open the envelope, and then held himself back: a message from a stranger to a stranger, handed to him in trust. He put the box back on the chest of drawers, pulled out some wrapping paper he'd kept in the closet for such occasions, and then went back to call Martine.

Her voice on her machine had the sound of someone walking out the door and closing it firmly behind her. "Hello, it's John. I just wanted to say that I'm looking forward to seeing Nicki next month. And I didn't forget your birthday. I actually went to the trouble of getting you something, in a place that would have meaning to you, and then, of course, forgot to send it. But it's on its way now, with my apologies and"—he paused to measure the words precisely—"my fondest wishes. California is very strange for somebody like us. Like a scene some child has drawn on the beach, which gets washed away every morning. Anyway, I hope you had a lovely birthday, and celebrated in high style."

Then, wrapping up the other present in his gold paper, he suddenly realized that he didn't have the number of Khalil's friend, in Santa Monica, or Barbara, or wherever it was. He went back to the suitcase, pulling things out in the same order as before—postcards of the Citadel, bottles of shampoo, names of professors Sefadhi had given him—and came at last upon the business cards he'd collected. On the back of one—it happened to be for a rare-book dealer, in the suq—he'd scribbled down the number of the woman.

"Hello?" came an uncertain voice when he dialed the number.

"Hello. Is that Ms. Jensen?"

"Yes. Can I help you?" She spoke demurely, with a curious formality: there was California in her voice, but also something farther away, more cautious.

"Yes, I think you can. I was just in Damascus, and I met a friend of yours, and he gave me a present to deliver to you, and I was wondering how best I might get it to you. Professor Khalil."

"In Damascus?" she said, as if the name were strange to her. "In Syria?"

"Yes. He said he knew you from an Islamic conference in Scandinavia, I think."

"Oh, you must be looking for Kristina. She's not here."

"Will she be back soon?"

"No. I don't think so." The voice didn't sound very sure of anything: he saw someone small, a little tentative, looking out from behind a barely opened door, and waiting for it to close again.

"Will she ever be back?"

"Yes. In a few weeks, I think."

"Maybe I could drop it off, then, and you could give it to your roommate—"

"Sister."

". . . your sister when she returns."

"Sure. Anytime."

"How about tomorrow, in the afternoon? I feel terrible hanging on to this for all these days."

"Sure, anytime is fine."

"Would three o'clock be okay? Tomorrow."

"Three would be perfect," she said, and then gave him some instructions for getting off at Mission, and following the parks and the schools till he came to the "blue house on the corner."

"I'll see you then," he said.

"I hope so," came the far-off voice.

The next afternoon, threading his way through the narrow streets that lie just behind downtown—the shadows that give it substance— he tried to make sense of her somewhat whimsical directions: "right one block after the oak tree, and then straight when you see the church, and then past the place where the girls are wearing green plaid skirts, till you see a white camper under a tree." There was no sign of the camper, but he found a blue house, and the numbers matched, so he parked on the street and walked to the door. There was no answer to his knock, so he tried again. He waited, looked around—we are never less ourselves than when waiting for a door to open, he thought, never more at loose ends. But the door never opened, and there didn't seem to be a bell.

"Hello?" he called out. "Anyone home?"

But there was no sound from within, not even a whisper. He walked around to the side of the house, knocked on a window, tried to see what he could make out through the sliding doors: just boxes heaped up, in a distant room, and books and papers everywhere. "Hello?" he called again. "Anybody home?"

There was not even the sound of someone trying not to be seen. He walked around some more, just in case she was in the bathroom, knocked once more on the front door, and then gave up. The driveway was deserted, and if he continued circling the house, some suspicious neighbor would no doubt summon the police. The perfume bottle didn't look expensive; he could surely leave it outside the door.

He put it beside the welcome mat, so she would see it when she returned, and then went back to his car, looking over his shoulder to make sure it was safe from the rain. As he got into his car and started up, suddenly there was a kind of clattering behind him, and a large white tank, as it seemed to him, so smeared with dust that it was turning grey, labored into the open driveway. At its wheel, he could tell from where he sat, was a young woman.

He got out and waited by the driveway, to make sure it was her, and for a long time heard nothing but someone struggling through the debris of the car. From where he stood he could see sweaters, newspapers, old dresses, and boxes piled up so high in the back that it was a miracle she could look out.

At last a small figure stepped down from the vehicle—it was a long way down for someone her size—and came up to him, flushed. "I'm sorry," she said. "You've been waiting. You must be the person who called?"

"I am. John Macmillan. I actually left the present on your doorstep—I wasn't sure you were coming."

"I'm sorry. I was running late, so I canceled the bank and gave up on the flowers and came back here, so I wouldn't miss you. And then . . ." For whatever reason, she looked bereft.

"No harm done. I'll give it to you now." He went over to the door, picked up the box, and brought it over.

"Camilla," she said, extending her hand. "We talked on the phone."

"I know." He looked at her—the long fair hair falling to her waist, the pale, clear face, and, more than that, the sense her hair gave her of someone taller than she really was—and said, "Sorry, I know this sounds stupid, but you look familiar. Might I have seen you somewhere before?"

"At the lecture maybe? I was there with my friend."

He thought of the woman alone with her plate of snacks and the unmet "friend" she'd come with—who was now, apparently, standing before him. Strange that she'd made the connection so instinctively.

"So—would you like an orange juice or something?" She brushed a few stray hairs away from her forehead, and he saw someone flustered, a little, as if she'd mislaid something, just when the telephone rang, and couldn't now put her hands on it again.

"Why not?"

She fumbled with the key for a few seconds, leading him round to the side of the house, and then into a small, too-typical Californian kitchen. There were counters on all sides, boxes of tea bags by the sink, a calendar with a picture of the Moorish courthouse. She had, in the current fashion, magnetized letters on her refrigerator, waiting to be turned into words.

"Would mango juice be okay? I seem to have run out of everything else."

"Fine. Excellent," he said, as she extended two dirty glasses that looked as if they'd recently been excavated from Pompeii.

"So you're a student of religion?" she said, to be saying something.

"Whatever that means. But, yes, here for a few years of graduate work. And you?"

"I'm a kept woman," she said, and again he sensed something strange in her, withdrawn: the answer came trilling out so easily he felt it was a standard ruse.

"Funny. I'd have thought you were an actress."

She looked up suddenly. "How did you know that? Have you been making inquiries?"

"No. It was just a lucky guess, I think. A joke." But she was look-ing away again, and he was reminded of how often conversations in California went like this: as if you were going through the lines of a play, which everyone knew and was used to performing, and then suddenly somebody fell through a trapdoor, and her words came back to you from very far away.

"That's so weird," she went on, alone in her own world. "Because I had this friend once, an old boyfriend, and one day I was writ-ing down his name, and he called me at that very moment—from Chicago! And this other time, I was in England, this was years ago, and I walked into a room, and there was the same person I'd met a year before. Somewhere completely different."

"England's a small world."

"Not that small." An unexpected sharpness.

"You were a student there?" he said, to bring them onto safer footing.

"Nineteen eighty-five," she answered with pride. "At Oxford. It was the most beautiful experience of my life." He kept quiet: clearly they were moving in opposite directions.

"And you?"

"The same. But that's what I've come here to get away from."

"We were probably there at the same time!"

"We probably were. Anyway, I should be off: I've taken up enough of your time."

"It changed my life," she said, and again he had the sensation of having tripped some wire so that suddenly she became a deeper ver-sion of herself. She went in and out of focus like the sun behind clouds. "It was the first place I'd ever been where they had real respect for the past. Where they valued where they came from."

"I'm sure," he said, and got up as a way to go. He'd learned long ago that the people here who longed for the Old World were the ones with whom he'd have least in common.

"And you're from Denmark originally?"

"How did you know?" Again, she looked startled. "Are you telepathic?"

"I don't think so. Jensen's a Danish name, isn't it?"

She nodded, obviously not satisfied by this. "Usually people say

'Norway.' But, yes, I'm the usual California mix-up: half Danish, half . . . something else."

"Well, I really appreciate your help. When you see your sister, please tell her she has a big fan in Damascus. Professor Khalil wanted me to pass on his warmest regards."

"They always do," she said strangely, and he was thrown off-balance once again.

"Thanks for the juice. Maybe we'll bump into one another."

"Maybe," she said, not sounding very confident. "Thank you for the telepathy." And somehow, as she sat in the kitchen, letting him show himself out, leaving him with the unmistakable feeling that he was abandoning her in some way.

That night, when he returned home, he found himself thinking about Martine. He took his glass of wine into the study, as usual, and looked out to sea, and all he could hear, for whatever reason, was her voice, the last night on the train. The couple next door was playing an old Dead album, very loud, and there were the usual shouts and barkings from the beach below, but all he could see was her eyes, pleading with him in that way that said she was so scared she'd prick him if he came any closer.

It was three, four in the morning now, in his head, and they were on the bench by the river, under the trees, with all the punts moored up, banging now and then against the bank. The sound of a live band far away, under the tent, and only a few couples straggling across the lawns or stealing, periodically, through the great iron gates, into the quiet and privacy of the trees.

She was stretched out as she liked to sit, her feet in his lap, he playing with the straps of her sandals. They'd both drunk too much, and when he moved his fingers under her dress, she giggled and squeezed and said, "Don't!" in a way that meant she didn't want him to stop.

He ran his finger under the bottom of her legs, and then along the inside of her thigh, across the warm expanses, and she relaxed as she could never do indoors, and when the moment was over, she kissed him gently, and then they were farther apart than ever. The creakings on the lawns, the bottles scattered around the Cloisters, she pulling her legs sleepily back as soon as it was light, and saying, "I ought to go."

"Me, too."

"Of course," she said. "That's what you're good at."

"The scholarship stipulates . . ."

"I know what it stipulates: I'm the one who helped you fill out the application, remember? I just wish you had the decency to acknowledge the real reason why you're going."

He walked out into the night, to try to put the distant moment away—to come back to California—but all the memories now closed everything else out: the long, long evenings in the country when the sun just rested on the horizon forever, and the whole world dwindled into a murmurous quiet; cows on the hill, the two of them stretched out on the grass somewhere, a bottle on the blanket, and she, occasionally, saying, "How can you want anything but this? Aren't you happy?"

No past and no future: just the suspended quiet of a summer evening that annulled a sense of direction and of self. Her eyes alight as it got dark, the bleary taste of wine upon her lips, the long nights when they never seemed to sleep. Until, of course, the past was so enormous that the only thing they shared was the sense of what they both wanted to avoid: it was as if the house they were building was coming apart, piece by piece, and brick by brick, and each day brought more packed boxes stacked up by the door. "If you mean there's no patient Penelope to put it all together again in the morning," she'd said, when he'd mentioned the feeling, "you're probably right. I never was very interested in sewing."

As he walked, a couple suddenly ran, singing, down the wooden steps of their home and out onto the beach. He watched them in the distance, running into the waves, hand in hand, and thought of the first letter he'd written her after he arrived. "Loneliness is a good thing, don't you think?"

.   .   .

The next morning it was clear—none of the coastal fog that usually enveloped them till one, two in the afternoon—and when he went to his desk, his mind started to run in every direction except the one he wanted it to go in. Something in the trip had left him unsettled, not himself; not anything Khalil had said exactly, but all he hadn't said. His reticence was so absolute, it gave the impression he had something to hide.

The scholar's fear—he was reminded every time the latest issue of the *Journal of Islamic Studies* appeared inside his box—is the scholar's dream, in a different key: that suddenly someone, somewhere, will make a discovery that turns the whole field on its head. If the discovery is his own, he can claim a victory of sorts, but even then it is a partial victory: every new development can turn years, even decades of research upside down. Like seeing a woman across a room, Alex had said, and throwing over your wife of twenty years.

He tried and tried to bring his mind back to the matter at hand—his paper next week at the graduate seminar—but a part of him was far away, and restless, the character in the fairy tale told, on no account, to look behind the last door on the second floor (and so unable to think of anything else). "The first line of Rumi's *Mathnawi*," he wrote now, but almost automatically, most of his mind in the maze-like streets of Old Damascus, "describes the cry of the flute, pining for the reed bed from which it was plucked. The Sufis, like all mystics, are singers of a homesickness that is a kind of hope; all of us are exiles in the world, they tell us, longing to get back to the place that is our rightful home."

Outside his window, the surfers at the point were riding the waves, masters of all they surveyed for a moment, and then abruptly vanishing from view, until they emerged again, in a scramble of pale limbs and bobbing boards, their bodies washed towards the shore like so many pieces of laughing debris.

"For the Sufis," he went on, trying to push himself back to the paper in front of him, "the heart of life is mystery: everything we don't know. We are even mysterious to ourselves, they believe: a part of us going through the rituals of our daily life, while another part, a deeper part, cries out for whatever it is that can take us back. The stranger whose voice we recognize as our own."

He stopped again, and got up to stretch his limbs. It was the whole point of the exercise, in a way: to learn to keep yourself out of what has been the consuming passion of your life. The scholar is trained to give himself over to a piece of paper, a riddle—an ancient crux—for years at a time, and told in the same breath to keep his feelings to himself: it is a training in living in the shadows.

He went out into the street now—anything to be free of the paper—and watched the usual dawdle of shirtless boys cycling past, and girls with ponytails flopping against their backs as they jogged. In his mailbox, for the first time in several days, a letter was visible through the slot, and when he pulled it out he saw a pale-blue envelope, Hafez Assad glowering in two colors from the right-hand corner.

Inside—he tore it open as he walked back into the room—was just a single thin piece of paper, the faded black seal of the Institute of Religious Studies in Damascus at the top. The short message looked like it had been tapped out on a manual typewriter almost as old as its owner:

> Dr. Macmillan:
> Javad tells me I was inexcusably rude when we met. I apologize. We have lost the habit of courtesy in my country. Conversation is something we fear—there is nothing good that can come of it. However, if I cannot help you in your researches, I recommend to you Professor Espinoza in Cádiz. He has spent many years tracing the flight of alleged manuscripts from our poets. I further recommend you make no mention of this to Javad. He and Professor Espinoza do not see the same way on many things.
> I hope this begins to make up for my lack of hospitality before.
>
> Your obedient servant in God,
> Adnan Khalil

He felt a quickening inside him, as when a door swings slowly open and you see a shiver of light behind it. He saw the old man in his dark room, the framed prints on his shelves, the dusty books inside the case. He heard the man speaking in code everywhere he went, the only safety he knew, no doubt, in the company of his poems. Then he reached for his address book, to write the new contact down—and realized, fumbling in the pocket where he always kept it, that it was gone. Since the trip to the Middle East—or had it started before?—he'd seemed to mislay everything he cared about.

When he dialed the number on the card—he'd had to go back to his suitcase again and sift through the row of books to retrieve it—a woman's voice came briskly on, and announced, "This is 964-3271. Please leave a message at the tone."

"I'm really sorry to bother you again," he began. "You won't believe this—" And then, suddenly, she was there, like someone who'd been waiting for him.

"Hi."

"Hi. I really apologize, you're not going to believe it—"

"I know. I've got it here."

"You found it?"

"You left it on the counter. I found it as soon as you left. But I didn't know how to find you, so I was waiting for your call. It looks like your whole life is in here."

"I think it is. Is there some time I could come by and collect it?"

"Name your time."

When he pulled up to the small blue house a few hours later—he noticed with relief that the car was in the driveway this time—he heard her calling, "Over here. By the side." When he arrived at the door through which she'd let him in before, she turned over whatever she'd been reading, as if anxious lest he see the title.

"I can't tell you how grateful I am. If I'd lost this . . ."

"I know. You'd have lost everything." She got up and handed over the small address book.

"Well, I shouldn't take up any more of your time."

"I'm not doing anything. Are you?"

"Well, I've barged in on you twice in a few days, and ..."

"That's fine. But you must be busy." She looked up at him and he saw, suddenly, someone with nowhere to go, living in somebody else's house and collecting the presents that people brought from far-off countries for Miss Jensen ("No: the other Miss Jensen").

"I've got something I have to do this evening."

"Good," she said, "so do I," though he felt, with a pang, that it wasn't true: she didn't have anything to do anytime soon.

"Would you like to go for a drive?" she went on in her vague way. "It looks really pretty out today."

"Sure. Why not?" He'd told himself, on coming to America, that he'd try to learn to be more open; the West was the land of unexplored horizons.

"Just give me a minute," she said, and he found himself alone at the half-closed door, waiting and waiting (she hadn't invited him in, he noticed), while Martine came into his mind again: suddenly, after all this time, she was everywhere. "It's almost as if you're hiding out behind your life." The Cloisters on a winter morning, their breath making ghostly circles in the air. "The poems, the strict routine, the books on your desk—it's all a way of keeping yourself away from what you really feel."

"That's why I'm going to America," he'd said, and she'd looked back at him as if he'd truly disappointed her, by closing the wrong door. Now, at last—it had been a long wait—the door before him opened, and the young woman came out, transformed: in a long white dress, with a dab of blusher to brighten up her cheeks, her hair let down to frame her frightened eyes. He thought, inexplicably, of the time a student had asked him for an appointment, to discuss her paper, and when she'd opened her diary, he'd noticed that all the pages were white, unclaimed.

"So—where would you like to go?" he said, not sure of what the protocol for this demanded.

"Anywhere would be great. Can we go up to the mountains?"

It was a surprising request—the mountains were so close, she could get there in ten minutes—but he looked again at her lumbering car, ill-suited, perhaps, to such ascents, and then opened his door for her, and drove along the foothills to the north. When they turned right onto the Pass, they began to climb the road that eventually cuts across the mountains and down into the valley beyond.

"When I was in England," she was saying as they rose, and he heard a blur of parties at Magdalen and lectures on Gertrude Bell, the time she'd gone to Paris to see some Ottoman prints, the class she'd taken on women on the Silk Road. It was as if she were playing a role, and one that she had calculated would play well with him, and yet one that made no sense in the context of her life. "I guess that's why England was such a liberation," she said, as the town began to fall away behind them, and they climbed and climbed, the hills below them dry and bare. At the top of the Pass, where it begins to descend towards the inland valley, he turned right, along the "Road of the Heavens," which twists and snakes along the top of the range all the way to Montecito in the south, and suddenly, as so often here, the weather turned, and they were in clouds so thick they could hardly see a few feet ahead of them.

"You never know what it's going to be like here," he said. "Like two different countries, almost."

"We've risen so high, so fast." She peered out into the fast-moving mist as if happy to be somewhere murky again, in the presence of chill. "It wasn't just testosterone, and people talking about their résumés," she went on, and he remembered that she was in the middle of explaining England to him. "It was as if people knew where they were going."

The trees were very close to them now, on both sides of the narrow road, and in the fog they seemed closer still, the only shapes they could make out in the grey, the only tokens of something real. The world had lost dimension here, and order, and even though he put on his lights, they could still see nothing but mist, an imminence of rain. Every slow turn and mountain curve bringing some new shifting prospect.

"I'm sorry. I didn't realize it would be like this."

"I'm not. It's amazing. Romantic. Mysterious."

As they edged along the road, they found themselves navigating between great boulders on the hill above, and sudden, plunging falls to the other side. Occasionally, through the clouds, the city showed up, shining, with the sea a rich blue behind, and the islands in the distance. Then the clouds would be everywhere again, and they would be alone with great stone markers, the outline of hillside brush. Here and there they could see a house above, someone's expensive dream constructed in the mist.

"This reminds me of the stories I used to read when I was a child," she said. "About transformation and magic doors and people who went through these hidden doors and came upon a hidden world."

"This was in L.A.?"

"Yes. But I imagined it was somewhere else."

As she spoke, looking for what would connect them, and reaching out, in her way—he remembered how she'd invited him in for juice—he began to prepare a small speech in his head: "Look, you're really sweet and charming, and I'm sure you have plenty of admirers, but I'm afraid . . ."

He was about to deliver the speech, but she was chattering on about her time in France and how she'd seen a cloud that made her think of being inside a whale, as if some instinct in her told her to keep talking, and to keep his speech at bay, and how she'd once played the lead in a local production of *Shadowlands,* the story of C. S. Lewis. The sense of imminence was everywhere: the clouds portending rain, the little lecture building up in his head, the hopes that she'd brought on even this brief drive, in her white dress, and makeup that sharpened blue-grey eyes.

"Look," suddenly she cried, and again his talk was lost. "Can we go and explore?"

It was a pile of bricks in the outline of a room up above them, just faintly visible through the clouds, like an eerie relic of something else. More new lives being constructed on this fragile slope.

"I love abandoned houses. You can make them anything you want to." And just behind the bright voice, some quality of wistfulness, as if she were trying to push down whatever it was she felt.

"I'm not sure it's abandoned. It looks like it's being built." But already she was scrambling up the slope, unexpectedly nimble, holding her dress by the hem and moving as fast as if she were going off to one of the places she'd read about.

At the top, when they came to the house-to-be, she picked up a stone, a piece of brick, and looked around her at the emptiness. "I guess there's still a lot of work to be done."

"I think so." He looked around for the place at which to deliver his sentences—he'd formed them perfectly by now—and then, unexpectedly, a face peeped out, out of the mist, and then another: two yellow-haired kids playing hide-and-seek around the corners of the unfinished house.

"This is ours," said the little boy firmly. "Daddy says this is going to be my playroom."

The little girl looked on in reverence.

"This is our home. Who are you?"

"We're just exploring," she said softly, not shy about putting herself down on their level.

"What's your name?"

"Camilla."

"What a funny name! I'm Skye and she"—he pointed to what was apparently his sister—"she's Cloud."

"Then it's your day," said Camilla, bending down so she wouldn't be above the two of them. "A day of beautiful clouds. You must be the queen."

The little girl beamed, glad to be on equal footing, and the boy ran off, upset, perhaps, to be no longer the center of attention, and she gave herself over to exploring the joinings of the brick with the girl. Crunchings, scramblings from the clouds told them the boy was not far away. It was as if a whole veil, of wariness and distrust, had fallen away from her, and when she stood up, smoothing her dress, her face was flushed with bright color, light.

"I think we should probably be leaving them to their games," he said. "We don't want to trespass on their dream."

She scrambled down the slope in front of him, and he came after, trying not to fall, the words ready in his mind, and the first few specklings of rain prickling the windshield. When he started the car, she said, "Look," and as the mist receded, giving way to rain, they saw other houses, in no set pattern, all around the hills, the slopes blackened in parts, from a recent fire, and the houses the reborn hopes of people who had lost everything they owned.

"I'm so happy here," she said, a girl again after her game. "I've wanted to come here ever since I moved into Krissie's house."

He didn't ask why she hadn't, and as he prepared his opening lines—"You're really nice . . ."—she said, "Tell me about you. I've been going on and on about myself. What about you?"

"Not much to tell."

"You're studying Rumi and Islam at the university. Why did you choose them?"

"I don't know," he said, searching for the right distance. "I suppose they're everything we didn't learn about in school."

"Have you spent much time in the Middle East?"

"Not a lot. Enough. You?"

"I never go anywhere. But my sister, Krissie, travels. That's how I know about the Sufis."

They had almost come to Montecito now, and the houses had become more extravagant, Palladian villas, great country mansions set behind gates, all the many dreams people had brought and placed on the Pacific's doorstep. As they descended, they drove into late sunlight, and because the day was darkening now, and he remembered he'd concocted an appointment in the evening, he said, "Is there anywhere you'd like to go?"

"Wherever you like the most," she said, and he flinched at the unsought intimacy.

"The beach." There'd be just enough time for him to deliver his regrets.

He parked by the chains on the dead-end road—the signs saying "Stop" and "No Trespassing" at every point, reminding them of the security companies shadowing their every move—and they went down the concrete ramp that leads onto the sand. The sun was off to one side now, and sinking fast, and the last few surfers were trudging up towards the road, wet dogs shaking themselves dry beside them.

When she stepped onto the beach, she took off her shoes and ran towards the sea, and again he was disarmed, as if he were keeping two people company at once: the heedless girl who, when she remembered where she was, put on a mask of knowingness. She brought him a shell where he sat on a rock, as if they were the kids they'd seen on the hill, and said, "Tell me about your studies. What's the single best thing about them?"

"They make me believe, and they tell me of mystery."

He hadn't expected that; he hadn't expected anything. Clearly, he was tired and the day had gone on a long time.

"Thank you. That's beautiful." She looked up at him with an expectant glow.

One of the first things he'd learned when he arrived in California was that everything was different in the pacing: he would be walking through a prologue while those around him were running towards Act IV. Everything changed fast here, like the weather in the hills, and people reached for things with the terror of souls not sure they'd ever see the chance again.

"What is it? You look shy."

He was piecing the words together again, as the light faded, and the occasional faces that passed turned gold.

"Nothing."

"It must be something." She put her hands in front of her, in a pantomime of good behavior, and leaned forward: she stared at him beseechingly, teasingly, as if to prize out from him a boyhood secret.

"No, the thing is . . ."

"What?" she said, coaxingly.

"I'm taken." He looked away from her expectant eyes, her glowing face, and realized that the words had come out wrong.

"You are? You're taken with me?"

"No. I mean, you're very charming and sweet, and I wish things were different . . ." Out at sea the lights were coming on around the oil derricks, so the far-off structures glowed like Christmas trees. The sky took on a rich dark blue, and looking out in this light, with few signs of the developed world, you could imagine yourself in some other place of navy shades and desert spaces.

"I mean, in different circumstances, I'm sure, but the thing is, I'm claimed."

"Was it that obvious?"

"I think it was."

She sat back.

"I appreciate it. No. Really. Thank you for telling me. It makes things a lot easier."

"As I say, I'm sorry."

"No. It's much better you tell me now. I could have gotten hurt otherwise."

It *was* better; but he saw her packing away her things with the exaggerated efficiency of a girl told that the expedition's over, and it's time to go home. He looked out to sea, to where the dark sky showed off the lights, and she followed his gaze.

"Is she very far away?"

"Far enough."

"Then we're okay?" And there was a hopefulness in her voice.

He said nothing, so she went on, "I understand. Really. I wouldn't expect you not to be claimed."

"Good."

"I appreciate your honesty."

"Good."

They sat there, at something of a loss, and he did what he could not to look at where the lip gloss was wearing off, and the natural glow that had replaced the blusher was starting to fade. It was beginning to grow chilly—a wind coming in from the sea—and he remembered the evening appointments they'd both made up.

"I think we should be going." Leaning over to kiss her lightly for goodbye.

They didn't say anything as they drove back into town, but when he got off the freeway and started to approach her house, she said, "Thank you for giving me all this time. It means a lot."

"It's no problem. I'm happy to."

"Maybe I'll see you sometime at the university?"

"Maybe. I seem to spend all my life there these days."

He pulled up to her driveway, easy to find now thanks to the dusty white car that looked as if it had driven across continents to arrive here. She sat in the passenger seat, making no movement towards the door.

"Well, I think my eight o'clock meeting summons."

"Thank you for a perfect day," she said, with more seriousness than he'd expected, and then got out.

As he turned round and drove away, he saw her standing in the driveway, in her white dress, looking for all the world like a child dropped off against her will after a custody weekend.

What is it about the Sufis that attracts you?" It was one of the many questions that he took to his desk the following morning, from the unexpected drive, unable to settle to the work he'd promised himself. He thought, for some reason, of winter afternoons in England, the sky so low and grey that it felt as if he were being conveyed to a tunnel that would never end. He thought about the Department, and the endless talk of careers and papers and openings and tenure tracks. He thought, for no reason he could formulate, of the men in the great hall in Damascus, their hands extended at their side, palms cupped as if to receive whatever the heavens sent down.

"You realize he's the best-selling poet in America," Sefadhi had said, the very first time they met, at the interview. "I'm drawn to him in spite of that," he'd answered, and clearly it was the correct response, for six months later he was the professor's prize pupil, working on Rumi. "Our mission," the older man had said, in the slightly conspiratorial tone he favored, "is to smuggle a little of the Sufi light into the smog of California." Neglecting, for the moment, the fact that Tehran is said to have the most polluted skies on earth.

"Keep it simple" was Sefadhi's only advice for the presentation. "The point of the exercise is not to show off the details and originality of your research. It's the opposite. Make these poets live for people who know very little about them."

Outside his window, the ocean was foaming and pooling around the rocks, and the summer fog erased almost everything: it gave a forlorn air to the strip of beach, as if the world had left it behind somehow and would never come back to collect it. He looked out into the mist and tried to recover the person who'd known nothing of the poets until Martine gave him the book of Rumi translations the last night in Istanbul, an undergraduate's token of love.

"The Sufis," he wrote quickly, "so-called for the rough woollen gown they wear, or *suf*—emblem of their austerity, their voluntary poverty, their anonymity—were a small group of Moslems who began to gather in groups, often secretly, at the beginning of the eighth century, soon after the Prophet's death. Their aim, quite simply, was to find a direct path to the divine, without the mediation of any Imam or cleric. Their goal was not to conquer the world, but to conquer themselves."

It was the most agonizing thing in the course, after all these years, to try to reduce the figures he'd been studying into formulae: whatever had stirred him, years ago, had had nothing to do with the Islamic history he'd known nothing about. But the point of the seminar, as Sefadhi had stressed, was to keep all real knowledge out of it—"pretend as if you're meeting them for the first time."

"Because they opposed everything around them, they always had the air of a secret group: in Shia countries, such as Iran, they are a minority group in a minority sect that has always defined itself by its opposition to the norm—the word 'Shiite,' as you know, means 'partisan.' And so I might best present them to you by telling you what they are not. For the Sufi, God exists not only in the mosque or madrasa; He is everywhere, not least inside our hearts. The jihad that all good Moslems undertake (and, as you also know, I'm sure, the word means 'struggle' or 'aspiration,' with none of the associations of 'holy war' the networks always mention), the Sufi sees as internal: his goal is to suppress the infidel within. The Sufi ideal is one of love, but it is not the love of the compassionate mother, or of Jesus, he speaks of; it is the ravenous, consuming eros of the lover inflamed."

How does one begin to describe fire? Describe its effects, perhaps, the light it throws off in the dark. He thought of the blackened hills they'd driven through the day before, and the houses bravely coming up in the mist; he thought of her, recovering hope enough to run into the surf as if she were a child again.

"All of this doubtless sounds strange at first; but, really, it's not so different from everything we read in the Kabbalah or Plato. Even from the visions of Blake and Coleridge. The soul is an abandoned girl, lost in the wilderness, and crying out for the home that she has lost.

"The cry of the Sufi is, quite simply, the cry of abandoned love. The drive of the Sufis is to find the hidden self, the secret soul, that has the capacity to take us back. They do not care whether you call the destination God or Truth or Reality or Emptiness. For the Sufi, man is not fallen, just fallen asleep; we are not lost, just temporarily obscured. Like stars that can't be seen in mid-afternoon."

He stood up and stretched. The fog was beginning to rise up the cliffs and dissipate as it reached the town; the impression he had—the drive still inside him—was of grey eyes and blue, one light giving way to another.

"In many ways, indeed, the Sufis are closer in spirit to the mystics of other traditions than to the mainstream of Islam. That is one of the things that make them seem so subversive. We know them mostly through their poems, short, enigmatic outpourings that are thrown out like hand grenades to explode our every assumption. Their goal, deep down, is to take us into a space outside of space, as you could call it, where time as we know it is stilled, and everything that is beyond time comes to light."

He imagined himself, thirty years from now, another McCarthy, fumbling for his notes and reading from them in the wrong order as he tried to expound the beauties of making sense of what you don't know.

"That is the reason, too, why they so famously use images of madness and drunkenness and love. They take the notion of surrender—the literal meaning of 'Islam,' as you know—and push it to its furthest extreme. Hence, too, their love of jokes and riddles, eccentric stories about the lovable bumpkin Nasruddin.

"In that spirit, I leave you now with a short example. Many of us, when we were young, heard stories of the Three Wise Men, who followed a star to the manger where they found the infant Jesus. But recent scholarship suggests that the men were in fact Zoroastrians, from Persia, star-watchers who'd been following the heavens from a mountaintop. And for a good Sufi, their story is a near-perfect allegory of the soul. The Magi follow a distant star to a forgotten, unprepossessing place, and inside it they find, not just a divine baby, but an image of their unfallen selves. To the Sufis at least, the tale of the Virgin Birth is, as much as anything, a tale of a new birth inside the watching visitors."

The next day, he went for his biweekly session with Sefadhi—Tuesdays at 4 p.m., they'd decided years before—and when he arrived, it was to see his adviser standing at his window, dark eyes keen, and such hair as he still had impeccably in place. Even after all these years, his professor was still the subject of constant rumors, some people saying that he had once been sentenced to death by Khomeini, others that he was actually an emissary from the Revolution: how better to bring the wisdom of Khomeini to the West? When anyone questioned him outright, the man himself would say only that he'd come to California "to protect our poets from what they might otherwise become in the land of the spiritual makeover."

As soon as he heard the knock on the door, the older man turned around—his ears were famously sharp—and picked up the thread of himself as if they had been interrupted only a moment before.

"Forgive me, please; I was somewhere else."

"I can see that. Sorry to have brought you back."

"Not at all. Duty calls." He motioned his visitor towards what earlier generations had called the "hot seat."

"So," he went on, when they were both settled in, "our friend with the broken heart is well?"

"Well enough. I'm going to argue that you need to break a heart to make a new kind of life."

"Really?" the professor said, tapping the tips of his elegant fingers together. "I look forward to being enlightened." And then, since more, perhaps, was expected of him, "We can be assured, then, that the taxpayers' money is being well spent?"

"I think you'll have to ask them about that. I'm not sure what any of this has to do with—that." From where he sat, he could see bodies stretched out on the beach like pagan offerings. The call of gulls, a dog's barking in the distance. The smell of kelp coming through the window, and the sight of Frisbees winging through the bright, blue day. The Sufis felt like an irrelevance.

"I apologize for Adnan," Sefadhi went on, redirecting the conversation as smoothly as ever. "Life is not easy in Damascus."

"I appreciate that." It wasn't like his adviser to say the same thing twice. "He gave me what he could."

"He did?" There was barely a flicker of sharpened attention. "He's not a man of many words."

"No. He told me what he could."

"So," said Sefadhi, whose pride prevented him from inquiring further, "no more business for us to transact?"

"I don't think so. He did say something about the Shiraz Manuscript, though."

"Of course. People will say everything."

"Though he couldn't really tell me much about where it might be now."

"How could he? People say this, people say that." Sefadhi shot his stiff cuffs, white as ever, to go with his red tie. "There are no doubt Shakespeare first folios in the country houses of Hampshire. As scholars we work with what we have."

"And he said something about a woman called Kristina." At this, however, his teacher refused even to be drawn.

"So," said the professor, getting up, "six more chapters, nine more months. The road is clear before us."

"It is indeed."

"I look forward to your presentation. My only words of advice: remember, please, to keep the poets higher than your thoughts of them. Don't pull them down to your level; let them draw you up to theirs." He paused, and began to turn towards the window again, as a sign of goodbye. "It is best to make sure always there is something in them you don't understand."

With that, his student was made to understand that he was on his own again.

It was raining when he came in from his morning run next day, and as he opened the back door, he could hear the phone ringing on his desk, and then his automated self, the voice double who stood in for him on the machine, announcing that he wasn't there.

"Hello," he said, cutting himself off in mid-sentence. "Hello."

"Mahmoun?" said the voice at the other end. "Is Mahmoun?"

He could hear some kind of chaos far away: children shouting, and foreign music, and a voice, wild and rough, trying to make itself heard above the clamor.

"No. I think you have the wrong number."

"Macmoun. John Macmoun?" As the voice went on, not ready to be shaken off, he could hear whispers behind it, urgent talk in a kind of Farsi he couldn't follow, and the words "Damascus," "Ferdows," something else.

"Sorry. Who is it you want to talk to?"

And then, abruptly, another voice came on the line, and the image of cacophony receded.

"Mr. Macmillan: I apologize. My cousin's new to the country. His English isn't polished." This voice was more than polished, clearly foreign, but with a finishing-school sheen to it.

"That's quite all right. Why did he want to talk to me?"

"It's all of us, Mr. Macmillan. We heard that you are interested in manuscripts from our country?"

One question, half a world away, and already the news was everywhere.

"Where did you hear that? From Damascus?"

"From friends." He paused for a moment, as if to retrieve his line of thought. "My father has a shop here—we are in Westwood—and we were thinking you might be interested in us."

"I'm a graduate student. Not a collector, or an expert or anything."

"A graduate student with Javad Sefaredi is not just a graduate student." The man spoke absurdly like a dark-suited villain from some bad movie, pronouncing Sefadhi's name in its original form: maybe it was the range of foreign tongues here, and the fact that nobody quite understood the others, but California gave him often the sense of having wandered out of real life, into some place where people acted themselves, and not always very plausibly.

"I'm not sure I can be of help in any way."

"Only because you are not aware of our situation. We have a manuscript here, and we were hoping you might care to look at it."

"For what reason?"

"Simple curiosity. You could see what it means. Maybe, if you are interested, you can look some more. You are not interested, you know someone who is."

"With a view to what exactly?"

"Only looking."

Clearly he would get no more from the man, and clearly, now the man had got his number, there was little sense in playing hard to get.

"When's a good time?"

"If you had time on Wednesday the twenty-eighth, we would be honored to receive you. My father's shop is at 9763 Westwood, near Ohio. Islamic Arts."

Mowbray had said something along these lines when first told about the fellowship: "You do know what you're getting into? Throw out a question, and you're liable to find people in every corner of the room coming up with answers."

When first he'd arrived in Santa Barbara, he'd made it his practice to go every morning to the first-floor room in the library where they kept the foreign newspapers. Looking at last week's copy of *The Guardian* had seemed a way of keeping up some kind of connection with home (even with Martine). Then he'd thought back to why he'd come here in the first place—saw his parents silently raging against the small house they'd inherited—and never returned to the room again.

The day after the phone call, though, almost on instinct, he went back to the small barred cell of fading print, and found a place among the homesick boys from Bangalore and the engineers from Taiwan, poring over their ideograms. The *Iran Daily News,* as it happened, was in the same aisle as *The Independent,* and as he lost himself in the exile paper from Los Angeles, he found himself with the Iranians to the south, doing everything they could, far from home, to keep alive some memory of a place they loved.

"Black became white for us, north was south," wrote a doctor from Shemiran, in the column the paper reserved each week for a reminiscence of Iran. "And all the things we loved were raped. Our Queen, we were told, was sending jewels, carpets, diaries to Palm Springs, and Jimmy Carter was reciting Saadi at a banquet in Tehran. The British ambassador was visiting the Pahlavis on Paradise Island, but he came to them with a false name, a false passport. Meanwhile, the people in the villages, in Qom, Mashhad, listened to the BBC World Service for news of their Hidden Imam."

Now, of course—the man hardly needed to spell it out—it was he who was most likely living under a false name and identity: doctors from Tehran were working as antique dealers in West Los Angeles, and antique dealers moonlighted as immigration lawyers. At night, it was rumored, they gathered in somebody's house, under cover of dark, and brought themselves together with their stories of escape: the nighttime flight across the mountains on horseback, the old woman next door stoned to death on the street.

He thought back to what Sefadhi had said, and realized that, as with all the professor's comments, it hid more meanings than he had seen at first. If so little was known of Shakespeare (whom he loved, what he wrote, even who he was)—this had been his implication— how much less could we know of poets from a culture that had not even seen printing till five hundred years after their deaths? To search for a lost manuscript was like searching for a silent whisper; and even if you did come upon something that might be valuable, to say where it had come from was like picking up a grain of sand and saying which part of the desert it had issued from.

The seminar the following week passed painlessly enough: the Sufis were in such vogue now in California—Gloria Steinem writing on *fanasha* as a symbol of female power, Demi Moore and Madonna said to be reciting Rumi verses on a CD to be put out by Deepak Chopra—that no one looked very much askance when he began speaking of the hidden liberator, the unlikely stranger in Sufism who turned out to be a catalyst. "Love for the Sufis is not so much blind as a kind of higher vision," he found himself saying, and one or two people around the table nodded. When he told the story of Nasruddin, the holy fool of Sufism, looking for a key under a lamppost, Elaine actually burst into laughter. Why did he look there? the eccentric old man was asked. Because, he said, though he'd lost the key indoors, there was more light to look for it out in the street.

"And, of course," said Sefadhi, a slight edge in his voice, "for the true Sufi, the looking is the key. Even if you don't know what you're looking for." Then, sensing that he'd gone too far, he stopped himself and said, "Questions: I'm sure what John has said has given you much to think about."

"It has," said Alex, and there was a faint stirring around the table that John's best friend should be the first one to challenge him. "You talk about this dissolution of self"—his eyes met his friend's—"as if it were water going down a drain." There was a scattering of laughter. "But how does it happen exactly? A poem, a meeting, and then you disappear?" The laughter became more generalized.

"Hardly. It isn't anything you can plan for. You just have to leave yourself open, the way you might leave your door open in case a friend drops by." He'd lost the battle already, he realized; he was sounding priggish and defensive.

"So it's more a kind of 'follow your bliss' thing?" said Debra, who could be relied upon to complicate the simple.

"It's more a question of knowing that you don't always know where your bliss may lie. Sometimes it may be in the most unexpected places." He was talking—he was thinking—in circles. "The Sufis often say that God is a hidden treasure who created the world so He could be discovered. They aren't solitaries: Rumi could never have come to an understanding of his better nature without the mysterious appearance of the wandering dervish Shams."

"There are no monasteries in Islam," Sefadhi summarized succinctly, and then there was more talk, of how "the bee thirsts for the honey that thirsts for him" and how his student had "translated the sweetest nectar of the East into a cordial for the West."

The object of the compliments was lost, however, far away; he'd let the tradition down, he knew. Somewhere, he'd lost the sense of compassion.

The minute Sefadhi was finished, there was a vivid, if discreet, movement towards the door, and a couple of classmates stopped by to offer thanks, congratulations. Dick wanted to know if he'd be free for their usual game of tennis—Thursdays at seven o'clock—and Alex asked him if he'd like a drink. Getting up and straightening his papers, happy never to have to look at them again, he heard someone hovering behind him and looked up to see a woman he hadn't registered before. She'd been sitting, he now recalled, in one of the seats against the wall reserved for members of the community with "special interests."

"Thank you for your candor," she said, and offered him a small smile.

"Thank you," he said, not sure what she was saying.

She looked at him for a moment, a trace of amusement in her blue eyes. For all the foreign elegance—the tumble of long dark hair, the ruby earrings—she had something familiar about her.

"I think you know my sister," she went on, and when he failed to respond, she extended a manicured hand. "Kristina Jensen. You helped me with a favor."

"Oh yes, of course. How are you? Very nice to meet you." Though by now, of course, it was too late. She seemed, in her worldly confidence, to belong to a different continent from her fair-haired sister.

"I'll let Camilla know I saw you," she said, in her faintly ironic way. "Thank you for the gift."

"Thank you," he said again, and then, as she walked away, realized that he didn't know if she'd been referring to the presentation he'd just given, or to the present he'd delivered.

. . .

Campus was more than ever like some sketch that nobody had troubled to fill in during the lazy days of summer, and as they walked among the buildings, the grassy courtyards set among high towers, no sound came up to them except, at moments, the massed, far-off chant of cheerleaders here to practice affirmations. Houlihan's, when they got there, was almost empty and when he claimed his usual place in the corner, Alex went off to get some drinks. He put the books down on the floor and thought: nine months from now, all this will be over.

"To new lives," said his friend, raising his glass after he'd sat down. "And undiscovered selves."

"To finished theses," he replied, and sat back against the wall. On the system, U2 were racing through the desert, in search of light, a lost redemption; they still hadn't found what they were looking for. At the bar, a girl pulled back her shoulder strap to show her companion a tattoo she'd just acquired beside her collarbone.

"That woman at the end," said Alex, trying not to seem too interested, as he cupped his lighter's flame in his elegant Recoleta way. "You've known her long?"

"I've never seen her before in my life."

"But she said something about a sister, someone you'd helped out?"

"I brought her something from Damascus. I met her sister once— no, twice."

"Only twice?" said Alex, squinting as he let a draft of smoke out. His enemies in the department—and they were never in short supply— held that Alex asked questions of others as a way of not asking them of himself; knowledge, for him, was a kind of power, they said, which was why he always tried to know more about others than they could know about him. Together with his air of imported sardonicism, it could have made him insufferable, except for the sense that this too was a cover, the disguise behind which he pursued his own interests: the rumor had it that he was completing a thesis on Castaneda—the first half would argue that all the stories of Don Juan were a fiction; the second half would argue that they were nonetheless essential works of mysticism.

"And you?" he said, to avoid his friend's cross-questioning. "You never tell me anything."

"What is there to tell?" Alex shrugged. "I labor like a medieval monk and hear students ask me if Borges was a Buddhist."

"Was he?"

Alex looked at him as if to say, "What do you think?" Then, "I thought you'd come here to get away from all that."

"I have," he said. "I don't have time for complications."

"So you're not going to see the sister again."

"I can't. I told her I was taken."

"Ah," said Alejandro, with a private smile. "The mysterious Englishman. Ashamed of nothing but his tender heart."

Around them the place was beginning to pick up. Amidst the smoke and noise, a hand placed just too high upon a leg; a laugh a little too loud. "I know this amazing place in the hills from where you can see the fires." "I have an audition coming up next week."

"You wouldn't want to lose your focus," said Alex.

"No," he said. "I wouldn't."

When he cycled back along the cliffs, many hours later, there was almost no movement along the street. He saw a police car parked outside his house, red light turning, and for a curious instant a foreign impulse flared up in him. Then he looked farther along, to the beach, and saw where a group of distant figures had built a bonfire at the point. It licked and spluttered between them.

When he got into the house—locking the door behind him—he could hear nothing but the sound of Jewel next door, singing of "foolish games": the surfer, no doubt, getting his partner in the mood. Going to the desk, he took down the books he'd be returning to the library in the morning. For the first time in months, he had an unobstructed view of the sea.

The next night, he got back late from the library—he couldn't afford a break with the deadline coming up so soon—and, walking into the terrace, saw a piece of paper curling out from the fax machine. He hadn't had any faxes for weeks, so he took it out, to find what looked to be a column, from the *L.A. Times,* sent, as far as he could tell, by someone in Westwood or Beverly Hills.

"NEW 'SCRIPTURES' UNEARTHED," said the headline, and underneath it, a subhead said, "Scholars ask, 'What does this say about "gospel truth"?'"

It was a two-column story, clearly buried in the back pages of the A section.

From Associated Press

AMMAN, Jordan—In what is coming to seem an increasingly common phenomenon, scholars working in western Jordan claimed yesterday to have unearthed a document that, they say, could add significantly to our understanding of the Christian story and may, according to one member of the team, "constitute a whole new gospel." Though full details of the discovery remain unclear, those in possession of it—members of an expedition from the University of Arizona—say that it presents the Christian savior in a radical new light, at odds with that of the canonical gospels.

"At last we're seeing the true Jesus, a more interesting figure than the one we know," said Donald Mulligan, the leader of the expedition. "The Jesus we read about in this manuscript is more akin to the figure we know from the recent gospels according to Peter and Mary Magdalene. The searching figure, almost Gnostic, who, in the Thomas gospel, tells us that if we bring forth what is within us, what we bring forth will save us. If we do not bring it forth, what we do not bring forth will destroy us."

More conservative scholars, however, remain unimpressed. "I find it surprising that all these so-called 'Gnostic Gospels' always say the same thing," said Father Kevin Doyle, Professor of Comparative Religions at Notre Dame. "If they are to be believed, Jesus was just a New Age seeker in disguise. A feminist or a proto-Buddhist. I question the virtue of throwing out the wisdom of 2000 years for the discovery of last night."

In response to such challenges, Mulligan points out that the Dead Sea Scrolls were discovered by Bedouin shepherds looking for a goat. The Nag Hammadi gospels, he says, were found by some local brothers looking for some fertilizer. "It's surely no coincidence," he said yesterday, "that the very way in which these texts have come to light is consistent with their message."

The deeper question, most scholars agree, is whether all the new texts—the Jesus Seminar has endorsed 20 such since the war—add to our knowledge of the Christian tradition, or only take away from it. "The principle extends to every faith," said Javad Sefadhi, Islamic scholar at the University of California at Santa Barbara. "If we accept every gospel that comes along, what does that say about 'gospel truth'? If there are 10—or 20—gospels, which one do we swear on in a court of law?"

He put the paper down again on the desk, and looked at it more closely, to see if there had been any greeting or further message erased, or written so faintly that it hadn't come through. But there was nothing. He dialed the number printed at the top, but, as he feared, heard in response only the whine of another fax machine.

A little later, work finished for the day, he poured himself a glass of wine and took a seat in his armchair: with the seminar behind him, he could treat himself to a small celebration. He'd been waiting for some time to take a look at the spiritual diary composed by Rumi's father, the mystic whose visions, some said, had laid the groundwork for his famous son's transformation. As he read through them— trying to recall what he'd read about how the word "desert" came from the Latin *"deserere,"* meaning "to abandon," and then thinking back to John of the Cross's claim that man had been abandoned by his God—he started as the phone on the desk began to ring.

Reflexively, he checked his watch: eleven-forty-three.

He picked the instrument up, bracing for late-night news, and heard nothing at the other end. "Hello," he said again, and again there was nothing—or only what might have been the sound of someone trying to be quiet as he put the receiver down. He returned to the armchair, and picked the same book up. Then, as he settled into it, the phone began ringing again—eleven-forty-five—and he hurried to pick it up, as if to catch the phantom caller by surprise. Nothing once again: only the sound of muffled breath, as of someone trying not to be heard.

When the phone rang once more—six minutes later, according to his watch—he let it ring and ring and took himself off to the living room so the machine could answer for him. He heard a click, his automated voice announcing he wasn't there, and then, to his surprise, he heard another voice come on just after. "Hi. I'm really sorry to be calling so late. It's just, I was thinking about our drive, and I guess I was wondering . . ."

"Hello." He was back in the study at the phone.

"Hi. You're there!"

"I usually am, close to midnight."

"Great," she said, as if she hadn't caught the hint. "Because I'm going to be driving up north this weekend, and I guess, I was thinking, if you had the time . . ."

"I probably have an hour or two," he said, thinking that, if he didn't say that, there'd be another call like this a week from now, next month. "But I'm feeling rather pressed at the moment, what with the deadline coming up."

"I understand," she said solemnly, and then waited for him to say more.

"I met your sister."

"Yes," she said. "She told me. Thank you."

"Thank you" for what? Somehow she seemed always to be presuming a connection he wasn't sure they'd made.

"I didn't know she was interested in Sufism."

"Sometimes, I guess."

"And you must be back in L.A. now."

"For now." As if to tell him that the more he asked, the less she'd say.

"So, if it would work for you, let's meet at three p.m.—at Follow Your Heart."

"The health-food store?" she said, and then, when he said yes, said, "See you then."

He pulled into the small parking lot a few minutes before three o'clock the following Saturday, but the white tank he remembered from the driveway was nowhere to be seen. He imagined her steering through weekend traffic, pushing back a strand of hair as she looked down at the clock that wouldn't be working, reaching in the glove compartment for a map that wouldn't be there.

The kind thing, clearly, would be to sit in his car as if he'd just arrived. He reached for the book of poems he'd brought along with him—just in case—and read the usual Sufi injunctions. "Sell your cleverness. Buy bewilderment." By the time his watch had reached three-thirty, though, he realized he was taking in not a thing: all he could register was the car that wasn't arriving. He saw a pay phone outside the store, and went across to dial his own number. When it answered, he heard, as he'd expected, his own voice, closely followed by her own. "Hi. I'm really sorry. I'll be there soon. I was going to be on time, and then something came up." Her voice almost cracked. "Please don't give up on me. Please?"

He put down the phone and took a long walk around the block. When he came back, though, there was still no sign of the oversized car made for family vacations. He went into Follow Your Heart and bought some dates—the treat, she'd said, her sister always brought back for her from trips to the Middle East.

Back in the car, he picked up the book again, and turned the pages without reading them. Then at last, a few minutes after four, he heard a thump, and saw the car that he remembered bump into the lot. There was fresh mud on its fenders, and its left-hand indicator was winking for a right-hand turn. It lurched into the small space and then paused, as if searching for a space that would be big enough. Then she eased it into a spot and for a few long moments there was nothing.

When she got out at last, he saw no one he could recognize. It was as if a pale facsimile of her had come up here, with all the spirit absent. "I'm so sorry," she said, as soon as she caught sight of him. "I was hoping and hoping I wouldn't screw this up."

"That's all right. You're here now. It's still light."

"It is," she said. "Thank you." And a little color came back to her face. "Thank you for not giving up on me." She took a deep breath. "Can we still go on that drive?"

"If you'd like."

"I'd really like. That road we went on before?"

She got into the car, and placed a blue overnight case at her feet. Then, as he began driving along the hills, she said, "Are you mad?" and jammed a tape into his system as if to drown out the answer. By the time he turned off the main road, and onto the narrow one that curls around the mountains—bare golden hills above them, and the city half lost in a haze below—Bing Crosby was singing about tropical sunsets and girls with flowers in their hair. Someone else, with an old voice that made him think of Fred Astaire, was hymning the Southern Seas, and the moon over Burma; there was a song about a cruise, a shipboard romance, the sadness as the port came into view.

She looked out the window, alert, expectant as a visitor.

"All these songs about traveling?" The traffic had thinned out now; Santa Barbara was a greyish blur in the distance.

"When I was young, I always thought I'd travel."

"And in fact?"

"In fact, I haven't." The trace of anger that lay just behind the eagerness.

"Well, you can make up for it now," he said brightly, and then realized that what he'd said could be taken in the wrong way.

"I will," she said. "I am." The light slowly returning to her voice.

The sky looked guiltless as they crossed the Pass, and each curve brought them some new outline of a house, barricaded behind gates and rebuking the ash-filled slopes all around. "Like phoenixes," she said, and he thought that she was right: they were indeed like mythical creatures of a kind, living far above the city, in a place where they were sure nothing bad could happen to them.

A man was jogging along the narrow, steep road, a dog bounding beside him, and the sea far below. Though it was a Saturday in summer, few other cars were to be seen, and, high above, the tumult of the town far away, it was easier to believe that you were in some previous California, before anyone had thought to call it Eden. The smell of wild anise, and the sky sharp over the lake to the north; an absolute emptiness across the classic Western landscape of ridges and orchards and valleys: California, before it had a name.

In the car, meanwhile, the men bowed in black ties and the ladies' dresses swirled around a dance floor off at sea. Lovers met under tropical moons, and reality was nothing that couldn't be wished away. He thought of his coming trip to Spain, and then, catching sight of her looking out towards the town and ocean, bit the truant thought back.

"You still wish you could travel."

"Of course," she said, with more conviction than the question had deserved. "I wish I could do many things."

"You can, can't you? That's what California is about."

"For some people, I guess." The wistful tone softened the traces of bitterness. "I believed all that once upon a time—"

"Now?"

"Now I don't know."

As they turned onto Painted Cave Road, an ancient canyon on one side, poison oak, thick trees, a gurgling stream at the bottom, they were taken farther from the world than ever, the road closing in on them on both sides and the rocks above enforcing a kind of sovereignty. The switchbacks were harsh, and up above, when they stopped beside the canyon, the markings in the Chumash cave showed scorpions, circles, snakes. Whatever you might believe about California was here, on this shaded road: the ancient signs, the open bright sky. Farther up, nothing but rolling hills and mountains in the distance, Cachuma Lake blue in the sultry afternoon.

"Can we walk a little?" she said as they went up higher, and her manner was so uncertain, so far from the local presumption, that he was touched; the way she asked for favors carried with it the tremor of an expected refusal. He parked the car under a tree and followed her, scrambling, up to a rough, dusty path that cut a thin trail towards a farther hill. They walked and walked, thirty minutes or more, everything falling away from them, and then the trail ended at what seemed to lie at the terminus of every mountain path here: a ruined house. Once upon a time, someone had tried to build a Roman villa here, it seemed, commanding the valley below, and so far from the city that no rules applied; now they could see broken bottles, torn condom wrappers, a few uneven stones poking out of the worn grass.

She took herself down to a flat open space—once a living room, perhaps—and slipped through the broken arches, bending down to pick up rocks now and then, or peeping out at him and smiling from behind a shrunken red-brick chimney. She loved to gambol through other people's spaces, it seemed, the actress again, free as long as no one took her for herself.

"Tell me a story," she said at last, having scoured the site thoroughly and settled down on a line of broken wall, the sun beginning to sink behind them. The wind had come up, as it always does on summer dusks in the hills, and with its bluster came a trace of chill.

The flat open space looked strangely like a tiny open-air stage, made for recitations, and so he went down to it, stood before her, maybe thirty feet away, and said, "There was once an old man, who was young in years, and who lived in the old city of Konya. He was a respected teacher, a father of two, a pillar of the local courts. He led a good and pious life and was famous for the judgments he passed on religious matters."

The words came easily to him, and from a place he couldn't name. Learn and master all the rules, Sefadhi had said, and then throw them all away.

"But one day, for the first time ever, without warning, the man of religion found God. It sounds like a dramatic thing—a thunderbolt from the heavens. In fact, it was a very simple thing: he met a stranger who gave him back a sense of who he might be. 'Who is better?' the rough traveler, much older than he, called out in the marketplace. 'The one who studies God or the one who is God?'

"It was a strange question and perhaps a heretical one, and it shocked him so much he became someone a little different from the person who'd woken up and left the house that morning. Someone, in fact, who thought only of his duties, his students, the case of the moment."

She was looking down at him happily—glad, he realized, just to be in this unlikely site with the sun setting and nothing else around. All the struggle and paleness was gone from her now: as if a storm had passed and she had come into a clearing.

"And then, as suddenly as the stranger had come, this new friend disappeared. The old man wept; he walked and walked to see if he could find him. He sang songs, wrote poems, even, when he heard the new friend might be in Damascus, sent his son there to bring him back.

"But then"—and here, to his pleasure and surprise, the story took hold of him, and he left everything real behind—"as seasons passed, it became clear that his friend was never coming back. That his purpose, in some sense, had been served. And so, picking up an old leather bag from beside his bed, he walked out of the house, out of the town, and up into the hills.

"The town of Konya is surrounded by mountains, and in winter they grow cold, impassable. Travelers stay in the inns till spring, and everyone waits for the first sign of wild flowers. But this man went in the opposite direction, climbing up the mountains in winter as if determined that no one could follow him.

"Days passed, his wife and children looked everywhere, but of course they could not find him. Neighbors muttered that they had been 'abandoned,' but his wife knew that in some sense her husband was just going home. He was not lost, she thought, but found, and now was on his way to a place as distant as the place where he had been born. Though shopkeepers searched all the places where he was known to sit and drink and talk, they never found him, and his wife never helped them in their search. 'He is not there,' she said, 'because the person you know is dead.' "

The wind picked up now, blowing her long hair into squalls and tangles round her face. She pushed away the strands that flew into her mouth, and he raised his voice to be heard over the whistle and the roar, his words filling and echoing around the abandoned space.

"The police sent horses and dogs, the best climbers in the town traveled as far as they could, children were told to look out for a ragged man where they played, but it was all, of course, in vain. He was beyond their calls now, and it was easy to believe that words were among the things he'd left at home.

"In time the search was stopped, and families returned to their usual rounds. His students became teachers, with schools of their own; his children became parents. One day, many years later, a traveler came down from the mountains, in February, when the snow was thickest, with a curious tale. He was a bedraggled man, of twigs and branches, and he said something rough and strange about a young old man, seen many years before, beating a trail into the mountains, to somewhere from which you could see valleys and distant lakes. Without saying a word, he had followed the man to a rock at the end of the last trail, where the path ran out, and seen him arrive at the ruins of what must once have been a large house. There was someone waiting for him there, as if they had planned to meet all along, and as soon as he saw the wanderer arrive, to be found by the stranger, he, the man who spoke to them now, turned round and came back out into the world."

A silence fell, broken only by the wind, the flapping of her hair against her cheeks and shoulders, the sound of his steps scrambling back to where she sat.

"That's beautiful. Where does it come from?"

"Here," he said, tapping his chest.

"Dangerous, too."

"I suppose it is. I hadn't meant for it to come out like that."

"I don't think everyone would be so happy about his abandoning his wife and family."

"I know. It must have come out of one of the texts I've been reading. You know how you read a story—about a pavilion in the desert, say—and then you dream about it, only better?"

She was holding on to her hair as it streamed about her face; the sky was on the edge of navy blue, and the first stars seemed imminent.

"We should be heading back. You must be cold."

She shook her head no. "I like it here. It's free."

An unexpected word to use, but he sat beside her on the rock, leaving her free to explore some more.

"A long way from Los Angeles," he said, somewhat obviously, as if words were less dangerous than silence.

She nodded and turned to him, expectant. In most people it is the eyes that tell you who they are; in her, the small pursed mouth, strangely prim and shy.

"Well, I'm heading back even if you aren't." He pulled himself up and began walking along the path: the afternoon was taking strange turns along the road, and he'd found himself in a place he'd never expected to visit. He held on to the thought of the Rumi story as if to prevent himself from losing balance.

She followed him as he walked, and when they arrived back at the car there were stars in the branches above them. The road was close to pitch-black, and it was easy to imagine that not a single car had driven past in all the time they'd been walking. Their own car looked touchingly brave and resolute, alone under the tree full of stars.

He unlocked her door, and closed it behind her, and when he got in at his side, he moved into a waiting silence. He didn't want to intrude on it—her quietness pulled him in as much as her chattering pushed him away—and he put on the heater and sat behind the wheel, waiting till she returned from wherever she was.

"Thank you for a lovely walk."

"My pleasure." Such observation of ceremonial courtesies in anything-goes California.

Then, after a few moments, "Do I get another kiss?"

"I don't think so. I'm taken, remember?"

"And not with me."

"It wouldn't be fair—in the circumstances."

" 'In the circumstances,' " she said, mocking the pompousness, and leaning forward to kiss him lightly on the lips.

She kissed, somehow, as if she'd never kissed before: suddenly the girl who listened to the songs of travel was in the tiny car beside him. It was strange to see all this just from the way she said, "You're so warm," and rested her head on his shoulder, but he could feel somehow the weight of all the things she hadn't done or thought, saving them up for a rainy day that might never come. She was like someone whose life had not begun.

"Thank you," she said. "You really touch me."

"I'm glad."

The words could hardly have been more inadequate.

"I could get in trouble with you, big trouble." The very girlishness of the phrasing making her point better than she could.

"You're lonely," he said, not knowing why exactly.

"In a way. As much as anyone. Like you, I bet." She turned to look away from him, out the window. "All the time I was growing up, I never seemed to belong. My parents were outsiders everywhere we went."

He didn't say anything, to leave her where she was.

When she turned back to him, her eyes were full.

"I'm sorry," he said, smoothing the fall of hair behind her ears. "I didn't mean to bring up painful memories."

"That's okay. I don't mind. As long as you make them better."

The strange, antique diction again, the sense of her removal from the world, and then, as if pushing aside what was fragile in her, she climbed over the gearstick—a tomboy on her way into the hills again—and sat in his lap. Her long hair, golden where it fell around her face, highlighted the hurt eyes.

"Eaargh," he said, looking up at her.

"What is it?"

"I'm starting to like you more and more."

"Somehow, I thought you would."

She looked down again to kiss him lightly, and he thought of how California did this to you: suddenly the rules were changed, and you had something fragile in your arms, and you weren't sure what to do with the weight of it.

"You grew up in an area like this?" he said, to retrieve his bearings.

"Except I was alone."

"Not in your home."

"Especially in my home. As soon as I opened my eyes."

He kissed her quickly for consolation, and then reached for the gearstick, so she'd return to her side and he could start up the car and drive back into town. Whatever would come after this would only smudge what had come before.

The engine spluttered and juddered, and failed.

"The heater, it's killed your battery."

He got out into the angry wind—rising while they'd been in the car—and she climbed out of her side, and they were alone in a howling whirl, the lights of the town far below. Above, there were so many stars the road was bright, in ghostly light, and so they began walking, towards more dead brush and empty hills. A few minutes later, the wind roaring, and the trees shuddering and bending in the dark, they came to a house, built on a turn, a house of spirits, as it seemed, with a rusty old pickup and a VW parked in the dust beside it, and no lights on inside.

"Anybody home?" she called out. "Hello?"

There was no one, and they walked on, brought together at the point where they'd been planning to pull apart. Farther down the road, there was another house, built on a ledge, a ship waiting to take off towards the distant lights, and as they drew close to it, a pickup truck pulled out. They went up to it, explained the situation, and soon were riding in the back, the stars above them through the trees, absurdly like two orphans lost at camp.

"Usually," she said, holding her arms around herself in the wind, "I mean often, I get freaked out just to be this close. But with you I'm safe, because you're taken."

"I hope so," he said, as if picking up the habit of uncertainty from her.

When the truck dropped them off at a small illuminated phone booth, sitting implausibly in a parking lot in the middle of the mountains, a shuttered country store beside it, and a broken piano outside the door, he called the emergency rescue service, and was told to stay where he was, they'd be there in fifty minutes.

"Lost in the mountains like the guy in your story."

"Except he was alone."

"Not at the end," she said, a mischievous light in her eyes. "What if they never find us?"

"They probably won't. All I could tell them was, 'We're in the abandoned parking lot somewhere near the top of the Pass.'"

He picked out a simple prelude on the piano, and she sat down beside him, kissing his neck, blowing on his lobe, the cusp of his ear, as he played. He looked over at her, and her eyes were thrilled, awakened.

When the tow truck came, a short bull-necked man, not delighted to be called out into the hills at eleven o'clock on a windy Saturday night, asked him to sign, and then drove them, his truck laboring, back to the tree full of stars.

When he dropped her off at her car outside Follow Your Heart, no words came to mind.

"Thank you for a wonderful day," she said.

"Thank you," he said, recalling that his story had ended strangely.

. . .

The next day, when he came home from the library, there was a message on his machine. "Hi," said the now familiar voice, curiously flushed, full up. "I hope you won't get mad at me, though probably you will and won't ever want to see me again. But I just wanted to thank you for a lovely day. I don't have so many of those in my life."

The abrupt lurch into something else, and the sadness she carried round with her like a coat. "You may think you've made the biggest mistake of your life, but I wrote you a poem. Here goes: please don't laugh.

> "We climb and climb,
> And from the peaks we see
> A space I might have called
> Eternity.
>
> The day winds down,
> The skies unravel wide,
> And where we are
> Is somewhere deep inside
>
> A home that never was,
> A place that has no name:
> Stillness in the dusk,
> No face inside the frame.

"I don't know what it means," said the soft voice again, "but I think I was inspired by our walk. Our walks. If you never want to talk to me again, I'll understand. Take care."

"Mr. Macmillan." It was Alex's voice now, feigning distance. "I couldn't observe you in the house last night. Were you unavoidably detained?" (It was Sefadhi's euphemism for students who failed to show up for seminars.) "I know your Sufis are a jealous mistress."

. . .

He played the message over again, and listened to her odd poem: as much Emily Dickinson as the Beach Boys, he thought, and not at all the simpler kind of lyric he'd expected.

He picked up the phone to thank her—it had been a long time since anyone had written a poem for him, let alone dared to read it into his machine—and then he remembered he didn't have her number. He could call Kristina, of course, but that felt like a violation of trust somehow. Besides, Kristina seemed involved with everything else in his life, Khalil and Sefadhi and the men calling from Westwood.

The only thing to do was wait. By the phone if necessary, with this new life set to one side of the desk beside the ancient poets.

He got up early on the twenty-eighth, and drove through Santa Barbara to the south. There were campers, boogie-boarders, German sightseers along the coastal highway, and on the strip south of Oxnard there was still an air of happy improvisation, as if no one had really settled down there yet and the beach still belonged to rock and sea. A few hardy souls were camping out in tents beside the waves, and occasionally figures would emerge from the beach down below and walk along the road, swathed in black, or bare-chested, as if they were characters from the Chumash caves. The impulse, always in California, backwards, away from established forms, towards whatever is primeval.

Now, besides, as he pulled into Los Angeles, all the ancient cultures of the world were streaming into the bright, forgetful city, bringing their runes, their songs and superstitions. There were more Druze here than in Lebanon, it was said; more Zoroastrians than in Iran. When he turned off Wilshire and drove towards Olympic, he found himself in what could have been a suq, selling homesick dreams; "Mexanesian" restaurants under palm trees, and Spanish pawn shops with their signs in Hangul script. So many different cultures crowded into the small space beside the desert that it looked as if the wind would blow and all of them would be scattered again, to the far corners of the earth.

On Westwood itself, the numbers went down slowly, past a long, half-broken line of places selling passports, immigration advice, dusty deserted restaurants offering what was billed as "Royal Persian Cuisine." From the windows of the stores old torch singers, from a generation ago, and a world away, looked back at him; pictures of the central mosque in Isfahan, amidst guitars and children's baubles. Old men sat on the sidewalk with their Farsi newspapers, sugar cubes set beside their glasses of tea, and on one side street an ancient man, in faded jacket and tie, was helping his wife across the road, her head scarf, her blond hair, the expensive leather bag she carried all speaking of other lives, far away, in the shadow of the Champs-Élysées.

The place marked 9763 looked hardly different from its neighbors, and when he went in, it was to be greeted by the smell of scented cardamom tea and only a few men in the aisles, browsing through magazines and books. The characters of Farsi rose and broke around him like waves in a foreign desert. Behind the counter, a man in a greying ponytail was conducting an argument on a phone—or just a Farsi conversation—and one or two of the men, some in suits, one even in dark glasses, looked up to see who had come to join them.

"Can I help you?" said the man from behind the counter, suddenly by his side, and looking piqued.

"I'm John Macmillan. I have an appointment with the owner."

"Is he expecting you?"

"I think so. His son's the one who told me to come here."

The man looked back at him in open disbelief, and then began walking towards the back of the store with the rolling gait of a wrestler. When they'd got halfway there, another man, well tailored, came to take the stranger over.

"Mr. Macmillan. Thank you for your time. It's good of you to visit us." The smooth voice from the phone, all Belgravia polish.

The newcomer muttered something quickly to the ponytailed cashier, and the man went back heavily to his post.

"My father's waiting for you," said the smooth young man.

They walked back through the narrow aisles to a small office in the rear where a man in a jacket and tie—a professor in an earlier life, perhaps—was paging through a large book. When they came in, he looked up from what he was doing, and the young man went over to stand by his side, as if to serve as a translator.

"My father wanted you to see this."

The old man opened the desk in front of him, and pulled out a large May Company box, about the size of a formal shirt. Then he extended it across the desk to the visitor.

He was meant to open it up, he guessed, and when he did so, he had to stop himself from saying anything. It was beautiful, so beautiful he wanted to take it away and lock it up inside his desk forever. It felt like the reason he'd begun studying these distant poets all those years ago, love song and prayer all at once.

The cover itself, clearly old, was heavy and green, with gold calligraphy across it, not far from the imperial style; when he opened it up, very carefully—the owners' eyes on him at every moment—it was to see poems written on every page, great swirls of racing dots and dashes, as urgently from the heart as if they were verses from the Quran (they weren't, his Farsi told him). Along the margins of each page were golden arabesques, as if to keep the meanings hidden, or safe. He thought, for no reason he could fathom, of the golden bars on the shrine in Damascus, the weeping women at its grille.

"It's beautiful," he said, aware that they were watching for his reaction. It didn't matter what he said, he realized; the purpose of the summons was to see how he responded to the book.

"We thought you might be interested in it," said the silky young man, who seemed accustomed to acting as an intermediary.

"Interested, of course. I'd give anything to have this in my possession. Even for a few weeks. But I'm not a collector. You understand that?" As long as you can't tell someone's motives, you're always a few steps behind him.

"We know that. We also know that you are a scholar. You have spent years with Javad Sefadhi. You've been to Syria."

He looked back at them to try to gauge what was going on. Clearly, they were testing him in some way, toying with him; he remembered how, with Khalil, he'd gone in with questions of his own and come out with the professor's errands.

"I hardly have enough money to buy my own textbooks."

The young man said something quick and rough to the older man, under his breath, and then looked back at him with a smile.

"If I had a chance to spend some weeks with this, a month or two, I could tell you something. But I'm not sure I have the time or"—he might as well speak their language—"you have the money. Anyway, there are a million people who know more about this kind of thing. Even in Los Angeles."

"They are not pure," the man said simply. "They know too much."

"Not poor, either. I'm sorry: I don't know what to say. It's beautiful, and in the right hands it could give someone a lot of pleasure." He'd keep things on the aesthetic level. "That's all I can say."

It was not an easy thing to put the book down: holding it even for a moment had felt like walking into a private room where something you've been looking for indefinitely awaits you. To have the prospect of new verses in his hands, to see them in a context that no one known to him had seen before—the scholar is a materialist in a different vein. He put it down, and looked to see what would follow.

"We are grateful for your time," said his urbane host, "very grateful," as another, still younger man came in with a tray on which had been placed three glasses of tea. "Maybe, if you are interested later, if you know someone who is interested, you can come back. You have our address."

He took the glass he was given, uncertain about why they were performing the formalities after the discussion, not before, and sipped. "How did you find me?" he asked. "I'm not the most obvious person to consult in such a situation." Men who spoke like characters from a second-rate thriller, an actress on a mountaintop at midnight: it wasn't so much that California lacked mystery, he thought, as that it wrapped it in the forms we know too well from movies.

The young man didn't say anything immediately, but opened a thin black leather wallet and pulled out a card, heavy and embossed. "It means a lot to us that you are interested in our culture." Then he led him back towards the door. "We are grateful, deeply grateful, for your interest." Thanking him for what he hadn't done—as, he realized with a start, Camilla often did.

Out in the street, abruptly exiled from the mystery, he felt at odds, restless and defeated: two hundred miles just to be caught inside one of the diaspora's intricate designs. He looked at his watch—it was still early—and he thought of Camilla, hiding out somewhere inside the grey sprawl. She'd taken care, he'd noticed, never to tell him anything about the specifics of her life—where she lived, what phone number would reach her, what she did with what seemed to be her free time. But he'd caught sight of an address, on the top right-hand corner of her address book, when she'd pulled it out to write down his telephone number, and even if it led to a parent's house or just a place where she'd once lived, it could only bring him closer to a sense of who she was.

He drove across the tangle of freeways in the angry, hazy morning, the streets a snarl of competing dreams, the roads themselves an emblem of what happens when everyone is free to pursue his hope, and they all fly off in different directions. The place gave newcomers a blank piece of paper on which they could sketch anything they wanted; but would the newcomers ever give the place something more solid to hold on to than a sheaf of decorated papers?

When he got off the freeway running south, closer now to the hills—he could smell orange blossom in the streets, and the mountains were just visible through the smog—he drove slowly down the road he'd mapped out in advance, a long, disinherited street of fast-food stores and gas stations, the occasional astrologer's shack offering futures at $25 off. Now and then, at intersections, a church spire poked forlornly through the trees, mocked in some ways by the small, colored buildings on every side.

When he turned off the main street onto the road whose name he'd seen on her book, he found himself in the kind of California backstreet he'd imagined in the Chandler books he'd read at school— a long row of low-slung Spanish houses, their curtains drawn against the world. The number he was looking for was painted in black on the sidewalk, but when he went up to the front door and rang the bell, there was no answer. He couldn't even tell if it had rung. Walking around the house, he imagined her in her bedroom, crying out for help and then barricading herself in behind locked doors and closed windows in case anyone actually came and responded to her call.

On the far side of the building from the road, he could just make out the grubby backs of curtains, cigarette stains on the carpet, and a mess of papers everywhere; beside the front door, a few wet bills and letters stuck damply out of a tiny mailbox. He walked through the garage on the other side, and came to a small garden, wild and overgrown, and behind one of the plate-glass windows, the curtains left a small space open. Peering in, he saw a wilderness of boxes, papers everywhere, plants, stuffed animals, old letters, a dress, a calendar from three years before. Everywhere he could see, a mess of objects once treasured, all thrown together so wildly you couldn't tell what was important and what was not (part of the point, no doubt). A stranger looking in would have said that a thief had been through the place; he imagined that the thief was her, throwing everything together so as to hide what it was she cared about.

"It's weird," she'd said suddenly, just before he dropped her off at her car after the long night on the mountain. "I'd really begun to think you were someone I could get seriously hung up on." The tense she'd used, the sudden rescinding of trust, the pulling away when minutes before she'd been clambering towards him—it all seemed a way of saying that she would always hide from what she liked.

Above the mess on the floor, he could just make out—not easily, through a dirty window, in the midday glare—a framed picture on the wall: a painting of an English house, he imagined, or a Renaissance madonna. He looked closer, trying to decipher it, and saw, or thought he saw, a painting, Near Eastern in origin, of a tiger, framed in black and golden lines: the kind of thing a caliph might amuse himself with on an idle afternoon.

"I'm sorry I missed you," he wrote on a scrap of notebook paper as he walked back to the front door. "I only wanted to say hello." Then, getting in the car to drive home, he realized that he was further from knowing anything than when the day began.

The morning in the Iranian shop had left him at a distance from himself, as if the life he was officially leading were taking place in a language he couldn't speak. He couldn't tell what impulse exactly had been awakened by the manuscript, sensual or professional or romantic, but it hardly seemed to matter: the Iranians, as no doubt they had intended, had set something ticking in his life, and now he could settle to nothing else.

"The thing you've got to bear in mind"—Mowbray, after being asked for a letter of reference for the fellowship—"is that everything in that tradition has a different value since the Revolution."

"Meaning I should be careful?"

"No more than any scholar is careful."

It was his professor's habitual warning, but underneath the note of caution lay something more particular: ever since the clerics had come to power in Iran, both the outer value of Islamic texts, and the inner, had been suddenly transformed. Manuscripts were streaming out into the West now at a faster rate than ever before, on their way to auction houses and private collections; but, more than that, something that was sacred, even esoteric, to those within the faith was being sent to people who saw it only in financial terms. And every time a book of poems was sent to Christie's, say, or sold off to some museum, something whose only real meaning was spiritual was being treated as just another *objet d'art,* or valuable antiquity. As if a price tag were to be hung around the neck of a saint.

Khomeini himself was remembered in many quarters as a latter-day Hafez, the "Defining Modern Mystic," as Pauline Davis had called him in the title of her dissertation: people spoke of how he lived in Qom in the early days, in a tiny room, surviving on rice and yogurt, and devoting his nights to writing love poems and to studies of the Gnostic scriptures. During the day, he would sit with his students on the floor and speak of the sufferings of the oppressed. When he spoke of God—Pauline had said this in her seminar—you could feel the fire of love burning through him.

But as soon as he came to power, like any leader, he'd begun to fear his own shadow more than anything. And any group that met under cover after nightfall, mystical or otherwise, could be seen only as a threat to the regime. The rulers of Iran would never take after Sanai or Saadi, two of their strongest attractions to the West (just as the Southern Baptists seldom bothered to attack Shakespeare, even if they did find him immoral); but any manuscript not authorized by them—and offering a different reading of the faith—could only be seen as a subversion. Especially if it came forth from someone outside the faith.

It was dark when he got back from the library, and when he opened the door—locking it behind him—the only thing visible in the room was the furious blinking of the red light on the answering machine. He pushed a button, and a voice came out that sounded as if it was very far away. "Hi . . ." He couldn't make out all the words that followed (she was in the desert, he guessed, her voice drowned out by passing eighteen-wheelers). ". . . just got your message. I'm sorry I missed you. Miss you, I guess . . . to Monterey this weekend. Any chance you might be free . . . It's 818-437-2962."

"Just" got his message? And driving up to a town three hundred miles from her own? In England people take you by surprise the longer you know them, and only slowly, often after many years, could you begin to make out the hidden staircases and false fronts behind which they conceal their treasures; here the surprises came all at once, and even the surfaces were variable.

He waited till it was a reasonable hour the next morning—she liked to roam at night, she'd said—and forced himself not to go out to the library, not even to take his morning run along the beach. When the clock on the desk said 10:00, he dialed the number she'd left for him.

"Hello," said the voice at the other end. It was groggy, and very male.

"Hello. I'd like to leave a message for Camilla Jensen."

"She's right here. Do you want to talk to her?"

"Why not?"

In a matter of seconds—too few for comfort—she was there, intimate as ever, inches from his ear.

"I hope I'm not disturbing you."

"You can disturb me anytime." Femmes fatales, he guessed, were not part of her onstage repertoire.

"Anyway, I got your message . . ."

"Are you free? Can we meet?"

"Perhaps for a short while. I've got a paper to complete."

"I'm driving north on Tuesday."

"Then why don't you come to dinner? I'm at 4657 Del Playa. You just get off the freeway at Los Carneros, and then drive towards the ocean. When you can't drive any farther, turn left."

"I'll be there," she said, and then there was a scuffling—the sound of whispers—and she returned to whatever was at her side.

"So when do I get to meet this woman you're not seeing?"

It was Monday evening—their usual time for darts—and Alex was picking up his implements from the counter near the table.

"In time. It'll happen."

Alex fired his darts—one, two, three—into the board, all elegant economy, and then turned to sip at his drink. "Is it something you think I'll see or something you think I'll say?"

"Neither. It's just that she's not at her best in public."

"The private treasure," said Alex in his characteristic way, and made room for him to take his turn.

His first throw landed in the outer ring.

"The Sufis don't tell you to live in your own head."

"I realize that," he said, and his second dart banged against the board and fell limply to the floor. "It's just that I don't have time for distractions with the thesis due next June."

"So you keep yourself hidden, and tell yourself you've got mystery in your life."

"I wouldn't say that."

His third throw scored a paltry 7.

Perhaps the most distinctive feature of the Shia faith," he found himself writing the next afternoon, determined to put all thoughts of manuscripts, and unsought friends, behind him, "is the principle of *taqiyya,* or sacred dissimulation. This notion, of sanctioned lying, is all that allowed the Shia to keep going when the Soviets converted the mosques of Central Asia into 'Museums of Atheism,' and all that allowed the Sufis to keep a flame alight when Atatürk turned Turkey into a secular state, banning the dervish orders that are now the country's most famous export to the world.

"There are, of course, many practical, and political, reasons for the principle of hiding what you truly feel, especially in a culture like Iran, where secrecy has always been a kind of second nature ('Conceal your goal, your destination, and your creed,' as the old maxim has it). But deeper than this, the principle of *taqiyya* stands for something more: it tells us that we're all other—better—than we seem.

"Indeed, as Ryan McCarthy has written, in defining religious discourse as that which covers its own tracks, leaving a trail only for initiates, it is a way of drawing a curtain—best of all, an invisible curtain—between those who are inside the circle and those who are not. To feign ignorance, as Peter did, in denying Jesus, is in fact . . ." and then the alarm clock that he'd put at the side of the desk went off, and he came back to his senses: three-fifteen Tuesday afternoon. She'd be getting in her car to start the long drive up here.

He walked out into the bleached sunshine, and untethered his bike from where he always kept it, by the wall. Then, going into the center of town, he went to the record store that had been his sanctuary when he'd arrived, and rummaged through the "Super Oldies" section at the back. At the supermarket he bought a jug of mango juice, and a bottle of wine like the one he'd seen at the sister's house, the first afternoon. Then, going home to tidy up, he put a copy of Rumi on the bedside table, and stopped to wonder what it was exactly he was doing.

He timed the spaghetti so it would be ready for eight o'clock, and give them a little time to enjoy the beach while it was light. He set the *Songs of the South Pacific* he'd just bought at the second track, with the PAUSE button depressed. He put the books he'd been packing for Seville away so she wouldn't be reminded of his coming departure. Friendship is in every case an acceptance of someone in all her mess and folly, he thought, but in this case, he had to take extra care to step around all the things she was keeping away from him: the house with all its clutter, the unexplained male voice at the other end, the stuff she threw behind her in the car as if it would all sort itself out in her absence. It was as if she feared the clearer person inside her.

At seven-fifteen, the phone rang, and, startled, he ran across to it, and answered softly, almost intimately.

"Mr. Macmillan." Alex, smooth as a late-night deejay. "Bertolucci's *Conformist* at Campbell Hall. Tonight at eight o'clock."

"I'm sorry. I have something else."

"Of course you do." Alex rearranged his pride. "Some other time, perhaps."

He went back to the sofa, and sat there at a loss, not sure exactly why he was waiting for someone who contrived to put him off in some way. It was as if she had a light, a fire inside her, and shied away from it by living in the smaller self she presented to the world. In most people you feel that they're showing their best face to the public, and keeping their shadows carefully hidden; in her it was almost the opposite.

He looked at the clock again—seven-fifty-one—and wondered if he'd given her the wrong day. But if he called now, he'd only get the man he was eager not to ask about, or give her another reason to be wary. Besides, she was on her way to Monterey, and he was taken, so he'd said.

At eight-forty-five, he put down the book on which he hadn't been able to concentrate—"Your real country is the place where you're going, not the place where you are"—and got up to push down the PAUSE button. He took the mango juice back to the refrigerator and turned off the main course. At nine-twenty-three—the clock seemed to be following him everywhere—he went into the terrace to collect the books he'd need next week for Seville.

Outside he heard a car slow down, then stop. An ignition turned off, and a door was slammed. Footsteps on the gravel, and then a knock at a door, next door.

He picked up the phone to make sure it was working—nine-fifty-seven—and then went out to the beach, so he wouldn't hear the sound of a knock, the absence of a knock. When he came back, having tried to extend the walk for as long as he could, there was still no car in the place he'd left open for it—he checked—and he went into the bedroom and turned off all the lights.

In bed, he was in Paris again, and the now ubiquitous Martine was at his side, watching the rain slant into the gutters, and the pigeons on the slate-grey rooftops, a red-and-blue umbrella far below, and a man pushing and pushing at a button. "It's what's so heartbreaking," she was saying as she turned away, and walked back into the room, the dark. "The sense that if you ever let yourself go, really let yourself go, something rather wonderful might come out. But you won't. And one keeps on hanging on, just in case."

Then she'd said nothing, and he'd remembered that her silences had always been much harder to answer than her words.

He saw another figure now, in her sister's kitchen, looking as if she were the only person on a long line of folding grey chairs in some institutional hallway. At the very far end, alone. He started counting the chairs to put himself to sleep—"sixty-one, sixty-two, sixty-three"—and then, suddenly, he heard a knock, so faint it sounded as if it wanted to take itself back already.

He lay where he was; the red digits on the clock said 10:37.

"Hello." A small knock again. "Sorry. It's me."

He lay and lay where he was, and then went slowly over to unbolt the door. "I'm sorry," she said, and he saw someone who seemed not to have filled herself in today. Her eyelids were red and bruised, and there was a stain at the side of her dress. She'd put on something blue, to match her eyes, but the light had changed long since.

"I got you this," she said, and pushed a card into his hand.

"What happened to you?"

"The usual." One word too many, he saw, and she would flee. "I was trying and trying so hard . . ."

"So hard you didn't even call."

"I wanted to call. Really I did. But then I'd have never come." She looked bereft, as if she'd thrown her hopes into the fire. "I thought you'd be mad."

"Why shouldn't I be mad? You're three hours late."

"I knew you'd be," she said, and there was almost an echo of comfort in her voice, as if she could relax into her fears again. "I knew if I tried too hard . . ."

"You'd go wrong."

She nodded, looking towards the ground. "It always happens like this."

"Well, you'd better come in, for a moment. It's late enough as it is."

"Thank you. Do you want to see your card?"

"Not terribly, to be truthful." He turned it over and saw an ornamental Persian miniature: a garden made to look like Paradise, a stylized prince and princess underneath a tree, the sky all around them a jeweled glaze of blue and gold. Inside, the printed message came from Rumi: "Lovers don't finally meet somewhere. They're in each other all along." She hadn't written anything inside it, but he felt touched and startled all at once: giving him messages about "lovers" when she'd hardly managed to bring herself to his door.

"It's on the back," she said. "I didn't want to take away from the poem."

He turned the card over and saw her writing, sloping and sprawling across the space, in the blotchy ballpoint he remembered seeing in her shirt pocket the first time, at the sister's house. "Thank you for giving me a chance," she'd written in her broken scrawl. "I'm sorry in advance if I disappoint you. I disappoint myself, every day, every moment. You're the first person in a long time who's given me a chance to show I might not be completely worthless."

It was like everything about her: proclaiming her unfitness in every syllable, and yet, in the proclamation, in the cry that was sounding just beneath the words—someone raising up a hand as if to be pulled up—it asked for something else and said she was staking everything on this. We are something more than the sum of our mistakes, he thought, and then completed the thought: "But that doesn't make the mistakes any less costly."

"I had some mango juice ready for you. Almost three hours ago." She looked down.

"A whole meal, actually. More than that."

"I'm sorry," she said, and her arms were around him, her head buried in his shoulder as she sobbed and emptied herself out completely.

"I always blow it." The force of her self-impatience heartbreaking to see. "I always do. Every time someone shows the slightest interest in me, I push them away."

"Why is that, do you think?"

"Why do you think? I'm scared. If I really want something, it'll be taken away from me. It always has in the past."

"So you try not to want anything?" She nodded, caught up in a small space with her greatest enemy. "Not the ideal quality in a friend. Even in an acquaintance."

"I know. I'm sorry. I know I've blown it."

"I should be getting back to sleep. If you'd like an orange juice before you hit the road . . ."

"Thank you. I didn't mean to let you down like this. All the trouble you've taken . . ."

He pushed the START button on the CD player, and somebody began to sing of the beaches of Tahiti when the moon is full. The mango juice was cool, and a little color came into her face; her fear had the capacity to erase her entirely, to turn her into a walking shell of some kind, and yet whatever was opposed to it, which came out more slowly, began to fill her face with light. She showed every last feeling on her face (strange, he thought, in an actress), and that made her more dangerous than anything: she could make you believe that you had the capacity to bring the light back to her pale complexion.

"You went to all this trouble. Just for me. People usually don't do that."

"I went to much more trouble than you can see. I wanted to make you happy. I'm going to Spain soon, and I thought this would be the last chance."

He was giving her a chance to pull herself away. And responding to her games, perhaps, with some of his own. The crooner sang guilelessly of stars in the Southern sky and how the trade winds made the coconuts fall to earth.

He looked unsubtly at his watch.

"It's getting late."

"I know. I don't know where to go. They're expecting me up north tomorrow."

He sighed, so she would hear it, and went into his bedroom to pull out a few blankets. He threw them, with little grace, on the sofa, and said, "The bathroom's over there if you need it. I'll be going out first thing in the morning. But you can let yourself out; the door will lock behind you. I realize that gallantry demands that I give you the bed and take the sofa myself, but, frankly, I'm too tired."

"Thank you. This is really kind of you."

He went back into his darkened room and willed himself towards sleep. Eleven-forty became eleven-forty-one. A few hours later, it was eleven-forty-three. He could hear scuffling in the next room, a heavy thump, a stifled curse. He could hear sandals being slipped off—so it seemed—and a light-blue dress being pulled over a head. He could hear everything more vividly than if it had been taking place at his side, in the bed.

At one o'clock he went into the next room, his mind as overbright as a video arcade.

"Hi," she said, stirring on the sofa.

"Hi. I just wanted to make sure you were okay." His excuses, he realized, were sounding as flimsy as hers.

"I'm fine. Just upset with myself. Empty and frustrated. You?"

"Not great."

He came round to where she was lying, and she sat up, wrapped in blankets, her hair—she'd obviously washed and combed it in preparation for the evening—falling straight down, and making her seem naked in some way, undefended.

"What is it with you?"

"What isn't it?" The bitter sound that always lay behind the brightness. "It always happens like this."

"What are you scared of?"

"Everything." It sounded like she could tear herself into pieces. "Frightening you away. Not frightening you away. Getting involved with somebody I care about, and ending up with my heart broken. Not getting involved with somebody I care about, and then regretting it the rest of my life. Everything's scary."

"You sound like a movie."

"Movies have happy endings."

Anyone could see how this would play out: she'd make her worst fears come true, and then the lowest part of her could say she was right all along. She'd push someone away till he hurt her, and then say she'd been right to know she couldn't trust. He thought, somehow, of what McCarthy had said, about the two different ways of seeing life: "The believer erects a temple in his mind, and that becomes the locus, the impetus, if you will, of his exertions. The unbeliever digs a hole, and then is assured of having no way out."

"What can I—what can anyone—do to help?"

"Nothing. Ever. Everyone gives up on me. Usually way before this point."

He smoothed away the moisture that was gathering at the corner of her eyes.

"What's the cure?"

"I don't know. If I did, maybe I could do something. All the time I was growing up, I was always sure I was going to be abandoned."

"By your parents?"

"By everyone. I wanted to shout out, 'Mr. Stork, Mr. Stork: you dropped me at the wrong house. Please come and take me to a place where they'll really like me.' "

It sounded like a child's complaint, but the sadness went deeper, if only because it had had twenty years to ripen.

"Maybe you can make the place where people will be kind to you?"

"I can't. When I was young, everything I did was wrong. Whatever I did, they'd yell at me."

She carried her frustrations with her everywhere she went, and then looked around her and saw the image of her frustrations.

"Camilla, I don't know what to do. Why don't you come next door, and I'll read you something to help you get to sleep? To help *me* get to sleep!"

She followed him, swathed in blankets, tripping over the edge of them once, and then taking smaller steps: he could see a white nightdress underneath all the layers, bare feet. She moved across the room as if under a spell placed on her by herself.

In the bedroom, he stacked the pillows up against the headboard, pulled back the blankets on one side, and said, "Here. I'll read you poems so boring they'll put us both to sleep." Picking up the volume of Rumi he'd put beside the bed, as if poems of surrender were the best way of making them drift off.

When the light came up, not many hours later, she was so deeply asleep that all the strain was gone from her, and her face was as clear as it must have been when she was feeling truly safe: for the moment, she had been taken by the stork to a place that was more accepting.

He left a tall glass of mango juice beside the bed, put the CD player on PAUSE at the song she'd said she'd liked, and picked up the book of Rumi from where it lay, facedown, pages splayed, on the bedside table. Then he set it down again, and took himself off to the library.

When he came home, in mid-afternoon, the house was immaculate. The dishes had been washed and neatly put back on their shelves. The counter had been wiped clean, and the blankets set back in the closet. The Rumi book—he noticed, though he'd told himself he wouldn't—had been moved a little closer to the wall.

On the coffee table sat an envelope, and when he opened it, he found another card, showing a close-up of an elaborate carpet, so rich with golds and blues that it seemed the cover of a Quran, a prayer that was itself a proof of a divinity.

"Let yourself be silently drawn by the stronger pull of what you really love," read the inscription (from Rumi, of course—as Sefadhi had feared, he was quickly supplanting Rilke and the Dalai Lama as the reigning king of greeting cards). On the back again, the small, looping scrawl. "Thank you from the bottom of my heart for putting up with me and helping me get to sleep and opening the door to me when I came. I'm not used to so much in my life."

Now she was gone again, out of reach (no address, no telephone number except the ones answered by machines, her sister's voice, some man he'd never heard about), and he was left to get his thoughts together before next Monday, and the conference in Seville.

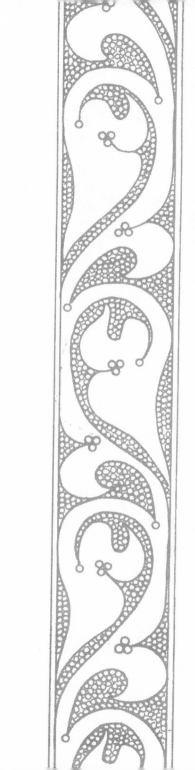

II

The famous manuscripts that so many of us are chasing now came out of Iran in two large waves," the German was saying, as he walked into the hotel banqueting hall a little late. "The first, as you know, was the wave sent out by the exiles, when they saw the Revolution coming close, the same exiles who sent their carpets, their jewels, even their children out into the world. The second group, more interesting for our purposes, are the ones that were smuggled out by the regime, after the Revolution had come to power." The large German started to cough, and the audience—the place was packed—leaned a little closer. Clearly, he was enjoying being the center of attention. "The old houses, the university, even the museums of Tehran, of Shiraz, were raided, and their treasures sent out in order to gain hard currency."

There was more along these lines—the Shah's sister herself was believed to have taken riches beyond counting to her house above the sea in Santa Barbara—and then, with a flourish, the scholar from Hamburg (a thick red beard, and a dark-blue corduroy jacket) said, "The problems of Iran are now the problems of everyone. Globalism has made of Tehran an international syndicate."

A few people asked questions—"Are you not projecting your own interests onto the regime?" from someone near the front, "What does it say about the Orientalizing impulse?"—and then, as if the room itself were exhaling its breath, everyone scattered, into their private groups, to discuss who was studying with whom, and what the Islamic Reformation, if it ever came, would do to their lives.

. . .

He'd felt, stepping off the plane, and back into the life that had been his a few months before, as if he were stepping into a play for which he'd forgotten all the lines; everyone else was in costume, as they were supposed to be, and only he was walking among them in civilian clothes, an outsider who might be taken for an intruder. Even the paper he'd been preparing for so long, on Rumi and John of the Cross ("Abandon: East and West"), seemed to have changed color or shape on him somehow, till the words themselves appeared to be turning on their heads. He'd been pleased, months before, to think of "being abandoned" as the perfect description of the mystic's state of transport and self-forgetfulness; but now, suddenly, "being abandoned" seemed to mean something quite different, closer to being deserted. He thought, without wanting to, of a young woman in her sister's house alone.

Seeing that he wasn't quite the person he was supposed to be, he went up to his room and drew back the curtains. Outside, beside the nearby minaret, a perfect crescent moon: the classic Islamic symbol, which reminds us that there is always more going on than we can see. Even when the moon is full. Then, going out into the street, as if to orient himself—a part of him was floating, high over the ground—he walked away from the main square, the noisy laughter from the bars, the sound of clicking heels for tourists and violently strummed guitars. Seville seemed almost an exercise in teaching one how to read: for those with eyes, there were Arab spirits hiding out even in the menus posted outside restaurants *("arroz," "naranja," "azúcar")*, even in the faint memory of the ghazal that haunted the guitars.

Twenty, thirty minutes later, he came to a residential quarter, much quieter, where he could catch, just occasionally, the sound of laughter from an upstairs window, a slip of light escaping from behind a heavy door, and, peering in, he saw a courtyard—a tiled fountain and a fruit tree—that seemed to tell anyone who looked that the treasure of an Andalusian house exists in all that can't be seen from the street. Going into a bar—on impulse—he did what he hadn't expected to do, and picked up a postcard from the cash register. Doves, and a pond shaped like a star.

Then, scribbling very quickly on the back, without putting a name at the top, he wrote:

Not by constraint or severity should you have
access to true worth, but by abandonment.

—HENRY DAVID THOREAU

When he came back to the hotel, the official life of the conference was over for the day; and so the real life was just beginning. He wasn't ready to sleep yet—his day inverted by the change in clocks, and something else in him pulling him along, the way an overeager dog might pull his owner—and he looked in on the bar on the second floor. There were one or two people he knew, or thought he knew, from conferences past, but no one he thought he could talk to now. Downstairs, in the basement, there was another pub, and when he looked in, he saw Hans Müller, the speaker of this evening, sitting at a small round table with someone he thought had been with him at SOAS, and a small dark man with a beard, whose shoulder bag made him think of an Islamic adventurer. In between them, a woman—Anne, he seemed to remember, from NYU—and the loud sound of laughter.

They made room for him when he came up, and soon the conversation was back to how America was in search of new enemies now that the Cold War was over, and how *Jihad vs. McWorld* was arguing that Islam would be the great enemy of the new postmodern order. Ever since the Revolution in Iran, their field had stakes, a new urgency; they were now, willy-nilly, people of the world.

"Sefadhi, too, right?" said the woman, though he couldn't tell how much weight lay behind the question. "Don't they say he's an agent for the government in Tehran?"

"They say everything about Sefadhi," he said, a loyal student, and a polished one.

"But you were in Damascus, I thought I heard," she persevered. "You must have seen Khalil?"

"Insofar as anyone can see him."

"What's he like?" Like many of the stars of the field, the Syrian scholar had the glamour of the seldom seen; he so seldom left his little cell that all kinds of rumors and mysteries gathered around him.

"Hard to say. I think he's learned to keep himself hidden from view."

"But he's an old friend of Sefadhi's, right? From before the Revolution?"

"That's what they say."

"And Azadeh, too," piped up the small man with the beard, suddenly engaged. "Ferdows Azadeh."

"Twenty years ago, perhaps," said Müller, not anxious to be left out, and then the talk drifted off, to why Sefadhi had chosen to put himself in Santa Barbara, so far from the Washington that most of the émigré professors sought out. The talk rose and crested around him, and he thought of a small room across the world, the ocean outside the window, someone hopeful and hidden lying across his bed.

As the evening went on, more and more empty glasses accumulating on the table, he felt a pressure, unspoken, from his right, and when he looked up, the woman beside him looked at him directly, and pushed her glass a little closer to his. Academics were natural spies.

"What's the real reason you're here?"

"The same as always. I have a paper to give tomorrow."

"I know that. But I'd heard something else." He didn't rise to that—Sefadhi would have been proud—and she went on, "Something about looking for manuscripts. Kristina Jensen and someone else."

The attempt at sounding casual was so strained, he didn't make much attempt to dodge it. "Everyone's looking for manuscripts. Just ask Hans."

The large German looked at them from across the table, attention caught by the sound of his name.

"I'd been meaning to ask you, actually," said the Englishman, seeing he had a chance now, "where exactly did all these manuscripts end up?"

"Everywhere," said Müller, more relaxed now that his paper was over, and it felt like they were only making conversation. "Paris. Vancouver. Los Angeles. Everywhere the people go."

"Those are the ones that came out early?"

"Why not? The ones the government steals, they send to Syria. Saudi. Through pilgrims on the hadj." He raised his mug and took a long swig. "The keepers of the Islamic Revolution selling its treasures for BMWs!"

Then, as if realizing, belatedly, he'd said too much, he stopped and looked across at him. "You are very interested in this topic. From where comes your interest?"

"I have a fiancée," he said, without thinking, "in Los Angeles. From Iran. She talks about them in the context of her family."

" 'Her family,' " said Müller, repeating the words as if to show how implausible they sounded. And then, eager to be rid of the questions, drew them back into the larger conversation.

He gave his talk the following morning—or someone who seemed to be standing in for him, a stunt double, delivered it—and then he went up to his room and fell into a deep sleep. When he awoke—10:07, it said on the little clock by the bed—he didn't know for a moment where he was, whether it was day or night. Then, stepping across to the window, he drew the curtains back and saw the Christian image of faith—he hadn't noticed it before—above the minaret. Beside it, as before, the Islamic moon.

He was feeling revived now, as if he'd slept through half a lifetime, and, needing some fresh air, he got dressed quickly and went down into the lobby to take a walk. As he stepped out, he felt a tentative hand on his back and whirled around to see who was beside him.

It was the small dark man from the night before.

The man nodded, as if it was natural that they meet again, and as he stepped out, the man stepped out beside him, as if, without words, they'd agreed to spend the evening together. As they walked down the street, neither of them sure what exactly to say, it felt, absurdly, like an assignation.

"You're studying in Germany, I take it," he said, in the voice that Martine always mocked. "Your English voice," she called it.

"Now," said the man. "I was in England before."

"Really? Where?"

Around them, the cobblestones of the central quarter, the old lampposts and balconies made up to re-create the city of Don Juan (the city that Teresa of Avila had called the most evil place she knew). Every now and then a couple came out of a bar, all elegant dishevelment: a hand around a waist, the sound of drunken laughter.

"I was in London," said the man, in his shy, strange way. "Then America."

He found the place he'd read about—there didn't seem to be a way to avoid a conversation—and they walked into a raucous pub, all student laughter, and, here and there in the corners, people they knew from the conference trying very hard not to be seen.

He got drinks for them both—the dark man wanted only a 7Up—and then they sat down and tried to find ways around the silence.

"You're originally from Iran?" he tried, and the man nodded.

"They called me a barbarian in England," he said. His conversation was strange; his accent was good, and he'd clearly spent most of his life in the West, and yet he skipped from topic to topic the way a bad needle would on an old LP. "They showed our class a map and said, 'This is where civilization ends.'"

"It's not a very hospitable culture."

"I didn't know where my parents were," the man went on, swerving again, though this was more likely a story he'd told often. "They were in Germany, they were in Turkey. Sometimes, for years, I didn't hear anything about them."

"It's sad," he said, inadequately.

"They sent me to America, like all the other people without a home. When the rebels took the embassy, they brought me in for questioning. The FBI office in San Diego." He had about him the quality that Persia had carried through all its empires, of melancholy, the sadness that accompanies a fall from glory. And mixed with that, a bitterness, that insufficient attention was being paid.

"You haven't been back?"

The man shook his head no. "You hear them in Santa Monica. These voices from eastern Iran, from places I've never heard about. Talking about what they had for dinner, what is happening in their

village, how they dream of America, the land of plenty." The bitterness again. "On the radio, the satellite. But the people in America are
singing Sufi songs, reciting poems, the same people who never went
to the mosque at home."

"The exiles, you mean?"

The man didn't answer. It was just a form of nostalgia, his silence
said, a way to try to keep the community going far from home.

Then, as if he'd come to some decision, the man leaned forwards,
with more attention. "I am hoping," he said, "that you can help
me." His voice went low, though nothing he was saying seemed to be
very confidential. "We have a group—it is an association—that is
working to collect the body, the documents of Islam."

"To bring it into one place."

"Exactly." He rewarded him with a smile. "FAITH. The Friends
and Associates of the Islamic Tradition and Heritage.

"And I am thinking that you can help us. You give us information,
you give us advice. You tell us what you see when you make research
trips."

"I don't think I'd have very much to say." The very sound—his
father's voice—he'd gone to California to escape.

"Sometimes you are inside a circle when you think you are outside
it," the man said, warming to his theme. "You send us e-mails. You
give us brochures. You help us to put together the broken body of
our faith."

"But I'm not necessarily the one who should be doing that."

"Of course we have enemies," the man said, though he'd said
nothing about that. " 'Colonizers of the truth,' they call us. 'Intellec-
tual mercenaries.' They want us only to accept their reading of the
tradition. But it is something important we are doing, I think you
know."

"I do," he said. "I'm glad to hear about it."

Then, as if he'd sat down in a seat that was being kept for someone else, he said—his formal voice again—"I think I should be going
now. I have something to do."

. . .

They walked back out into the street, and he said something implausible about having to check up on an Islamic building in some distant corner of the city. He tried not to look at the man trudging back to the hotel alone. The brief encounter had shaken him in some way he couldn't explain to himself—like walking into a friend's house and coming upon the friend in the kitchen, in a deep embrace, eyes closed.

He wandered around, to clear his head, following this lane, and then that one, into a very different area from the one he'd seen before, and everywhere around him were bolted doors and unlit lanes. He turned into a smaller street and felt as if he were walking past a line of fortresses. Just before a crossing, though, there was a sliver of light from behind a door, and, going up to the entrance—it was a small church—he pushed at the heavy bronze door; to his surprise, it gave.

He walked into a tiny, cold chapel, thick with the smell of incense.

At the altar was a body of thin white candles, wavering; around the sides of the place, taller, thicker candles, illuminating old canvases of Judas, Peter, the Last Supper. The Madonna's sad, undefeated eyes followed him as he walked in and around the pews.

Then, sitting down—he needed to catch his breath, to put the evening behind him—he closed his eyes, and suddenly she was there, inches away, eyes narrowed and her hair let loose. She was working at something with her fingers, unclasping, unbuttoning, and her voice was at his ear, saying his name over and over.

He opened his eyes again, and there was nothing. Just a row of sacraments at the front of the altar—he hadn't noticed them before, behind the candles—and the pictures of the Virgin on every side. Pulling out a postcard he'd bought in the hotel—the archways of the mosque in Córdoba, hidden inside the Catholic cathedral—he wrote, as before, without thinking:

> *Yearning makes the heart deep.*
> —AUGUSTINE

. . .

He had a few hours free before the train to Granada the next day, and, pulling out the letter he'd brought with him from California— the faded seal at its top more faded than ever—he called the operator to find the number of the Arabic Department at Cádiz. When he dialed the number she had given him, a woman answered, and, disconcerted by his fumbled Spanish, she transferred him to another woman. This woman seemed to have even less time for him, and soon he was back at the first. Finally, another voice came on, more commanding, male.

"*¡Hola!* Hello?"

"Yes. Professor Espinoza, *por favor.*"

"*Digame.*"

"Yes. You don't know me, but I'm here for the conference in Seville, I'm a student of Sufi poetry, and Adnan Khalil . . ."

"You study in England?"

"In America, at the moment."

"Where in America?"

"In California, as it happens."

"You study in Santa Barbara?"

"Yes, for now. But what I wanted to ask you was . . ."

"I am sorry." The voice closed every door he might have imagined open. "Please give my regards to Javad. I am very busy at this moment. I wish you success with your researches."

The phone came down into his waiting ear.

He'd told himself he'd use his one day off to go and see the Alhambra, the most powerful reminder of Persia, so they said, still visible in Spain. He knew it was best to go when nobody else was around— you can only see the Alhambra when you can't see very much. So he waited till the early afternoon to take the train to Granada. When he arrived, in late afternoon, he lost himself in the narrow whitewashed lanes of the Arab quarter, boys in thick sweaters kissing one another noisily on the cheek, and following with their eyes every woman who walked past.

From inside the cafés came the scratchy, plaintive sound of Arab love songs: a man crying out for his beloved, and ready, in his desolation, to start a riot.

The light fell slowly over the city, and when it was almost dark, he got up, paid for his mint tea, and began the long ascent of the hill. The hotels on both sides were full of noise and animation—the excitement of people who had made the building's acquaintance— but the street itself was surprisingly deserted; few people knew that the palace opened its doors again on certain nights in the summer.

He walked up into the dark, towards what presented itself as a citadel, and as he came within a few hundred yards of the kiosk where they sold tickets—a tired face behind the bars—he saw a smaller building between the hotels, with a light still on. A young man, shaven-headed, was standing under a dim naked bulb, appearing to be reading. There was no one else in the place; it had the feeling of an afterthought. Drawn towards it by its very emptiness, he opened the blue door—a bell jangled dully above him—and walked in.

The man barely looked up, gave an almost imperceptible nod from the cash register next to which he was standing. As the visitor took stock of the shelves around him, he saw what seemed to be books about secrecy and love; a worn piece of paper on one of the shelves read, in fraying handwriting, "OCCULTISMO." He picked one of the books up and opened it, and saw what seemed to be diagrams of human evolution, and whole sentences written out, too emphatically, in block capitals. Pieces of the text were in Aramaic, or some other esoteric language, and here and there there seemed to be astrological charts for what looked to be whole cultures.

"There is an Interworld," he read, in a book in French (though it had been published in Geneva), "that belongs neither to the realm of gods nor to that of mortals. It is a separate zone, not real and not allegorical, and in it each one of us has a daemon, a guardian angel, if you will, who watches over our higher self while the lower struggles through its duties." These things are known only to the elect, it went on, and at some point he felt as if he'd come upon the love letters of an acquaintance; he put the book back, feeling he'd stepped too far.

Then, walking towards the back of the shop, where works in English seemed to be kept, he ran his eye quickly along the shelves devoted to tomes in his native tongue. As he did so, almost perfunc-torily, he happened to see the book he'd been looking for all along. *Poems of Shiraz,* said the title—gold lettering on a crimson spine, dating, he guessed, from around the turn of the century. He passed it by and quickly examined all the other titles, lest his ever-eager eyes be deceiving him. Then, at the same volume as before, he saw it once again: *Poems of Shiraz.*

He picked the book off the shelf and for a moment did not open it. He was shaking, as he did whenever he was coming closer to an answer that might end a quest. Then, very carefully, he opened the cover, and began turning through the pages. There were poems on every one, through almost the whole length of the book. Poems by Hafez, turned into English by Gertrude Bell. Beautiful poems, myste-rious and deep, he could tell, yet tamed somehow in their Edwardian quatrains, reduced into something a clergyman might read to his sis-ter before retiring for the night.

He put the book back and considered himself chastised.

To step into the Alhambra after nightfall is to step into patterned moonlight. No one else was visible except for the woman at the kiosk, and nothing could be heard but the sound of water everywhere. The occasional footsteps of a guard, making his regular patrol.

He stepped into the first room, to find it lit by a single candle, so that as much was in shadow as in light. An arched window let in the smells of the night, a faint breeze; far below, the lights of the city. The next room was a little dimmer, and the next one darker still; he felt as if he were on his recent drives again, the nights in Santa Barbara, each room less well lit than the last, and for that reason more myste-rious, inviting.

He walked in from chamber to chamber. The doors were set at the sides of the rooms, and their archways—Damascus again—were low; so low he had to bow to walk through them. The sound of water everywhere, like a reminder of something you forget at your cost.

When he came to what seemed to be the innermost chamber, a candle at each side of it, he sat down against a wall. The steps of the guard approached, and then receded. The smell of oranges came from the garden. The sound of water. "It's weird," she'd said, not long before she fell asleep. "Did you ever notice there's a 'Camilla' hiding out inside 'Macmillan'?"

Pulling out a piece of paper, he wrote:

Dear Anagram,
Can you hear the sound of water, from the courtyard? Smell the orange trees outside, feel the early night wind? Can you hear the guard in the distance, almost as if you were here?

I hope you can, because you are.
Fondest regards,
John

When he stepped out of the terminal in Los Angeles, she was, of course, nowhere to be seen. There was a girl with long fair hair, stepping into a dark man's Porsche; another in a sky-blue dress, leading along a child who stopped to gawk at every foreigner. People bumped into him, as lost as he, perhaps, and then apologized; a girl was saying, "I'm sorry . . ." in just the way she did, but it was someone different, darker-hued. She must have got distracted, he thought, or suddenly frightened; her life seemed to shoot forwards and then stop again like a car in the stop-and-go traffic.

He waited for a bus that would take him home, and when he stepped into the house, three hours later, the light flashing on the machine had a plaintiveness that might have been hers. "Hi," the recording said, "I didn't know if you were coming. Or if you'd decided you were done with me. If you haven't, I'm at 818-416-3775."

He dialed the number and she answered on the first ring; she'd been waiting.

"It's you," she said. "You're back."

"I am. I said I would be."

"I know. But I thought—anything could have happened."

"It did. It didn't. I'm here."

"Will you tell me about your trip?"

I'll put away my fears, the voice said, if you'll say goodbye to yours.

He opened the door at the sound of her knock—night had fallen, and the ocean was just foam around the rocks—and when she came in, for a moment he didn't recognize who she was. Jet lag, he said to her wearily, but it was the effect she often had on him; as if—he thought to himself—he needed to turn and turn the lens till it came into sharpest focus and the blur resolved itself into a person he knew.

She was wearing a long black dress, with a heart-shaped piece of jade around her throat. When she hugged him, perfunctorily it seemed, he felt her trepidation: a sister looking in on a brother with whom she'd never much got along.

"You look well," she said, though not happily.

"I am. It was really something."

"I'm glad," she said, and then looked away from him, as if to orient herself and remind herself where she'd come.

"Scared, too."

"Scared? Why should I be scared?"

"I don't know," she said. "You tell me."

He looked at her, but she was browsing, with ostentatious casualness, through the book he'd left by the armchair.

"You said something about a production of *Emma*," he said. "You were trying out for the lead?"

"Don't change the subject. It won't make it go away."

He took a deep breath. "Orange juice? Some wine?"

"You tell yourself you're not frightened and then it's worse. It rules you from the dark."

She was like someone who drives two hundred miles, he thought, to have someone say, "I don't want to see you." And he, no more mature, like the person at the other end, who says, "I do want to see you. You'd better go home."

He went into the bedroom, brought out the book he'd bought for her—the story of Ibn Arabi's encounters with Sufism and romance in Seville—and when he handed it to her, she smiled briefly and put it down.

"Do you want to take a drive?" In the car, he knew, she could let her defenses fall away a little; there seemed less danger of sudden closeness.

She nodded, and they went out to where he'd parked, and drove towards the south. When they hit the freeway, she sat back and closed her eyes, and he could almost see her settling back into herself, and taking off a layer of camouflage. The light backstage that made one put up with the acting.

The fog was coming in from the ocean by the time they rounded the great open turns that led to the Rincon; there was almost no traffic, and it was as if the whole great stretch of coastline was about to close down for the night. The little huts above the beach looked like birds, looking for their next perch, and the faroff pier, in Ventura, the branch on which they could alight. But by the time they drew closer to it, even the houses were gone from view, and all they could sense through the fog was the ocean, coming to shore a few feet away.

They drove through the sleeping town, and then he turned off the freeway and they followed a country road down to the neglected main street of Oxnard, its sad line of fallen pool halls and cantinas. The workers had come in from the fields long since, and from out of the bars and jukeboxes came songs of *palomas* and *sueños*. As if he'd just turned off the main street in Seville and ended up in an orphaned side street.

She picked up his hand as he drove, and as he threaded his way through the broken festivals of the farmworkers, they came to another road that ended suddenly at the beach. A souvenir store with illuminated seashells in its window. A liquor store with a few pickup trucks in front of a neon sign that said, LIQR. A café of sorts, where three men were walking around a small fenced garden, singing the day's last love songs.

They took a table in the garden—white Formica tables, and some flowers forgotten by a previous customer—and as they sat back, breathed the night air, they heard the sound of *"Heimat"* from the street: a German woman walking back to her motel. From farther down—the beach—the sound of Sting, lying down in fields of gold.

"You hardly need a manuscript when it's as beautiful as this," she said, and he said, "Yes. But views don't last for long."

She turned away, and he realized he'd said the wrong thing. Soon she'd be talking about fear again, and the headlines. People aren't ashamed of all the things they've done, he thought (not certain if he was thinking about her, or himself); they're ashamed of all the things they haven't done. Embarrassed by their innocence, in a way, which they try to dress up with knowingness and glamour.

They got back in the car, and drove back along the deserted road to Santa Barbara. Occasionally a pair of lights would shoot at them through the dark, and then there would just be two red dots disappearing in the rearview mirror. The sound of the sea through the fog, the world of men effectively erased.

She pulled down the window, and the night air came in, so damp it felt as if it was on the brink of tears. Chill, too, as if to say that summer was now ending, and another cycle ready to begin. When he got to the house, she hesitated, and he realized she was wary of what was expected of her. "I've got to find something in my car," she said (and he thought: The person she was before? The person she thought I might be?). When he came out, after many minutes—she was still struggling through the debris at the back—she said, "It's here. I'm sure it is."

"I think I ought to sleep," he said, and felt a whisper of gratitude as she kissed him on the cheek.

When he awoke, long after midnight—close to midday now in Seville—he went to the edge of the bedroom to see if she was awake. "Anyone there?" he said, as softly as he could, so as not to rouse her. "I don't think so," said the figure on the sofa, and she struggled through the blankets to sit up. He came over and sat beside her on the couch, and, putting on the kitchen light, which wouldn't be too strong, saw her hair falling all around her face, a golden tangle.

"Did you find what you were looking for?"

"I don't know. I've lost a sense of what it is."

She shivered, drew the blankets around her for extra warmth.

"What are the colors there?"

"On the surface, white and brown. Deeper than that, lapis, gold."

She nodded, blearily. "Like Isfahan." He remembered, with a start, that she'd been studying the area before he'd even heard of it.

"I wrote you a letter, actually. Two. Though I didn't know where to send it."

She said nothing in response to the opening.

"How did it make you feel?"

"On the surface, calm. Deeper than that, abandoned."

She didn't respond to the word, and he looked over to see what she was saying.

She was breathing deeply, eyes closed, away from him again.

In the morning, when he went in, she was already packing, with a foreign air of purpose.

"You've got a rehearsal today?" In all the time he'd known her, she'd never said anything about an audition or a production, or anything that might pertain to a real life.

"No. Something you don't want to know about."

"A meeting? A secret boyfriend?"

"No," she said. "I've got a manuscript to collect." When he said nothing in response, she looked up at him, as if surprised. "That's a joke."

"I know. But I'd like to see you act in something."

"You will."

"In L.A.?"

"Wherever," she said, and then she was kissing him briskly and on her way.

. . .

He watched the car struggle to the end of the road, turn away, towards the mountains, and then went back into the house, to clear up. He hadn't unpacked yet, and he needed to get things in order before he visited Sefadhi. He collected the stray glasses from the table by the couch—the orange juice he'd brought her when he woke—and as he did so, he noticed a piece of paper peeping out from under the sofa. He picked it up and saw it was a page from her notebook, her hieroglyphics all over it. In one corner, what looked to be phone numbers, from West Los Angeles, scribbled down as she listened to the radio, perhaps. A list of names, he thought, in another corner. "T. E. Lawrence. Isabelle Eberhardt." Something that could have been "Jensen" or "Javad."

At the bottom, what might have been notes to herself, the outline of a letter. "Feels like a new me. Except more like an old one. Need to tell him why he's scared. If I don't see you, it's not because I don't want to. The opposite. Your regretful, wine-dark C."

He put the piece of paper down, and then—suddenly fatigued (the hours were playing tricks on him)—he fell asleep. As he did, he saw a crowd, dark men all around, with beards, turbans, and someone was saying, "He knows she's dead. He just won't acknowledge it." And someone else, "She's only pretending to be like that. It's what they do abroad."

Then, almost violently, he was awake again. Cries from the beach, and the sound of muffled music from next door. A dog's bark, the sound of laughter. Someone shouting something about the coming football season, and a revved-up sports car in the street. He picked up his books, went to take a quick shower and then took himself to the department, to make his report.

When he climbed the flights of stairs—the way he traditionally braced himself for Sefadhi—and got to the site of his advisor's office, he found the door closed, as it almost never was. "A visitor," said Eileen, trying to sound as casual as she could. "He could be quite a while."

"That's fine. I'll wait." In the last issue of *Islamic Quarterly* there was a report of people going to Rumi's birthplace in Afghanistan, to see if they could find traces of manuscripts that might have gone missing. The long-dead poet was a big commodity now; one such discovery, and matters both financial and political could be taken care of. He fumbled through the pages—they might have been written in Turkish, so little could he summon interest in them—and then, after thirty or forty minutes, the door opened and a figure stepped out.

She could hardly have been less like what he expected to emerge. She was in her mid-twenties, he guessed, with a long rush of streaked hair, and an air of worldly elegance. She nodded to Eileen as she left, took him in quickly, and then walked down the corridor—on her way, he could more easily imagine, to a cocktail party in the eighth *arrondissement* rather than any academic office.

"A friend," said Sefadhi, as if some explanation was called for, as he came into the office. "From another life." Then, realizing how that sounded. "Tehran. Many years ago."

"I'm sorry to interrupt."

"You interrupt nothng." Though the smell of expensive perfume was everywhere, and a plate of pistachios sat on the desk.

"So," his advisor said, and fell into the guise he usually wore. "The world of intellect proceeds, I think."

"Like a treadmill." He thought back to the whispered conversations in the bar. "You're lucky you weren't there."

"I was, I'm sure, in conversation." It was his teacher's way of issuing a warning: speak carefully.

"I heard about Minasian, the curse he said hung about any manuscript that was sold instead of passed on. I got a list of the books he gave to Oxford, and the ones that went to UCLA. But no one had anything to say about fugitive manuscripts."

"They won't," said Sefadhi. "They can't. There's nothing for them to say."

"But if I could go to Iran, just for a week . . ."

"You'd find nothing. There's nothing to see in Iran."

"But a sense of context at least. A background for the poems."

"You can get that in West Los Angeles." It was, ironically, the same thing he'd said to Martine when she'd asked him why he would ever go to California to study Sufism.

"But the landscape, the inspiration for the words."

"I don't think I ever told you about my uncle." It was so unlike Sefadhi to say anything about his private life—even to acknowledge that he had a life outside of his office, his role—that he knew the offering was not casual. "He was born in Russia, many years ago, like my aunt. And then, when the Russian Revoluton came, they had to flee to Iran. Then, when the Iranian Revolution came, they had to flee. To Canada. Now they sit in Canada, in Toronto, and every day they wait for the next Revolution, so they can flee again."

"It's not a field for dilettantes."

"Your words," said Sefadhi, tapping his long fingers together. "Not mine."

Back home, he thought back to the sudden, strange story his advisor had offered him. The dates didn't match—how could Sefadhi have an uncle alive at the time of the Russian Revolution?—and the whole story had the artificial air of a set piece: a packaged lecture a professor might offer to any student who showed signs of being too inquistive. And yet the fact that his teacher had issued it seemed more important than its substance: it was as if the more he pursued even the ghost of the manuscipts Khalil had alluded to, the more Sefadhi would try to throw roadblocks in his way.

He picked up a book to read more about Shiraz—the famous city of nightingales and poets that had long been the cultural center of old Persia—and then, putting it down, recalled the images that had come up on TV in Syria. All day long, on the cable channel from Syria: just figures, dressed in white, walking silently around the Qa'ba. Great masses of them proceeding down the passageways of a mosque, taking off their shoes, preparing themselves for the ritual ablutions. All day long, amidst the chatter of the other stations, these silent images. No speech or music on the soundtrack: only the sound of their shuffling, their prayers.

It was part of what made the faith so unsettling to the world at large. That sense of massed devotion; almost an accepted madness. People coming from every direction, at the end of day—he'd experienced it once in Arabia—old men, young, men in white, men in sandals, coming from all sides to file silently into the mosque together. And five times a day, if you were a good Moslem, even if you were eating or talking or making love, the call to prayer rose up and then . . .

The phone on his desk began to shrill.

"Hello."

"Johno. It's Nicki. Is that you?" Her voice still had the faintly regimental air that blurred around the edges in Martine. As if, even now, you could hear generations of officers in the tropics bringing the sepoys to the front, or making sure all the trains were running on time.

"It is," he said. "Are you coming?"

"Yes," she said. "On Friday, if that's all right for you."

"Friday, I'm actually rather tied up. Would Thursday work?"

" 'Tied-up'! I can't believe how American you sound. Martine's never going to . . . Anyway, what shall we say, then? Thursday at eleven?"

When the rap came on his door, at the stroke of eleven, he was back in England again, and a place where people pose their statements as questions for very different reasons from the Californian. She offered him her cheeks to kiss when he opened the door, and then handed him some flowers. "Perennials," as she told him, while she came into the house and began looking round.

"The famous lair at last," she said, and before he could orient her, or offer her a drink, she was wandering around, as if casually, taking notes, he guessed, for the report she'd be sending back to England. "So this must be your bedroom," she was saying, and he imagined her looking around just long enough to note the color of the curtains and how the pillows were arranged, "and this must be where you get all your great work done." She was in the study now, taking quick note of how many books were there, and where. "And this"—she walked past him again, in the corridor, so close they almost touched—"this, I'm assuming, is where you sit and think of England."

"When I can."

"It seems such a large place just for one."

"Two, if you count Rumi."

"Yes," she said. "I do remember that part." There was a pause. "Martine used to tell me."

She stopped her circling then and he looked at her: a long sleeveless yellow frock, as if for a picnic, and a pricking of something floral at her pulse points. Her sister was, of course, the one thing they had in common, and yet she was also the one topic they didn't know how to broach. She sat between them as if she were sitting in the middle of the room, in a golden cage.

"Have a seat," he said, but she said, "I've been sitting for ages. I'd rather stretch my legs."

"Something to drink?"

"Anything cool," she said, and then turned her back on him as she went to the terrace, as if to savor the view. She'd always been his strongest supporter in the Chancellor camp, he knew; were it not for the claims of family loyalty, he and she could have been close.

"So, how are you?" she said, when he came back with the drinks and a bowl of nuts. "How's the New World treating you?"

"Well enough. I'm just trying to get my thesis done before the beginning of next summer."

"So you can do what exactly?"

"The usual. Look for ungainful unemployment far from home and try to make myself useful in some way."

"The Johno we know and love," she said, in the tone he recognized. "Still a terrible creature of habit, I'm assuming."

"The opposite. I don't know where I'm going."

"I see," she said, just as her younger sister would have done. "You're not seeing anyone, then?"

"No time, alas. The thesis looms."

"Yes, I do remember that part, too."

She was opening the book by the table—*Vineland*—to see if it offered any clues.

"What about you? Anyone in your life?"

"You know me," she said, looking up. "I've always got someone wonderful in my life. The only trouble is, he never comes out of my head and asks me to dance."

She straightened the narrow straps on her dress, and he felt she was about to say something more. She didn't, but looked at him directly, almost plaintively.

"He will one day."

"One day when I'm eighty years old, perhaps." Then, suddenly, there was a terrible crash from next door, a great silence and, after what seemed like minutes of no movement, the sound of whispers, people picking themselves up and conferring, as if about to make a new home in the middle of the debris.

"No thoughts of coming back, then?"

"That would be going backwards, don't you think?"

"Yes. I suppose it would."

He went into the kitchen to fetch the salad and when he came out, she was saying, in response to the commotion next door, "I do so love it here. All these places called Xanadu and Lotusland, aren't there? With frightful battles going on behind the bougainvillea."

"Like anywhere," he said. "Only in England, it's the nicer parts people always hide."

"Yes," she said, not sounding very convinced. "It's what you're writing on, isn't it?"

"In a way. The idea that what we have inside us are not just repressed demons and all that, but something radiant. Exalted."

"Mmm," she said, suddenly fascinated by her lettuce. "Wherever did you get this dressing?"

It was a way of telling him, in effect, why he could never go back to England: anything can be forgiven there except the longing to be better.

"More wine?" he said, but she was lost to him now, and he realized she was already thinking about how she could cut the meeting short. He'd startled her, frightened her, by sounding serious, and now she couldn't be sure he wouldn't do it again.

"I wish it weren't so late," she said, the minute she was finished. "I have a million things to do today."

"You can't stay for dessert?"

"I only wish I could."

She looked at her watch, though there was no need of that, and when she'd finished helping him take the plates into the kitchen, she picked up the scarf she'd draped across the sofa when she'd come.

"My love to Martine, please, when you're home."

"Absolutely. I'm sure she sends hers back to you."

"And to you, too," he said, and she turned away. "You're sure you're taken care of for the day?"

"Oh, more than taken care of, thank you." She knew her part, her voice was saying; she'd soldier on regardless.

The next day, as he sat at his desk, thumbing through the book about Shiraz—night had fallen, and he hadn't got anything planned (he'd only told Nicki he was "tied up" to show her she couldn't have her way in everything)—he heard a knock on the door by the back steps and he looked up from what he was reading.

"Surprise," said the familiar voice. "You weren't expecting me."

"I wasn't."

In someone else he'd have imagined she was here to check on him; but with her, it was almost as if she were trying to catch herself by surprise. If she didn't make plans, her reasoning went, she'd have no time to be apprehensive.

"I've come at a bad time."

"Not at all. A usual time. I was just at work."

She came into the room and looked at the books that were scattered across the desk.

"What on?"

"The usual. How the haunted are dangerous in some way. And how their fear, their anger, comes out at anything that happens to be in their path."

She looked at him to see what exactly he meant, and he said, "That's why the Islamic world is such a threat to us," and, deciding that she'd be satisfied with the answer, she went past him into the living room. As she did so, he saw her shoulders stiffen.

My ex-girlfriend's sister," he said, realizing she'd caught a trace of an earlier visitor. "Here to report on me to London."

"This isn't the one you're taken by?"

"No. Not exactly."

She turned around to look at him—she had to protect herself, she'd said on the phone—and then, as if determined to put her reservations behind her, she went on to the couch and claimed a seat.

"You want to see what I've brought for us to look at?"

"I'd love to." From where he stood he could see candles, cards, books, all in one undifferentiated pile in the overnight bag she carried with her; she had enough to keep her going for days.

"There's this," she said, and as she pulled out a glossy catalogue from the bag, he realized it was an invitation to sit. She wouldn't run away just now. When she handed over the pamphlet, he saw a picture of the mosque in Jerusalem, under the title, *Hidden Treasures*. Inside were glossy pictures of all the romantic old cities in the world—Cuzco, Angkor, Luang Prabang. "There's also this one," she said, picking out a very similar catalogue from the Bay Area, and he turned through it to see misty sunset pictures of Petra, Dunhuang, Isfahan. The places she'd studied in college, he thought (the places she heard about her sister going to). Around the margins were scribbled phone numbers and names here and there; certain sentences in the text had been highlighted with a yellow pen.

"So many places you've never been."

"They're nicer than any of the places I have been."

She looked away, and he said, to pick them up, "Some juice? Any wine? What can I get you?"

"Just you would be plenty." She looked at him, and now it was his turn to look away.

"It's getting dark. Maybe we should go out while there's still light?"

She smiled, as if some supposition had been confirmed, and then walked ahead of him down the steps to the beach. When she got to the sand, she leaned down to untether one shoe, and then the other, and handed them to him as she went off, away from him, down the beach, following the trail that the ocean had made, hopping back now and then when the tide came in around her feet.

She walked and walked, away from him, all the way down to the point. Then, when she got there, she scrambled up onto the rocks— he could see from where he followed—as if to gauge what was ahead, around the corner, versus (she turned back now) what was behind her, where she'd come from. Then, as if she'd come to some decision, she started walking back to him. By the time they were a little apart, the sun was fire on the water and her face was gold. It looked as if she'd walked free of something, and her face was open now, relaxed.

"You like to stay where it's dry," she said, and he, not knowing what it meant, said, "Only when it's light."

They went back up into the room, now dark, and when she sat on the sofa, she curled her bare feet under her, a spot or two on her skirt where the water had caught her.

Then, closing her eyes, she put her head back on the sofa. "It's nice here. Safe."

"You're where you're meant to be."

She opened her eyes and smiled; after nightfall—the books on his desk said—you can be anyone you choose.

"I have a question," he said, since it seemed she was relaxed and a better moment might never come.

"What's that?"

"What's the nicest thing that ever happened to you when you were young?"

She thought and thought, as if not many candidates came to mind, then said, "You first."

"I lost my way in the woods and got saved by a fairy god-mother."

She looked at him strangely—he had no more idea of why he'd said it than she did—and then, very slowly, "Someone called me 'Dove,' once. In fifth, no sixth, grade."

"Because of your eyes?"

"Not only that." He remembered how she'd said she'd never fit in here.

"That's strange. I was just reading this." He picked up the book he'd taken out of the library after McCarthy's lecture and, in a voice not quite his, and not quite McCarthy's, read,

" 'O my dove, that art in the clefts of the rock, in the secret places of the stairs, let me see thy countenance, let me hear thy voice; for sweet is thy voice, and thy countenance is comely.' "

She looked at him as if to see what he'd intended, and he said, "I hadn't recalled . . ." and then stopped. Hadn't recalled how the words sounded in the King James translation, he might have said. Or hadn't recalled how he had such a gift for saying the wrong thing with her.

"I used to write, too," she said, as if forgiving him the intrusion.

"Poems?"

"Stuff. Silly things."

"What kind of things?"

"I'd make a poem, and every line would start with one of the letters of my name. So the first line would begin with a 'C' and the next line with an 'A' and the next line with an 'M' and so on. A verse form for narcissists."

"And your parents didn't approve of it?"

"My parents only approved of me when I was sitting in my prison at home."

She was coming into focus, as the darkness in the room intensified, but he was careful: jog her once, or say too much, and, as in a Polaroid, the image would blur forever.

"When I was young," she said, and the words carried strongly in the unlit room, seemed more full of weight, "I always thought that every one of us had a place, a secret place, even if we never found it. Like *déjà-vu* in advance."

"You don't think that now?"

"Now I think you've got to be very lucky to find your place. It's certainly not going to come and find you."

"But it could be something else, couldn't it? A book. A song. Even a person."

"I believed that once upon a time and I almost died of sadness."

It was the kind of thing she said that sounded as if it came from one of her plays. And yet the way she said it was not studied, but startled.

"The Sufis believe that everyone has a home, hiding out somewhere in the world, and all we have to do is find a key."

"They obviously haven't met my mother," she said.

"She can't be that bad."

"She's worse. She's evil."

And then, realizing, perhaps, that she'd gone too far, she fumbled in her bag and brought out another offering, wrapped in dark-blue paper. "I brought this, too."

He went across the room to turn on the light, to see what she was extending, and when he got back to her he saw she'd unwrapped what looked to be a dome, midnight-blue, with gold stars around it: a desert sky. Then, getting up again to fetch a box of matches, he applied a light to the wick of the dark-blue sphere, went over to turn off the light and they were alone in a lighted room, reduced to a shining dome.

"It's beautiful."

"I thought it would remind you of your poems."

"The best part of them, perhaps."

She sat back again, rested her head against the couch, and said, "If you could have anything in the world, right now, what would it be?"

"I don't know," he said. "I'm fairly content, I think."

"There must be something." Nothing more distrusted in California than the impression of settledness.

"I suppose I'd like to make a discovery in my field. See something or find something that nobody's ever seen before."

"You're such an optimist," she said, as if looking at some souvenir he'd brought back to her from Spain.

"It's not me, it's them. They're apostles of hope, the way I see it."

" 'Apostles of hope,' " she said, as if turning the phrase round in her hands. "You have such a bright way of looking at things."

"And you? If you could have anything?"

"I'd get a new me. A new life." She didn't say it dramatically, or with any emphasis; just matter-of-factly, as if it were something she needed from the supermarket. He extended an arm along the back of the sofa, and she came a little closer, rested her head against it. Since the evening on the mountain, they'd stepped back in a way, but closer, too, as if passing up the illuminated entrances on a hillside to search for something darker, deeper down.

"So," she said, and her eyes were closed and she was clearly as relaxed as she would ever be, "tell me about this woman you're taken with."

"I'll tell you about Martine. That's safer."

She said nothing, so he continued.

"She was bright, funny, full of life. Though she liked to hide it behind a tough exterior."

"Sounds familiar."

"And we got on well enough for a while."

"And then?"

"Then, I don't know. I think there was always something in me—a restlessness, a kind of distance, perhaps—that was unsettling to her. She used to say that I was faraway even when I was next to her. I'll never forget this one time, in Turkey, soon after college, we were staying near the Hagia Sofia. And as soon as the day's first call to prayer went up, I went out, to see what the mosque looked like at dawn. I wanted to see it at its purest. When I came back, it must have been seven-thirty, eight, I realized I'd done the wrong thing: gone out to see the mosque when I should have been with her."

"Did she say anything?"

"Not then. We went on with our tour, had our breakfast. But a few weeks later, after we got back to England, there was this call, in the middle of the night, and it must have been a boy in his teens, very shy, polite even, but persistent. 'Mister Macmillan, I'm calling to say I saw your friend Marty last week. We had quite a big time together. She told me she was going to call you herself, but I didn't think she would, so that's why I'm calling. To tell you we had a big time together.' He didn't need to say any more, though he did, being young, and somehow I felt that he was being completely straight with me, was an innocent in his way. And Turkey had been the cause of it."

"So you let her go?"

"The opposite. I held her closer than I'd ever done before. We went, the next time we had some time free, to Cephalonia, this amazing island from Homer where you can feel the gods and ghosts of Odysseus's time all around you. A dazzling blue sea and white buildings everywhere so you just disappear, fade into the brilliant light, and olive trees and shepherds that might as well have been there four thousand years ago. It was beautiful. But it was already too late, we both of us knew. Something had been broken, and there was no putting it back together again.

"The last day, in Athens—we were back in the Plaka, in a small hotel—she said, 'I'll never be complicated enough for you. I couldn't be. I'll never give you something to get your teeth into.' And that was more or less the end."

"You drifted apart?"

"Not in so many words, but yes."

"And Rumi became your consolation."

"Not exactly. But he was reliable. And reliably uplifting. That was another thing Martine could never get over. 'How can I ever compete with some legendary old man who's been dead for donkeys' years? I'll never be as mysterious as he is. I can't be. He's got seven hundred years on me.' If there were anything she could do, she said, she'd do it. But there wasn't."

"So how can I compete?"

"By giving me something he couldn't. By being yourself."

He'd done it again. Like when he'd leaned in to kiss her goodbye on the beach, or reached for the Song of Songs when he'd only been trying to pass the time. Somehow with her he seemed to have a genius for saying more than he intended and coming out with lines he'd have laughed at in the Cineplex.

She turned her head a little and kissed him now, deeply, imploringly, as if to try to summon up someone deep in hiding. Her hair fell around their cheeks, their mouths, and they were tented in its golden fall.

Then, remembering how quickly she took flight, he pulled back a little. "Maybe we should wait."

"I'm sorry," she said, as if the fault was hers. "It's been a long time since I was intimate with anyone."

The words she used, like the Alice band with which she kept her hair in place, her high-buttoned dress, its whites and pastels—all of it issued a warning more forcibly than anything she said. As if she were a vase only inches behind a velvet curtain. Move one inch too far, and she'd be broken.

And yet her face, when she forgot about herself, was filled with an ancient light and clarity. He thought of the time, as a boy, when his mother had dragged him around the Uffizi in Florence, and he, a typical schoolboy of nine or ten, had yawned conspicuously with each new room, and looked in the other direction. Then they'd come into room 10, the madonnas of Botticelli, and something had caught at him. It wasn't the cackling cherub at the center of each painting; that seemed almost a joke. And yet the girl who cradled him in every picture was almost painfully alive. Half glowing with a mother's pride, half holding back, as if startled by the light with which she'd been entrusted. Half moving towards the Angel Gabriel, to hear what he was whispering; and yet half withdrawing, as if not sure if she wanted this new destiny.

He hadn't known at the time that Botticelli is the obligatory favorite of every romantic schoolboy; hadn't even heard that Simonetta Vespucci's uncle was the one to find America. He'd known nothing about the Angel Gabriel's connection with Mohammed. Yet what he'd seen had been more real than any of that: a girl awakened to a light she hadn't known about, and fearful, disconcerted, now, lest her life would never be the same.

"What are you most afraid of in the world?" she said, and the spell, for the moment, was broken.

"Of losing myself. You?"

"Of losing everything. Being alone."

"Being abandoned, in a way."

"I guess," she said, and then turned away, as if the interlude was over. "Anyway, that's safer than any of the other answers."

In the morning, when he forced himself to the library, she was sleeping. Stretched out, even when he returned in late afternoon, in a happy state of trust. She never slept easily at home, she'd said the night before, the conversation drifting on till dawn, and the two of them, without seeming to intend it, moving from the sofa to the bed. Yet sometimes all she wanted to do was sleep and sleep so she'd never have to look at the life that was waiting for her.

When she heard him come in, she stirred, and opened her eyes.

"You deserted me."

"For a few hours."

"To do what?"

"To surrender." He hadn't expected that.

"To what?" she said, and she pushed the sheets back just a little.

"The usual. My poems."

"Words on the page."

"Why not?"

"Possession is nine-tenths of the love," she said, as if talking to herself, and then he noticed that her face was flushed, and her lips were faintly parted.

"For them," he said. Whatever she needed—whatever he needed— he thought, came at some level deeper than the body.

She looked up at him, clearly piqued that the moment had been lost.

"You never talk about your parents."

"There's not much to say."

"They're in England?"

"They were. Not now."

She looked away. "I'm sorry. I didn't know."

"You needn't be. I never told you."

"So that's why . . ." and then she stopped herself.

"That's why I'm the center of the Macmillan empire," he said, to bring them up from the deep.

She didn't laugh, though. She looked at him and looked at him, and then looked down, as if she was shaking.

"What is it?"

She shook her head, eyes full. "It's too poignant."

When he returned from the library next day, she was gone.

The darkness came on much earlier now, and soon the first winter storms were slashing through the town: two, three days of agitated skies, the sound of unrelenting rain, and then the streets outside were silent again, and pockets of blue could be seen in the white. Pieces of a broken pot, and the clouds just rimmed with light. Then, as suddenly as it had come, the storm moved on, and he awoke one morning to find the world as sharp as if it had just been slapped awake.

Early winter was the magic time in California, the days acquiring an edge, a form of sharpness, that they never had in the bleary summers. Voices soft and low in the sweatered dark, heat lamps on the terraces at six o'clock and around everything a kind of definition, a startled clarity, that gave the sunny days more meaning. In winter California became an older place, with secrets.

He called her occasionally to try to bring her back, but all he got was the sound of a phone ringing and ringing, now and then a male voice saying shortly, sharply, "This is 437-2962. Talk!" Then, a few days later, three hectic beeps that told him that the tape was now full: no messages could be taken in any case.

"We run from our fears," he wrote, pushing himself back into the papers on his desk, "and so run from the very place where our transformation might be hiding. We wall ourselves in with what we think we know, and then what we don't know, which is what can save us, is left knocking on the door." Then, wondering what he was really writing about, he tried to open the books on the desk to bring himself back to the matter at hand: the fact that Rumi had signed half of his poems with the name "Shams"—the bedraggled stranger he had claimed as his own—and the fact, on top of that, that this was a metaphor as well as an ancient gesture: in Persian, "Shams-suddin" means "Religious Sun."

"Five hundred of his poems, more," he went on, "Rumi ended

with the word for silence. As if to say that words or poems can only take you so far, and no farther. At some point you have to cast off from reason, say goodbye to the things you can explain and then . . ."

And as he began to finish the sentence, as seemed to happen every time he was back in his dissertation now, the phone on the desk began to ring.

He let it go unanswered, not eager to come back through the centuries to hear a telemarketer make his sales pitch (or, what seemed little different, to hear a well-meaning classmate talk about a manuscript that had shown up in Herat), and then, as the unknown caller continued to talk—no click—he turned the volume up to see why the intruder was going on so long.

On the machine, the voice he least expected to hear: ". . . the unwarranted intrusion," Sefadhi was saying, "but if I don't hear otherwise from you, I shall expect to see you at six p.m."

He played the whole message back again, the volume higher, and heard what might have been a practical joker, or a trick concocted by some Department prankster: what sounded like his adviser summoning him for an "informal meeting" two days from now, on the beach. So informal that he was fixing a time and place. In all the time they'd worked together, Sefadhi had made it a point never to meet him outside the office; if anything, he'd tried to screen him off from any glimpse of a private life. When, once, one of his graduate students had summoned the courage to ask him about this, he'd just said, in his characteristic way, "Limits are what give meaning to affection."

It sounded so much like a ruse that he wondered what could lie behind it. Was Sefadhi concerned that his most loyal student was running after manuscripts that didn't exist, moving in the opposite direction from his thesis? Or did he have some message to impart, about where real manuscripts might be?

When he arrived at the Beachside Bar on the appointed day, a few minutes before six—Sefadhi was ruthless in such courtesies—the waiter led him out onto the terrace, and he saw his teacher sitting alone at a round table with a white tablecloth on it. As soon as he heard the approaching footsteps, the older man looked around and stood up to greet him, and his slightly informal wear—an open-necked white shirt and sweater—made him look as he seldom did: forlorn.

"What will it be, John?" he said, taking care not to sit down till his student had done so.

"Just a Coke," he said, knowing that his adviser would never drink in public.

Around them it was already dark, and the waiters were stepping from table to table to turn on the heaters. The tables with their white linen, laid out in front of the sea—the islands outlined in the distance, and fading into the dark—looked like a party someone had arranged for friends who would never come. Sefadhi asked him in a desultory way about Seville, who had asked after him, who had not: all the questions he could have asked, and didn't, at their debriefing session. Then, as if casually, he told him a little about what had happened to Uwe while he was away: the Department was still alive with the news of the Dutch student who, six months before the completion of his doctorate on Scientology, had suddenly taken flight. Slowly, almost imperceptibly, the word had it, his life had begun to turn into a television melodrama. His cat had been found dead on his driveway; his children had been handed notes at the day-care center; someone had even said that he'd gone and done the Witness Protection thing, taking a name from an old gravestone, and living now under another identity in a far-off town.

"They found out about his thesis, I gather."

"Or somebody told them," said Sefadhi, pointedly. "What about you? The manuscripts you were so excited about."

"Not excited now. They don't seem eager to be found."

"No one's been of any help?"

"The opposite. The people who know something seem the last ones to talk."

"And the ones who know nothing talk and talk."

He guessed, from his professor's joke, that he'd given the right answer.

"And if I did find something . . ."

"It would be worse."

"I know. It's better that I don't."

"A complicated field," said Sefadhi, jangling a few nuts from the small white bowl in his palm as he spoke. "I never really told you, I think, about Leila."

"Your first wife?"

"My only wife." A flash of steel behind the curtain. "The reason I'm here. The official reason, at least: SOAS, California, my life in the West"—he contrived to give the last phrase the feeling of inverted commas—"the whole thing."

"She worked here, I think I heard. Or studied here at least."

"Worked, yes. After a fashion. Before I knew her. By the time we met, she was in London, at the embassy."

"A diplomat?"

"In a sense. In London she was first secretary."

It was unclear to him why Sefadhi was saying any of this; the more he said, the less clear it was why he was saying anything at all.

Then, playing with his stirrer, and rubbing his hands together to rid them of the dust of almonds, he said, "What you have before you, John, is that most implausible of figures in your English spy novels, the unsuspecting husband of a spy."

"That can't be."

"Why not? We always had a large presence in London; it was there long before Mossadegh. Many of our people were working covertly. And I, a student, became that unhappiest of clichés, a spy's half-knowing spouse. A funny thing to be, in both senses of your word."

"Everything okay with you gentlemen tonight?"

The waiter was standing at their side—he'd seen that the older man's glass was empty—and Sefadhi, shaken from his story, ordered a second soda water while his student shook his head no. Around them, as the wind blew in from the sea, the waiters were bowing down to try to light a candle on every table.

"As you can imagine, it was not easy. I could ask nothing, I could know nothing. When she was late at the office, when she was called away to an overseas trip; when she went out and didn't come back for three days . . ." The new drinks arrived, and he paused. "Of everything I could know nothing."

When someone entrusts you with a secret—this had been Alex's wisdom, years before—he's trying, as often as not, to keep you from some deeper secret. If someone tells you he's the husband of a spy, it may be a way of keeping you from thinking that he's a spy himself.

"So you never knew anything?"

"Nothing. If she took meetings in a hotel, if she went suddenly to Europe, if she disappeared without a word, I could know nothing. It was nothing dangerous or difficult, she used to tell me, but it was better for me to keep my innocence."

He said nothing, so Sefadhi would continue, but his adviser seemed to need no prompting.

"She could have been enjoying a contact that was 'extracurricular,' in your words. She could have been making deals with Iraq, with Hafez Assad. She could have been reporting on me to the authorities. I never even saw her passport."

"And this went on a long time?"

"I met her in '73. It ended in '79."

"I'm sorry."

"She was called back to Tehran, shortly before the change in government. I never heard from her again."

"You don't even know if she's alive?"

"I know nothing. If I am a married man; if I can take another wife. What happened to her house near the Winter Palace—she used to show me pictures. Her grandparents near the border, the cinema they ran. Nothing. It's better, perhaps. If I knew something, it would be worse. If we had both been in Tehran in '79 . . ." and then his voice trailed off, even his grammar and syntax falling away.

Neither of them said anything for a moment, and then, feeling that his teacher was waiting for him to draw some conclusion, he said, "There's a virtue in keeping quiet."

"A virtue in remembering what you're up against." Sefadhi sounded like himself now, as if they were back in his office. "These men are not gentlemen."

"Things have consequences, in other words."

"Always. Unintended consequences."

The older man drained his second glass quickly and then called for the bill; when it came, he drew out a black pen with gold trimming, elegant even in this casual meeting. "I know I can trust you to keep this to yourself," he said, as he calculated the tip and signed. "A private consultation between student and teacher."

"Of course."

They got up, and as they began walking out, suddenly the older man slipped, and grabbed onto the tablecloth to keep himself from falling. A glass of water spilled its contents across his sweater.

When he came out into the parking lot, more steady now, it was as if the man so in command of things in the office had been replaced by someone more faltering, more poignant; someone not sure of what part he was meant to play. "Next time, our usual place, our usual hour," said Sefadhi, collecting himself as he went over to his car. As he unlocked the door, the older man seemed to be shivering a little in the winter night.

When he got home, unable now to settle to the reading he'd promised himself, he pulled out a piece of paper from the bottom drawer and, in the precise and meticulous way that Sefadhi himself had taught him, began to make a diagram of the forces gathering in his life, a "star map," as his adviser would have called it.

On the one side, there was Khalil, who'd somehow led to Kristina, then Camilla, and then whatever lay beyond Camilla; on the other, the men from Westwood, the strange fanatic in Seville, whoever called him up to say nothing, or sent him unsigned faxes. As he looked down, it seemed that the drawing was beginning to look like a maze, one of those puzzles Camilla so loved to toy with. How thread your way to the center without repeating your steps at any point? And how link one side to the other without noticing that the only thing they have in common is the one person you tell yourself you are not growing closer to?

"Make a list of what's important"—it had been Sefadhi's injunction, in his first year here—"and then eliminate from the bottom."

He drew out a piece of blue letter paper from his desk and began to write.

Dear Benedict (if I may, after all these years),

It's been a long time since I was last in touch and I know that generations of new disciples must be clamoring at your door. But I did want to say hello again, after all this time, and to tell you how things are going over here. Also (as you've no doubt guessed), to solicit your advice on something: you can be assured I'm not completely disinterested.

You told me when I chose to go to SOAS, and implied the same when I asked for the reference for the Scholarship, that I should be ready for a "hall of mirrors," as I think you called it. I was, of course I said, and of course, as usual, I didn't know the first thing about what I was getting into. I never realized what a strong division separates those who are party to this world from those who aren't. I feel at times like a kind of neophyte in some kind of Underworld. Except that the Underworld is the real world, and I have to find my way in it. Like when I was in Damascus, not long ago, and every little lane I turned into in the Old City seemed to have a blue sign on it that said "Cul-de-saque." Wasn't it you who told me that in medieval Cairo half the roads were cul-de-sacs?

In any case, the images are catching, rather, and one doesn't know where to stop. But the reason I'm writing now is that I've begun hearing, here and there, about certain manuscripts, not widely known of in the West, that might have come out of Iran in recent years. They could be in France, though more likely they're somewhere here in California. People seem so reticent about them that I'm sure there must be something there—even if I'm hardly the person to make sense of it all. Those who care about the manuscripts, of course, as well as those in possession of them, all have considerable reason to keep their cards very close to their chests and to keep them out of public view.

I know this isn't strictly your field, and I realize I'm not giving you very much to go on. But if I did come upon one of these anthologies, what exactly would I do with it? Especially when others regard the texts as a matter of life and death. I suppose I come to you largely because you're not in the field: you're an innocent, in that way. Everyone else has an agenda, to the point where one is least inclined to trust the people closest to one.

Might you have time for a chat when next I'm in England? I don't know when that will be, but for now I wish you and of course Miss Mowbray all happiness and health. I also hope you'll enlighten us on St. Teresa. What was she doing on all those long nights alone? I hope you'll tell us.

With every best wish,
John Macmillan

Then, picking up the telephone, and looking again at the list he'd drawn up, he dialed her number and when he heard the voice again on the answering machine—"This is 437-2962. Talk!"—said quickly, directly, "Camilla, I'm going on a trip, up north. Any chance of your being free for a small adventure?"

The next day, she arrived just as it was getting light—in her ineffable fashion, the only way she could find to meet him in the morning was by driving through the night and then camping out near his house until dawn. The sensible thing would have been for her just to come and stay overnight, but already they were both moving warily around the memories of dinner appointments lost, his waiting and her worrying. To be insanely early seemed safer all around than being dangerously late.

She piled her things into the back of his car—things and more things—and then they headed north, past the last stretch of undeveloped beach in the area, driving through almost rural parts of suburbia, and great meadows that ran along the freeway, the sea beyond the train tracks blue. After a hundred miles or so, the road trickled into the coastal highway again, and we drove along a single-lane emptiness, with cows grazing above the road to one side—placid as creatures from an older world, going nowhere—and a lighthouse here and there set among the rocks and the foaming ocean on the other.

Long stretches of virgin beach ran along the cliffs, and the colors were primary and stark: green fields, high blue skies, patches of flowers, and the greenish sea. Years ago, in another world, this was the place he'd dreamed of when he thought of California: a territory still unclaimed where people lived among eternities. No history, no tradition, no society, no preordination: only whatever the rocks and the light and the changeable sky seemed to determine.

At his side, he thought, someone who longed for nothing but history and tradition and a role: someone who had even become an actress so that people would tell her what to say and do, as if she could escape from a haunted house into a studio apartment that was empty, ready to be furnished according to someone else's taste. She put on a cassette of Celtic folk music, looked out at the expansive sky, the rocks and sense of unvisited space. He felt as if something at last was moving forward: with each mile away from Los Angeles, she grew younger and freer, more full of animation. As if, in some child's coloring book, the outline of a face was being filled now, and made piquant, by red, yellow, gold.

As the road climbed and ran high above the ocean, the sense of spaciousness came and went, sometimes to their left nothing but clear air, not even a speck on the horizon in the distance; sometimes a sudden grove of trees, and a valley shadowing its darkness. Battered mailboxes in front of torn fences, as if milestones in the wilderness, and the lowering of trees making each sudden expanse of space and light a quickening.

Finally, the trees and the shade grew more intense, and, after crossing a creek, everything woody now and gold, green and brown, the floating surfaces of Southern California far behind them, they pulled off at a little inn, tucked into a grove of redwoods. You could hear the gurgling of the creek from every room. Tall trees moved back, back towards the mountains as if pulling you towards something ancestral. There was a sense here of being in one of those sleepy hollows along the coast—Pynchonland—where the real world is forgotten and one slips into some other order, behind the rolling mist and in the protection of old trees.

The meeting he'd fixed up was two hours farther north, so they followed the road up, the groves of trees thickening, enclosing them from the world, and then suddenly giving way to sunlit fields, a silver road above the cliffs, and great suspension bridges that seemed to bring them back into the world of men and moments.

Then, as they began winding around the small rural trails that run like whims or quickly arrested thoughts around the Santa Cruz mountains, he veered right onto a dirt path—she reading the instructions he'd taken down over the phone—and, bumping along a pot-holed road, came at last to a small house built in a dark grove of trees. An aging Citroën and a motorbike were parked outside; a trailer ran alongside the main house; and behind it, as if it were a back room entered only by invitation, stood the woods.

Talmacz was waiting for them, sitting on his porch nursing a beer and looking more like a rancher than a translator of Islamic poems. His yellow hair fell to his shoulders, and his shirt was partially unbuttoned; he seemed closer to the woods than to any library one might imagine.

"Come in," he said, "you're just in time."

They followed him through into a cozy rustic room—rocking chairs and pillows and a few Islamic rugs here and there, eyetooth locks on the wooden doors as in a fairy tale.

"What are you drinking?"

He brought back a beer and a glass of wine and sat back in his rocking chair, moving with a deliberateness that enforced their distance from L.A.

"So what is it I can help you with?"

"Pretty much everything. You're the only real person I know of in this field."

"That's why I'm not in the field," he said. "Like to keep my distance."

In another light the man would have seemed too much the laconic cowboy to be true, a Marlboro Man come into the candlelit room of someone who spent too much time reading. But in the context of Islamic Studies, he was just incongruous enough to be plausible. Ten years or so ago, having wandered into the field from his studies of Whitman and Longfellow, he'd started translating Sufi poems in a rangy, uncompromising vernacular that spoke right to the dancer down the street and the organic farmer over in Capitola. The books had begun selling and selling—Sufism, they said, the Tibetan Buddhism of the new millennium—and the academics, who for the most part distrusted him, began calling him the "Alan Watts of Modern Islam" or the "Ruminator of Santa Cruz." Instead of finding obscurities in the poems, he dared to come out with simple, universal truths.

"But where—if you don't mind my asking—do you get your texts? How do you know they're authentic?"

"That's a professional secret," Talmacz said. "If I told you that, I'd be doing myself out of a monopoly. But my advice to my students is, 'Stay well clear of it. The whole thing's such a mess these days, you need an industrial-strength shovel to go into it.'"

"Because of all the new translations?"

"There's that. There's the Sufi boom—all the world getting off on these guys now, though most of them don't know the first thing about what they mean or who they are. Even the scholars don't know their asses from their elbows. Nicholson—the granddaddy of Rumi scholarship, the one who broke the whole thing wide open? Some of the poems he includes in his edition weren't even written by Rumi! And the new guys you see, producing instant Rumi tapes and Top-Forty ghazals, they wouldn't know a Farsi verse if it played a kazoo on their stomach. Even the Iranians: they see a market and they're back in the bazaar again. There's a guy doing Rumi now, native speaker of the language, he translates 'two planes of existence' as 'two pairs of buttocks.'"

She broke out in a laugh, her demureness suddenly forgotten.

"I mean, it was always bad round here. All the poems getting copied out for five hundred years and no one knowing what's being added or altered or taken out. And the guy himself cranking out so many poems, it's no surprise most of them got lost. But now it's even crazier. The biggest Rumi book out there now—its cover design is from Portugal! But they don't know; they don't care. People are grabbing at him here, translating from him there, grabbing pieces of the true cross like he was Dylan or something! 'Give me a line I can use with my girlfriend, Jalaluddin!'"

The way he pronounced the name—as if he were speaking of "McIntosh Jallaludin" in the Kipling story—showed that this was a cover, the mask he'd developed to pre-empt the criticism he heard. The leading modern translator of Rumi wasn't the most obvious person to be talking of the Islamic tradition as if he were a backwoods hack. But people in the New World have their own defenses and strategies, and simply practice *taqiyya* by calling it plain-folks honesty.

"You must be tempted to get out of the field into something else?"

"Tempted, sure. I've gotten out, the way I look at it. I've translated the best poems and left the other scraps for the hyenas. I don't think I'll be doing much more Sufi work for some time to come. Students come up to me all the time and say, 'I want to study Rumi; I want to learn about the Sufis; blah-blah-blah.' I tell them, 'Stay where you are. Do Ezra Pound instead.'"

"But how did you get into them in the first place? It wasn't the most obvious field to study."

"No," said Talmacz, speaking a little more slowly now. "I don't have your adviser's vested interests, shall we say." He drew out the syllables as if to stress their significance. "But I do have a regular person's interest." It was as if he'd been talking automatically before, and now the answers came out more deliberately. "It was the sixties, there was all this stuff in the air—Malcolm X, Marcus Garvey, Muhammad Ali, all of that. And the Moslems were always the big bad wolf in every story. I guess I just figured we were so busy making all these jokes about how they called us the 'Great Satan,' we didn't stop to think we were calling them the 'Great Satan' ourselves. Except we didn't have the balls to use words like 'Satan' and 'infidel.'"

"It was politics, then?" She'd offered, on the way up, to start asking questions if that would put their host at ease.

"It was politics, it was economics, it was everything. I guess I just figured we picked on them because they had a belief, to the core. We just kind of said, 'I know what I believe. I believe I'll light up another joint.'"

"But you're still teaching them, after all this time?"

"Sure. No sense in keeping them to myself. But I don't really teach them anything. I just take them places in the woods. Give them Blake, Dickinson, give them these flashlights they can use. First class of every semester, I say, 'This is a course in Farsi epistemology. Anyone who wants to study mysticism, go somewhere else!' That usually weeds the crazies out."

"And the secret poems, the ones that are in L.A.?" It was the first time she'd shown him her acting skills.

Their host fell silent again. Then, looking straight at her, he said, "I'm not into any of that stuff. Way I see it, we've got plenty of good poems already. Too many. What do we need any more for? The regime figures Rumi and his buddies are the best PR tool they've got, outside of the cinema, more power to them. But you go looking for new poems and you might as well write a few yourself!"

He took a long drink from his can, and they realized, suddenly, that the interview was over. They'd made a friend of sorts, and lost a contact.

"I didn't know you knew Sefadhi well," he tried, but by now it was too late.

"Guess I should be going back to my shop." He'd kept his poems safe from prying eyes for decades now; there was nothing they could do to smoke him out.

They drove back along the coast as the sun sank into the sea, and soon there were stars everywhere, promiscuous. There were few lights on the road, and the whole area was so undeveloped that there were almost no lights between them and the sea. They passed along the thin winding road in a world of stars, the foaming sea, silver places on the hills where fire had burned the bush bare, or where the moon happened to find a rivulet of stone.

"So now I know what you'll be like ten years from now," she said, as a way of saying they were close. "Ornery and cranky and pretending you like nothing except six-packs and your gun."

"Except—being English—it'll be port and my cigars. Comes to the same thing, though."

"It's funny how all of you in this field seem so into pretending you're something you're not. Pretending you don't like the work you study, pretending you're after bigger game. Like teenagers who don't want to let on they like girls."

"I suppose it is. What's your father like?"

"The same. I never know who he really is, what he loves. Love is for his study, which we were always told when we were growing up was forbidden ground. Life is for what happens outside. Which means us."

"But he looked after you, didn't he? In his way."

"In his way," she said, and he got the sense, as he often did, that the more he asked the less he'd know. "He just didn't like us knowing too much about what he did away from us."

She put her head back against the seat, and he saw it as a way to let all talk fall away. Once, as they went round a sharp curve, headlights catching only a few feet of asphalt before them, they saw a deer, stationary, standing on a ridge a few feet above them, and then turning, running away into the woods, as if a tutelary spirit vanishing. The rest of the time there was only the ocean, flat as a plate beside them, stars above the hills, the outline of pine trees, and occasionally, very far away, a red light disappearing around a turn.

They passed a small cluster of cabins as the trees began to close in on them again, and, off to the left, a sudden burst of lights, and Japanese lanterns hanging from a great building that sat upon the cliff like a spaceship waiting to take off into the dark. A little later, the small wooden sign, hand-carved, beside the road that told them they had arrived at their temporary home, and they turned up the short driveway, walked up the creaking stairs to their room.

The place came with heavy comforters instead of telephones, and no televisions or keys, but odd pieces of whimsy: a straw doll in the closet, a book of Anaïs Nin left with a candle by some previous occupant. She buried herself under the blankets, and he went to the window, then came back: outside, the gurgle of the creek and, here and there, the lights of occasional cars, suddenly shooting through the trees.

"It's funny," she said. "It feels different here. Like somewhere older." Her sentences themselves had slowed down, and she'd gained the gift of concentration. "I feel like I could be anything I want to be here: the prettiest girl in class or the person I was abroad."

"You are," he said. "The prettiest girl in class."

She kissed him on the nose. "I think it's difficult for you—for someone with a normal family—being with someone like me. I don't think you can understand what it's like to be like this."

"All families look normal from the outside." And then, when she said nothing, "I think I understand your fears, the ways you've been hurt."

"It's more than that." A car turned the curve on the road, and its lights lit up the room. Then darkness again, and the sound of the stream. "It's a lot more than that. It's like"—she fumbled for the words—"like I'm living in a hornets' nest. All the time. All these things buzzing around me, and there's no way I can ever be away from them."

"We all get like that sometimes."

"Not all the time. Not every hour of the day. It's like this war going on inside me, and there's nothing I can do"—the small voice cracked—"to keep the enemies beaten back."

"You need help," he said, as tenderly as he could, and then realized that the sentence meant many things at once.

"I know I do. I appreciate it, really I do."

She pulled herself closer into him and closed her eyes, as if to shut the whole world out. He remembered the time after Cephalonia, the last real night with Martine, when, in the small hotel in Athens, suddenly, with no warning, something had come over her. Her voice had gone low, and everything she said had been designed to destroy. She was possessed—a creature in a low-grade horror movie—and all he could feel in the small room was that he was with something dark, full of venom, so full that it wanted to tear apart everything it saw. He tried to expel it, but what can a young and undefended student do against a force that comes from somewhere at the core? Another reason, perhaps, he'd chosen to study the great poets of affirmation and alchemy.

"What about you?" she said, and he could tell she wanted to be free of thinking about what she'd come up here to leave behind. "Did you have a place where you could be safe?"

"I think the whole world is like that, in a way. I mean, I think things are benign, deep down."

She looked at him, and the brimming at her eyes offered wonder, envy, pain. "That's why we could never be together."

"That's why we have to be together. To round one another out—the black spot in the white circle and vice versa."

She got up and went into the bathroom, ice-cold in the night in the unheated cabin, and when she came shivering out, and running back to bed, something had turned in her, in even the short moment.

"I think you just lie to yourself about it. You've set up your barriers so efficiently that even you can't see they're there."

"Maybe." Thinking that this impulse in her, to read the world in terms of darkness, was the true reason they could never be together: they spoke a different language, in which nothing carried, and all he could do was wait for those moments when she allowed the girl in her to claim a tiny victory.

"It's like your adviser," she went on, "all the ways he tries to keep you guessing."

"I didn't know you knew him."

"I don't," she said quietly. "Except through you."

Then, sitting up, she looked down at him, and he could tell they were at a crossroads. She would never be calmer than she was now, but further discussion would lead them back into a forest after dark. He leaned forward and kissed her on the pulse of her throat. She shivered, as an actress would, and pulled him closer. Her neck when he unbuttoned her shirt was warm, and flushed, and when another car came past, taking the curves very fast—a sudden shaft of light into their room—he saw the person of whom she was most afraid, rapt and stainless as a madonna.

"I want to believe you, really I do."

"We'll have to work on it," he said, and, looking at the brightness in her face, he saw how easily it could be answered by going a little further and erasing everything they could see of past or future. A long kiss, a slipped-away sheet, a loosened self, an act of love would make everything better right now; but the next day, when they woke up, they'd have crossed to the far side of an abyss, and there'd be no way, ever, of finding their way back to the innocence they'd lost.

California taught that lesson, if nothing else: restraint, and the meting out of pleasure, lest soon you'd be exhausted and have nothing to look forward to.

In the morning, something was already gone. The day was fresh and reborn, and when he opened the door and looked out, they were in a pastoral clearing: someone was chopping wood outside a cabin, set at the top of a path that led into the trees, and early light came through the grove of pine trees to make the creek below sparkle. The world still had the dew on it (as she had, too, the night before). But with the weight of their imminent departure he could feel her running away again, back into the safety of her cave, and nothing he could do would pull her out.

"What would feel nice?" he said. They were in bed, the sun was streaming in through the windows, and the rest of the morning yawned before them.

"To stay like this. Forever."

"And failing that?"

"Failing that, we could"—she thought for a moment—"go to a place where you'd never have to let me go." She spoke as a girl to make the wish come true.

"But right now, right here, at this moment, what would feel good?"

"You could tell me we'd never be apart."

"We won't, for now. I brought you this as a small token of that." He got out of bed, walked across the room, and took out from his case a small box. She took it from him, and inspected the top.

"You can open it, if you like."

Inside was a bracelet, and a pair of earrings the color of tiles in the Alhambra. She put them both on, and then jumped up and twirled herself around, as if modeling the new person she could be. The room was washed in sunlight, and she smiled as if she'd never cry again.

"Thank you. It's lovely." She came back to where he lay, and threw her arms around him. Her cheeks, he felt, were wet.

"What is it? Did I upset you somehow?"

"Only by making me happy."

"But unless you think things could be better, or imagine it . . ." And then he stopped, because optimism is largely learned, like any other kind of trick.

"It's like these poems have given you a pretext for belief. An excuse. Which is fine for you."

"But for you, it's no help at all?"

When she nodded, and said nothing more, he said, feeling he was flailing, "Maybe that's why we're here. It's a way to step outside our usual lives. We can be different." But the words sounded hollow even to him, and by the time his reassurances got to her, he could see, they'd lost their meaning. In the poems there were rooms outside the world where something was suspended; but in the world itself?

On the way home, they drove slowly, to keep their parting at a distance, stopping at an art gallery built around a redwood tank, dawdling around the hamburger stand that sat on the cliffs, in an area that grew emptier, less developed with every passing season. The only stretch of the coast he knew that slipped back into the past, as if the present were not holding on to it tightly enough.

When they crossed the mountains and came in sight of Santa Barbara, passing the illuminated phone booth, the piano he'd played the night they were stranded, the city looked like a circuit board beneath them, a grid of colored wires that they could rearrange at will. He left the car running at the house—she had an "errand," of course, unspecified, in Los Angeles—and when she turned to him, it was as if she was losing a foothold somehow.

"See you soon, perhaps."

"Perhaps."

"You can come back anytime."

She didn't say anything, and she showed no sign of moving, so he turned the ignition off, and they waited in the silence.

"I tell myself it's my imagination," she said slowly, not looking at him. "And I can return to it even if you're not around."

"You can," he said, with a sureness that made her look more frightened still. "If you see another space, you're not trapped in the one where you are."

"No. Only trapped in the space you want to get to."

He said nothing for a long moment. "Maybe you need to be shaken up. Be thrown into something so foreign that you forget all your usual fears and step away from them without even knowing you're doing so."

"Easy for you to say. You're used to living far from home."

"You could be, too."

She looked away again, towards the sea. "It's something I've always wondered about you." The words came from very far away.

"What's that?"

"What you'd be like if you'd grown up with two parents, siblings."

"Very different, I'm sure."

She only asked these things when it was drawing close to time to go: it was a way of hanging on. "Well, I should let you go."

"I think you should. You have a long drive ahead of you."

She turned to look at him, her hand sliding up his leg, and he saw how she had kept men around in the past.

"I think we'd better go. Before we both freeze to death."

"Can you give me one more minute? To write you something before I go?"

"Now?"

"So you can see what I look like when you're not around. When I'm at home, waiting for the next meeting." She'd come upon the one invitation he could not resist: a tangible reminder of her presence.

"As long as it doesn't take too long." He got out of the car, and as he did, he saw her fumbling in her case for a pen, a card, whatever it was she had brought in preparation for this moment.

He walked along the road to the small patch of grass that sits above the sea—an adult's playground, as he'd thought of it when first he'd come here—and then walked back, as slowly as he could, to where the car was parked. Catching a glimpse of her through the windshield, he realized she was right: he could see the person who came out of hiding only when alone, bent over her book, frowning in concentration. Biting down on the top of the pen, and looking out into the dark as if counting syllables to herself. When she turned down again towards her card, her hair fell all about her face, and she had to brush it behind her ears again. She saw him looking at her through the window, and smiled as if the day were just beginning.

Finally, just as his patience was about to snap—it was cold and it was late, and he could feel Sefadhi nearby, the poems on his desk, the thesis deadline drawing closer—she rolled down the window. "Okay. Come and get it."

She handed him the Oriental card, and he read, "Dear John," though the letters were already smudged, crossed out here, a word added there, so many squiggles and second thoughts around the lines that it was already almost impossible to make out.

I still wake up, several times a week, and tell myself it can't be true. That anyone who's normal—kind of—with a normal life, could have any time for me. And sometimes I don't wake up at all, and then it's even better.

When I was young, I told myself that if I closed my eyes, everything in my usual life would disappear. My mother, my father, everything. And then I did, and opened my eyes, and everything was the same it had always been. I wasn't in Samarkand, riding horses, and there wasn't anyone coming along who thought and felt like me. Once I opened my eyes and there was someone coming along who felt like a part of me, but he had a different story in mind, and I had no place in it.

Now you tell me I should come out and open myself up to you. What can I say? If I say yes, maybe I get something good until it stops being good. Anything could happen. It's like driving along the freeway with your eyes closed. If I say no, I get the same as usual: no happy ending, no ending at all. You've always got some poem nearby that talks about the beauty of surrender, but in real life surrender comes at a cost. I know.

So what do I do? I don't know, and you don't, either: you just tell yourself you do. But until you get well and truly sick of me, I want to say thank you for giving me a chance.

He put it down and, as ever, had nothing useful to say; the saddest thing about the sad is that they can see what's going on at least as well as any onlooker. He looked at her briefly and kissed her on the brow; she got out and walked to her oversized truck, to drive away.

He'd put Rumi aside for a while, the way you try to put aside a song that's going through your head—or, more likely, to drown it out, by playing something else. The something else right now was the famous perfumer Attar, Rumi's inspiration, whose *Conference of the Birds* tells of thirty birds flying off together in search of their lives, whatever is lost within them. The hero of the story, the hoopoe, is prized in desert countries because he can see where water is running underground (as, he recalled, an early translator of Rumi had called one of his works "The Soul of Goodness in Things Evil").

Now, though, he seemed to have lost his taste for explanations—everything he'd told himself about Camilla (and his adviser; even about himself) so wrong that everyone became less and less visible as the days went on. He turned instead to the last chapter of his thesis, about the influence of the Islamic poets on the modern world. The Arabs, of course, had given us the way we count and drink and hide—"alcove" and "alcohol" and "alchemy"—and the Persians were the ones who had given us the word "Paradise." When Dante committed the Prophet to hell (to be eaten by pigs, no less), it was tempting to say that every good poet tries to bury his father (as Harold Bloom had said, half burying Freud); the obvious reason for Dante's rancor was that his *Divine Comedy* read like a Christian version of the Miraj, or celebrated Night Journey, of Mohammed (and who was Beatrice but a displaced Shams?). Much of the world, in fact, if looked at with certain eyes, resembled a carpet with Islamic threads in every corner. The Sikhs, the Cathars, the troubadours—all of them were said to have got some of their ideas from the Sufi notion of a hidden order. Almost 250 pages of Emerson's journals—someone had shown him once in the library—were devoted to homemade translations from the Persian.

And yet, he found himself writing now, not as he had expected to do, the real contribution of the Moslems to the outside world was not in the numbers they gave us, but in the ways they'd seen the limits of arithmetic. More precious than any of the numerals they invented was the "zero" they'd imported from India and Babylon; and, more than that, the sense that one plus one could equal zero. If two beings throw themselves fully together, they can so lose themselves in something higher that the result is what looks like nothing. In Attar—he turned back now—the dominant words were "die" and "abandon" and "burn." Die to every notion of yourself, the birds kept saying; die even to what you think is good or pious. Abandon every notion you've ever had of faith, even of what the faithful say about abandonment. Burn everything you have, even if it is what you most value, not only in the world but in yourself.

All Islam asks is that its servants give up everything, beginning with their lives: he thought of the photos he'd seen of the Martyrs' Cemeteries around Iran, their endless rows of headstones in the desert, small pictures of the teenage boys who'd given up their lives for the Ayatollah on every one. Yet Sufism, as ever, went even further. The true Sufi gives up his very faith, his reason, everything he understands, of faith, and burning, and abandonment. "Abandon the search for God"—the Gnostic Monoimus's words had stuck—"and the creation and other matters of a similar sort. Look for him by taking yourself as the starting point."

He made his way, next afternoon, slowly along the bike path, over the scrubby grass, bald in summer but now richly green, and along the top of the cliffs; down below, birds pecking their way across the sand, tall surfers, a few lovers sitting among the rocks. Everyone in his own private dream; and hoping, somehow, that the dreams would somewhere intersect.

Sefadhi's practice was to have his students read their essays aloud to him, "to take responsibility for their beauty and their foolishness," as he was wont to say: a hangover, some said, from his days in Qom, and the last of the medieval disciplines. Words are important, it was a way of acknowledging: something more than markings on a page. You claim them formally, publicly, as if they were your children sent out into the world.

This time, reading what he'd written of Attar and the power of abandonment, the sentences coming out with more fluency than usual, he read himself into a state of near intoxication. When he was finished, his tutor looked at him, for a long, long time, and said nothing. There was nowhere he could turn his eyes except to the impeccably coiffed figure, his few hairs neatly combed, his cuffs and red tie immaculate, his black shoes polished every day.

"Well," his teacher said, and looked at him again. Outside, the usual desultory cries, the day drifting on towards its end. "I admire your conviction," Sefadhi began his assessment, slowly, "your willingness to incarnate, shall we say, the emotions and resolves of your subject. Your facts, insofar as you include them, cannot be quarreled with. This is a rendering of Attar that some of his disciples might be happy with. In the context of our project, however, it is"—he paused—"more unsuitable than I can say. As a piece of scholarship, it can be compared only to the ravings—or the pantings"—he made the words sound like a curse—"of a lovelorn boy."

The professor moved his chair around, as if to collect himself, and looked away from him, as if not to see the damage he was inflicting. "You write—you write as if you are writing to some beloved, someone you care for more than you should. It is a rhapsody, a call to love, a gust of wind. As an offering to my colleagues, however"—he swiveled back—"and to myself, it could more easily be taken as an insult."

There was nothing he could say to this; the man was his teacher, and born into the faith besides.

"You realize it's all a fairy tale?" the older man said to him, as if holding his anger back. "You realize it means nothing, in the context of our thesis?"

"We have documentation for most of it," he said feebly. "I haven't departed from the record."

"You haven't departed in the few facts you choose to share with us. You spare us outright falsehoods. But to turn Attar—or any of his fellows—into a California surfer boy is worse than committing any falsehood. It is to translate him into a tongue in which he has no meaning."

"I use his words, not my own."

"And your meanings, not his own. For those who know and love this poet, what you've written is a kind of obscenity. Everything is there except what is everything to him: his God." He paused to try to steady himself; both of them knew he was in no hurry to antagonize his most faithful student. "You have, if I may say so, smeared your own feelings all over him like a kind of paste. A graffito over the building he has taken pains to construct for us. You remember when I spoke about 'textual rape'?"

He nodded and said nothing. Perhaps, he thought, his teacher was trying only to spare him from a grilling at more hostile hands, to give him a taste of what he might expect from the less sympathetic members of the Department. And perhaps his unease, volatile at the best of times, had been made acute by the confession at the beach, and all the sudden, unwanted talk of smuggled manuscripts. A part of this might just be personal, the moment and the mood talking. But the bulk of it, he knew, was not.

"You've worked hard on this, John, I realize that." He was a doctor now, mapping out strategies at the dying patient's bedside. "You have a perspective, even a depth of involvement, that is tonic. But you cannot turn these poets into mere carriers of fire without taking them away from everything that's important to them. These poems are fragile things, esoteric in their way; to strip a text of a context is to leave nothing but a pretext."

He recognized the line from a long-ago preface—Sefadhi's own youthful excesses—but he felt he was in no position to answer back.

"What do you suggest, then? How can one begin to write about 'mystery' without trying in some fashion to unriddle it?"

"I suggest you keep your life quite separate from your studies. I further suggest you think of your audience: a generation of scholars training the next generation of scholars. I suggest that you leave your explanations behind and content yourself only with the words, the very particular words and meanings, of a poet whose meanings are far greater than you or I could aspire to. Rumi, Attar, Hafez, they are wise men in a complex tradition; please do not bring them onto your daytime television."

Afterwards, there was nothing to say. He cycled back along the track, the light now going fast—the beach was already almost deserted—and, back in the house, it was all he could do to pour himself a drink and take it to a study that now seemed deeply empty, abandoned by its governing spirits. In his mind, arguments (lover's arguments, lawyer's arguments—the same) began to form: "If you weren't so nervous about how Iran is seen in the West . . ."; "If you didn't bring your own past and sufferings into this . . ."; "If you hadn't been so wounded in love, and determined to box it out of your life . . ." But even he could see they were foolish, spiteful things that he had to say only so he could throw them away. He composed a four-page rebuttal to his teacher, and then put the treatise away in his desk and thought back on the evening just past. "You sound tired," she said when she called, late that night. "Has something happened?"

"Nothing much. Just the usual labors with my thesis."

"Do you want to tell me about it?"

"No. It's just the usual departmental stuff. Nothing important."

"If it were nothing important, you wouldn't be sounding like that. I guess I'm not the only one who's bound by pride."

"I guess not. Anyway, we're on for tomorrow, yes?"

"We're on for ever. Just stay where you are, and I'll come and make it better."

She arrived at his house just before dawn, as if to advertise her eagerness to help, but when he opened the door she didn't come in. "Come on. I'm going to take you away from this."

"It's six o'clock, Camel. I haven't even got up yet."

"That's why I want to get you now. While you're fresh. You need a break from all your books."

Letting her minister to him, he'd begun to see, was the best way to take her out of her troubles; like acupuncture of a kind, healing the soreness in some part of her by releasing the brightness and compassion in another part. He put on his clothes and got into the passenger seat of the truck, she flinging books, brown bags full of sandwiches and little bowls of pasta into the back to make room for him. Then they drove up into the hills, on the old mountain road they'd never been along before.

It was still early, the sun hardly up, and the roads were almost empty. Here and there an older man in a bright tracksuit walking fast around the curves, a dog running up ahead. A pair of cyclists, shocking in bright yellow and purple suits, whooshing round the turns from the mountains above. In the fast-food stand where she'd stopped to pick up coffee, two gulls were perched above the speakers, and you could smell the sea, feel the presence of kelp and seaweed, with the day yet unborn.

As they drove higher around the turns, towards the Pass, they saw more and more bulldozers, sleeping on half-deserted slopes, or resting in some valley, in a circle of brown earth. Contractors' signs sat in front of every other driveway, next to the blue warnings that told of some security firm's surveillance. He'd never been in a place where watchfulness and hopefulness were in such alliance—the construction of new lives everywhere, and hidden cameras, unseen watchers on all sides to make sure they didn't slip back into the soil. Churches, companies, new institutions coming up everywhere, and every few years a fire or flood or earthquake to send them all back into the earth. Life could make no impression on this soil.

As they proceeded up towards the very top of the hill—a red light winking from a satellite far above, she peering over the huge wheel like the captain of a very uncertain ship—suddenly they hit a bank of fog again, the cloud level, and when they turned a corner, coming into blue skies once more, she pulled abruptly up a steep driveway, and they found themselves on a crest.

"What are you doing? What's up?"

"I want to look. I've never been up here before." The truck was alone, at the edge of a steep slope, amidst fog and winter chill and silence. She got out, and the slamming door resounded in the emptiness. He followed, and they found themselves, in the mist, on the flat ridge, in front of the outlines of a house. There were no curtains on the windows and plate-glass doors, and they could see that there were no real divisions in the house yet: just planks everywhere and cellophane, chalkmarks, measurements scrawled in black, the outlines of a life.

"Let's check it out," she said, walking towards the ghostly place, marked out the way policemen in the movies draw silhouettes of bodies when there's been a murder. "No one's here yet."

"They will be soon, I think."

But she was away from him now, walking around the house, peeping through windows, tapping on the walls, as if she were a county inspector, stopping now and then to yank at a door clearly locked from the inside. He went the other way, inspecting this strange place, alone on a hilltop, of expectations, and few memories.

Then, suddenly, through the chilly, misty early light, "John. Over here. Come quickly."

He went over to where he could hear her voice coming from, on the far side, down a rocky slope, at what must be the lower level, and when he got to where she'd been, she was nowhere in sight.

"Come on. In here." The girl in her, whatever was hopeful, stealing into a place—apparently one door had remained unlocked—and making it, for a small while, her own.

Her steps were crackly on the cellophane, and the wooden boards were cold underneath his feet. The rooms were still dark in the absence of natural light, and as they walked they had to move carefully, not to smudge the figures and marks chalked up on the floor here and there. The corridor that linked the rooms was close to pitch-black.

"What do you think?" Her face was radiant. "Our very own house."

"Until they come back. A few minutes from now. I imagine they start working at seven or eight."

"Just five seconds more," she said, not pleading but walking away from him again, so he couldn't pull back, and tiptoeing up a small flight of stairs to a space so huge that it would surely one day be the living room. Large windows on three sides admitted them to a world of fog, and against one wall were the outlines of a fireplace.

"A whole house from scratch," she said in wonder, "according to their dreams."

"I don't think their dreams included us. We should come back sometime when we know they won't be coming."

He turned and walked down the stairs again—a hint—but she went on, marking the territory as an animal might.

"I'll only leave if we can come back tonight," she said, catching up with him at last where he stood in the mist outside the door left unlocked.

"Of course we can."

Back in the house, he went to his desk (the way a ship might go back to port), and she, stretching her arms and closing her eyes, said, "Mind if I watch?"

"Not at all."

He posted himself at his desk, and she curled up in the armchair a few feet away. He looked at the book on Hafez, but all he could see was someone drawing a brush through her hair, again and again and again.

"Do you need anything?"

"I'm fine," she said. "Am I disturbing you?" Over and over, almost absently, long fluid strokes that caught the light.

"No. It's fine." He threw himself back into the books, almost physically, but it was useless: always, at the edge of his vision, someone pulling out a strand of hair and looking at it cross-eyed, or combing and combing, to let all the tangles out.

"What are you working on?"

"The usual. Why Sufis believe in the dark—as the place they can see the light."

"Like us. In the car."

"I don't think so." Sefadhi's harangue had been hard to forget.

"What do you think they'd say if they could see us now?"

"They'd be appalled. We're about as far from them as anyone could be."

"They believed in ritual and order," she said, and he thought of how the two of them had arrived at the same door this morning, but coming from different sides.

"They believed in everything this place negates."

She stopped what she was doing. "You don't think you'll ever find anything that no one's ever seen before?"

"I'll be lucky to find a single sentence no one has ever written before."

An hour or so after dark, they drove up again into the hills, in his car this time, which took the curves more easily, she, in her customary way, making it a ceremony, a secret rite, by bringing a bag in which she'd packed provisions. The fog had lifted long ago, and when they pulled up the sharp driveway to the ridge, they were looking down on lights now, hovering, the winking red blinkings of small planes, coming down to land at the airport by the sea, the presence of islands out beyond.

The streets of the small downtown were long yellow lines, only a few cars buzzing along them, and for a moment he felt he was in Granada again, in one of the Alhambra's dark rooms, sealed off somehow from the lights of the town, and so in a position to appreciate them more.

When they were inside, though—the door gave again, easily (a measure, perhaps, by which the construction workers ensured they'd never get locked out)—it was pitch-black. She'd brought a blanket, a small flashlight to guide them through the darkened rooms, but the reach of it was small, and the house, the wind gusting around, seemed very large. As they walked, they bumped against pieces of wood, bruised shins against objects that hadn't been there in the morning, so it seemed.

"This can be our special place," she said, after leading him up into the large space among the open windows. "We can come here whenever we want to. Our very own abandoned house."

"It's not abandoned. It's getting more occupied every day. And we can't come anytime we want."

"After hours, then. When it's dark."

For her, he thought, an empty space; for him, a place coming up and taking shape every day. In their different perceptions, all the distance that lay between them.

Through the windows now, surrounding them, there were lights. A shiver of yellow from the sleeping town below; stars intermittent in the skies; the bright-red lights of cars behind, pushing through the mountains.

"I've brought candles," she said. "A bottle of wine. We can be anyone we want here."

"Within reason," he said, and then realized how wrong that sounded. She was trying to pull them away from boundaries.

"It's like undressing in reverse," she said, as she pulled out a box of matches and lit a candle.

Her face was eerie in the small light, hollowed out, ancestral (the word seemed constantly to be coming to him now). She was previous, in some way: previous, perhaps, even to all she'd suffered in her life. The light caught ridges, different angles in her face; her eyes were bright, her hair was loose against the dress she'd brought.

He had a premonition of being here before, and wondered whether it was dreamed, or just a trick of consciousness: a moment ago remembered as an eternity. Her voice, when it carried to him through the dark, was mysterious, charged; everything is intimate when it's whispered.

There was a strange intensity about them now, impossible to doubt: the scooped-out faces in the thin light, their bodies making shadows on the naked wall across from them. No furnishings but the lights below, and the wind gusting along the paths and making the windows shake.

"Closer," she said in the near darkness. "Over here."

He followed the sound of her voice—she'd moved the candle round to the other side of her—and then felt a hand steadying him, lips on his neck, the fall of hair.

She smelled of something exotic—he remembered the bottle of ylang-ylang she'd put into her bag—and her hands were nimble, active in the dark. What she'd said was true: they weren't themselves in this light.

The wind came up again outside, and they could hear small bushes and pieces of debris being pushed along the walkway. The windows, the screen doors rattled, and it felt as if the wind would send the house itself gusting and howling over the edge of the ridge. "Is this what your poets taught you?" she said, very close to him in the flickering light, lips, wrists, hands wet with oil all around. "Let's see what it is we're not allowed to do."

Shortly before dawn they got up, replete with the sense of something they'd touched that they couldn't understand. Again they'd come close to the edge of something, and he'd turned back, and she, looking at his eyes, had turned back, too; around that corner, whatever they knew would be greater than what they didn't. They got in his car and drove back through the waking world, and when they let themselves into his house they saw what they'd gone away to put behind them: a red light blinking on the answering machine.

"See who it is," she said. "It could be urgent."

"That's why I don't want to see who it is."

"It could be for me," she said. "It could be anyone." But he knew this was the one number she'd never give to anyone she knew.

In mid-afternoon, while she slept, he got up and tiptoed over to the machine, curiosity alight. It was probably someone from England, he thought, calling to invite himself to stay. Or Alejandro, eager to convey some piece of droll wisdom, about how the person you have to look out for is the person you say you're not taken with.

It was none of that; it was his most frequently unexpected caller now, Sefadhi, with a brief and purring message. It was as if his passionate essay on Attar had somehow roused an animal from its lair, and now his professor was stalking him, or trying to pursue him back out of the light.

"John," said the urbane voice, composure recovered since their uneasy meeting by the sea, "a little something has come up, in India, next week. Something I think you can be helpful with. A Christmas present from a Moslem, if you like. If you could call Eileen to confirm your acceptance, I would be most grateful."

He dialed the number reflexively, keenly aware that he was being asked to accept an offer that hadn't even been presented to him yet, and Eileen, when she answered, sounded nervous. "I'm sorry. He's caught up in a meeting right now. No. For how long, I don't know." So nervous he felt he could see his adviser by her side, gesturing furiously as she spoke.

"Will he be free later on?"

"I can't promise anything," she said, still anxious, and then, from the other room, came a sleepy call. "Who is it? Someone for me?" And he realized what it was his adviser was trying to pull him away from.

She was looking up eagerly when he came in, her face washed clean of all its usual doubt. All she needed, he'd come to see, was a place where she felt protected, and then she could claim the stronger person who was waiting for her, inside. She looked at him, and he saw the opening she was beginning to occupy with her mind; a vacation, he away from his books, she away from Los Angeles. And the abandoned house in the hills the first place they'd come upon where they could leave behind the world—and the pasts that seemed confinement.

"It's just," he said, trying to find the words, "something has come up. Nothing important. But I have to go and check in with my adviser. I'll be back soon."

"I'll be waiting," she said, and he looked away from the hopefulness.

He took the long way round to the library, to give himself time to think, and when he went in, he walked up, with sudden purpose, to the new second-floor computers. Years before, when he'd arrived, he'd told himself he should learn everything he could about his mysterious adviser, and had started to spend long hours with the card catalogue (no computers in those days); then, after a week or so of this, he'd told himself that if they were going to work together it was better to know nothing. The same tendency, as Alex had pointed out, he seemed to be exercising with her: what you don't know can't hurt you.

Now, however, he had a purpose, and when he typed in his adviser's name, the computer whirred a little, told him to wait, and then threw up a long list of green codes and titles on the screen. He scanned them quickly, and saw what he expected: all the stuff, in fact, that had made him decide not to explore too much before. Many of the items referred the reader to obscure journals in Farsi, from around the world, or Festschrifts to which his adviser had contributed; one entry noted a piece written with a Frenchman, in a magazine from England, another some contribution to an anthology. The topic, in almost every case, Sefadhi's special interest, poems from Isfahan not widely known of in the West.

He pushed the button that led to the next screen, and there found more of the same: not a single mention of Shiraz, or Rumi, or anything that might have come as a surprise to him.

Then, getting up to stretch his legs, he walked up to the eighth floor and back, and something in the movement jogged his mind: years ago, Pauline had said something about how Sefadhi, once upon a time, had written a few pieces under his father's name. No one knew why exactly, whether this was a custom of some kind or a precaution—akin to the Anglicizing of his family name, Sefaredi—but it had made his bibliographers' lives a misery, she said.

He tried to retrieve now the father's name—it was one of the commonest in Iran, he recalled—and then, going through the options on the screen, he saw the one he recognized. "Ardeshir Sefaredi, 1953–." He tapped at a button, and, a few seconds later, a new list of entries appeared, much shorter than the first, and none of them more recent than 1985. Many of the pieces weren't translated yet (or transliterated ineptly by some unknown programmer).

As he scrolled down the list, he could detect nothing out of the ordinary—once shaken out of their code, these items were much the same as before. Close to the top, however, was one entry that looked different: from 1984, the computer said, and from something called Persiflex Press (an exile concern, he assumed, in Los Angeles). Its length was unusual—thirty-six pages only—and its title, not in Farsi, announced, almost defiantly, "The Desert of the Sacred, the Desert of the Profane."

He followed the call numbers up to the fourth-floor extension, and when he came to the Iranian section, he found a large anthology of Isfahani poetry (never checked out, the slip on the back page told him), and another book on the conventions of Isfahani literature. Slipped between them, slim as some secret message a student had left for his beloved, was a pale-blue pamphlet, hardly larger than a theater program.

He took the pamphlet to a nearby carrel, and when he opened it up and began reading, something in him seemed to stop. It was not that the content was so surprising, or different from what he might have expected, but the manner, the voice in which it disclosed itself bore no relation to the elegant figure he knew. The sentences were rough, unruly, passionate—it felt as if they had been scrawled out very quickly, after dark—and they hardly seemed to care who was reading them, or what another scholar might say. They read, in fact, like the utterings of a man possessed.

There are two kinds of desert in the world—this seemed to be its thrust—the desert of faith and the desert of anarchy. "In one place, people search for water, look for what materials can sustain them; in the other, people look only for themselves." He thought back now to the parable of Attar's that had loosed such invective in his teacher, and wondered if the source of his adviser's rage was a kind of recognition: nothing unsettles us like the sound of our own voice echoed back to us. "In one desert people gather around a mosque, a walled city, or a circle," the text went on, "in the other they never stop. They move and move, towards a horizon they can never reach. We might almost say that the people who gather are the ones who wish to be found by God, while the people who seek are the ones who wish to have God found inside themselves."

It was an edgy piece, unhinged in some way, and what gave it its particular charge, he saw, was some kind of division in its writer: as if the man longed to affirm one form of order, yet found himself drawn to another. Or was somehow trying to articulate, or exorcise, his betrayal in these pages, as if to thrash out the impulses that were leading him away from the world he sought to defend.

The history of Persia, the piece went on, more unexpectedly, was the history of the war between these visions, the Green Revolution taking over from the White, one group filling the emptiness with the gaudy tents of Persepolis, the other with the glittering shrines of Sufi saints. "In the old days we drank in public and prayed only in private," the young writer went on, more conventionally. "Now, on the far side of the world, we go to the mosque every Friday, and drink and weep in secret. Two kinds of treasure we have about us, an outer and an inner, and the one is concealed within the other."

It was the kind of thing that was likely to make sense to almost no one but a close associate; at times it sounded like one of those preachers who appeared on the airwaves on Sunday mornings to rail about fire and brimstone. But this demagogue wrote of what came after the fire and brimstone: silence, uprootedness, uncertainty. On and on the ragged aphorisms went, for many pages, less and less interesting as they continued (a fire is most commanding at first glance), and then, at last, they subsided into a final comparison, not surprising, of the land of exile ("a place of modernity, disorder") and the beloved home left behind ("a land of secrets").

At the end was a dense appendix, referring to some professor of astrology in Los Angeles and his work on stars, and another, bizarrely, describing the hours of an initiate's day, as outlined in a ninth-century handbook. At the very end, a final Appendix, C, on what a more secular soul might have called "The Sufi Way of Healing."

This included more talk about the cult of discipline and the virtue of doing without, and then drew a comparison between a culture of ease and of struggle. "In the one there is the belief that suffering is the enemy of life, that which we must expunge; in the other the sense that suffering is the source of life, the cradle of our wisdom. The only tragedy in the world is a young culture that believes in comedy."

Finally, in the very last words of the pamphlet, as if rising to a grand summation of everything he'd said before, the fervent young believer wrote:

We live, some of us, in exile, in a culture that speaks of therapy, as if therapy was not with us all the time, in our God. The therapy culture tells us that everything we do is the product of a trauma, where we tell it that everything we do is the consequence of God. The therapy culture says that we are formed by family, community, upbringing, we tell it that we are the creations of the Divine. The therapy culture offers confessionals for those who have turned away from God; it says that everything has a reason, an earthly cause that can be yielded by analysis. We tell it that our cure, our source, our reason can only lie above us. We enter the causeless and find ourselves by losing ourselves in a Greater Self. All that we are is what we cannot name and cannot know.

Written in the year of the Prophet, peace be upon him, Most Merciful and Just, 1362.

He turned the final page, and sat for a long moment at the desk. Around him, two young Japanese girls were giggling; a tall bronzed boy in shorts was passing a note to a girl with long fair hair, and she was biting her lower lip and looking back at him. Outside, a few gaggles of students walked through the courtyards in the direction of the sea. The eucalyptus stood along the sides of the lagoon, and then there was open space and light.

When he got up at last, his legs crumpled beneath him for a moment, and he almost fell; he had been sitting in one place so long that they'd gone dead. The kind of abandon his measured teacher had chosen to confess to the world at large, even a decade ago, was itself a shock; but more than that, there was the fact of his writing all this in English, and allowing it to be printed and kept in the library for anyone who looked. It was less a treatise, he began to think, than a call to arms.

When he arrived in the Department a few minutes later, Eileen looked up and greeted him with a smile that seemed uneasy.

"He's not expecting you, I think?" she said.

"I told you I'd be coming. I'm answering his summons."

"I see," she said, unhappily. She put through a call, taking pains to say nothing in reply to what was said to her; then, not many seconds later, the door to the private office opened, and Sefadhi emerged.

"I just got your message," he told his adviser, and then recalled, strangely, that he'd heard the same phrase, said to him by someone else: she, calling from one of her hiding places, a few weeks before.

"Come in," said Sefadhi, leading him into the office, and pulling out the creases in his trousers before he sat down.

"You've decided to take up my offer," he said, as if he'd given his student a choice, and not a command. "It's nothing urgent: just one of those things that come up from time to time."

"A nothing urgent that is sending me across the world."

"You don't want a free vacation?" asked Sefadhi, knowing the question was rhetorical.

"I'm not sure I've got much choice."

"You will enjoy it," his teacher pronounced. "There is a manuscript that someone has found in Jaipur. Not of great interest to us, I have no doubt, but similar, perhaps, to the books they keep in Delhi and Lucknow. A relic of the time before they returned to their original homes."

"Then it's of no use to us."

"No obvious use, no. But the owner of this text, a Mr. Hussein, has asked that we help him place his book."

"And tell him what he doesn't want to hear."

"And tell him nothing," Sefadhi corrected gently, no doubt catching the implication in his student's voice. "He has a manuscript, and it is no doubt of value to him. That is all he needs to know."

She was waiting for him when he got back, sitting against the propped-up pillows, her face alive with all the places she'd scrawled across a pad: plans, projects, all the things they could do together in the few days off.

"I'll be there in a second," he said, and took himself off into the study to collect himself.

"What is it?" came the voice from next door. "Anything I can help you with?"

"Not now. I'll be there soon."

"You're preparing something," she said, her voice heartbreakingly free of the veil it usually carried with it.

He went into the room where she was, the receding ocean leaving the sand behind outside, and sat by the blanket under which she'd stretched her legs.

"What is it?" she said again.

"Bad news."

Instantly, without a further word, the color went out of her face, as if this was what she'd been waiting for all along.

"You're leaving me."

"Not exactly. Only for a few days."

"You're leaving me," she went on, "just the way I said you would." She didn't think of sudden calamity or earthquake or death; only the drama she knew and had played out a dozen times before.

"I'll be back by the fourth of January."

"You leave when?"

"Two days from now."

She counted the days off on her fingers. "The twenty-third. Just before Christmas."

"Sefadhi's found some manuscript, in some old house in Rajasthan, and he says it needs authenticating before the new semester begins. He, of course, has other plans for the holiday, so his most faithful student—or the one most beholden to him at least—gets the call."

"He can't do that. It's Christmas. It's New Year next week."

"He can do anything he wants." He put his hand on the leg underneath the blanket, and she pulled it away. "Without him, there's no fellowship. Without him, I can't even stay in the country. He can do anything he wants with me."

For a long moment she said nothing; he thought of someone whose car has gone off the road, and then, in the shock immediately after, starts throwing out flares, whatever distractions she can put up in the road.

"He's going to see his daughter, I guess."

"Who told you about his daughter?"

"You did. The first time I met you."

But he was sure he hadn't.

"He's going off to some Iranian gathering. And he knows I have no such excuse."

"You don't?" she said, and then got up from where she lay and began to collect her things. "That's fine," she went on. "Greg said something about Palm Springs. I'm sure he can come up with something."

"I'm sure he can. All I can say is that, if you're disappointed, I'm even more so. I've been looking forward to this since . . ."

And then, when he said nothing, she turned to look at him, and everything in her softened. He had only to hint at all the holidays he hadn't spent, with the family he didn't have, and she was defenseless against him.

"It's just . . ."

"I know. For you this would be the trip of a lifetime. I should dress you up and you could talk like me and say you're John Macmillan."

She didn't laugh, though, and went on pinning up her hair, while she proceeded to look around for whatever things of hers were still lying around.

"Well," she said at last, gathering things up in her arms to take to the bag in the next room, "I hope your trip is a roaring success."

"I hope it's over before it starts." He remembered the paper he'd seen in her notebook once in which she'd listed all the cities she dreamed of visiting.

"We'll go somewhere one day, I promise."

"Maybe," she said, and then, with more feeling, "What if I can't sleep without you again?"

"We'll have to make sure I'm always around."

"I'm serious," she said. "What if I miss you and miss you and you're off looking for some inspiration? Or doing some stupid chore for your adviser?"

"I won't be, if the inspiration comes from you."

"So clever with your words," she said, and took the things she'd gathered off into the next room.

The light had fallen as they'd been talking, and the room was now pitch-black. He sat there for a few moments in the dark, the sound of the ocean outside, distant cries from near the point, while she, he could hear, was throwing her things together. Then, suddenly, the phone began calling from the study, and he ran to pick it up. Maybe the whole thing had been a test, one of Sefadhi's elaborate devices to see how committed his student was? Maybe it had just been a joke of some kind; or he hadn't managed to acquire the visa he said he'd scare up overnight.

"Hello," he said, picking up the phone.

"Hi," said a voice, almost familiar, but not quite. "How are you?"

"Very well," he said, trying to find his ground. "You?"

"I'm well," she said. And then, after a pause, "You don't remember me, do you?"

"Of course I do."

"Who am I, then?"

"Someone I know."

She laughed at the feebleness, and he began to put a face to it. "Kristina Jensen," she said, to take him out of his cloud. "We met at your presentation on the Sufis."

"Yes," he said, "of course. How are you?" But he'd already said that once, and now, almost reflexively, he was looking back at the living room to where someone else was collecting her things.

"Am I disturbing you?"

"No, not at all. I was just—well, preparing something."

"The reason I'm calling is Camilla. We were worried."

The "we" the most sinister thing she could have said.

He didn't say anything, so she'd have to make clear her intentions.

"We haven't seen her for a while, and we were beginning to worry. I wondered if you'd seen her recently."

"Not recently," he said, willing the angry figure in the next room to be quiet, "she could be anywhere," and he was rewarded with the conspirator's laugh again.

"You'll tell us if you do see her?"

"I'm sure I will," he said, suddenly realizing that his new friend's fears were not imagined.

"Good. We appreciate that," she said, and he waited for the inquisition to end before the voice in the next room could respond.

"Who was that?" she said, pretending not to be interested when at last he put the phone down. "Your secret girlfriend?"

"Hardly. Just someone looking for something." He didn't know what to say exactly.

"Did you give her what she wanted?"

"Not yet. It was something I care about."

By now her things were set in a neat stack by the door. Her face, as so often, broadcast the wish to run away playing off against the longing to stay.

"Can I ask you for something?" she said, once her preparations were complete.

"Whatever you like."

"I wish it were." And then, after she'd made sure he'd caught the implication, "I think it's better if I ask you for something you can give me."

He didn't say anything.

"Just hold me? Till I get to sleep? At least I can have one night of calm before you go."

He went in and cleared a space for her on the bed, smoothing down the sheets where she'd been lying before, and when she came in, he held her and embarked on a long, winding story to help her get to sleep. About two people who follow a road of dark curves up and up into the hills, and then find a space that has never been claimed, and start to make it their own—a private space outside the city, uninhabited—and then climb up into the large room, lights visible through the windows . . . but by the time he got to the empty, dark space, her breathing had fallen into a regular rhythm, and he could tell she was far away.

He followed the couple a little farther himself, in his mind, into the empty space, up to the wall against which they could sit, the intimation of Spain, the Alhambra in the lights outside, and then, as he began to fall asleep, suddenly he felt her clutching at him, desperately, as if clawing.

"What is it?" he said. "What's happening?"

"There was this, I don't know," she said, "this figure all in black." Her nails were digging into him, and it was as if she were still asleep. Or taken up, at least, in some other place. "I was saying, 'Go away! Get away from me! You're evil!' But it was coming after me, and I went home, and then it was coming out of the bushes. It was after me, it wanted to get me."

"It's okay," he said, waking up. "It's all right. It's just a dream."

"It was, I don't know . . . We were wrestling in my room, and then I was saying, 'You're evil. You're black!' And my mother came in, she had a knife, and she was drawing it across her hand."

"It's all right. It's just a dream. I'm here. You're okay."

"Like this person who had no color, no color at all. And I was saying, 'Leave me alone! I don't want to see you. Leave me alone, can't you?'"

And then she was sobbing, great speechless sobs, and it was another person he'd never seen before, squeezing out all the things that had been trapped inside her. Choking now and then, and talking through her tears in words that came out muffled, incoherent. "You see?" A great gasp. "You see what I've been telling you? Anytime anyone starts getting close to me, I get like this. I become the person they most want to run away from."

"It's all right. It was just a dream. You're better now."

"Now you see why everyone gets sick of me."

Then, as abruptly as she'd clutched at him, she got up and made to walk towards the door, where all her things were stacked.

"You can't go now. It's four-fifteen."

"If I don't go now," she said, and she didn't have to complete the sentence. You'll never want to see me ever again.

"Then come back as soon as you're feeling a little better. We can have Christmas in advance."

" 'In advance,' " she said, as if it were a nice thing for other people to believe in.

In the morning, as he'd half suspected, there was no sign of her. He checked the answering machine, he opened the door, but there was nothing. He stayed in from the library, didn't take his run, but the apartment was more silent than if there had been no one there at all.

The following morning, very early, he put his things into a bag and drove south. The sky was the color of steel above the sea, light-threaded, and along the coast the traffic was sparse: people had already begun staying in for their Christmas celebrations. The last time he'd come along the road, he thought, seeing the occasional surfer come in from the sea, he'd been on his way to Westwood, the Iranians and their manuscript, her house full of clutter under the smog.

"I look at you sometimes"—her voice in the cabin near the creek, the light from occasional cars shooting through the windows—"and all I can see is this hope, this boy's hope, that everything will work out okay. I can't share in the hope, I can't believe in it, but it seems like a good thing to have, not terrible at all. And then, sometimes, I see you at your desk, or when you're running along the beach—I see your back—and all I can see is this incredible vulnerability. As if the slightest wind would knock you down."

"It's the language they speak here," Alex had said, years before. "It's the Californian addiction. The only thing they recognize is weakness."

But then she'd gone on. "That's why we're perfect echoes. You see in me the things you'd never admit to in yourself."

"I'm glad you can see it like that."

"I'm not. But if I couldn't, I wouldn't believe I had anything to give you."

At the departure gate, after checking in, he called the most recent number she'd given him, and heard the male voice dispense its command. Then, trying to frame his words carefully, so they'd reassure her without throwing off anyone else who might be listening, he said, "This is a message for Camilla Jensen. This is . . ." and heard a click.

"Hi. I was hoping it was you."

You didn't come, he might have said. I waited and waited; I went out into the streets in my pajamas at dawn. Instead, he simply said, "I can't wait to see you again. We'll celebrate Christmas when we meet."

"By then . . . ," she said, but whatever came after was drowned out by the sound of the announcement of his flight.

III

British Airways flies through the night to London, and then through another night to Delhi. When he arrived, in the dark of 1 a.m., there were figures coming towards him out of the mist, shrouded in blankets, only their eyes staring out through the phantasmal chill: "Sir, please, sir, come with me." "Sir, best price for you." It was always like a graveyard outside the international airport—he remembered even from his trip in college—and the number of figures had increased, moving without direction in the brown light, wrapped in turbans, their dark eyes sharp.

He got into a broken-down Ambassador, some of the shawled figures getting in on all sides, turning around from the front to smile or gawk at him, scrambling into the back seat to sit beside him and guard his carry-on. As they drove into the spectral capital in the night—it was 2 a.m. now, local time—he felt as if he were moving through a battlefield at the end of some medieval war. Here and there, figures were sitting by small fires along the side of the road, their eyes wild as the headlights caught them, while others plodded along with bullocks in the middle of the half-deserted street. The air was brown, over everything a kind of filthy mist, and the buildings that came occasionally looming out of the dark, illuminated, looked more unreal than ever, like painted models. India had the one thing that California lacked, he realized—the theme of all his research coming back to him—native ghosts. Everywhere the sense of unseen and unburied spirits taking over the imperial city while the people slept.

He took an early breakfast—one thing they still did well here—at a hotel Martine had told him about once, scribbled off a card to her, and then returned through the fog, less mysterious now the sun had risen, to catch the early flight to Jaipur. At the other end, pushing his way through the confusion of the small terminal, all the mystery and menace of the throning crowds gone in the morning light, he found a man, impeccably got up in dark suit and tie, holding up a sign on which "Mr MacMillane" had been written.

The man led him farther out into the clamor, and opened the door to a grey Mercedes. Hussein was putting him up in a hotel near his house—his way of showing that he knew foreign tastes—and so they drove out into the town: huge billboards with large women spilling out of saris and men dancing around miniskirts, little stalls that looked like they'd been swept forty years ago towards a wastepaper basket they'd never quite reached, the commotion of cows and bicycles and ringing bells made many times worse by the sudden profusion of cars. In such a world, he thought, who wouldn't want to gather in secret at dead of night and take himself out of all this? The human impulse to escape would never go away: God has to be understood in the context of everything that is not Him.

As they drew away from the town—the clangor and the big streets quickly fading—the driver put on a tape (another sign of Hussein's wish to be seen as sophisticated, or else just his habit of directing everything), and the blowing winds and uprising sands of desert music came up as they passed, almost instantly, into open spaces. Already the villages around them were nothing but mud-baked houses, children crowding over fires, the wind outside sending red and orange and green and blue scarves fleeting against their faces in the dust. Dark eyes watched the carriage from their fairy tales move past, beseeching, angry, startled, and soon even they were gone, and there was nothing but brown earth, brown walls, dry stone—an ancient space of almost atavistic emptiness.

At last they came to a large driveway—he could have been in California, he thought, in Palm Springs or some other garish attempt to fill the empty space—and pulled up to a huge house, crumbling but clearly elegant. Hussein was waiting for him at the door (the driver having called ahead when they were two minutes away), and came out to greet him as if they were oldest friends. Talk, he recalled, was never difficult in India, especially for an Englishman people were eager to impress.

He was led into an old-fashioned reception room—the stuff of Indian fantasy, he thought—and Hussein circled around the topic at hand, asking him about the flight, offering him a drink, so perfectly slipping into the part he had chosen to play that it became quite impossible to see him. He, too, had become archetypal—the employer's prerogative—and every last urbanity seemed like another veil thrown up, or a kind of fog. He could no more be identified than the men looming up in the mist the evening before.

"You must be exhausted," he said in that Indian way that was more warning than commiseration. "And absolutely famished. Let me get you something to take the edge off your hunger before we have a look at the manuscript." He was daring him, he realized, to see him as cliché; in India, a man in a house like this would do everything possible to insist on his distance from the role, so as to lure his visitor into an assumption and then leave him at a disadvantage. The first prerogative of power is to do as it chooses and not even look at the rules it is breaking.

"Of course I don't expect you to come to any decision right away. In fact, I wouldn't want you to; haste would be a kind of waste, don't you think? Besides, this is India." Every sentence reminding him of where he stood and whom he was seeing. "But I'd like you to take just a peek at it. Before you return to your hotel. So you can think about what you have to work with."

They walked into a library—again, it looked like a Sherlock Holmes movie, with a huge spherical globe at the center and nineteenth-century editions covering all the shelves, a scattering of dust—and the man extracted a key and pulled something out from a desk. "Here, don't be shy," his host offered, and he came around and found himself looking at a book like none he'd ever seen. A few Arabic characters were printed on the cover, framed by curlicues, and inside were pages upon pages of small script, written as tightly as a Quran. As in an illuminated manuscript from England, some characters were written in red, and gold had been used unsparingly.

"It's beautiful."

"Isn't it? One of the few things that didn't get carted off to the British Museum. In any case, I don't, as I say, want you to say anything now. Mum's the word. Just take the image back to the hotel, join me for dinner, and you can look at it properly in the morning."

The whole thing was a charade, of course: he recalled Sefadhi's advice to authenticate nothing, however impressive it looked. His job was only to give the man a little time. "It doesn't really matter what he has"—the professor's final words. "These old palaces in India are full of everything. The important thing is that the awareness that he has something does not get out. That we keep it to ourselves."

Bearing this in mind, he checked into his hotel and lay out in the sun. Outside the walls, the desert wind blew, and at dusk the lights came on as in a miniature. For all the otherworldliness of the setting, he ran a long bath in his cabana, and thought of her; he called, once it was late enough, but all he could hear—this was still India—was her tentative "Hello? Hello?" and then a startled putting down of the receiver: she must have deemed it an intruder, or someone from her past.

He dined with his generous host, heard about Mountbatten and the Travellers' Club, pulled out such pieces of his past—Oxford, Wodehouse—as were part of the local currency, and, in the morning, returned early to spend all day with the text. Whatever it was, it was beautiful—he thought of the dome of the mosque in Damascus, of Persian carpets he had seen, and the Qurans so small they fit inside an earlobe. Not all the script was intelligible to him, but it didn't matter: he was walking through another world, of cool courtyards and the sound of water, and above everything there was a patterning of gold and peacock blue.

The book might have been drawn up by some loyal retainer a generation ago; that would take nothing away from its radiance. The centuries collapsed in India, so no one really seemed to care what was new and what was millennia-old, any more than they would worry about whether this copy of *Reader's Digest* came from last week or a century before.

On his last night in the place, after dinner, Hussein asked him if he wanted to see something "absolutely unexpected," and he followed him up some small, narrow, winding stairs to a rooftop, where his host (ever-surprising) kept a telescope. Lights were intermittent from this vantage point, but the older man fumbled and cursed at the lenses till they could see the planets as clearly as he had seen her, a few days before.

"You've come to some conclusion about my manuscript," said the man, screwing up a lens.

"Not at all. All I can tell you is it's beautiful, which you know already. As you also know, the likelihood of its being original, or worth anything, is next to nothing, I'm afraid."

The man held on to his demeanor as if he was remembering what the English said about sangfroid.

"What I'd recommend is keeping it here, with all your other treasures"—a nice touch—"and enjoying it whenever possible. Whatever you might get for it would not be worthy of it in any way."

This had been Sefadhi's suggestion, and again it seemed to work: the Englishman from across the seas had somehow converted disappointment into something to be cherished.

"You wouldn't recommend other appraisers?"

"Obviously, it wouldn't be in my interests to do so. But even to be disinterested for the moment"—"Be an Englishman with him," Sefadhi had said, "that's all he wants"—"I think too many hands would only injure what is, whatever its provenance, a gesture of love."

These were just the right words to use, and the man smiled again, flattered at the quality of the messenger, if not his message. "Jolly good," he said, in that engagingly antiquated way the foreigner remembered from his other visit. "Shall we go down and celebrate with a cigar?" The "celebrate" a gesture of thanks to him.

On the way back to Delhi, he stopped off in Agra, as he'd promised her. "I know it made me almost fall asleep with disappointment when I was a teenager," he'd said, "but our eyes change. Grow up. Before, I didn't know that the gardens were a diagram of Paradise, and I couldn't read the inscription on the dome. I knew nothing about Shah Jahan's connection with the Sufis—the way his son had had the Upanishads translated into Persian, and his daughter had been so ardent a mystic she would have been a sheikh if she had been a he. I was like a nonbeliever staring at a sacred manuscript. I think I'll have grown into it, in a way."

When he walked through the main gateway this time, he thought of the court chronicler of Akbar, centuries before: "Through order, the world becomes a medium of truth and reality; and that which is but external receives through it a spiritual meaning." Amidst the dust and the noise and the crowds of the city around, the cab drivers with their whispers, the boys with their carpet shops "close close," the squiggled commotion of nonlinear India—surely no clearer when Shah Jahan was on the throne—the building made a different kind of sense. In its way, in fact, it seemed a kind of Sufi parable: while the visitors thronged into the main chamber, bright with lapis and carnelian and jade, letting their voices echo around its great dome, the real meaning of the place, Martine had told him, was all underground. "You've got to go there at dusk," she'd said, "after the heat's gone down, and the crowds have begun to thin out. Just before the gates are closed. If you're lucky, the small gate will be open. The whole point of the Taj is what you can't see."

He went back to a hotel for lunch, having taken in the details and oriented himself, as meticulous as any spy circling around his prey—every Sufi poem has a face it shows the world, and a secret life that is its own: a Sufi building is a model of the soul. Then, in late afternoon, he went back through the great gates, paying again, just as lights were beginning to come on across the Yamuna, and water buffalo were gathering along the far shore to drink. The crowds of villagers in flaming orange and scarlet and golden saris—antidotes to the deserts where they lived—were just about gone now, subdued into murmurings, and as the sun declined into mist across the polluted river, guards were walking about the benches with torches, making sure no one was hiding in the dark.

As he hovered around the great entrance, trying to make himself unobtrusive, suddenly, amazed, he saw a faint light—a naked bulb only—shining from the bottom of a flight of stairs plunging down. He descended quickly, so quickly he almost slipped on the recently washed steps, and at the bottom he came out into a strange inner chamber, hushed and small, where two men were pouring water on the floor.

One of the men—both dark, and dressed in the clothes of the poor, dirty white shirts and grey trousers—shuffled over to one of the great caskets in the room, and placed a lighted stick of incense on it. Then a rose. A few moments later, he took another stick of incense and a rose and put them on the other casket, built like an afterthought on the side, housing the man who dreamed up the palace, now beside his wife. The decorations on his tomb were flowers, on hers verses from the Quran.

Above them, just faintly coming down the steps, were the last voices of sightseers trying out the echo, amazed to have the great dome talk back to them and no one else. Their voices climbing up towards the rafters, and then reverberating around and around them in circles. But the caskets they were so busily serenading were empty ones, ruses to distract the world from the real spirits buried in this underground place.

The men said nothing, just went quietly, devotedly, about their task. He was the only other one in the company of the tombs. His feet on the marble floor—Damascus again—were cold. He felt in some way that he didn't try to explain to himself, or even to make clear, that being here was a large part of what reading his poems, seeing her was about. Under the public exterior, there was always an unvisited deep vault.

In his hotel room, lit only by oil lamps now that the electricity had failed again, he turned over a postcard of the false tombs and wrote:

> *Is it the gods who put this fire in our minds, or is
> it that each man's relentless longing become a
> god in him?*
>
> —Virgil

The next day, flying towards England, he tried to imagine how he would begin to tell her of the experience: one in which nothing had happened externally, but certain locks had fallen away. One of which he had no photographs and which he could not explain by way of any postcards or posters of the Taj. One, in fact, that he had been pointed towards by the woman with whom he was in some ambiguous way "taken."

"You go into a mosque," he heard himself telling her in his mind, "and it's empty space: water and shadow and light. In the desert, water's worth more than rubies. The smallest glint of color almost blinds you. You walk into a prayer hall and it's so vast, so empty, for all the people praying and chanting and chatting there, that you get swallowed up. You disappear: become a particle of light, a wisp of smoke.

"You're in a place so safe, and yet so rapt, that you lose all sense of you, and become the air."

Getting out another postcard, he simply copied out a sentence he'd found in a bookshop at the airport.

Heart is the name of the house that I restore.
—Mir Dard

I missed you more than I can say; more even than my silence could communicate.

J.

The next morning, making his excuses to Nigel and Arabella ("I still think you've gone bonkers. A little while in California, and you become—I don't know—Timothy Leary or something"), he took an early train to Oxford and walked through the muddle of dusty red-brick streets, as changeless as the buildings around them, to Mowbray.

The man was getting on, of course, but he still kept up his full load of teaching, and every afternoon, or even late at night, after a Formal

Dinner, he'd get on his bicycle and go along South Parks Road all the way to the flat he shared with his sister, off the Bardwell Road. "Home" was probably putting it too grandly: it was a typical North Oxford encampment, with astrologers in the basement, and the sound of Tibetan chants coming up through the gratings now and then, to mingle with the bicycles, odd language students with pasty faces slipping in and out of doors, a piano teacher whose errant students served instead of Muzak, and a few very dark men who talked about the LSE but seemed in some form affiliated with the university. In the middle of the ragged chaos, Mowbray seemed content in a small second-floor flat, offering *"ex officio"* advice to anyone who sought it.

When he walked up the steps to the porridge-grey building and rang the white button three down from the top, a small figure appeared, a few minutes later, looking worried, and Alice Mowbray showed him the way up to the room. In all his years of knowing the scholar, he'd never penetrated the secret sanctuary before.

"How are you?" said the professor, getting up from his armchair, a little unsteadily.

"Very well. You?"

"I survive. You've brought something for me, I see."

"Nothing much." It was a book he'd found in the hotel bookshop in Delhi, surely out of print here, and redolent of a time when Mowbray was himself a student. An exploration of St. Thomas's work in southern India, by one F. W. Pickering Smith, M.A.

"Thank you, thank you: I knew his son," his old professor said, not entirely unexpectedly. "And you, how is life in California?"

It felt absurdly like a le Carré novel, but he told him anyway. "Almost exactly as you'd expect."

"A good thing and a bad thing, then?"

"Exactly."

"But it agrees with you? You're happy?" Ruthless about essays and excuses, he was always disarmingly kind—undefended, almost—when it came to human things. "He pours his strength into his scholarship and keeps his vulnerability for his life," as Parkinson had said once.

"Enough. Sefadhi's a brilliant tutor, and the place is beautiful to look at. It's never lost that Gold Rush feeling, though now all the prospectors are shrewd enough to say it's 'spiritual gold' they're after. But ever since Pagels, I think, they're all out for hidden treasure." He wondered how much he was talking of himself.

"And you're off doing heretics?"

"In a sense. It's bracing."

"I should think it would be," the old man said, with the ambiguous air that had left generations of students unsure of whether they'd been patted on the shoulder or put in their place (or, more likely, both at once).

"Thank you, my dear," he said, as his sister brought in a tray with the tea and milk and sugar and a stack of digestives.

"I got your letter, of course," he went on—now that the biscuits were here, the formal session was deemed to have begun—"and would be glad to help if inexpertise is no hindrance."

"It's not at all. I mean, I don't want to put you on the spot, and I know it's not your field, but I keep running into hints, all over the place, about so-called secret manuscripts—unpublished things, verses kept in family homes and the like—that came out of Iran in '79, or soon thereafter. I was wondering if you'd heard anything about that?"

The older man broke a biscuit in his hands, and dipped it in his tea. His pride was evident in his terror of making even the smallest mistake in a scholarly attribution, and the visitor was reminded that, for all their affected vagueness, English academics are as much double agents as any of their colleagues, knowing how to hide their intelligence behind practiced masks of ignorance.

"It isn't my field, as you say: I've never been drawn to it myself. I think it would be foolish of me to say anything."

He sat back, as if waiting to be prompted.

"Anything would be a help, really."

"I think the only thing I can give you that might be any use would be this, which fell into my hands quite recently. I know nothing about its origins, or its author, but, whatever the reality of either, it'll be of more help to you than I could be." He picked up an offprint that was lying on top of the books on his table, beside the chair, and handed it over. Clearly—characteristically—he'd hunted it down and set it aside in anticipation of this meeting.

"Otherwise, I can profess only uselessness. All my students these days seem more keen on the Reverend Moon and the swami on all the television shows." Oxford still appointed its Regius Professors of Divinity by means of official letters from the Palace and trips to 10 Downing Street, but religion was held to be such a part of life that it was not always recognized as a subject. Those who studied it, like Mowbray, had to pretend to be anthropologists.

"Well, I shouldn't take up any more of your time," he said, feeling that he'd given his old professor a taste of California to share with his colleagues and sister, and the old man had given him something in return. "I expect you have loads of essays on Hare Krishna to read by tomorrow. It's very good to see you again, and I'll profit, I'm sure, from the article." The benediction had been given; his job now was to make himself scarce.

When he got back to the house near the river—Nigel did everything he could, through the carpets on his wall, his trips to Yemen, even his fencing lessons on Wednesdays, to show the world (and himself) he hadn't become the person he used to mock—he took himself off to his room, and went slowly through the article his old professor had given him. He'd actually taken it out of his briefcase in the train, and then, for some obscure reason (the field must be getting to him), put it back in, lest anyone see what he was reading. Not that an offprint from an issue of the *Journal of Asiatic Studies* from two years before was likely to set many alarms ringing on the 17:23 to Paddington.

The title of the paper was "Missing in Action: Sufi Manuscripts and the Second Revolution," and the first few pages, as was the convention, were devoted to saying how little the author knew, and how much was still unknown, and how indebted he was to fellow scholars, even while offering himself as a sovereign authority. Sufi, Bahai, and Zoroastrian scholarship had all been thrown into disarray when the Second Revolution (as the paper always referred to it) came into being; great buildings had been renamed, memories of the old regime had been purged, and history had been subjected to an instant "retrofit" (the French author clearly eager to show himself conversant not just with École Normale Supérieure English, but with all the nuances of Santa Monica).

Overnight, history and literature had been sent out of the country, like a second Holy Family: forced to hide out, affect modern clothing, even go to enemy countries until the storm subsided. Treasures had been hidden in secret compartments in suitcases; hundreds of trunks, firmly sealed, had passed through the hands of dockworkers in Bandar-e-Abbas. The scene had been as "unruly," the article said, in its slightly precious way, "as when an earthquake shakes a house, and its inhabitants run into the cold, taking what treasures they can carry.

"The age of late capitalism," it went on—and here he began to pay more attention—

is the age of global scattering: heirlooms, secrets, flying across the planets as when a vase is shattered. Myriad pasts find their way into every present. A Dzogchen sutra is as likely to be found in Santa Fe as in Paris; to see Khmer Buddhas, you are best advised to proceed to the fourth story of the River City Mall in Bangkok; most of the great treasures of the Song Dynasty are said to be in a home in Palo Alto. The very bricks and mortar of the civilizations that made us up are now up for offer, in real time, at sothebys.com.

What this means, hermeneutically, is that texts have shed their authors, as much as they've lost their readers. They float, without names, without addresses, like refugees with only transit papers moving from airport to airport. Words, poems, spells, are just part now of the postmodern diaspora. In our own field, we follow the Sufi path by going to places that have never heard the name "Hafez" and committed none of Maulana's verses to memory.

Yet the history of any tradition, the way it has lived and colored minds, is to be found not in the Sheldonian, nor behind some mock-Tudor mansion in Bel Air. And the poems of the great Sufis will disappear not because they are erased from the earth, nor even because they are uprooted, and can now be uploaded in an instant. Rather, they will fade from view only if those who have eyes to see them fade. If they get translated into languages that have no word for "fire" of the Sufi kind. If they get paraded before the ignorant as once women from Egypt, or Chinese men, were paraded before the laughing crowds of Europe. If those who have keys to their secret doors disappear, the poems will shrink into love songs, or cries to drunkenness and dissipation. When the eyes that understood the Nabytean rites of Palmyra, when the priests who were aware of the hidden codes of Karnak disappeared, then, and only then, did their cultures lose their meaning and their power. Sufi manuscripts are everywhere, we know; but do we have eyes with which to read them? The meanings never change, only the people who seek for them.

It was a typical piece of evasion, clotted and muffled and oblique, with a tremulous current of outrage running just below its carefully maintained tone of academic neutrality. True to his thesis, his assumptions, the author gave away nothing about his own background or interest; it was only the name and the address in Paris that suggested a male Frenchman. In many ways, he seemed more interested in the "postmodern postmortem" he claimed to find—"where Ronald McDonald is knocking at the gates of Qom, and the people of America are hungering for Kabir"—than in what the poems contained.

But in a curious way, the paper gave him hope. It spoke on behalf of underground manuscripts, he felt, and its message, unexpectedly, was the same as hers, reiterated so often: "Don't give up on me, please. Please don't give up on me yet."

When he came out from the Customs area, into the bright winter light, she was, as before, nowhere to be seen. Girls in halter tops and miniskirts, going this way, going that, girls with fair hair not their own, frightened women stepping into new lives and looking for the loved ones who ought to have been waiting for them but were not: everyone except a girl who'd seemed closest to him when he was far away.

He trudged over to the nearest telephone, under a fast-rising escalator—could feel himself lifting up a weight again, as seemed to happen so often with her—and then, suddenly, he felt a tap on the back, and turned to see her standing there, as if she'd been waiting there for weeks. It was part of the perverse hopefulness of the place, he thought, kissing her, and smelling the shampoo in her freshly washed hair: the fact she bore no sign now of the haunted woman who'd left him less than two weeks before. The virtue of living in the moment is that old moments can be erased, in an instant; she looked at him as if she'd never heard of someone frightened by a nightmare.

They walked into the multilevel parking structure—her car, encrusted in new dirt, straddling the space next to it—and then he brushed the hair off her face, and kissed her with a new directness. She softened into him, for a moment, as if something had been released in her in his absence, the way, sometimes, one goes to sleep with a question and awakens, mysteriously, with the answer. Around them, people walked past, just released from Mexico, Armenia, Iran, and put all the hopes they'd packed into the backs of cars they'd never seen before, and drove off towards new lives.

Climbing up at last into her cockpit, he leaned over, as she put the key in the ignition, and kissed the space behind her ear, her neck. Something had come free in him, too, and he felt that if he didn't press the moment it might never come again. Her shoulder blades, partly exposed by the black dress she wore; the top of her chest, flushed with color. Around her throat now, the silver necklace he'd brought back from Jaipur.

"You seem better somehow," he said. "As if you've come to some decision."

"You're back," she said, unanswerable as ever.

"You didn't have bad dreams?"

"I don't have to now. You're back."

By the time they reached Malibu, night had fallen. It was still blustery and cold, the sea squalling and throwing tantrums, and when it began to rain, fogging up the already dirty windshield, he made things worse by circling and circling, with his finger, the cool parts of her skin, where the sleeves began, taking a finger of her nondriving hand and putting its tip between his lips. He wasn't sure who it was who had come off the plane, who it was who had met him, but there was a feeling of momentum, as if they'd been freed somehow by displacement.

"We've got to stop," she said, and he couldn't tell if she was referring to the vanished visibility of the road, or the suddenly visible, palpable presence by her side. She was going too fast, she might have been saying; she needed to slow down.

She pulled the car into a parking lot beside a bikers' bar in Trancas, and the wind howled and screamed as they ran into the warmth. Inside, under colored lamps the shape of mushrooms in the Disney movies, a few tall men in ponytails were playing pool in one room, reggae drawling, drifting through the ancient system, while a handful of others—Harley jackets and baseball caps—were sitting at the bar. They sat apart from the regular customers, high chairs around a small round table, and when the drinks arrived, the new him, more decisive, put a finger in his rum and drew it slowly down her throat.

The rain was coming down so hard now that the wooden rooftop of the bar began shaking and the music was almost impossible to make out. Every time the door opened, a great gust of cold damp came in, and it felt as if the whole structure would creak and split and give out. When they had finished eating—he'd told her only about the Taj, the lights burning under the romantic cover—they went out again, through the pelting rain, and sat in the car, breath lost, as if they'd run for miles along the ocean. The windows were fogged up, and the heater gagged and protested when she pushed a button, so they knew it would not cooperate. The space in the front seat was hardly bigger than a confessional.

"You're sweet," she said, as if to keep him at a distance; the word put a pleasant cage around the feelings. Outside, brown bags and paper cups blew and skittered across the parking lot. Branches beat against the windows—she'd parked under a tree in the hope of staying dry—and the wind howled and whooshed as if crying to be let in.

"A long way from Jaipur," he said, as if to acknowledge that some distances remained.

She started the car up and they drove very slowly along the nearly abandoned road, hugging the side and crawling through the short distances that were all they could see in front of them. At the great curves before Point Mugu, boulders lay strewn across the asphalt, and when a car came round the turn towards them, very fast, she swerved and almost lost control. The rain was unrelenting, and he placed a finger on her legs, her thighs, and she held it there as if to say, "Yes. But no more now."

"Do you know where we can go?"

"Anywhere it's dry."

"Big Sur is too far away."

"Your house is too full up."

He knew what she meant, and he let her take control. When they got to Santa Barbara, she drove all the way through town, and then up, towards the mountains, as if she knew where she was taking him. The car labored and resisted as they arrived at the steep road, and the way itself was blocked with thick branches here and there, dust and debris fallen down from the slopes. He took a guess at where she was taking him, and why; there were no lights there, and they were edging through the dark.

She felt her way around the curves, tense, alert, he wide awake in his different universe (the sun above the desert in Rajasthan), and then, at last, they saw the grey mailbox by the road, the sudden private road up to the ridge.

When she stopped, he handed her his jacket and she ran, through puddles and dust and branches, to the door they always used. He came after, and within seconds they were in the dry and dark. Silence everywhere around them.

"The one time we need a flashlight . . ." he said.

"No need," she said, and led him out into the corridor.

They fumbled upstairs, moving slowly in the dark, and then came out into the great open space of the main room. The wind shook the windows and the doors, and the storm was so intense they couldn't see the lights below, the stars.

"It's like a place outside the city walls."

"I know," she said. "That's why I chose it."

She sat down against the wall, where they'd sat before, and he sat down beside her, the jacket placed beneath them.

"I made a New Year's resolution," she murmured, in the dark, not choosing to light a candle as she'd done before.

"What was that?"

She leaned over and kissed him as if every reservation was forgotten. No words, no hesitations.

"You're sure you want to?"

"This isn't going to be ours forever."

She lay down on the jacket, and, in the dark—the rain beating on the roof, the wind sounding like it was throwing over the world—she unbuttoned her dress, and he kissed her throat, down the sides of her, to where the last buttons eased away. A warmth spread through her body, what felt like weeping down below, and when he met her there, she let out a great cry, and then began sobbing, holding him close with her muscles and wrapping him up in her as if he were her winding cloth. "Thank you, thank you, thank you," she said, the sound of something terrible, like fear or loneliness, discharged from her at last. "Thank you, please, yes, thank goodness." And the cry in her throat so naked, it brought tears to his eyes, too.

They slept. For a long time, so that when he stirred—or knew that he was stirring—he could see that the blackness all around had been replaced by greyness all around. A damp and sogging nothingness, so thick he couldn't see a tree, a house, the road below. "They'll be coming soon." He turned, to where she slept. "We should move."

"It's Sunday, remember? We can stay."

He lay back beside her on the floor, a traveler deposited in a new place he couldn't quite put words to yet. The old expectations, the way they'd kept themselves going forward for so long, gone now, and asking them what they'd be replaced by.

"So how was the manuscript?" she said at last, as if she saw what he was thinking, and wanted to help him free of it. "What did you find?"

"I found that people put a lot of hope on these things. Stake their lives on things they can't understand."

"Like you."

"Perhaps."

He drew a hand around her waist, slipped off the blanket she'd unearthed.

"Was it beautiful?"

"Very. Which doesn't make it old, or authentic, or valuable. But it's a beautiful thing to have. He seemed a kind man, the right man to have it."

"And your own manuscripts?"

"The ones I've never found, you mean?"

She nodded.

"The same as ever. Incredibly potent because I don't know what they are. They could contain the secret of the universe."

When your mind is intent, possessed—when something below your mind is more than intent, possessed—everything you say voices the same theme: anything he said about the poems now, he was saying about her, or them, or whatever it was they'd entered.

"Will you be happy if you find a manuscript that no one's ever seen before?"

"Probably happier thinking about it. Alex thinks it's just a device I've come up with to keep myself interested."

"And you—what do you think?"

"I think that these old men, all that time ago, were on to something. The only way we can see God, feel what it means to be beyond thought, protected, loved for what we are—"

"Is right here."

He nodded, glad that she'd completed the dangerous thought for him.

She sat up, explored the house in the pale light—they'd never really been here in the daytime, and even though the day was all fogged over, they could for the first time see the outline of what it would be, and make out the shapes the rooms would take. For the first time, in the grey new year, the rain dripping from the eaves, puddles on the bricks outside, the few growing things nearby green, green, they could walk through the mind of the man who had designed it.

"Let's try here," she said, finding another room, empty, with windows on two sides, closer to the mountains (on a clear day, you could see the ocean from here).

"You think we can stay here all day?"

"Why not? It's ours, for now. No one can find us here. It's the space outside all space."

She loved her games with words, ways to remake the world and give it a different meaning, ways mostly to run away from it, into another universe, where things had symmetry, made sense.

They sat now against what would one day be closets and book-shelves; not the most comfortable place for tired arms and backs, but enticing, somehow, in the thick fog, with the sense of animals—gophers or whatever else lived in these hills—beginning to prepare to come out again.

"I like it when you can't see the horizon," she said. "You can't see to the end of things. It feels safe."

"Though limited."

"I like limited," she said, and he fell silent.

Then, pulling him away from the dangerous topic, "Let's play a game."

"What kind of game?"

"The second-best place in the world."

"Okay. If you could be anywhere in the world, right now, where would it be?"

"In Cortina," she said. "High up. On a late-spring day. In a meadow, under the sun."

"You've been there?"

"In my head. You?"

"I'd be in Isfahan. Watching the blue so strong it makes your eyes sting."

"You'd want to go to Iran?"

He felt a sudden hardening in her limbs, as if the relief had gone away from her. "For what I study, it's the place to be."

"But they stone women in Iran. They kill writers who don't say what they want them to say."

"That's the government, now. Persia, though, is different. It's the home of the mystical romance."

"You can't mean that," she said, and already, without moving, she seemed to be edging away. "You don't know a thing."

"I know about the restrictions there, I know it's unfair to women, and to dissidents. I'm just saying that its poems—the gardens and paintings—moved me once upon a time. That's why I chose to study it."

She didn't say anything for a moment, and he went on: "I know what you're saying. About the Revolution and its dogmatism, the way they believe what they believe with a vengeance. But when I was growing up, in school, it was just the opposite. The one thing we were taught was never to have belief. Or admit to it, at least. It was a sign of weakness, of delusion; you were allowing people to get at you. As long as you didn't believe anything, you were safely behind the walls of the castle. Nothing could hurt you."

She looked at him now, where they lay, and he felt the softness slowly return. Outside, the water dripped down and down, from the roof, from the tall trees, the eaves and windowsills. Her lips, even now, were soft, and her breath was sweet. They put the world behind them once again.

The day drifted on, and the clouds showed no sign of lifting. It was as if they could be there forever, outside the reach of anything. There were no clocks or divisions in the house; it held no memories or hopes. Only the walls that kept them from the world outside, the windows, the different spaces, each with its different configuration of light and silence, the small set of provisions—toothbrush, crackers, cookies, towels—she'd brought in her blue bag. Accustomed to staying in places not her own, she had the gift of making anywhere a home.

They chatted in a desultory way, walked out into the mist, their breath making new clouds, letting the damp air awaken them. She pulled out the bottle she had brought before, candles, a book of Yeats, a small transistor radio on which to play music. The floorboards were cool beneath them, and the rooms were large enough to be filled with anything.

Inside her was another country. After all the time they'd spent shying away from the fences they'd made, turning back at every crossroads, now there was a sense of flooding, and as he looked down at her, face turned, eyes tightly closed, the color rushing into her cheeks and neck, he felt he could see all the people she'd ever been: the girl in the woods, telling herself stories so she wouldn't have to go home; the young woman turning away from everything that moved her; the woman who hid behind the giddy girl and only came out now, when he ran his mouth along the unexplored places. All her sweetness, her sadness, everything she'd put away and kept in cobwebs till this moment, brought out into the light, and when he moved more deeply, she laughed and laughed and laughed as if walls were collapsing inside her.

After, he fell into a deep sleep, and saw a mosque somewhere: perhaps the Isfahan of which he'd just been speaking. The cry of a muezzin from a tower, men passing through a narrow door. The masses of bodies all turned down, identical, at group prayers, and some strange music that cut at him, and drew blood.

When he awoke she was fast asleep, smiling every now and then in her dreams, and saying words that meant nothing. The fog was all he could see through the great picture windows dominating the room, and the small sounds of rain, the day collecting itself, the afternoon gathering. When he fell back to sleep, he fell into a different kind of dream, a wrenching, and when he woke up his eyes were wild, he knew, and he was sobbing.

"What is it? What's happening?"

"It's nothing; I'm sorry."

"It's something. You're shaking all over."

She held him—happiest, always, when she saw signs of how fragile he could be—and he felt, irrationally, absurdly, that he couldn't see enough of her. Hungry for her, desperate, though she was right here, and they were spending all the day together.

"You've got it bad."

"I know; I'm sorry. It's sort of a ravenous need that nothing could begin to fulfill."

"Thank you for being ravenous." Though it was the "need" she was happiest to hear.

When she fell back, and into a sleep again, he got up and stood by the window, the world immediately in front of him alight, intense, with everything erased. Somewhere out there the thesis that was going unwritten; the exiles with their complicated hopes; Martine and Nicki and Sefadhi. From the road came the sound of a car—or a truck, more likely—gears grinding as it went slowly round the curves. It could be a rescue vehicle of some kind, like the one they'd summoned months before; it could be the builders, convinced that the fog had lifted sufficiently for them to go on working, even on a Sunday; it could just be a neighbor returning to his house.

He sat against a wall, from which he could watch her sleep, and wrote her a letter, as she liked to do for him. By late afternoon, the mist was climbing up the mountain, leaving behind little strips of road, small patches of hill, as a tailor might leave behind snippings when he's patching together a coat. In the far distance they could see a small light in the hills, and more cars now were beginning to brave the narrow road.

"Are you okay?"

"I'm fine," he said. "It's been a strange day. Momentous, in its way."

"You're not thinking about where you should be?"

"Only one place," he said, and she looked at him warmly, and kissed him for thanks.

"Before last night I was scared to say how much I missed you. In case you never came back, or the plane crashed, or something—I don't know—happened. It seemed like opening up a space and maybe it would never get filled again."

"I'm here. I'm not going anywhere. We can't, in any case."

The light was fading now, and the fog, though intense, was less close than before: occasionally, as night fell, they could make out small lights, red and yellow, on the mountaintops. Evening became night, and night became early morning. They fumbled, explorers on a new adventure, through different rooms, testing them all for size and shape. In some they could see—or imagine they could see—the faint outlines of the mountains through the windows; in others, the city below, the sea.

As the day began to draw closer—they could feel the dark lifting, and the mist had almost evaporated by now—he heard her return to Los Angeles in her voice. To singleness and fear and a kind of watchful skepticism. She was already in her usual life, and angry at him, at herself, for allowing the transition to happen. In both directions.

"I wonder," she said, making circles on his arm, pulling the hairs now and then in her distractedness, "what place I have in your life."

"You have a place right here."

"Right now I do. But what about later? When you have time to think about things?"

"That shouldn't change a thing."

"You have a life," she said, and there was a trace of envy in her frustration. "Things to do. People to see. You have a thesis to write, an adviser to visit. What about them?"

"I'll still be with you."

"You're sweet," she said, for the second time since his return. "I know you mean well. You don't want to hurt me. But you will. You can't share yourself with me while you're attending to your life—no one's found a way of doing that."

"I share myself with you and I get the things done. Not necessarily at the same time."

She went back to picking absently at the hairs on his arm, comparing the colors of their skin, pressing her hand against his so she could admire how well they fit.

"I know you mean it: you really believe we can get the better of things. And you have every reason to think it. But what have I got?"

"You've got many things. Sweetness, innocence."

"If you're around, perhaps. But if you're not—you saw me at the airport, before I found you."

He knew that anything he said would only be a provocation.

"And if I try to be with you all the time, I'll push you away."

"Then we have to find you a direction. Not mine, but ours."

"I don't want a direction; I just want to be with you."

A child throwing a tantrum, and saying she'd never come down to dinner again in her life. And he, having encouraged and allowed the retreat from the world, become a child himself, was in no position to say a word.

When they went out of the house at last, the air was fresh and rinsed, with the singing, stinging clarity that comes only after a great storm. The town below looked as if it was being seen through a sharpened lens that had recently been polished, and you could make out every ridge and pattern in the islands far away. Above the mountains there was a silver-and-pale-blue light that gleamed like polished iron.

As they began making their slow way down the mountain road, they watched the world coming to life: occasional disheveled cars poking out of driveways, dusted and begrimed; a creek rushing through the valley where days before there'd only been a dry riverbed; and people looking out of houses like survivors from an earthquake. Each turn put Eden farther behind them, and brought the desk, the campus, a little closer.

"I'm sorry if I spoiled everything. It's just—"

"I know."

"I don't know how to be." Tears of frustration, as well as something else. "I want to give you everything, but if I do—"

"Just be yourself."

"You sound like my shrink. That's what she says, and then the little clock goes off, and my time is up."

The sea below them was a richer blue than he'd seen before; the town gave off glints and sparkles, as if it were a mirror held up to the sun. He looked at her as she looked out of the window, turning away now, towards the green hills, the shining cars, and wondered how fear could ever be magicked away. If he were next to her for a hundred years, she'd worry about the hundred-and-first. The same way nobody could ever tell him not to be afraid of snakes.

When she looked towards him again, she said, "Thank you for a wonderful time." It had the knelling sound of a valediction.

"The trick will be to take that time into our daily lives."

" 'The trick,' " she said, mockingly, and with a bitterness the house had covered up.

When they got to his home, he said, "I wrote you a letter while you were sleeping before. Do you want to hear it?"

"Thank you. Maybe later."

"I think I'd better go," she went on, as he got out of the car. He thought of her sudden disappearance before, and the impossibility of ever finding her once she was gone. It was a pointless mystification she threw over everything, but if she didn't feel protected in that way, she'd never venture out at all.

"Stay for a while. Just to get your strength back. If it helps, I'll take myself on a walk and leave you alone."

"Just for a few minutes, then."

He prepared the bed for her and went out to the sand. There were unsightly clumps of seaweed all along the space now, pieces of driftwood, kelp, branches thrown for dogs and never recovered. In a few days of rain, everything had returned to chaos, and he thought of Martine playing at being a cleaning lady in Oxford, " 'This room looks like a storm has hit it.' "

Here and there, pink shells were glistening in the freshened light, and as he followed the beach along, farther than he usually walked, he came to a place where the sand suddenly cracked, and a small river opened up, just too wide to jump.

He could take the long way round, going all the way up to the road, or he could roll up his trousers and walk through. He thought about it a moment, thought about the nights they'd just spent, and rolled his trousers up, walked across the rivulet, and then, when he came back, walked across again.

When he got back to the house, she was sitting on the sofa, at peace.

"You got a chance to rest."

"I did. It was what I needed."

"You're strange: you wear the colors of the last place you've been on you."

"And you don't show any trace at all."

"A difference between us, I suppose."

"I wrote this for you. You were gone a long time."

The miniature showed a man with a princess in a pavilion—"lovers in dalliance," as the captions usually said—and above them, from another window, a woman (the same one, or—given the generic style of representation—another, even a rival?) aiming an arrow at the sun. The princess longing to keep the day at bay? Or her enemy venting the anger that came to her, as she sat within her tower, in a kind of prison?

Inside, she had written, as if it were a poem,

> My body water, you flow through me like a foreign river.
> Some part of me fire, kindled in this room alone.
> The sky inside, above the angry sea,
> The silent, raging storm.

He had never found a way to say anything to or about her poems; they showed him the person she was most shy of revealing the rest of the time.

On the back, a shorter offering:

> Ice inside me as you pass.
> The rocks under sighing trees,
> Touch me where I weep.

He looked across at her, fallen in some way, and then she was walking out to her car, and there was the sound of the great beast revving into life.

The very next day, and he couldn't tell if it was circumstance or pattern (a pattern he couldn't see), he got a letter from the person he least expected to hear from. As if, far away, Martine had been with them in the house during the storm, watching everything that was unfolding, and now, on cue, as reminder or sanction, her letter peeped out of the mailbox.

John,

I got your present. It was kind of you to remember, thank you. The only way I could think of to reciprocate (you were never the easiest person to buy presents for) is by passing on something Madame Duvalier told us at St. Mary's. When Montaigne was a young man—she always beamed as she told us this for some reason—he met a man, a man who'd written a book called *Voluntary Servitude*, of all things. And this man, a stranger, seemed so much like a lost part of Montaigne that both of them were rather turned around.

Of course Montaigne was hardly a radical, being a mayor and all that, so it wasn't as if anything illicit—Madame Duvalier always had problems with that word—went on between them. But each rang a familiar chord in the other. Montaigne felt as if he were leaving everything he knew for some better, truer place which was the place where he really belonged. At this point, our teacher would be shaking (some girls unkindly thought, with the memory of what she'd lost).

Anyway, soon sonnets began pouring out of this stranger, sonnets so passionate that they might have seemed to come from love. And then, after scarcely four years of fellowship,

Étienne de La Boétie, the mysterious stranger, died. Madame Duvalier always looked a bit hysterical at this point. Montaigne of course was devastated, and all he had now, he wrote, was "smoke, nothing but dark and tedious night." And so, with nothing else to do, desperate to keep the memory of his absent friend alive in himself, he began to write. Words came out of him as once they'd come out of Étienne.

Does any of this make sense? And do you see why I'm writing it? French lessons from the Sixth Form aren't what I expected to be sending you, or, I'm sure, what you expected to receive from me. But I thought it would be what you wanted to hear: Nicki said you felt very settled in your unsettled way.

Fond wishes and thanks again,
M.C.

He hadn't expected enigmas from her, she was right; one of their problems had always been the way her directness glanced off his indirections. And yet she was giving him a present, clearly, of the deepest kind: something that wasn't of interest to her, but might be to him. More than that, she was all but handing him over to what had always been her greatest, and least trumpable, rival: Rumi, whose story this so clearly reflected. The most selfless gesture of all: she was telling him to keep going, in a way, even if it was along a road that would take him away from her.

He put down the letter and wasn't sure where to turn: our questions, the stories we carry with us through life, never really change, he thought, even if we wear different clothes for them, and think our circumstances look different. We're really just in eternal syndication, as they'd say round here, playing the same parts over and over even if we think we've left all that behind. Here he was, on the edge of the New World, falling into a new relation—with everything—and he'd ended up, so it seemed, exactly where he'd been amidst the thirteenth-century cloisters in England.

He thought of calling Dick and asking him if he wanted to play tennis at seven o'clock, or perhaps making up the missed *Conformist* with Alex. He thought of a drive up to the temple in the hills, where he'd always gone to collect himself. But he didn't want to carry ghosts up, of a kind that temples like that were meant to screen out; and he didn't want to start talking to Alex or Dick about exactly what he ought to be keeping to himself. He turned on the computer, and decided it would be best just to still his mind by doing some routine work that required nothing from him at all: transcribing notes, perhaps, from one file to another.

He scrolled down the list of files on-screen, looking for the last one he'd opened, checking by the date, and as he did so, he came across what had to be a mistake (though computers don't tend to make mistakes): one file had been opened today, the machine said—01-04-1996, 9:11. It couldn't have been, he thought—he'd been away in India for eight days, and then in the rainy house with Camilla: he hadn't even turned on the machine since the previous year. But the day's contours stared up at him from the screen, telling him he'd already been on-line this morning.

He clicked on the file to open it—it was called ABANDON—and when it came up, saw the notes he'd put in a year or so before, while writing on de Caussade: the book whose title he'd been so taken by *(Abandon à la providence divine)* that he'd checked it out of the library on a whim.

"Abandonment," he read now, and found himself going back to what seemed like another lifetime,

is the crime that God is accused of by man. Abandoning us to our fate, our sorrow, those not sympathetic to Him might say, as a negligent father leaves his children to the storm outside. Even Jesus on the Cross raised the same complaint: "O Father, Father, why hast thou abandoned me?"

Yet what if we take the word a little differently? What if, let's say, God's abandonment is not that of an indifferent parent, but, rather, that of a composer, a creator, so carried away by the forces that race through Him that He forgets everything around Him and lets the story run away with Him? What if God gets so lost in the delight, the forgetfulness, of creating that what He's making somehow takes on a life of its own, as we say? What, in other words, if the abandonment that God is guilty of is not that of desertion but, rather, of rapture, the neglectfulness of an artist who lets the work take over?

Is it possible? Could it have happened that Man, the highest work in God's creation, according to the Moslems, might have got the better of his Creator's plans for him? As Iago might have run away with Shakespeare? And God, in whatever sense the word has meaning, "lost Himself" in creating us and so, in a way that could not have been foreseen, lost us? God's very abandon leading to our abandonment, not just on the level of a clever play on words, but much deeper, as when, surrendering, we give ourselves over to what we could never have expected? And so the beings He was creating acquired colors, or destinies, He could never have imagined, and the world became much richer, more full of contingency, than was planned.

It's heresy, of course, to say that the purest Creator of all might be subject to the impulses of the very beings He created. And yet it tells us that we are never more God-like than when we give up—give up control, give up expectation.

He looked at it now, and tried to remember the different person who'd written this, in a momentary flight all those lives ago. Speaking for the very principle he wouldn't embrace if it came to him in life.

At the bottom of the text, he now saw, was something he was sure he hadn't seen there, and was sure he hadn't put there: "Abandon everything," Dionysus's words to his followers. "God despises ideas."

The next week, thanks to some of Sefadhi's maneuverings, an Iranian was due to come onto campus to deliver a talk on passion in Islam. He was a complicated man, according to Sefadhi, who'd been forced to leave Iran in a hurry, and had lost everything he owned; but he has "wisdom you will be the better for. Even the thorniest rose has fragrance."

His own research, though, seemed to be moving ever more in circles, as if the Rumi he thought he knew had turned into someone else, just as—McCarthy said—your room becomes something different as soon as you install a different kind of light. He'd taken Rumi for years to be the great laureate of love, in some ways giving voice, and spiritual elevation, to the excitement every teenager feels when he steps outside himself. But now, as his thesis drew towards a close, he saw that really he was writing not about love but about loss.

The great majority of his poems had been written (was this what Martine had been telling him, too, with her letter?) after his beloved's absence. Their theme was not so much the intoxication as the more resonant and lasting question of what comes after. How do you begin to turn absence into presence and loss into a kind of discovery? He'd thought the poems were about passion; now he saw that that was true only insofar as passion, in the Latin, meant "suffering."

As soon as she came back to his house, three days later, they put all words aside; and went in their minds to the rainy house again. He could ask her about the sentence at the bottom of the file, or whether she'd gone to Palm Springs with Greg; he could force her into the smallest box he could find (and diminish himself in the process). But the only point of their being together, it seemed, was to climb and to fall into something else.

Hands and mouths were flame, and everything that had been held back, pushed down for so long, seemed to come loose now, in a rush. She shuddered even when he touched her neck; he jumped around her like a madman, said things he couldn't fathom. A door had sprung open, and everything came out.

"I can't believe how well we fit together."

It was the usual lover's sentence, in the usual lover's light: the sea was tugging at the shore outside, and their lives lay on the floor around them. Distant calls from far along the beach, and the light, as from a festive house, of the single derrick out to sea.

"You mean like this?"

"Like everything. The letters in our names. The circumstances of our lives—all the times when we could have been in the same room without knowing it. The way I felt something inside me and never guessed that it was you."

The same things that every pair of lovers say when they're ushered into the impersonal. She was lying on the pillow, her face turned away from him, caught by the light as it rose outside the window. Her hair was a wet tangle, and the skin around her neck, beneath her ears, was damp. His mouth was at the dampness, on the faint golden down on her back, at the hollows and arches down her spine. His voice was at her ear, and he was calling her name over and over and over.

The next day, when he awoke, he was nobody he could recognize; nobody he could even trust. His thesis overturned, his adviser forgotten, the letter from the library recalling the book on *Rumi's Passion* thrown under a pile of scrap papers on the desk. He came out of the bedroom and into the study, and wondered how much he'd become her, in a curious way: the person he'd longed to be when first he came to California, though no one that anyone could get on with very easily.

In the kitchen the clock said, "9:45"—too late for his morning run, too late for a desk in the library. Whatever he knew of anything seemed not a searchlight now, but a kind of screen, a wall that stood between him and a truer knowledge. And the person he'd thought he might become seemed locked up in someone else's house, and all he had to get by on was a set of clothes that belonged to someone else.

He looked in on her where she lay, at perfect peace, but sure to be frightened, rattled when she awoke—the farther they went along their road together, the more terrified she would be (the more she could see how much there was to lose)—and the more obliquely they would have to move. He remembered the early afternoon on which he'd told her, "You take leave of your senses almost as if you were a mother seeing them off at the station. Waving and waving as the train pulls slowly away."

"And you," she'd said, "don't take leave of them at all" (though in that respect, at least, she had been proved as misguided as he).

He thought of calling Alex, the way he'd always brought himself back to shore before, but then he remembered the last time they'd spoken. Alex had called to ask him why he hadn't heard from him for so long—why he'd canceled all their meetings—and he'd said something vague and unpersuasive about being preoccupied. "You're not falling subject to Religious Studies Syndrome?" his friend had said, and he, unable to resist, had said, "What's that?"

"Suddenly," said Alex, in a faintly operatic way, "you see all the noble ideas you're writing about—'the dissolution of self,' the 'hidden stranger,' the 'unexpected liberator'—embodied, very conveniently, in the person you're claiming not to see."

"It isn't like that," he'd said.

"Of course not," his friend had said. "I just worry. You may not see this story of the dithering Englishman and the flighty woman as being about this, but she will do so. I can guarantee it." Then, as if he was truly worried, "You can't use a poem to get closer to a woman. You know that, don't you? And you certainly can't use a girl to get closer to a poem."

Since then, he'd been wary of his friend, but now, newly emboldened, he remembered Alex had said something about their going together to an exhibition downtown, of Islamic paintings from Washington. He drove over to his friend's house, a few blocks away, on Embarcadero, and knocked at the door. There was no answer.

Strange: this was the time when Alex was nearly always home. He walked around, knocked at the side door, but still there was nothing. Shrugging, he took himself downtown, and parked by the rambling gardens of the Courthouse. The sound of water playing from a nearby fountain.

He went through the Spanish-style courtyard, past the strummed *canciones* from the Mexican restaurant, the early flowers in the sun, and went up the two flights to where they were showing the miniatures. The room was kept dark—a sort of visual hush—and most of it was empty space: each tidy rectangle hung in a small area, hardly larger than that of a magazine, and around it there was mostly emptiness. Yet each of the paintings held a world in it. A pair of lovers waiting in a pavilion; a wounded deer; a royal hunting expedition: all the archetypal scenes of Islamic art through the centuries. In many pictures, a woman sat alone, in an upstairs room, waiting for her beloved on a night of rain.

In every one of the pictures—it was easier to see when they were all together like this—the same figures reappeared, as if, across centuries and continents, every painter had tried to draw upon the same pool of images. Indeed, as if every painter had tried to draw the same face, as if he was the same person. The artists had nullified personality, in both themselves and their subjects, till all the figures—types, really—seemed no more human than the script in gold, written on black panels at the bottom, or the ornamental frames that held the images in a cage.

He went from one room to the next, then back again, and found himself strangely calmed by the quiet, the darkness of the space. All kinds of worlds and environments soothed into this simple, unchanging order. And in every one, the world was seen, famously, not as we would see it, with its particularities and imperfections, but as Allah might (which is why you could see what was going on in every room at once). The celestial viewpoint was part of what accounted for the stillness in the paintings, the sense of calm. Even the scenes of bloodshed were strangely without drama.

At the very end of the second room, the curator had chosen to include three paintings from Venice, to show how the tradition had come up against a wall, and turned a corner, you could say. These pictures were notably different, because they had proportion, individuality. In Venice, rulers had asked that they be painted larger than their background, that they be shown as exactly who they were—the persons that their wives and mistresses saw. They'd even demanded (a small notice explained) they be painted in the middle of each frame. Pieces of the classical style were still apparent, but the heavenly serenity of the other paintings had been replaced by the jangle and vividness of the real.

There was a quote from *Othello* at the bottom of the last caption, and he thought of Iago and Desdemona fighting for the Moor's soul, in Venice. The one whispering in the foreigner's ear, to doubt everything he knew; the other, almost wordlessly, urging him to be worthy of his native majesty.

She was still in bed when he got back, but it was dark, and when he lit the candle by the bed, he saw for a moment a face from one of the last paintings. Then, blowing out the candle, he lay beside her in the bed and put his arms around the dark.

A few hours later, she awoke, and at some point in the night that followed the two of them disappeared. No he or she, any more; no cause or effect. Just the sound of the ocean outside the window, the moon occasionally catching something on the water.

She reached for him where he lay, and then turned back to light the candle on the bedside table. Outside, through the window, the lonely single light of the derrick out to sea.

"When did you first know, do you think?"

"I didn't know. It never began."

"But when did you first think?"

"As soon as I said goodbye."

A little later, there was more darkness around them. The last planes had come in to land by now, and there was only the shape of their shadows, coming together, moving apart, on the wall.

"Are you warm? Are you cold?"

"Not warm. Not cold. Not anything."

"But you're shivering? You're shaking."

"Not shaking. Just breathing."

"You're frightened in some way?"

"How can I not be terrified?"

Then, as the light began to seep into the room again—she blew out the candle, and they were just shapes in the dark, nobody they could easily recognize—

"Lie still. Just there. Don't move."

"Hang on. Don't stop. Just there."

"Let go. Go wild. Don't stop."

"I'm gone."

It was afternoon by the time he got up, and Debra's seminar was due to begin in twenty minutes. He got ready quickly and cycled across campus in a kind of trance, hardly noticing the figures on the beach, the dogs with twigs in their mouths, the smudge of tar on the sand, but seeming to see everything that was inside them or around them, the networks that were part of them. He wasn't himself, he felt, and his feet weren't touching solid ground: a box of lightbulbs stands on a factory floor—he'd met the image in a book by McCarthy—and the bulbs are all individual, mortal; but turn them on, and the light they transmit is not particular to any one of them.

Debra had chosen to talk of Zen mindlessness—"no mind," as she chose to call it—and as she spoke, all he could see (the lover's self-absorption, he imagined) was his own poems, translated into a different tongue. The Zen student, she was saying, seeks to set a torch to every image or abstraction behind which he might hide: the long nights of meditation, the crack on the shoulder with the wooden stick, the mindless repetition of routine—it was all a way of trying to break through the mind to what lay beyond it. "If you see the Buddha along the road, you must kill him."

"You could almost say the Zen monks are Sufis who never move," he said when she was finished, and there was laughter around the room. But he'd been serious. At some level, as with all these disciplines around the world, the names were not important.

"That might be a useful beginning," said Debra, taking his comment and already putting it into the tidy frame of her thesis. "But for the Zen student, as for the Buddhist—hence the confusion between the two—the ultimate truth is emptiness: *shunyata*. Whereas, for your Sufis, from what you told us in your enlightening presentation" (she was laying the ground for a compliment in return), "it's more a case of affirmation. They believe in something, it's just a something so far beyond their categories they don't have words for it. Except 'the Beloved.' "

Yet what, he thought, as he cycled home, did any of it have to do with the shadows on the wall, the candle she'd set back so they wouldn't knock it over? He thought of his father, working so selflessly year after year for a company that would repay his faith only with occasional bonuses. Giving himself so fully to what he knew could never sustain him that when he woke up it was as if he'd dreamed through all his life.

Along the ocean, as the light began to fade, a woman in a black catsuit was walking along to the distant point, a surfboard under her arm. A prehistoric ruler, he thought, in his altered state, off to lay her offerings on an altar for the gods.

When he walked into the house, she was getting her things ready, to go back to L.A. again—fearful, he guessed, of how far they were going. "I've got to work on something at home," she said. "I can't tell you because you're a part of it."

He followed her out to the car and watched her drive off into the distance. "Mysteries are not to be solved"—it had been his favorite line in Rumi once upon a time. "The eye goes blind when it only wants to see why."

He had to track some books down before the Sufi came up next week—if only so he could know what questions to ask—so, getting in the car, he drove towards Chaucer's. He sped through town, and then, looking up, realized he'd missed the turn; the places he knew were remade for him now, and he in them a stranger.

He turned around and doubled back, feeling foolish, and when he got to the bookstore parking lot, found it full as ever. Edging along to find a place, he suddenly saw someone he thought he recognized.

"Alex," he called out, rolling down the window. "Is that you?"

"John." His friend didn't look pleased.

"Hang on. I'll be there in a minute." He went round the corner, and parked in the handicapped zone near the post office—apter than he knew, he thought—and then ran back to check in with his friend. He'd felt bad that he'd been ducking him ever since Alex had said something about *"folie à deux."*

Then, coming up to where he'd seen him, he realized something else had been going on. She was very young, with bright red lipstick, wearing a thick fur jacket even on the unbuttoned California afternoon. Her short blond hair peeped out from underneath a small black cap.

"It's been a while," he said to Alex, and when he got back nothing but a shrug—Alex, too, didn't seem himself today—he realized he would have to take the initiative himself. "John Macmillan," he said, extending a hand towards the stranger.

"Enchanted. Sophie Rajavi." She offered in return a soft and ringless hand, a jangle of gold bracelets dancing around her wrist.

"Now I know why Alex has been so busy," he said, though nothing came back from his friend but a tight smile.

"This must be the friend you've been telling me about," said Sophie, not ready to be deterred by her companion's silence. "The one who keeps you sane."

"Of course," said Alex strangely. The pressed jeans, the cashmere scarf, the leather jacket were all as they always were; but the figure inside them seemed fraudulent somehow, as if he'd got into the wrong self today.

"You're just visiting?" he asked the girl.

"For my vacations. Six weeks."

"And you're friends from France, I take it."

"From USC," she said, looking sharply up at Alex as if he'd let her down. "Alejandro must have told you."

"He did, of course," he said, recovering too late, as always. "The European girl who was keeping him from his studies."

"No," she said. "That was the one before me." She skipped around misunderstandings as gaily as a girl in a sunlit meadow. "What was her name, Alejandro? The one before?"

Their friend said nothing.

"From Denmark. Catrina. Candida."

"Camilla?" he tried, and she rewarded him with a smile, poking Alex in the ribs for his silence. "Camilla, yes. She was the one before me."

"It looks like John is busy," said Alex. "I think we should let him go."

"Of course," she said, popping forwards, and kissing him lightly on each cheek.

"I hope you enjoy your stay here."

"I will," she said. "*Ciao.*" And, hooking Alex by the arm, led him off to their next adventure.

He walked towards Chaucer's and then, when they were out of sight, turned back and went to the car. But when he got in, he went nowhere. Whenever they'd talked about her, Alex had seemed to know everything: the Latin philosopher of love, as he'd implied. "You sound like you're in love with her poignancy, not her." "You can't make yourself weak for a picture of a tiger." But he'd never mentioned the picture of the tiger, he thought now; he'd never betray her in that way.

He drove home, hardly watching for the police as he accelerated, and, as soon as he got in, went to the desk and began making notes. It was like the time Sefadhi had said something about how he couldn't explain the poems until he'd decided whether they were addressing a "mystery" or a "Mystery," and suddenly he'd seen everything he thought he knew transformed. Now, going back over their conversations, he wondered what Alex had really been talking about when he spoke of the "sad and lonely victim of New World possibility." Or the time when he'd suddenly asked him what he thought of the coming star Gwyneth Paltrow, in the new Jane Austen movie.

"It's nothing," his friend had said on Halloween—it must have been two years before, the waitresses at Houlihan's dressed like Marilyn Monroe, with red tails on their backs, while the men who were drinking were got up like vampires or ghouls. "I thought I saw something there, but I was wrong." And yet the way he'd said it suggested that he hadn't been wrong so much as wronged; he'd given up the opportunity only once it had passed him by.

Every time she'd said she was on her way back to Los Angeles, he thought now, she might have been driving only a few blocks away, to Embarcadero; and the time Alex had called to invite him to a movie—the first night she was due to visit: maybe it had been a test of some kind (devised by him, or her, or both of them?). In private, he decided crazily, they discussed their common English friend in Spanish.

After a long while, he picked up the phone, and began to dial his friend's number, and then he saw Sophie on the couch, reaching out a long, tanned, slender arm to answer, and put the phone down again. He picked up a piece of paper and began writing a letter to her, and then wondered what it was he was really saying. "You can't take a leap of faith by degrees." It had been he who had said that to her (over and over).

He picked up the phone again, to call her, and then, without planning to, or knowing what he was doing, he dialed a somewhat longer number, one he hadn't known he had by heart, and was rewarded with a strange, old-fashioned jingle, and then a bleary voice, clearly not happy to be disturbed.

"Hello," said a woman's voice, and he saw eyes closed, a darkened room.

"Hello," he said. "I realize it's the middle of the night there, and this is probably the last voice you expected to hear. . . ."

"What time is it? Where are you?"

"It's late afternoon; I'm here in California. I'm sorry to wake you; I was sure your answering machine would be getting rid of me."

"Then why call in the middle of the night? Some of us have jobs to go to, you know."

"I know. I'm sorry. I'll call back later if you like."

"I'd not like, frankly. Having been got up in the dead of night, I'd much rather you didn't."

He felt reassured in some way: the almost instantaneous alertness, the empty bed beside her, the refusal to let him off too easily. "Anyway, what is it? Why are you calling?"

"I wanted to wish you a happy New Year. And to thank you for your letter; it meant a lot to me. I tried to call from Heathrow, a couple of times, but both times I wasn't sure you'd be happy to hear from me."

"What makes you think differently now?"

"Nothing. In fact, I have good reason to think I was right. I suppose—I suppose I just wanted to hear your voice again. And I wanted to tell you: I did go to the Taj, just as you told me to. You were right."

"You did? You went there?" Something softened in her voice, and he came closer to the person he knew, as if she'd opened the door at least, and let him into the hallway.

"A few days ago. It was amazing."

"You saw the vault, the place down the steps?"

"I saw it all. Just as you told me to."

"I wouldn't have thought you'd remember."

"I always did remember the wrong things."

"Yes. I do seem to recall that." It felt now as if he were back in the living room, though for a moment she'd thought of leading him down the hall. "How's California after all this time?"

"I don't know," he said, thinking of the person who'd come to stand for the orphaned state around her. "Complicated, I suppose."

"But that's what you wanted!"

"I suppose so. But it's easier to imagine than actually to meet."

There was no sound at the other end. "You get to Paradise, and you begin to think it's probably the last place in the world where humans can actually live."

"I see." She'd never been very impressed by his moments of wisdom. "You're not getting all religious, are you? Nicki was a bit concerned."

"The opposite."

"What's the opposite of religious?"

"More sure of what I don't know. More clueless."

"I see." She was wide awake now, and he remembered the person who'd always told him he had to break free of England if he was ever going to put his family behind him. "Is there a significant other in this ambiguous Paradise?"

"I think there is."

" 'Think there is.' Surely you can do better than that, Johno?"

"Yes. There is, for now."

"This isn't some poet who's been dead for a million years?"

"Hardly. It'd probably be easier if it were."

"I'm sure." And then something tender came into her voice again, and he felt her on the verge of cracking: one more sentence, and she'd cry. "Well, do wish her well for me. And tell her she's got her work cut out for her."

"I think she knows that."

"And, Johno"—very close again, somehow—"don't let her go, will you?" So close now that she was at his side, and they didn't know what to do. "Set the double negatives aside for a moment, and hang on to her as if your life depended on it. Or hers did, at any rate."

"Thank you. I appreciate it." He stopped talking, but she said nothing to fill the silence.

"How about you? Who's suffering in your life?"

"Me, mostly. Nothing ever changes; I just get better at whingeing about it."

"Are you seeing anyone?"

"Myself, in the mirror, for the most part. Not a very pretty sight. I'm thinking of putting myself out to pasture one of these days."

"Don't do that."

"I'll try not to. But—I wish you had called, whenever it was you were going to. It would probably have been the only call I got that day." She stopped, as if she'd stepped too close, and he heard nothing else; she'd never be as undefended as Camilla was—England didn't work like that. But the pageant that kept on playing out in public, in the streets, wasn't always much help when you were alone at night in your room.

"Anyway, give me a call now and then, if you're so moved. Preferably not at one a.m."

"I will."

"And don't turn into Christopher Isherwood, if you can help it."

"I think it's Aldous Huxley you mean. He's the one who was legally blind."

She broke into a quick, unexpected laugh, and he was reminded of how it had always been the ultimate reward with her: she lived so far from politeness with him that every rough guffaw felt earned.

"I hope Miss Right can remain Miss All Right for a while."

"Thank you. I hope you can find the happiness you deserve. Truly."

"That's sweet of you. Thanks."

Then the awkward goodbyes and he was alone again, the disorientations of the day seeming, for the moment, to be part of another universe.

He worked late into the night, and did what he'd always done when he'd felt thrown off: treated his life as if it were an assignment, which he could put right as he might the next day's homework. He pulled out the star chart he'd drawn before, after the unexpected drink on the beach with Sefadhi, and tried to revise it to match what he knew now. Alex ought to be in the diagram, too, he thought, though he didn't know whether to put him in the part that was linked to Kristina, and so Khalil and all the others. And then he tried to remember whether Alex had ever said anything about Sefadhi, or Sefadhi about Alex. How did this begin to account for her sudden appearances in Santa Barbara—at the lecture, originally, and in Kristina's house the first day? And why had Alex asked so searchingly about Kristina after the stray meeting in the seminar?

It was long after eleven o'clock by the time he'd summoned the resolve to pick up the phone again, and, not knowing what moved him—was he expecting her to be there, or not to be?—he dialed the number that, months before, had led to the sleepy man, apparently lying by her side. "Hello," said the wary voice at the other end, small and distant, and when she heard his voice, she lit up in a moment, as if she'd thrown the windows open to celebrate a new year.

"It's you! I was hoping and hoping you would call. I wanted to call myself, but then I thought it might be too late."

He was chastened. "What's up?"

"I'm plotting. But I can't tell you, because you're the victim!"

"The victim?"

"Tomorrow. For your birthday. I've been working on a surprise for you. Not a complete surprise, now that you know about it, but I'm planning to abduct you."

"My birthday," he said foolishly: he'd stepped so far outside of time, or anything that was real, that he'd lost track of the day. It was almost a reassurance now, that he could forget not just other people's milestones but his own.

"You get to be my slave," she said. She'd heard the wariness in his voice, and decided not to be cowed by it. In fact, she was doing what he'd been telling her to all along—throw her reservations to the wind.

"So what do I do? How long does the abduction last?"

"As long as you'll let it. If I told you any more, it wouldn't be a surprise." Then, obviously realizing that if she didn't tell him more he'd bring along Sefadhi and the poems, she said, "Just pack enough to last you two or three days. I'll be there at three o'clock."

"I'll be waiting."

"Thank you," she said, more quietly at the other end, "for giving me the chance."

He put a few things in his carry-on, and waited for her the next day on the couch. He still had the sense of having come loose, somehow, so he was weightless: heady and off the ground, unable to make out distances or have any sense of solid earth beneath his feet. He'd talked and talked about the "empty room" that lies at the heart of Sufi thinking, the place outside of time and space where something deeper than the personal comes forth; but he'd never expected to step into even a facsimile of it. He'd meant to be meeting Dick this morning, for coffee, and he, the one who always planned things so meticulously, had forgotten to show up: bits of his life were flying away like papers on the desk on a blustery morning when the window was left open.

It was just before four when she finally knocked, but he hadn't noticed the time; when he opened the door, it was to see a figure ready for a Brontë novel: a high-collared black coat he'd never seen on her before, a black dress that showed off the gold hair she'd loosened, high black suede boots, and hoop earrings so unlike what she usually wore, it was like a costume from onstage. He thought of the strange meeting with Alejandro, and then remembered: "Sorry: it's been a long time since I was intimate with anyone."

"I thought you'd never come."

"And I thought I'd be here on time. So we're even." Nothing would unsettle her today, she was saying. "Compromised, in fact." And the play on words was a way of saying she'd try to be her most guileless and unguarded self today.

"I wish you'd given me a call."

"Then I'd have been even later." As if she were the one with the logic. "Anyway, I'm in charge, remember? Anything I say, you've got to do." She looked back at him, and he saw something pleading, just behind the bravado. The girl he loved was standing on his doorstep before him, begging to be given a last chance; the girl he distrusted was only in his head. He followed her out to the lumbering white vehicle and she wrestled for a few moments with the ignition, turning the key back and forth until the great animal sputtered into reluctant life. No hands on the odometer, he noticed; the gas tank could be empty or it could be full.

They took the coastal road south, the colors flamboyant above the gusty ocean, and the light began to fail by the time they passed into Malibu. The "magic hour" was always the bittersweet time in California: a last great flare of gold, and then the darkness fell around them.

She cut across the mountains to the clotted, choking freeway, and they joined the great procession of cars juddering towards the bowl of lights coming to life in the brownish air. The lights almost infernal through the haze—before it was truly night—so one could imagine oneself's entering some Dantean procession.

"You're taking me to the place you're most afraid of in the world."

"I've been waiting for this forever."

"It can't be for . . ." and then he stopped, because it could.

"I really hope you've never seen this before." He imagined, for some reason, someone stringing her house with Christmas lights and setting up a small tree with an angel on the top, for a holiday she'd be celebrating alone. It wasn't the poignancy, he'd told Alex months before; it was the hope that sat in the middle of it, refusing to go away. To turn away from hope is to commit a kind of sin.

She turned off the main road again, to get away from the congestion, and they followed a winding canyon, past hippie shacks and secessionist stores, rainbow flags flying from little grocery stores and strings of fairy lights coming to them through the trees, until they descended into Beverly Hills. Even in the near dark the quiet residential streets were immaculate, their flowerbeds laid out in front of mock-Arabian castles, and reindeer gallivanting across perfect lawns. People told themselves they could stage any drama they liked here, if they had the money, but the brown earth, the constant droughts, suggested something different.

She made a sharp left—they were very close to where the Iranian bookdealers were—and they found themselves in a small, neglected parking lot.

"Where are we?"

"We're here," she said. "We've arrived."

"Wonderful," he said, looking around in the dark. "Just what I've always wanted for my birthday."

There were only a few cars around them on the asphalt—the over-all impression was of emptiness—and at the far end was what looked to be a church. One of the large, serious Californian places of worship that he could never imagine being used for its original purpose. Brick, with stained-glass windows, a red door at the side, and, at the top of a few steps, in front, a ceremonial black door.

"You still won't tell me where we are?"

"You'll see soon enough. I really hope you like it." He thought, as she pulled at the handle and pushed her weight against the door to open it, of the time he'd asked her to read him something—he wanted to see what she looked like as an actress—and she'd chosen a play about a woman in World War I telling her young daughter that the little girl's father would be back soon, though he wouldn't. All she needed, he'd thought then, was someone to take care of, and she'd emerge from her dark maze without even knowing she'd left home.

"I hope there's still room in the front. They said that's where it's best."

He followed her up to the entrance, and saw that it was a Unitarian church they were entering. On a black bulletin board, which faced the street, someone had put up a quote in white letters: "Perhaps everything that frightens us is, in its deepest essence, something helpless that wants our love. —Rainer Maria Rilke."

Inside the hall, they were on the far side of the world. Although there was nothing outside to suggest it, the interior, faintly lit, was done up like a Moorish castle, gold and blue and silver. Inscriptions from the Quran ran up and down the pillars between the chairs and covered the majority of the walls, so that it felt as if the whole building were pulsing with prayer. At the top of what must once have been the space above the altar, someone had painted a high blue vault, with gold stars on it, so one could imagine oneself looking up into desert skies. A fountain played unceasingly on one side of the aisle, and on the other, black curtains had been set up, perhaps to veil whatever had been there before.

There were only a very few other people in attendance, filling up most of the first few rows of a group of chairs lined up at the front. Men, mostly formally dressed, with dark beards and expertly barbered hair. One or two women dressed from head to toe in black. All sitting in an expectant silence, as if getting themselves into a state of readiness—or, he suddenly realized, practicing a kind of prayer.

"What is this?" he said, under his breath. "Where are we?"

"You've got to wait." She enjoyed being the one in charge for once, and he let himself go: "Live in the nowhere that you come from," as his favorite poet wrote.

A few minutes later—and he understood her dark, formal clothing now, even if the freed long blond hair gave her away—a man came to the front of the hall, serious and well dressed, and said something in a language he couldn't follow: Turkish, perhaps, or a dialect of Arabic he'd never heard before. Nobody said anything; they hardly moved.

Then, in silence, a few men proceeded in from a side door. They were dressed, all of them, in long blue cloaks, with loose white shirts. One man, all in black, took a position on the floor, on an ornate red carpet. Four or five, carrying musical instruments, took their places silently along the side.

Then, without a word or prompt, one of the men, and then another, began to turn. A strange arrhythmic melody came up from the wings, and the men, as they turned, showed nothing on their faces: no joy, no emotion or possession. They simply turned. One hand extended towards the heavens, the other reaching down to earth. Not "whirled"—there was nothing furious about their movements; just something slow, hypnotic, almost inevitable.

The man in black passed between them as if to control the trance, to make sure each one was poised between surrender and control, and the men, in their precise way, turned and turned, as if hardly responsible for their movements. So out of themselves they did not even choose to be dramatic or spectacular.

Occasionally, someone began to move a little faster. The music sped up, and there was an intimation of being taken into something intense, like the final furious climaxes of a raga. But then the music would slow down again, fall into a pattern so narcotic that it threatened to pull you into another order of being, beneath the sea. The men's faces were thrown back, and their eyes were closed or, if half open, impossible to read. Whatever mounting ecstasies they felt were inward.

Then, as abruptly as it had begun, the whole performance ended. One moment, the dancers had been turning, the audience as much part of the pattern as the men who moved, and the next moment, they were separate again, and there was silence. The dancers walked away as they had come. The musicians packed away their instruments and followed them out. The onlookers got up—there was no chatter, no one said anything—and disappeared. By the time the two foreigners had made it to the parking lot, an old man was closing the doors behind them, and theirs was the only car in sight.

They didn't say anything as they walked towards her car, and she went over to his side to open his door before moving to her own. Around them, as they pulled onto the street nearby, there was still a banner saying "Happy Days" in front of one house, and lanterns picking out the driveway of another. New Year felt far away, but the decorations were still up outside many buildings, as if the celebrations were perpetual.

"So what did you think?" she said at last.

"Of the dancing? I don't know. It was different."

"Different better or different worse?"

"Different better, I think. Less dramatic. Less passionate than I expected."

"More mysterious," she said, and he said, "Yes, that's it exactly."

"I don't think it's something they put on for tourists."

"Nor do I. We were the only tourists there."

"I've been waiting and waiting to show you this. I know you must have seen things like this before—"

"I haven't. I've never wanted to."

"But you don't mind?"

"I don't mind."

They'd come to a larger intersection now: traffic lights, and an intricate labyrinth of tunnels and freeways, going east, west, north, south.

"How did you know about it?"

"I know more than you think." Then, as they passed onto the freeway, she said, "Now for Act Two."

. . .

"I know," she said as they headed out into the desert, the lights falling away quickly, almost without warning, so that suddenly they were in a darkness broken up only by an occasional cluster of fast-food stores and gas stations. "I know you've got a million things to do: the lecture next week, the last four chapters, everything else. But you've got to give me one chance at least."

"I will."

"You've got to trust me; I won't take you away forever."

The settlements were infrequent now, and the only other cars along the freeway were occasional trucks beginning the long trip cross-country, their boxes of lights shooting past into the dark. To drive away from the coast in California is to drive towards simplicity; with each few miles, the bright artifacts felt more and more like something that never existed, and they were in the presence of something ancient.

"It's like being in the Sahara. Or some postindustrial Sahara at least."

"Have you been to the Sahara?"

"No. But close enough." With Martine in the suq, the men chattering in the alleyways of Fez. She said nothing, and the weight of all the places she hadn't been seemed to fill the front of the large vehicle, already cluttered in the back with old newspapers, books, plans she'd never complete.

"Away from Babylon and towards the Holy Land," he pronounced. A fatuous comment, but the longing for conversation had disappeared in the wake of the performance. It had left him feeling as open, as depthless, as in the dreamless moments after love.

Close to midnight—they'd been driving for two or three hours at least—they rounded a turn and saw a sudden flood of lights in the distance, much farther than they seemed, but as they drove on and on, the lights never seemed to come any closer. More than an hour had passed by the time she pulled off onto a smaller road and started to thread her way through a grid of straight and sleeping streets.

"You know where you're going?"

"I think so. They gave me the directions somewhere."

Surrender to whatever is greater than you, he thought, and something comes forth in you you haven't seen before.

She pulled into the back of a lot behind a low, deserted building, and they stopped.

When first he'd arrived in California, he'd felt as if he were walking into an ancient version of Spain, done up again, brand-new. The names of the streets, the mellifluous sounds, the citrus trees, the white buildings and red roofs, all spoke of a far-off place that had left its jewels draped over the hills and scattered along the beaches. He'd come to take it all for granted then, until she started taking him round Santa Barbara, showing him the Moorish spirits that hid out behind the muscle cars. The tiles and designs on the Courthouse, the downtown cinema built in the thirties to resemble a courtyard in Spain, with whitewashed balconies along the sides, lavish dressing rooms, even a twinkling star or two set up on the roof, so that people watching movies could fancy themselves in Andalusia.

Once, driving a few miles down the coast, they'd suddenly come upon a large Moorish palace sleeping by the ocean, and when they'd made their way past the gatehouse speaker, through the gates, to the real-estate man presiding over the estate (three-piece suit on a Sunday afternoon), they'd stepped into another life: tiled courtyard, indoor swimming pool, archways out of Córdoba. Now a twenties-era fantasy that could, as the man in the suit said, "make a great fixer-upper for the well-to-do family with kids."

Now, as they stepped into the low white building, they stepped into Morocco. The man at the front desk offered them mint tea, in decorated glasses, and the room they entered was all white, with divans by a terrace, and kaftans instead of bathrobes. Lights all around, when he pulled back the curtains, and the sound of water, endlessly falling, as from a courtyard.

"It's like the place you always dream about," he said.

"That's what California's good for. Dreaming of other places."

"It's completely—completely unexpected."

The adjective was so weak she kissed him on the cheek. "You're sleepy. You should rest."

"Sorry. It's been a long day."

"Don't apologize. I like you when you're sleepy. You're most touching when you're vague."

He reached towards her where she lay, and she put a finger to his lips.

"No. I'm the boss tonight. Relax."

By the time they woke up, the temperature was already close to three figures, and the sun was screaming through the flimsy curtains. They ordered breakfast in the room, and savored the freedom from telephones, from books.

"It's funny," she said, breaking a croissant between her fingers, and licking the butter from her fingertips, "you never talk about your past. Almost like you think you could erase it."

"That's what people come to California for."

"But then they find that Californians have lots of pasts. Even if they can't always remember them."

She sipped at her orange juice, hair wet from the shower.

"You, too," he said. "You tell me about the ways you escaped from things when you were very young, but the rest . . ."

"Is what I'm trying to escape from now. That's why I love being with you. You give me the chance to be something different."

"But you can't pretend the past doesn't exist."

"That's what I was saying to you just now."

She looked away, at the terrace in the sun, the white houses with their expensive cars, the tiled fountains and their ageless music. She was speaking in innocence, and he not.

"What would you like to do today?"

"Find out what you've done." He didn't know why he said it, but clearly the previous days had not been entirely forgotten.

"What do you mean? This is your birthday."

"I know. That's why I can do anything—including asking you anything I want."

"One question—and then we'll go."

"Okay. My question is"—he paused—"what happened with Alex?"

She looked at him, and looked at him, and then it looked as

if she were falling. Her eyes filling up with what could only be frustration.

"Why do you want to know?"

"Only curiosity."

She paused for a long, long moment, as if to collect herself. Then, continuing with a change in her voice, "The same thing that always happens. He got tired of me, and ran away. He wouldn't even take my calls any more."

"Why not?"

"Ask him. Why do they ever get fed up? Maybe I wasn't interesting enough, or exotic enough, or strong enough. Maybe I didn't match his idea of the perfect woman. He always liked me well enough when he could look over the table and admire me, as he called it. *'Mirar es admirar'*—something like that. He liked me when he could show me off to the world. But soon he didn't like me in any other way."

"But you didn't think to tell me any of this?"

"Why should I? It's got nothing to do with you and me. That's what I was saying. You and me are different. That's why it gives me hope."

She was on the edge, he saw, of tearing up everything she'd hazarded, and going off forever.

"If you'd told me, we wouldn't be talking like this. On the one chance we have to get away from it."

"I'm sorry. Really I am." She looked terrified, like someone at the top of a cliff who feels the stones falling down into the emptiness below, and sees that soon she'll be falling, too. "I met him through my sister, and he seemed funny and mysterious and intelligent, and now, I'm sure, he never thinks of me at all."

"And that time at McCarthy's lecture?"

"I never expected to see him there. I told you: I was there for Krissie."

"Who's always away when it counts."

"Don't I know it!" She'd finally conjured hope, and instantly—so it might seem—it had been pulled away again. Her demons could say, "I told you so."

"Look," she said, and he could see she was fighting more strongly for them than she'd ever seemed to do before, "if you really want to throw me over because I knew Alejandro before I had the chance to know you, you might as well drive home right now."

"It's stupid, I know. Give me time to think about this."

He secured his bathrobe tight around him and walked out of the room, to the pool. Then, through a narrow corridor, into the parking lot: a slap of desert heat, the blinding glare coming down onto fenders, hubcaps. When he touched the door to her car, his hand pulled back as if it had been burned. Birdsong is a way of reminding us that Heaven is all around us, the Arabs say. But it's only we who can find the ears with which to hear it.

"Shall we see what else there is to look at round here?" he said, going back into the bright room.

They talked very little as they drove back in the evening, passing the industrial fields, the muffled lights of Ontario. If it really meant so much to him, he thought, then he could have asked her any number of questions, months before; clearly he was hiding from something, too. Why punish her for something he'd almost asked her not to divulge: like Greg, or whatever it was she did when he wasn't around?

As the road dwindled into twin lanes just before they came into Santa Barbara, there was a sense of coming to a forking of the paths.

"Do you want to stay?" he asked as they drove towards the university, the red lights of the airport, his home nearby.

"I think I should go. I have stuff to do tomorrow, in L.A."

" 'Stuff' meaning auditions? Rehearsals? A trip to the doctor, or your parents'?"

"Stuff. The usual mystery."

"But I'll see you before the lecture?"

"You'd see me every day if you wanted to."

"Thank you," he said, as they turned off the freeway, and onto the small road that ran along the sea. "Thank you for a wonderful escape."

"My pleasure," she said, leaning over to kiss him, but not turning off the engine, as if it was she, now, who had to look after him, walking into a house where the red light was winking furiously.

For a while, after he returned to his desk, everything that had come free on the long and unexpected excursion—the dance, the drive across the desert, the confrontation at last, the silence that had come after it—flowed through him, and he felt as if the poems on his desk were opening to his touch. As if he'd come to know his way around them now, the pressure points, the places where they were soft—the back of her neck, the area between her right breast and her throat—and when he pushed them now, they broke open, and he walked into a field of light. Don't even look where you're going, they said, and you end up somewhere truer.

The pages of the thesis came freely now, as if they were writing him, not he they, and when he went out onto the beach in the crystal light, it was as if the place he'd sought had come into sharpest focus: the aluminum glinting on the bicycles, the light flashing from Storke Tower in the distance, the sun catching the patches of tar left over on the beach from the oil spill years ago. The place was chaos and sadness and confusion, a vague idea no one had ever bothered to clear up, or even to work up into an argument; and yet all the spaces around it, within, above, across, were like nothing he'd ever seen at home. The only abiding sadness of California, its daily ache, was that it could always be something better.

When she came down again for the lecture, he felt the restlessness in her as strongly as in himself. She was tossing and turning even when she was lying still. She asked about his thesis, he talked about the deadline, she said something about how time was running out, and now and then they turned off the lights and he heard and felt and touched someone he couldn't analyze away.

"The body is dark"—it had once been his favorite line from Rumi. "The heart is shining bright."

The next afternoon—it was one day before the lecture now—she said, "Can I ask you for a favor? And you have to say yes, because I gave you a treat last week."

"What is it?"

"Our house. In the hills. Can we go there again?"

"Of course. When would you like?"

"Tonight. After dark." They still had one place that was unblemished; nothing bad had ever happened to them there. "It's like the place you described to me the first time we went up to the hills," she said, and he was touched, because she'd remembered—and caught the implication.

They got into his car after nightfall, and drove up into the hills. The old road they'd come to think of as their own had acquired even more pieces of debris since their last visit, and the potholes after the winter storms were so deep the car shook and shouted as they drove. The transmission groaned, and the axles banged against loose rocks as if the car were crying out against the ascent.

Above them, far above, the satellite dish, as ever, on top of one of the mountains, sending unintelligible signals off into the heavens, and receiving them back. The road so clear under the full moon that it looked like a thin ribbon of grey thread unspooled around the hills to take their measure.

It wasn't hard to follow the turns in the strong light, and when they came within sight of the house, he thought he saw a shadow moving in one of the windows, an outline against a screen. Then put the thought away: surfaces were deceptive when the moon was full. But he had a sense of the hillside's being in motion and alive around them; when they stopped, and got out of the car, on the silent ridge, there were stirrings in the bushes, as if something other than themselves was going about its business.

She went down first, as was their custom, and he came slowly after. When he walked down to the lower level of the house, where she always waited for him, he found her standing there as ever. But when she looked up, her eyes were full.

"It's over. It's locked. We've lost our secret place forever."

"It can't be. Let me try."

He pulled at the door, and tried to jiggle the screen that protected it. It didn't budge. He got out a paper clip and fumbled ineffectively with the lock, but nothing turned, or yielded to his wishes. He banged against the window with his fist.

"It's gone," she said, almost inaudible. "It's locked forever."

"I'm sure it isn't. Let's try the other doors." They walked around the house, stopping every few yards to pull at a screen, to see if an upper window would give. It wouldn't. Around the far side, she found a screen door only partially obscured by curtains and said, "Look. Over there." Light fixtures on the walls, a carpet on the floor.

"It's been a while since we were here last."

"Too long." Though it had been only a couple of weeks. "The one place we could trust, the only place that was ours, and now it's gone."

"I'm sure we can find a way in." He left her in the driveway and walked around the house clockwise, the way they'd never done before. He pulled at doors, tried to unriddle locks. Nothing moved. In the driveway now he saw a small blue sign warning of the security company that kept watch over the house; on the side of one wall, a dull red security alarm waiting to light up.

"Shall we try again tomorrow?"

"What good will that do? There are lights now, carpets—there'll be people living here before long."

"We could try."

"It'd only make it worse." She went and stood by the passenger door of his car, and he thought it was a phantom waiting to get in. All the life was gone from her, and she looked spent. He'd told her to come out of hiding, her face said, and as soon as she had, her door had locked behind her. He was just like all the rest.

The next day, the lecture hall was almost empty. A few loyal souls had shown up, doubtless to help Sefadhi, and a handful of others sat here and there in the middle rows to give the impression of fullness. But the vast majority of the seats were unclaimed. Esfandi had for some reason entitled his lecture "Fire and Surrender in the Islamic Way," as if not remembering, or even caring, that Islam was hardly a popular subject around here. If he'd substituted the word "Sufi," there'd have been blondes in the back row.

When the guest of honor followed Sefadhi through the side door, to the front row, the student watching them caught his breath: he'd seen the man somewhere before, he was sure of it. At the store in Westwood, months before? The assistant to the suave young broker?

The stranger was dressed in a light cotton suit, with a white shirt that set off his dark eyes and thick beard, and there was nothing about him that was relaxed. He didn't smile as his host chatted with him, and even when Sefadhi went up to the podium and delivered his usual encomium to the latest messiah, the man registered no smile of recognition or self-effacement. He sat, arrow-straight, in the front row, a dark oath, and when the introduction was over, he went straight up to the lectern and began to speak.

He had no notes and he gave no preamble. He just began to speak, in a high-pitched, piercing voice that sounded like a flute.

"Sometimes," he began, "you have been in love. You lie awake in the dark, you pace and pace through the night. You get up, you lie down, you comb your hair again and again. You know no world but this world, and you know no sound but the one you're listening for.

"When you know this feeling, you know you will do anything for your love. Nothing is too much for you; you will protect her with your life. You are not yourself without her; you do not have interests except her interests. Anyone who threatens her, you will punish, even to the death.

"Please think of this—please think of this again—when you hear of suicide bombers in the Middle East or 'acts of terror.' Please think of how you will do everything for those you have promised to protect forever. When you hear your journalists speak of our jihad, and people who will shed blood to protect their temples, please think of this. Love is not the place for compromise. Who half protects a love?

"The Sufi is the same as this. But his love is for a force that never dies."

Nobody in the audience stirred, and nobody whispered. The man's accent was strange, and his diction didn't fit; but the concentration of his thought was absolute.

"The Sufi's home is the lover's home, which is the paradox that stands beyond all reason. I am rich because I have nothing. I am full because I am no one. It is daytime for me when the world is dark, and midnight at bright noon. And because his world is everything that is not in the world around him, he cries out only for annihilation. 'Kill me now,' Hallaj told his friends; 'I long to be with the One I love.' "

The words were coming out fast, too fast in many cases to be understood; it was like seeing the holy verses in the mosque, a swirl of lines rising so high so fast that soon their meaning disappeared and all you could feel was their fury and their beauty.

"When you are in love—you know this, all of you—you are not yourself. You have no self. The world is a grid of shining correspondences. And the correspondences sing like angels. You cannot defile them with your intentions. You cannot undo the order that is suddenly revealed to you. All you can do is become a part of it and move in hallowed light.

"Your friends make jokes about your absentmindedness. Your parents tell you you're deluded. All the people around ask you to come back to the person they know. But you are dead to them. The world has no meaning to you. Everything you once cherished is irrelevant, and you are far above it. The only truth you know is the truth around you. And you know, more than that, that whatever you love, you cannot fail to love. You can no more be argued out of your devotion than a compass can be told not to find the north, the tides instructed not to follow their moon.

"'Don't come to me with reasons,' you tell your friends. 'Come to me with prayer bowls and songs.'"

She looked at him and he saw terror in her eyes: the man was pulling them towards everything that would take him away from her. He was speaking for the poets who were changeless, and the very words that once would have seemed a description of what they shared had now changed shape—or direction, rather—so they seemed to be an argument for separation. The visitor was talking of a love that never disappoints.

"In your tradition," the man went on, "Jesus comes to you as a reflection of God's grace on earth; in our tradition, all the world is such a reflection. The entire universe is God's messenger, and all life is our redeemer. We look on Paradise when we see a Persian carpet. We walk through Paradise when we enter the garden outside an Islamic palace. We lose ourselves in Paradise when we read the verses in our mosques and open ourselves to the dome above. To the lover, all the world is blessed.

"In your tradition, also, you speak repeatedly of God's love for man; in our tradition, it is more moving to speak of man's love for God. We long for that to be bottomless and without end. And for the Sufi, the longing that we feel for God, He feels, too: God longs for us, as a hidden treasure longs to be discovered.

"You do not come to the Sufi way through your mind. The mind is a knife, useful only for cutting apart. You do not come to our path through your heart. The heart is a shield, for defending yourself against truth. You come to it through grief. Through the shock that breaks you open.

"In your tradition, you speak of loving the one who is the source of all your joy. In ours, we speak of loving the one who is the cause of all our sorrow. Our hearts are broken open, and then we know real loneliness.

"Our word for this is *bala*. *Bala* in our language means 'affliction.' *Bala* also means 'yes.' We say yes to affliction, and in affliction find our faith. Thank you."

There was a stunned silence, and already the man was at his seat, hardly acknowledging Sefadhi and staring straight ahead of him as before. Clearly he was a practiced speaker, even in a foreign language, used to taking his simple, burning message (memorized, perhaps) to schools and auditoriums everywhere. Yet the impact was like that of seeing a sleek train streaking across a far horizon, under snowcaps. Nobody knew what to say.

"Mr. Esfandi has graciously agreed to take questions," said Sefadhi, ever the smooth peacemaker, but seeming more displaced than usual. "I am sure there is much you want to ask him."

No hands came up, however. The man returned to the stage and stood before them, looking down with his burning eyes, but nobody ventured a word. At last, one slow, unsteady hand went up.

"You spoke, so passionately, so eloquently, about the possession of love, if we may call it that." It was an elderly man he'd never seen before—a colleague from another department, perhaps, here to lend Sefadhi a helping hand. "You talked about the uselessness of judging it by earthly terms. Do you think we could relate this to the riddle in *The Merchant of Venice?*"

The man said nothing and looked back at him, unmoving.

"That is, if you seek love for what it can give you, if you seek love because of what you think is due you, you are lost. You have to give yourself over to it even if your love looks like a piece of lead."

There were a few laughs from those present, eager to have the atmosphere lightened, but not from the man onstage.

"I think so," he said, and looked around for further hands.

Debra, always reliable, complied.

"This annihilation, this *fana,* you speak of, right? Isn't it better to say that it's like an 'unbecoming,' in Schimmel's words, not a destruction so much? More like an unraveling, a going back to roots? Schimmel says it's not an 'ecstasy' so much as an 'instasy.'"

"Yes," said the man, now as silent as a few minutes before he had seemed possessed by words.

"I think we have time for one more," said Sefadhi, and the plaintiveness in his face and voice, his unsteadiness as he stood up, gave a weight and dimension to his dapper manner that made him seem what he seldom seemed before, touching.

He put up his hand to help his teacher out. "Your talk was billed as 'Fire and Surrender in the Islamic Way.' Yet you haven't mentioned 'fire' once."

"Exactly," said the man, and he stepped down from the podium, already looking for the door.

There was a scattering of bemused applause, and people looked around them as if for prompts or affirmations. It was as if a hurricane had passed through and now was gone except in the tremors it left behind.

"Give me a minute," he said to her, and then hurried to the front to make contact with the man before he could make his escape. "He can help you with these Sufi riddles," Sefadhi had said, and the very fact that the man looked so familiar (the fact that they might have met before, in an entirely different setting) gave him hope. The two men were just heading out the side door when he caught up with them—no one else had tried to detain the visitor—and he thrust out an awkward hand. "Excuse me," he said, his hand ending up on the other man's arm. "John Macmillan. I study with Professor Sefadhi here." His adviser gave a watery benediction. "I was just wondering if you might have time while you're here for a coffee, a brief discussion. I'm wrapping up a thesis on Sufi poetry."

"I'm sorry," said the man, as if he'd never seen him before. "Perhaps my cousin will have time." He gestured towards another man, standing a little behind the two professors, young, with an even thicker beard.

This second man, whose fleshy face gave the appearance of friendliness and accessibility, said, "Yes. Shall we go now?"

He went back to where she was sitting, and the three of them followed the professors out into the winter sun. "Your cousin is quite a speaker," he said, sounding stupid even to himself; the lecture had made all words sound stupid. Around them kids in tie-dye T-shirts, on skateboards, mountain bikes, with surfboards in their hands. Asian students gathered under trees in earnest conversation, teenagers more undisguised than most, holding hands or leaning into one another, giggling.

"You grew up in Iran together?"

"No," said the man, in a way that did not encourage further questioning. He looked away from him, and the questioner thought: a brother, truly a cousin? A beloved?

"But you've known one another a long time?"

"Long enough." With a slight smile. In Westwood the men had veiled themselves behind courtesies; here they seemed to be hiding out in public.

"Coffee, over there," said the man, pointing to a cappuccino stand that sat beside the steps leading out from the library, and the three of them shuffled, in no set pattern, to the fresh-faced boy and got their drinks. She'd seemed uneasy throughout the afternoon, and their new guest gave no impression of being any happier.

"So," said the visitor, as they found a low brick wall on which to sit while they sipped their drinks, "you study our tradition?"

"As much as I can. It's not easy."

The man nodded, sipping at his coffee very fast, as if to get away as soon as possible.

"The tradition doesn't always like to be studied."

"It studies you," the man said, in the cryptic, portentous way that could seem enlightening if you had patience for the Persian way, infuriating if you didn't. "That is its message."

"You don't go to Iran now?"

The man shook his head, cappuccino foam around his beard.

"It's terrible over there, I've heard," she said, and they both looked up. During the lecture he'd watched her playing with her hair, and drawing in her notebook—fairy towers and crescent moons and princesses in elaborate dresses out of Napoleonic balls, with hair falling down to the waist. But now, suddenly, she was engaged.

"It's inhuman, what they do. There should be a law against them."

The man looked up, though not at her, and it was as if something had come unlocked in him, too.

"There should be more than a law," he said. "Whatever you have heard is only a fiftieth of the truth. It is worse than you can imagine." His eyes had a faint light in them, slow fire, and, as so often in California, a casual conversation between immigrants congratulating themselves on having found themselves here touched on the politics of a faraway country, and suddenly a door swung open to reveal a house on fire.

"And the way they treat women," she went on.

"The way they treat everyone," said the young man with the affable face. "Like pigs. Against everything in our holy book. Against everything the Prophet, peace be on his spirit, told us. Against all the words spoken by our teachers, about the reverence, the deference for women. All things." He was alive now, and speaking as if in the streets of Isfahan.

"But we hear in the papers about a loosening up—"

"You 'hear in the papers,'" he said with contempt. "Of course you hear in the papers this. Our leaders, our government, they are not—forgive me—innocents. They are not young men. They know everything you want to hear. They will talk of Hegel and Kant and moderation. Of 'détente' and 'new relations with the West.' On CNN. What else can they say? What have they got to lose?"

"But that's better than before, surely, when it seemed we were headed for open warfare."

"Better to pretend friendship than to have a war?" The man looked at him as if he were very young indeed. "I'm sorry. Maybe in your country this is a good thing, you can smile and shake hands and pretend all is happy. In my country, no. These politicians are very clever men; ours is not a young civilization. They speak English, they make jokes about religion. They talk about 'hardliners' and they say they are doing something different. You see their new suits from Paris and you think they are your friends."

The whispers, the fears, the suppositions of home ten times more urgent and desperate when they're abroad.

"In the last year, two years, eight—no, I can say nine—of my friends have been killed. Taken into a field and shot. My own mother and father, in Tabriz, they cannot walk out of their home. They live like dead people already."

"I'm sorry."

"Of course you are sorry. You in the West are always sorry, very sorry for the sadness you have caused. You are excited because the 'moderates,' as you call them, come on the CNN and say all the things the West wants to hear. They are devils who know how to act as angels."

The cappuccino was finished now; the man burned with all he hated.

"And the people live no better than before?"

"The 'people,'" he said, spitting it out as if it were something that tasted foul. "The 'people' think only about one thing, and that is tomorrow. 'How will we get food? What will happen to our children? How will we live tomorrow, and the next day?' They will love the government only if the government stays out of their lives. If there is no war against Iraq, no war against Washington, no modernization campaign and new temple at Persepolis, they are happier than before. Like animals."

"And Soroush? We hear he's making a new kind of Islam, compatible with the West, trying to bring Islam into a better"—he searched for the right word—"understanding with the modern world."

"You think they would let him speak if they didn't control him? You think they would allow him to make this 'better understanding' if he were speaking against them?"

There was nothing left to say. She had fallen quiet, but she looked more sorrowful than he had ever seen her in public before; the man had finished his drink, and whatever they'd hoped to get from him, they'd gotten.

"Well, thank you for your time. It means a lot to us."

"Thank you," the man said, throwing the cup away. "For your listening, thank you."

They took their leave of him, and walked towards the car. As they did, suddenly he was at their side again, importunate.

"Excuse me? You have heard about the *mujahedin,* perhaps? They are in the airport, they tell you how terrible is our government, how they want to make things better? Like before. If they come to power, every one of us will be dead. Even our grandparents, our grandparents' nurses. Everyone who is not a young man, they will kill."

She was fighting back tears now, he could tell, and the man, seeing this, pulled himself back. "I am sorry to tell you these things. But is better you should know."

"Thank you for your trust."

And then he was away again, in the sun, and they were alone in the bright plaza, with students all around, talking about the next night's party.

When they got back home, there was another topic they could no longer speak about, and they walked around each other as if there had been a death in the family. "I'm sure it can't be as bad as he said," she said, sounding a little disappointed, as she always did, when all her fears were confirmed.

"I'm sure it could," he said, unable to conceal his unsettledness. "It makes you grateful to live where we do."

"That's why they come here, too, I bet," she said, with a nurse's tenderness; if he suffered, she did.

"At least it's better than it was. When they had brigades on hand to block out pictures of Margaret Thatcher if she appeared on the cover of *The Economist* without a head scarf."

"It's much better than it was," she said, and he had the feeling, suddenly, that it was she now who was giving reassurances, because she knew much more than he.

At his desk, Bach playing on the system to give him spirit, he felt himself more than ever going backwards, to someone alone in a darkened room, making patterns, doodling as if he were she during the lecture, drawing mazes, towers, boxes that soon became as tangled as a kitten's ball of string. He'd been planning to write on Hafez now, but it all seemed more and more irrelevant. "She's crying out for something," Alex had said (about the "European girl," he tried to remember now?). "But it's nothing any mortal soul can give her."

He got out a piece of paper to write on the theology of the Sufis, and then found himself making word games, seeing how he could find "fade" and "dies" hidden in "Esfandi."

"What's going on in there?" he heard her calling from the next room. "You sound suspiciously quiet."

"Not much."

"Are you busy making mischief?"

"I wish I were."

"Can you stand a visitor?"

"I think so, yes."

He heard her get up, and then she was standing at his door, her hair tangled from where she'd been lying on it, and her face sleepy and open, as if she hadn't yet come up through all the levels of herself to the surface. Her feet were bare; her hands clutched the glass of lemonade he'd left for her as if too small to hurt a soul. "What is it? You look distraught."

"It's nothing," he said. "Just stand there. Like that. Nothing more."

Early spring is radiant in California, and in the first few weeks, before the sharp light of winter is bruised and made fuzzy, the skies, blazing blue, look down on Persian carpets: the hills an arabesque of golden poppies and purple lupines, with blue-blossomed white lilac around the edges. "I tell myself sometimes that California is the place where Man plays God and locks himself out of Eden," he wrote to Nigel, thinking of the Nasruddin story from his seminar. "It's as if all you can see here sometimes is people walking around, looking at the ground, searching for something as if they'd just lost a contact lens, and saying, 'It's got to be here somewhere. I had it just a minute ago. Where can it be?' And then the spring comes along and suddenly they find the key to the heaven they've locked themselves out of—except, being mortal, they let it slip again, and then they have to start searching all over again."

They drove up into the hills and saw houses on every side coming up with new alacrity: the builders had decided that the year's final storm had passed through, and now they could complete their constructions with impunity (until fire came, or mudslide, earthquake or flood). As they drove along the old road towards the Chumash caves, suddenly a black BMW with its top down veered out of a driveway— the driveway that led to "their house," he realized—and a woman with affluent skin the leathery brown of an expensive handbag cursed at them as she swerved and drove towards the town.

"It makes me want to go to church and pray sometimes," he said.

"What does? All these houses being built on such treacherous ground?"

"All of it. California makes me want to say a prayer for the undefended."

She flinched away from him—she'd caught the hint—and then held on to his right hand as he drove up.

"Why did you come here, then?"

"Because it's beautiful and free. It allows you to be something else. I only meant that, when you listen to someone like our friend from Iran, you remember how the rest of the world is living. Here it's almost as if everything—even the hills and the rocks and the weather—is set up for us."

She drew away her hand, and he could tell he'd gone too far. Someone from the outside world comes to California and finds it intoxicating; and then, the morning after, wonders what he saw in it.

"It's something I've always wondered about you," she said, a few turns later, and he could tell from her voice, all careful innocence, that she was hurt and wanted to push him away.

"What's that? Why I don't go somewhere more real?"

"No. What you do for church. What religion you practice. You're always talking about it, and I know you're a professional student of religion"—like everyone, she couldn't help putting heavy quotation marks around the phrase—"but I've never seen you do anything that's religious."

"If it's religious, it's probably private. You wouldn't see it."

"You're avoiding the question. Do you do it? Do you believe?"

"Of course I do. I believe the universe makes sense; that everything that happens, happens for a reason, even if it's one that we can't see. That everything—everyone—has the potential for some good. I trust things."

"And I don't."

"That's the difference between us," he said, though the real difference was more profound and more desolate. She thought the angels he encouraged in her were temporary; he hoped—he had to hope—the devils were. Though they never talked about it, and in part because they never talked about it, they'd somehow put what was most essential to them, the very premises on which they'd built their lives, at stake here, and for either of them to admit defeat would be as much as to dismantle the whole structure of a lifetime. The little differences they talked about were ways of not acknowledging what was central.

They had reached the top of the old road now, and when it continued they were on the same road they'd come along their first time up here, in the mist. But more treacherous now, because they were driving into a past—and a comparison with the present—and every turn brought not new vistas but old ones, and questions about what had changed.

"It's lovely in this weather," she said. "You remember before. . . ."

When the twisting road ran out, it came to the "Road of the Heavens" that runs along the back of the hills like a line on a palm. He was tempted to remind her of the time she'd picked up his hand and seen whole heavens in it, found stars and crosses of fate, and said, "Your lines are so clear! Mine are a mess." But any reference to the past is tricky when you don't know where you're going, so he simply said, "What's your pleasure?"

They could drive up towards the mountaintop, where the air was high and chilly: his choice always. Or back towards the things they knew. Two people look at a stretch of road—he thought of McCarthy's example in his lecture—and one sees an opening, the other the terror of the unknown.

"Let's go down today," she said, and he thought how perhaps she preferred to be left in her unhappiness because it was what she knew: she knew the rules and how to make her peace with them. The first time they'd come up here, there hadn't been choices or metaphors: they'd only been nosing through the mist, trying to while away an afternoon.

As he drove back towards the city, they passed the illuminated phone booth, drab now in the sunlight, the shuttered country store ("FOR SALE" chalked up on its window), the broken piano he'd played in the cold night.

"Do you mind if we get out for a moment?"

"Of course not. Let's stop."

He paused by the road, and she got out and ran up the hill, as if to be away from him, or the car. The meadows were a field of color, up the slope, passing over the top of the hill and all the way down to the lake beyond, the inner valley. When he caught up with her, she was standing in a sea of orange, triumphant.

He caught his breath, and she sat against a tree; in every direction, the space went on and on.

"What would feel nice?"

"A story."

"What kind of story?"

"A story like the one you told me before when we were up near here."

"There was once a man," he said, making sure to think about nothing and just let the words come through him, out, "who was a careful and respected religious teacher. He had two children, a wife, a group of students; he was famous for his skills as an interpreter of the law."

She sat with eyes closed, the sun sweet on her pale face.

"Then, one day, out of the blue, another man appeared. He was a wandering dervish from far away, and as soon as the two of them met, they knew: each was the hidden key to the other. They talked and talked—everything rushed out of them, as if it had been waiting for this moment; not exactly as lovers of one another, but more, and better, as two lovers of the same sight. The same books, the same thoughts, the same beliefs. Their talk made them feel as if they were climbing through mountains, through the mist, into fields full of flowers, and high sunlight. They looked around at the place where they had arrived and recognized it as the place they'd been coming towards, half thinking of, all their lives.

"But the ones who were left behind when the teacher disappeared into the mist, the ones who had enjoyed his company and were suddenly deprived of it, were less happy now. Who is this new stranger who's taken our loved one away? they said. Why should we wait, after all this time, while he gets to have him to himself? They plotted and plotted, and, one morning, when the teacher woke up, he found his new friend gone.

"For days he was bereft. He searched and searched, he asked in the marketplace, in the mosque: everywhere. But the friend was nowhere to be found. Then, at last, when he had quite given up hope, he had a dream that the man was in the oldest city in the world, a place called Damascus. He sent his loyal younger son to find him, and there the man was, in a tavern, exactly as in the dream. He returned with the younger son, and the two old friends fell at one another's feet, weeping."

There was a light wind in the mountains today, but otherwise everything was silent. They were the only travelers on the mountain road on this weekday afternoon, and, eyes closed, she was surrendered to the story, the wind blowing all around.

"Again the friends lost themselves in talk, more fervent and grateful than ever now, having come so close to losing everything. The religious teacher found a woman in his household for the traveler to marry, to ensure he'd never have occasion to leave. The two of them lived in the same house, and, especially at night, when everyone else was asleep, they talked of whatever was secret in them, which was not a dark thing but a golden one.

"But the students, of course, grew more restless than ever, cut off from the one they loved. And one day, when the teacher stepped out, it was to find his friend—his image of the Beloved—dead on the doorstep. The rumors said that the teacher's own second son had organized the murder."

"And so the man was left bereft?"

"He was left, after the grief had worn out and grown tired, ecstatic. He was left full up with all the things he wanted to say to the absent friend, all the pent-up feelings for which he had not found a voice before. For whatever they shared could not be lost; indeed, his friend was more present to him now, more durably so, than ever before.

"Poems came out of him, and songs: great poems of triumph and surrender. He could never be cut off from his friend now, and, more important, never be pushed out of all they had worshipped together. They were linked irreparably. So much so that he found a new companion—an old unlettered goldsmith in the marketplace, a friend for decades. He took a new wife, cultivated new students and protégés. He lived in the knowledge that no one could take away from him what he had known and shared."

There were tears in her eyes when he came to the ending, and he didn't know how much he'd touched her, how much offended. "After all this time, you choose to tell me the true story."

"You knew it all along, though. Even when I told the other one."

"Of course I did. I've heard about Rumi and Shams; I was at that lecture the first afternoon, remember?"

"Then you knew I was making something up before? The first time we came up here."

"That's why I loved you. Because you were kind enough to give it a different kind of ending. To protect me. Why did you have to tell me the true story now?"

There are many ways to be cruel, he remembered Martine's saying, and he wondered if that was what coming to the top of the mountain meant, too. To tell her the truth—that they were drifting apart—was an unkindness; but to tell her a lie—that everything would be all right—was an even deeper act of cruelty.

Soon after it was light, the next day, she slipped out—"shopping," she said vaguely, but it was clear she just needed to be away, if not from him then at least from her sense that everything was unraveling between them. He went to his desk and worked a little on his revisions, to incorporate the new material that had been unearthed by an Iranian at USC, and yet all he could see was the phone at the edge of the desk: the magic object in the children's story that, if you touch it, leaves you scalded. He'd tried and tried for months not to think of the business card from Damascus, lying among his papers; to call the number on it seemed a betrayal. Yet not to call the number now seemed worse.

"Hello. Kristina Jensen," said the voice at the other end, as brisk and efficient as if it were in the office.

"Yes," he said. "This is John Macmillan."

"Camilla's friend," she said, and let the ambiguity hang in the air.

"That's right. And the reason I'm calling, actually"—he tried to make it sound slow and natural, though he'd practiced it time and time again—"is that I'm going to be in Damascus soon, and I wondered if you needed anything taken to your friend."

"Damascus?"

It was a paltry fiction, but she seemed in no mood to call him on it.

"For my research. And I think I'll be seeing Khalil."

"Oh," she said, as if she was somehow relieved. "You haven't heard."

"Heard?"

"He got taken in. For questioning. I don't think we'll be hearing from Professor Khalil for several months."

"I see." And then, as if he knew what she was talking about, "His activities?"

"The usual," she said, either because she took him at his valuation, or because she pretended to.

"Well, if you hear anything . . ."

"I'll tell you. I'm sure Camilla will know where to find you."

"If she knows where to find herself." She laughed, as she'd done the time they'd talked before Christmas, and he felt a twinge of guilt.

"She's never been the easiest sister to keep track of."

"But she does have a job, doesn't she? A steady source of income?" If he didn't ask now, the chance might never come again.

"Oh, she's well taken care of as long as my father is around."

"And she does act now and then?"

"In her mind, perhaps." The voice that had been keeping Camilla company all her life.

"And the degree at Oxford must have helped?"

"Oxford," she said, and there was quiet for a moment. She spoke about her sister as if she were a banker, talking about a troublesome account, in debt; and as she paused at the other end, he thought he saw someone in a marketplace, wondering exactly how many beans to place in the scales. "We think, sometimes, that Oxford's where the problems started. She went off on this course that took her away from us, from everything. After she came back, she was never really in sync again."

"But she had her degree, new qualifications?"

"Oxford was her great escape," the cool voice asserted at the other end. "'Women adventurers in the Middle East.'"

The voice, again, that had been putting Camilla in place since girlhood; he felt, suddenly, as if he were on the wrong side of the table, with the police, informing on Khalil.

"But it doesn't pay the bills," he said, to bring them back to the safer ground of cliché.

"It doesn't," she said carefully, and then, noticing perhaps that he'd been doing all the questioning, "What about you? Someone told me you were looking for Sufi manuscripts."

"Was looking."

"You didn't find any?"

"If you're in a desert, the most dangerous thing you can see is an oasis."

"You sound like Sefadhi," she said, with a small laugh, and he, surprised she'd left an opening, pounced.

"You're a friend of his?"

"Not really. Anyway, I'll give you a call if I hear anything from Damascus."

"Thank you. My regards to your father." Since, every time she spoke about him, he was always "my" father, and never "ours."

He really had put all thoughts of manuscripts aside; the visitation from the passionate Iranians had worked on him like a slap in the face. He looked in on her where she slept as he went to his study one morning (she'd returned the previous night), and wondered how he could ever make a connecting corridor between the two rooms. The poems seemed to have no meaning unless they could speak to someone like them, in a different century and culture; and yet they, he and she, had no value unless they led to something beyond themselves, more durable. Mortal and immortal lover weren't just different as *"amor"* and "love" were different—separate words for the same thing. They belonged to different worlds.

And yet (this, too, had been the point, surely, that the lecturer had been making) one can be an image of the other. As a man, seeing a picture of Isfahan, is taking the first step, in his mind, towards understanding what the place means, and seeing it more deeply. Even if the man is a woman, in Los Angeles, sitting in a cluttered room with the curtains drawn.

He sat down at his desk and, less than ever like himself, drew out a fresh piece of paper and wrote, almost triumphantly (defiantly), "EPILOGUE: THE HIDDEN JIHAD." The words that came out were mad, excessive—not unlike the young Sefadhi in his pamphlet, the part of him that was sane might have said; but the part of him that wasn't sane pressed on, about how every battle in the world (between left and right, between Old World and New) is just the same battle, between the part of us that thinks the world is capable of redemption, and the part that sees it as fallen. "One reason we turn to the Sufis today," he wrote, "is that they give us a sense of angels in a culture in which we've consigned most celestial beings to the New Age shop (and the darker ones to the Cineplex). They tell us that we are subject to something outside ourselves, though able to remake ourselves at any moment (the angel is within); there are, of course, more angels in the Quran than in any holy book.

"This hopefulness does not seem fashionable in the modern world. Take Goethe, for example, the very Goethe who loved the Persians so deeply that he learned their language in order to read the poems in the original. Before he got to that stage, though, the same Goethe, author of *Selige Sehnsucht*, or 'Blessed Longing,' gave us Mephistopheles, a devil who can play on a man committed to freedom and movement. The Sufis, by comparison, give us a counter-Mephistopheles, an image of a stranger who, instead, calls us back to our rightful, better nature. And in a culture in which we have no gods but plenty of beliefs—or, as commonly, no beliefs but plenty of gods—and where happy endings disappeared with faith itself, what we need more than anything is . . ."

He heard something stirring at the far end of the room, and looked up.

"You look strange," she said, standing at the door, for how long he couldn't know.

"Not strange. Just preoccupied."

"You look different," she said, walking over to him. "More like Sefadhi the longer you study this stuff."

"You hardly know him."

"I know enough," she said, and sat down on the armchair, picking up an old copy of a magazine.

"What is it? You look scared."

"I haven't seen this issue yet," flipping through the old *Rolling Stone*. "Is there anything I'd like in here?"

"What's happening, Camilla? Are you scared?"

"Of course I'm scared. I'm always scared."

"But more than usual?"

"I can feel what's going on." She put down the magazine and looked at him. "I'm not stupid. I can feel you spending more time in here every day. I can't blame you. Every day I give you some new reason to be done with me."

"That's why I'm here. To make sure we don't get into that position."

"But you're alone. How does that help?"

"I'm trying to find a way we don't have to fall apart."

She looked down, everything vulnerable in her (of hope and fear) playing at the corners of her eyes.

"Come here."

She got up and made her way to the desk where he was sitting. There was brightness on the beach outside, a surfer at the point. "Close your eyes," he said, and she did. He ran a finger slowly under her shirt, down with the unclasping buttons, around her sides and up again, along her back. Her body relaxed a little, and there was a soft sound from above. Then, out of nowhere, racking sobs.

"What is it, Camel? What's happening?"

Up on the desk now, papers, notes, all pushed to the floor.

"What is it, Camilla? What's happening?"

"You touch me in every way. How can I not be terrified?"

The afternoon passed, and then the evening; small clouds settled on the ocean, and the night began to fall. Everywhere they looked, when they lifted themselves up, papers, index cards, piles of magazines and staples; a vast scattering of what had once been orderly and concrete. An argument reduced into thin air.

He went into the bedroom, when the terrace had lost all light, and brought back a blanket so they could lie beside each other on the floor: a version, though a poor one, of their abandoned house in the hills. The ocean was outside their window, after all; though here, unlike in the hills, they could hear its ceasings and recessionals.

She pushed herself deep into him, so there'd be less chance to say anything, and he lay on the ruins of the argument he'd so carefully constructed. Their bodies, where they were moist, smudging or blurring the words. The peace in the room existed outside the reach of words, and beyond the grasp of any of the notions he'd so carefully mapped out. It was the frame within which the high sentiments reposed.

"What is it?" He could tell she wanted to say something.

"Nothing. I feel better now."

"Me, too."

"I was thinking about what you told me about the nights you had at school. When it was light." She stirred against him, and the movement was the only event in the room, in the strong moonlight, music coming from the house next door. "I know what you mean. I had days like that, too."

"In England? When you were a student?" Beginning to edge back, since the places they had in common, in their separate lives, would only lead to separateness.

"No. Before that. When I was younger. This one time, when I was in high school, junior high perhaps, we went to see my aunt, from Denmark. She was living way up in the north—the Faeroe Islands— in a little house near a lake. It must have been eleven o'clock, twelve, late at night. I was in her garden, and we were waiting for the sun to set. Except it was June, and so the sun never set. It just went down for a while, sat on the sea, and then went up again.

"It was mysterious. Nothing very dramatic or special. But I can still remember the feeling—even though it was cold and I was with the people I was most scared of, and this was a strange place, a long way from California. It was like being told there were other things in the world they'd never told you about at school. The fact that the sun could never set for days and there'd be no night, no stars, no anything. The kind of thing we thought only happened on the moon."

"You stayed there all night?"

"I tried. But my mother came in and noticed I wasn't in bed. Noticed I was happy, I guess. So she made sure we returned to Copenhagen the next day, and never went back to her sister's house again. The one thing she could never forgive was my being happy."

He held her close, invited her to bury herself in him, erase.

"That's one of the times she taught me my lesson. That I should never care for anything. Because if I did it would be taken away."

"You weren't into acting then?"

"Unh-unh."

The strange sentences he'd written earlier in the day were underneath them, illegible in the dark and perhaps never to be read again. The space on top of the desk was almost clear. The days were lengthening, and the last winter storm seemed to have passed through; they were moving into the expansive time of the year when they had first met.

"And the hiding went on?"

"Not always. There was another time, a few more times. Once, I remember, at a lake, when I was lying on a blanket, on this great green meadow, by the water—sounds stupid, I know, like I got it from some video. But I was alone, or felt I was alone. Whoever I was with must have gone off exploring or something. And I was just lying there—there was a light wind, it was a summer day—and watching the clouds. They looked like horses and dragons and wolves. And then, at some point, everything went still. I wasn't looking at clouds. Clouds were looking at me. And I fell through something, like Alice or one of those kids I read about, and became someone different for a while."

"So you know what I mean."

"In a way. But I don't think it's something you can write about. The thesis you're writing, the lecture that guy gave, all that stuff? I don't think that's got anything to do with it. Look at your adviser:

he's been living with these poems all his life. But whatever is real in him is something else. Which only his daughter knows."

"Maybe it's just an excuse for us to spend all day thinking about these bright ideas."

"Maybe. I knew when I was at the lake I never wanted to come up into my regular life again."

They lay on the floor, wrapped in blankets, and for a while it was as if they were in their cabin in the woods, or the room outside of time. He willed and willed the phone not to ring, and for a while at least it complied. There was a chance for making a space outside the world even here, in his study, with the papers scattered round like rags after something spills.

"Are you hungry?"

"Not hungry. Just happy. Not anything."

A little later, she took his hand and put it where she was warmest. A wet field in early morning. "'The secret path,'" she said, mischief curling at the edge of her voice. "That's what they call it in Vietnam."

In the morning, not unexpectedly, the homily (or hidden letter, or whatever it was he had written the previous day) was gone. Crumpled here, misarranged there. Fully lost to posterity. Which was a good thing, all in all: for Sefadhi it would have been akin to a piece of burning paper, a torch held up to all the chapters they'd completed. And she had answered everything in it without having to look at it. We build our great monuments of words, and then the earth shakes, the fires roar down from the hills, and all of them are gone except the parts we carry inside.

The days of spring went on, flowers ablaze in the mountains, the skies cloudless and exalting, the foothills so full of wild mustard that at times it felt as if they were walking through avenues of light. The whole state on fire, rejoicing, while the two worlds in his life he tried to bring together both seemed to recede and pull away from him— his thesis recalcitrant, as if his distrust of the words had transmitted itself to the paper; she needing at the first touch to jump back, like a girl who's put her finger on the stove.

"All this time together and I still don't know what's important to you," he said one day, when they were lying together in the afternoon, the room washed with light and silence.

"I don't know myself. If I did, I'd tell you."

"But you must have some sense."

She looked at him as if he hadn't understood a thing. "If I found out what I cared about, I'd have to bury it. Otherwise—I don't know—it would bury me."

He watched her in the mornings—she nearly always woke up hours after he did—and collected all the reasons he'd ever had to love her. She was a good sleeper, hardly stirring where she lay. She gave herself up to the peace and then held it close for hours and hours on end. When she faced the light, the sun caught the gold in her hair, just where it framed her eyes; her small mouth looked not just content, but able to be itself, shy, with not a trace of self-consciousness. One of the things she'd taught him, as he watched her fear give way at times to radiance, was that self-consciousness is the exact opposite of self-confidence.

When she began to smile in her sleep, and he saw her rising up towards the day, he fetched lemonade or juice for her, and waited by the bed so that he would be the first thing that she saw; she was trustful when she woke, fresh with all the places she'd been, and forgetful of herself: if they couldn't come to an understanding then, they never could. He pulled back the thin shades that filtered some of the light; she reached for him, pulled him under the covers, turned from the light, and buried her head in his chest, his shoulders.

One day, when she was in this open state—he couldn't try it any other time—he said, very slowly, quietly, "Do you think I could meet your mother sometime?"

She stiffened and he felt ice. Everything on her body grew hard, tense, and the way in which she answered was not panicky or terrified, but cold.

"Why would you ever want to do that?"

"Because we're stuck. We can't go forward until we've come to terms with this great weight you carry round with you everywhere you go. I feel I'm always in her company even though I've never met her. At least if I do, maybe we can work towards an answer."

"She hates me," she said simply. "That's how she gets her life. That's what she feeds on. She's everything that makes you want to run away."

"Then the only way to be rid of that fear is for me to come to terms with her."

She pulled back so she could look at him. There was a touch of gold in her blue eyes, and their shape, faintly Eastern, touched him; but the eyes were closed to him now, everything that was soft in them turned off.

"I know what you're going to say. I see why you say it."

"Then why do you bring up exactly the thing I've come here to get away from?"

"Because I think she's the part of you we have to look at and get past."

"You mean the needy and pathetic part?"

"I mean the part that's scared of its own beauty."

She stopped at that, and turned away from him so all he could see was her hair, her back: in her, not the part that spoke of hope or vulnerability. Her back was rigid, chill; it was what was used to being pressed against the wall.

"I only mean that, as long as you keep her as this kind of monster you carry round inside you, she'll always be there, and there's nothing we can do with her. Or about her."

"Tell me about it."

"And your father's not going to help us, from what you say."

"My father's perfectly happy as long as you leave him alone. All he wants is to be left in his own orbit."

"Would it help, do you think, if I met him?"

She looked as if she'd just been through a sudden death.

"If you met him, you'd become part of them. You'd become everything I'm trying to avoid in my life.

"I think it's hard for you to understand." Her voice was softer now. "You don't have a family. You're off in your own world, on some kind of mountaintop, alone. I'm not. Everything I love, they try to destroy. Anything that makes me strong or independent, they want to take away. Once, when I was very small, I came home from school and I found that all my animals were gone. Every single one of them. My mother had gone into my room and put them in a trash bag and taken them away so I'd never see them again."

"Because she worried you loved them more than you loved her."

"I came back home, it was early afternoon—I was six or seven—and everything in the room was different. I asked Silvia—the woman who cleaned our house, my friend, the only one I trusted in the house—and she said she hadn't been in my room at all. And then I knew that anything I tried to love, my mother would destroy. That the only way I could have a life was by shutting the door and pretending to care for nothing."

He said nothing. He could say that California was the place where you could put the past behind you, and that nothing need be as complicated as we like to make it seem. He could tell her of all the blessings of her childhood, in this privileged place far from all the Iranian had told them about his country. He could talk about the promise, the Sufi poets, and the feeling—she couldn't deny—that there was a light running through everything, and that it was true as the dark.

But to do so would be to do what she could never forgive in him, and to bring out of her the mother who was in hiding. For what he couldn't say to her was that the only times she described herself perfectly were when she talked about her mother; and that to call her mother "evil" or dark or irredeemable was to say some very dark things about herself. Better to assume the woman was just lonely and embittered and scared, frustrated with her life, and living through the only person she felt she could control—the daughter who took after her—than to say that the woman was a force of evil that nothing could cure.

The dialogue between them, though they never said it out loud, was a theological one, about possibility; and it hardly even seemed funny any more that the person from the Old World was the one who was telling the one from the land of promise that things could be improved. He thought of Kristina and realized that whatever was in

Camilla came from Camilla and not her environment. And yet the notion—the part of her that feared being like her mother—was like one of the great boulders in the road that came down after a storm: as long as it was there, no one could move past it, forwards, and every time they reached a certain stage in the road going up, they'd have to turn back and go down once again. Into everything she feared.

He took the long way round to Sefadhi's—a trick he'd learned from her, he thought—and as he made his way across the fields, he saw the students around him disassemble their lives and cast out from shore. Old now, in their nineteen years, they were ready to move on; the very street on which he lived was being pulled down, as a stage set might be, so that it could be made new again in the fall with the latest group of hopefuls. As the semester moved towards its close, and summer, young lovers wandered into something more serious, or splintered off and fell away; mattresses moved out into the streets again, and the boxes that had disappeared inside the makeshift apartments and lives started coming out again.

Sefadhi was as much responsible, legally, for the thesis as he; and yet more powerless as he saw it slipping further and further behind. "I am tempted to wish you had found those manuscripts now," he said, handing him a tray of pistachios and shooting his cuffs. He would never lose hold of himself in public, at least no more than he had done that evening on the beach: his discipline had taught him that much. And yet his anxiety, his disappointment showed in the way he turned away from his student after the handshake, looked down towards his calendar as if to take stock of how many weeks were left before the summer.

"I thought I was losing you to a spy novel before: a novel written by an Englishman." The English still being the root of all evil in Persia, a euphemism for "infidel," though it was something they had agreed to ignore till now.

"Instead you lost me to"—he corrected himself in time—"an emptiness."

"Is there anything I can do to help?"

"No. I think this one I'd better conquer alone."

"Numbers will be crunched. Figures will be counted up."

"I'll try to get something done. I've lost the thread somehow."

"I realize that. I try to tell them that."

His voice dropped, to something gentler. "Just give me something. Anything I can work with."

"Give me two more months."

"University regulations decree that I give you two more months. They further decree that I give you no more than that. Find a new translation of Eckhart, *The Cloud of Unknowing*, use it as a flashlight to train on Rumi. Write on Peter Brook's transmutation of Attar, his carrying of *The Conference* to the farmworkers of California. Write on anything, just so I have something I can give my colleagues, my superiors.

"Just give me something."

Out in the corridor he bumped into a familiar figure, hurrying away in another direction, and realized that he hadn't spoken to Alex since the surprise meeting in the parking lot. It had been a long time since they'd gone so many weeks without talking.

Alex looked as startled as he did, but he was never one to duck a confrontation. "You have time for a coffee?"

"I'd like nothing more. Let's go."

They talked of deadlines and fellowships and summer plans, everything but what they were thinking about, as they made their way to the café beside the lagoon. On the terrace the light was munificent, coming in off the sea and across the water between the eucalyptus trees so it seemed to wash over them like a private blessing. The reason they'd both come here, in a way, all around them: the smell of the sea, the sporadic gulls, the sense of long horizons.

"Sophie's gone home, I take it?" It was as good a way as any of moving towards what concerned them.

"For her studies. She's young."

"I'm sure she likes it here."

"She loves it." He smiled, to be using the word he usually danced away from.

"And Ixtlán?"

"It prospers. It grows and expands and builds new towers. No place that is nonexistent ever seems to go into decline."

It wasn't true, but he sipped at his coffee and said nothing.

"You? The deadline comes this summer, no?" It wasn't like him to be so tentative.

"Unless I get an extension. A lifeline to save me from the deadline." He was sounding like her, he realized, hiding out from truths behind words.

"You sound strange these days."

"How so?"

"The more time you spend with the Sufis, the more you sound like a Hollywood wise man. Speaking in riddles like the mysterious stranger from the East."

"It's probably her influence, too."

"You think so?" He had clearly been waiting for the question for weeks; his answers had been well prepared.

"What happened between you?"

"Nothing." Was Alex for once trying to be kind? "It was nasty, brutish and short."

"You never met her parents?"

"Never. We saw one another a few times, three weeks, maybe four; and then no more."

"What happened?"

"I saw her house one day, I thought about where she came from, and I realized it was hopeless."

"Like all the rest."

"So she said. I told her that in B.A. we have ghosts and bad dreams already. We don't need to come to California to meet more."

"And she said what?"

"She looked sad. She didn't say anything."

It sounded true, like everything she'd told him.

"Brutal as ever, eh?"

"Brutal is better than sweet." A softness, almost a solicitude, came into his friend's voice. "You know that, don't you, John? Giving someone like that hope is a kind of cruelty."

The talk with Sefadhi should have been the prompt for him to go quickly through the ritual movements and get his thesis over and done with: it was only a formality, a kind of ceremony in the church of scholarship, and no more was required than that he come in, kneel before the altar, and then be gone. But to do any of that seemed obscene when she was in the next room, crying out for help. Four months from now, the poems would be behind him, and he'd be looking for a job. But she, wherever she was, would be somewhere very close.

He got up and looked in on her as she slept, and thought again how it was only when she was truly calm that she could begin to acknowledge that she was haunted; only when she felt encircled that she could face the "demons" she talked about. Paradise is truly lost, he thought, as soon as a subtext snakes beneath every sentence.

He went to fetch her morning juice, and when she reached out for him reflexively, eyes closed, he said, "I've been thinking. . . ."

Instantly she was on full alert, her eyes looking straight at his.

"No, not like that. Something you'd be happy about." She closed her eyes again, as if it had been just a dream, and he thought that it must be like living in Beirut: always waiting for the next explosion.

"Mmm," she said, stroking his chest from where she lay, as if to get him to stop talking.

"Do you want to take a trip?"

Again she opened her eyes and looked at him, everything in her apprehension. Maybe this was his way—his roundabout way—of trying to get rid of her? Maybe he was planning to introduce her to somebody else? What was the small print she couldn't see?

"What kind of trip?"

"Nothing very dramatic or exotic. But I've got to do some research" (it wasn't true, but it would put her at ease), "and I thought maybe you'd like to come along. I told you we'd go somewhere together one day."

"You mean it? Really and truly?" When she was young, she'd told him, her mother liked to give her presents. But if ever she really seemed to be enjoying one, her mother would wrest it back from her, as if to say, "Fooled again!"

"Really. You're always talking about the places you'd like to go."

"When do we leave? For how long? Where?"

"The where part is a secret; the when part could be tomorrow. Soon, in any case; my deadline's coming up."

"What should I bring? Would the black dress be right? Or that one I wore for Christmas? Will I need candles? Have you seen my *Calling All Angels* tape?"

It was touching, always, to see how ready she was to try again: it was the California he'd imagined from afar, eager for the next possibility—though when he'd imagined it he'd never thought that possibility could be just a way of stepping around reality.

"It's only a few days, though I wish it could be longer. But it's a simple place: just bring yourself."

She kissed him quickly, then began to get her things together—the lack of emphasis from him was itself a reassurance—and as she did, she said, to show him she was happy, "I think I have a few days. Would the rest of my life be long enough?"

Next morning, she woke up early and started moving things into his car. It was like a military operation—a packed bag, a carry-on, a shopping bag bursting with books, so many contingencies and possibilities that she couldn't use them all in a month. As if she were staking everything on this. He looked around, and saw that the chaos of her car was now all over his; even the map was buried under a pile of old magazines, a scatter of cellophane bags, a blue swimsuit, and a pack of cards and some goggles.

They got in and started driving, and he saw in the mirror dresses banging against the back window: the cocktail dress she said she'd wear for a special occasion, a nightdress she'd bought for some long-ago romance—"peach satin," as she called it—the black dress she'd worn for the dervishes, all stacked on hangers in the back like the characters she might play for him. In England, he thought, people have costumes, but no chance for changing their roles; disappointment is hardly possible.

They drove east, off the freeway, on small country roads that ran through avenues of trees, the signs on the sides of the road, handwritten on cardboard, offering strawberries, melons, avocados for 99 cents or 25 cents each. The pickup trucks parked by the fields, the smallness of the shops and roads all taking them back to another country, farther south, where everything moved to a slower rhythm. Then the small road leaked into the interstate, and they began driving through the desert on a long empty stretch that led all the way to the Carolinas. Nothing but tract houses, laid out in occasional rows, like the flimsiest of hopes, inviting people to try new lives for themselves in the emptiness. Or sudden oases of coffee shops and gas stations, and then long stretches of just nothing.

He always had a sense of hopefulness when he was driving with her—the illusion, at least, of breaking through—and all he had to do, he thought, was turn flight into quest: make sure the place they were driving towards was better than the one they left. When they crossed the state line into Nevada, an hour or so after the place where a Sufi was building a circle of mud domes in the desert, suddenly the signs all spoke of new fortunes, windfalls of tumbling coins. Put your savings in the slot, they said, and a whole gush of gold pieces would make a new life for you. In Arizona, a few hours later, the motels were shaped like teepees, or Conestoga wagons, as on a children's mini-golf course, and people could fancy themselves someone else for a night. Escape, the open spaces said: make yourself new.

They drove into the parking lot of a listless two-story motel—it could have been anywhere—and after securing their anonymous space, they walked out into the late-afternoon glare. A long straight road, with fast-food signs and coffee shops, stretched into the nothingness beyond it. Teenagers drove by in trucks, and after they'd gone past, everything was silent. For as far as they could see, a kind of vacancy.

The next morning, they left early, before the heat could grow stifling, and the skies became distinctive, the cars and settlements looking scrappier than ever, so that it felt as if the heavens were the only imperial presence here. In the sharp-edged light it was hard to tell if they were driving into autumn or into spring.

"Where are you taking me?"

"You'll see soon enough. It's a secret."

"But it's scary, going into all this emptiness."

"You'll like it when we get there. You have to trust me." Around them, nothing but long road, deserted mesas, and light.

"Can we play a game?"

"What kind of game?" It would never be the dangerous kind, the kind where you ask another person what he most dislikes in you, or what he most wants to tell you but can't; it would be a game that tried to magic reality away.

It was. "We choose words, and then we make them into something else. And the closer they are to us, the more relevant they are to what we're doing, the more points you get."

"Points from whom?"

"Points from the referee who isn't here." She was changing "could be" into "is," he thought, and "never again" into "occasionally."

"Okay. You start, so I can see what's going on."

"NEXT GAS 91 MILES," said the sign they passed. Occasional names in the emptiness Indian or whimsical or meaning nothing at all.

She looked out at what wasn't there, and he could all but see her spinning letters in her head. Then, extended as if it were a gift, she said, " 'Rain.' And 'Iran.' "

It didn't seem a great triumph, and he wondered what she was really thinking of. "You know that 'rain' is a word for grace in their tradition? It's what they most pray for?"

"Of course I do. It's a desert," and, not for the first time recently, he was reminded of how much he underestimated her. She knew at least as much as he did about the Middle East.

"It's your turn."

He let his mind wander as he drove. He saw her bright face as she took him to the dervishes, and then through country as desolate as the one around them now. He saw her sobbing, and backing away from him, the dark spirit in her dream, even when she hadn't dreamed it, at her side.

" 'Rumi,' " he said slowly, choosing the very first word that came to him. "And 'Muir.' John Muir must have been here once."

"Lame," she pronounced, as it was, but he could tell she didn't want to stop. "It hardly has anything to do with us." He heard the "hardly" and saw again how she was beginning to wear his colors, his cadences: she sounded more European the longer they spent time together, and he wondered if finally she'd become so close to him that all the novelty and difference would be gone. The problem with actresses is that one never knows—maybe they never know—when their parts are chosen ones.

She said nothing, as if she were trying to push as close to him in her mind as she could, and then at last she announced, " 'Eden' and 'need.' "

It was a dangerous choice, both of them knew; it all but dared him to think of the things about her that were most unsettling.

"Well, the 'Eden' part at least is relevant. I don't know about the other."

"Now you."

"You're too good at this."

"You can't give up so soon."

"Okay, let me see if I can come up with one more pair." The light across the far mountains was more than ever like something in some old allegorical painting, about heavens and the fight with earth.

"You're going to laugh."

"I won't."

"Okay. 'Sufi' and 'if us.' "

"That's awful," she protested. "It means nothing. It's terrible. And it's two words. You can't do that."

"You never told me the full rules before. Anyway, it's relevant."

"Just barely. It doesn't mean anything at all."

"Shall we stop?"

"One more. A last one." And very quickly, as if she'd been planning it all along, she said, " 'Sacred.' And 'scared.' "

He looked over to see what lay behind the choice, but there was so much in her face, of delight and apprehension, and the wish to put herself on his side, that he said nothing. "You're too good. I give up." The long, straight road stretched on before them.

The game had beguiled a few hours, and the afternoon was moving on by the time they came to a small road in what seemed to be a blank nowhere: a narrow, two-lane path between high mountains and the occasional adobe house along a thin dirt road. The sky was throwing its punctual late-afternoon fit of pique, and the skies around were turbulent and visionary. He pulled onto an unmarked trail, and the car began jouncing and juddering over potholes and bumps. The path was unpaved, and the car found itself hurtled into puddles, and propelled this way and that across the rough ground.

"This can't be right."

"I think it is."

"You really know where you're going?"

"I think so. I hope so. This must be the right road—there aren't any others for miles."

As they bounced and bumped from side to side, the heavens turned jet-black above them, and suddenly, from what had not long before been a cloudless sky, a furious, penitential rain came down, as if announcing the end of the world. Hailstones beat against the front of the car, the windshield, the windows, and the roof, and as he drove into what seemed to be a downpour of small rocks, the car careened to one side of the road, and he stopped underneath a tree.

Pebbles continued beating against them, as if flung by angry children on every side, and when they abated the rain came angrily down, so strong they couldn't see a thing. The road ahead, the road behind, invisible.

"It's scary," she said. "I feel like we're in the Old Testament."

"We seem to be drawn to clouds. We're always in a storm." And she said nothing.

Then, again, "You sure this is the right road?"

"Absolutely. They don't have signs where we're on our way to. That's one reason people go there."

Then, as suddenly as it had come on, the rain desisted, and the storm moved over the mountains far away. He started up the car again, and they began to proceed once more towards their unknown destination, the puddles wider than before, and deeper, the car more buried then ever, the skies above all a furious radiance.

"You've never been here before?"

"I came close once. I was here to look in on the Penitentes, during the crucifixions they stage at Easter."

"In the Sangre de Cristos."

"Yes."

"And was it what you'd hoped it'd be?"

"I never got there. They aren't so keen on scholars coming to see them, as you know. But I got to know the area a little, and I heard about this place."

"How come you never came?"

"I wanted to keep it in reserve. For sometime special."

She said nothing, and the silence in the car grew richer.

"I thought that if ever I needed to think about something, in peace and quiet, this would be the place."

As he drove, he saw tears gathering at the corners of her eyes. As they often did, but with a brimming fullness now.

"And then, last week, I thought it might be better to be here alone together. If you see what I mean."

"I'm touched," she said, and then said no more, because she was shaking in some quiet way, at the fact he hadn't given up on her, quite yet.

"I'm sorry. I didn't know you'd be upset."

"Don't be. I'm really touched."

The sun had nearly disappeared over the mountains by now, and already the heat of the day was leveling off.

"That—that you'd want to come to a special place with me," she said, and then she couldn't say any more at all.

They passed over a rickety bridge, gold in the sky now, and lavender, the imminence of dark, and when they pulled into a clearing, it was to see six or seven cars lined up, neatly, on a patch of grass. The air was singing when they got out, and the silence pulsed around them. She wiped her face clean, and they walked into the small bookstore that served as a reception desk, and the monk on duty, shrouded in a full white cowl, said, "Welcome. How was the drive?"

"Tumultuous."

"Yes. If you go along quickly now, we'll be singing vespers in five minutes."

A straight path passed through the darkening desert, the chill of night coming on, the first stars above the peaks, and they walked into a clean, open space, with five wooden benches in a row, and a fresh, modern opening at one end. Behind the single cross that represented the altar was a large picture window that opened onto nothing but red rock. As if the real altar of the place was the cliff itself, its officers the light just visible at its tops and the noises, early lights of the desert.

There were ten or twelve monks lined up in rows, facing one another, at the front, and when they began to sing it had the sound of frail petitioners in the wilderness. Not rich and full and silvered, as in Westminster Abbey, but starker somehow, small and thronged, in this intimate, remote young space. The hymnal the two of them shared was old, cracked in places, and the words were all of warfare and blood. But the small space in the shadow of the cliff seemed consecrated to something other than the psalms. The monks bowed, as to the rock, and then, after a quick valedictory, proceeded in a straight line out into the dark, followed by the dozen or so laypeople in attendance. The sky now abundant with stars.

Dinner was served quickly, silently, in a room of blond wood tables, with windows everywhere: thick soup, large bowls, the lights of the desert outside, and the dark, making them feel as if they were dining with the heavens. When they walked out, they could just make out a silver trail of water running beside the "Enclosure," as it was called.

They put their things into the room assigned them, and then, not wanting to smudge the place with talk, went out again, and walked into the desert night.

"Do you want to see what the chapel looks like in this light?"

She nodded, and they followed the path, lit by stars, to the large structure that towered over the whole community. A single candle glowed at its entrance. Another sat under a Virgin, by the altar; another under an ancient depiction of the Mother and Child. There seemed nothing but candles in the place, and they sat in chairs, on far sides of the room, and closed their eyes, caught their breath, said prayers.

Then he stepped out, and she came soon after. They made their way, saying little, to the stream, and walked beside it for a few minutes. They could hear small animals—a squirrel, perhaps, or rabbits— in the undergrowth; the water made a soft song as it ran over rocks in the dark.

"It's calm here. It's hard to think of anything else."

"And when you do, it seems better than it really is."

She smiled, and went exploring, picking up rocks, bending down to see how deep the water ran, and what was caught inside it. Far away, the few rooms in a circle sat with their faint lights in the dark. The sound of foraging, of water running over rocks, water everywhere in the distance, as in Granada.

"I like the person I am when I'm with you."

"I'm glad."

"You like the parts of me that I like. I guess I've said that before."

"Not in the same way."

"It's never happened before."

Then her voice stopped, and he didn't pick up the thought. They sat, together and apart, on the rock, by the stream, the rooms in the distance. When it seemed time to go back, the little cell they entered was furnished with starlight and silence. Its two simple beds were pressed against opposite walls, and above each of them, on the wall, was a cross. A lectern sat by the window through which the stars, the desert came. A short typed list of rules asked for respect of solitude and silence.

When they awoke, the light coming in through the uncurtained windows, there were bells ringing with jubilation in the distance, and when they stepped out for breakfast, the day was immaculate. There was a desert sharpness in the air, and the monks were everywhere, going about their rounds, preparing food and cells, as precise as a regiment going through a well-practiced maneuver.

"I think I'll go and explore," she said, and he was touched by the gesture: a way of leaving him in the aloneness he'd said he'd wanted once. He sat in their small room in the morning sun and tried to think himself into another desert, where man felt vulnerable and alone with presences far greater than himself. The vast open space the mosque re-created.

When he looked out, towards lunchtime, she was sitting far off, against a rock, in a broad-brimmed hat, a sketchpad before her, intent. She had found the courage here to let go a little, and sat in her flowered dress, hair falling to her waist, like someone who'd kept D. H. Lawrence company. "I'm going off with Hilda," she said when they met at lunch. "She knows a way into the mountains," and he thought how wary she was of new contacts in her usual life.

In the evening, when they made their way back to the rocks on which they'd sat before, she said, "It's amazing. I feel cleaned out."

"I'm happy. That's what I hoped."

"And you?"

"Me, too. Like a cup left full of water in the sink, and all the impurities come to the top."

"It's what you write about."

"Write about, but don't experience."

It became their daily rite, to walk out after dark to the rock and share what the day had brought, though their words grew more sparse with the passing days, and soon it seemed there was no need for any at all. They sat across from each other on the rocks, and nothing moved but stars.

One night, as he bent down to pick up a pebble, she stole up behind him and kissed him on the fleshy part of his ear. The sudden tingle went through him like a shock; the latent sensuality of the place released in a torrent. It was an arousing site, with its restraints, its barriers; it took them back to their early nights together.

The next night, when he slept, he was walking by some holy place beside a river—Greece, perhaps, with its great rocks and high blue skies—and then, for some reason, the person he was with, trying to make patterns out of words, was gone. He could see the answer she'd been looking for, and he hurried to go and tell her. But by the time he stepped into her room, she was gone. And he was left with a curious knelling sense about him. The same dream as before, in Damascus: he'd had the answer, but it had come too late.

When he drifted back into his waking self, he knew, with the certainty of dream logic, that they were over. They couldn't be together. He looked across to where she slept, her hair spread out beneath her (she didn't tie it up here), a faint smile on her pale face, and saw her perfectly at peace. The straps of her nightdress had slipped off her shoulder blades, and they looked so pale, so vulnerable in the faint light that he went over and kissed them, one time each.

She stirred in her sleep but didn't wake, reached for his hand, and clasped it to the space between her breasts. Her skin was warm there, and he didn't know how much she was in the room, how much somewhere else. He stood by the bed, his hand on her chest, her hand on his, and then, suddenly, bells were ringing everywhere, marking vigils.

He went out into the dark, she still asleep, and saw the single line of monks, in white, all hooded, walking towards their prayer.

Their last night there, both calm and happy to forget what awaited them when they got home, they went to the rock they had appointed as their own and looked up at the stars, across to the mountains, following the trail of the silver stream for as far as it would take them. "On this rock I build my church," he said, half joking, but serious, too, because the words were catching here. "That's what I need," she said. "Not a church necessarily; but a rock."

The silence fell between them, they heard movement in the brush. It was the first time, he thought, they'd been out in the world together, presented themselves to others as a couple. This was not the real world so much as its annulment—its transcendence—and yet it was a start; they had the beginnings of a public life outside themselves now.

She had begun throwing pebbles into the stream, and it was he now who put a hand on her arm, lightly, to point out the star shooting across the skies. The pebbles, one after another, sent ripples all the way out to the bank, and then there was no room for anything but stillness; they were her way of saying she was happy, didn't want to go. The place had not cured her fidgetiness, her habit of looking this way and that, so life wouldn't catch up with her; in a sense it had agitated it, as if by reminding her of what she didn't have. But she had been transfigured in the light—there was no other word for it—and a whole face she carried with her, of anxiety, had fallen away.

"It's amazing," she said at last, throwing the pebbles into the stream, again and again, watching the moonlight shake. "I feel really moved to be here, privileged in some way."

"I'm glad. You're moved by the place?"

"By the place. By you, by me, by everything."

"By me?"

"I get to see you in your element here; what you're like when you're alone. I get to see the person who sits at his desk and prays for everything to work out right. And really believes it will."

She looked across to him from where she sat, the world black and silver around them.

"But you look worried somehow?"

"Of course I'm worried."

He reached a hand towards her. "Can I do anything to help?"

"No. You're the problem."

"But you said a minute ago . . ."

"I know I did. I said I was touched, and I am. Deeply touched, by everything I can't be myself. I see you here, and you're so content—yourself—so full of things you want to do, so free, and it makes me feel like a rock around your neck. Petty and unworthy and clinging. You don't need me."

"Of course I do. That's why I brought you to a place I'd always thought I'd come to by myself."

She looked at him, aghast.

"How can I take you away from this? You're happy here. You need your time alone."

"I'm happy with you."

She went back to throwing pebbles in the stream, and he thought that the person whom he could speak to best in her—womanly and full and calm—was the one who was calm enough to see they couldn't make it.

"It isn't you. I mean, it is you. But it isn't only you; it's everything. I feel opened up here—I can say anything. And when I can, I see . . ."

She let the thought trail, as did he. In their cell that night they lay, each in a narrow bed alone, facing the same direction.

The next day, when they stopped in at the bookstore to say their goodbyes and offer thanks, she started talking to the monk on duty, and he could see that she was trying to do anything she could to keep them here. This more than ever for her a departure from what she saw as Eden.

"I feel stupid asking you this," she said, though the monk was clearly not surprised, and was used to seeing people sorry to go back into the world, "but I couldn't help thinking. You live here all the time, so I guess it's not Paradise for you, but, I know it sounds crazy, and I'll bet everyone asks you this . . ."

"They do," he said, "and you're right. I do miss things in the world. As much as you would; more, perhaps." His face was tanned, but the glow in him seemed to come from something else. His words came out distinct and clear as pebbles he'd pulled out from the stream. "I'm not the master of all our disciplines. I never will be. Sometimes I wish we could sleep in. I wish there were more people to help out around the refectory, the store. This isn't a peaceful place or an easy place, however it may seem to you. I have all the usual human wishes." The sentences had been polished by the silence all around them.

"But"—now he looked almost embarrassed, for the first time— "if you asked me what I really miss, more than anything, I'd have to say, the chance to share the blessings of this place with someone I care about. There are all the brothers, of course, and the prior—we see him on a regular basis. But they have blessings of their own. I wish there were some way I could transmit this—whatever it is—to the people who need it most."

"That's where we come in," he said, because he felt the monk had said all he wanted to.

"You do. Come in again. And drive safely home."

After they reached the main road, and turned back in the direction of the interstate, they said nothing for a long time. Not out of emptiness, but the opposite: a fullness that doesn't want to be disturbed. They were back on the early drives, he felt, up in the hills, or in the early nights, long, wandering explorations till the light came up. In the part where they were silent, there'd never be any difficulties between them.

They were still in the desert when night fell—it was a long, long drive—and at times they couldn't see any other lights in the night around them. When they reached California, and the narrow roads of orchards and artichoke stands, she rolled down a window and let the wind come in, extending her legs into the darkness as they drove.

When he touched her thighs, as they passed through darkened villages, she raised her hips, so more of her was available to him.

As they arrived at the coast, however, and turned north, the lights, the signs growing more familiar, they could feel their daily selves waiting to take them in, devouring and unstoppable as in-laws, waiting to pull them back into the old pleasantries and arguments. "It's like when you're young, not wanting to go home again," he said, and she said, "Not only when you're young."

At last they saw the small light of his house, fragile against the large expanse behind it, and, parking on the street, began taking out the boxes. "We can do it in the morning," he said, because they were tired, and the air of finality would be too clangorous. When they went in, the red light was blinking, desperate, and there were letters on the table collected by the man next door.

"Welcome home," she said, as if to say that the end had now begun.

. . .

The desert had cleared something out in them, even if it had left them in a seeming emptiness with no external props or supports. "It's funny," she'd said, as soon as the sanctuary began to fade from view behind them. "It's like being lonely together. Except there it's okay, because you're not alone." "I know what you mean," he'd answered, for it was true: in the company of bells and monks and high, vaulting skies—the cliff itself a place of worship—it felt as if they were companioned in the deepest sense. But by the time they'd entered his house, their lives were cluttered again, and there was no way of being in this room (where the books lay, the thesis, and any foreseeable future) and that one (she sprawled across the sheets) at once.

When he turned towards her in the bed that night, she was flame, her skin so hot he thought she might be running a fever; but afterwards, when he turned away to sleep, he felt ice everywhere. As if the fever had passed from her to him.

"I ought to go to the library," he said next morning, seeing her still in bed, and she, in her instinctual way, burrowed deeper into her hole of blankets and pillows and sheets. "And there's the seminar this afternoon. Do you think you'll be here when I get back?"

She had buried herself under the covers.

"I just want to know, so I'll know whether to hurry home or not."

"No need to hurry." The voice came up to him from her hiding place. "I have something in L.A." After all this time, back in the wariness of the first afternoon, when each of them made up appointments that didn't exist, as if afraid to step out into a clearing. Though now the wariness was not habitual, but earned.

"If you could just leave the key by the stove when you go."

"Will do. Have a good seminar."

He tried to find the perfect line from the poets, to make them laugh, to sweeten the moment. But nothing came to mind.

He had nothing really to do once he got to the library—it was just a way to be away—and when he arrived, the thesis further away from him than ever, he went up to the eighth floor, where no one thought of Sufis, and sat in one of the chairs overlooking the sea nearby. "In space things touch, in time they pass," he thought, though why Adela Quested was coming to him now, just after the shock of the Marabar Caves, he couldn't tell. "Man is in love and loves what vanishes, / What more is there to say?" When they'd learned the famous line at school, none of them had known the first thing about love or loss: it had been easy to quote Yeats.

Sefadhi had sent a message, through Eileen—he'd always choose to apply pressure indirectly—that an article in the *Persian Review* assessed the state of Iranian studies in the light of all the new materials that had come to light, now that the community was global. Texts had even been dug up in Italy, of all places, and there was an expectation that more would show up in California; but, having seen how his adviser frowned on such possibilities before, he knew it would be a mistake to rise to the bait now.

He looked out at the great open spaces that lay before him—what had brought him here, in a way. California had never learned what to do with limit; and yet without limit there was no faith. It was the loss of Shams that had caused Rumi to find faith in the truest way, not just the finding of Shams. It's not dreams that belief gives us—that's the easy part—it's the strength to deal with the abolition of dreams.

Anyway, Rumi had never had to see his love grow old—or his Beloved; the death had saved them both from that. And then, looking at his watch, he saw it was two-fifty-eight. The seminar would be beginning in two minutes.

He raced down the steps, taking them two at a time, down eight floors, and sprinted across the campus, past the lazy clusters of kids at picnic tables, looking up at him in surprise from their yawning days. By the time he'd run up to the fourth-floor conference room, too much in a hurry even to wait for the elevator, Kevin was already well embarked on his talk on "Religion as a Grown-up Fairy Tale," drawing, no doubt, on his years with Bettelheim.

"Even as children," Kevin was saying as he came in, looking around for a spare chair, "even as children," underlining with his repetition the intrusion brought upon them by the latecomer, "we have some intimation of a world beyond our own, another realm behind the garden wall, as you might say. We do not have to see it or describe it; we feel it in our bones. We are captive to what you might call 'metaphysical nostalgia.' The longing, as C. S. Lewis might have said, for the far side of the wardrobe."

He looked around so all could fully appreciate the wisdom, and then prepared to continue. But just as he was starting up, the disheveled intruder suddenly broke in. "Children haven't been told to act as if this is the only truth there is," he said, and he saw several heads look up, as if startled. The rules of the seminar were so well known they didn't need to be spelled out. The speaker read his paper, and only when he was finished did questions or rebuttals begin. As the interruption subsided, looks stole around the room: "John Macmillan's well and truly lost it."

"We might therefore provisionally assert," Kevin began again, trying to find his footing, "that religion is at some level a sanctioned fairy tale through which society transmits its lessons to the young. It is the story told around the campfire, by which the elders pass on and down their customs and beliefs."

A few students were taking notes so furiously that it was a safe bet they were jotting down ideas for theses of their own; others looked at Kevin with such rapt attention that they were presumably off in Vietnam or the Amazon, collecting data from their field trips. "Religion, then"—the speaker pushed his way on—"is the way we ritualize and encode, the way we sanctify, you could say, the stories that bind the community together. The gods are myths enjoining us to act as if the stories of the gods were true."

Kevin paused again, to let everyone take in this cunning formulation.

"Hence my phrase, 'Religion, the Grown-up Fairy Tale.' Religion is a fairy tale for those of us ostensibly grown up. Religion is the fairy tale that's grown up with us, our companion. And religion is a fairy tale that's grown into a structure so enveloping we could call it the institution of society itself. It is, we might usefully say, the spiritual equivalent to the Bill of Rights—or the Highway Code, at least."

"But there's more to it than that." He couldn't seem to stop himself, though again people looked up (Sefadhi, in his seat, discreetly looked away). "Stories are more mobile than that. They change as we do, assume different colors depending on how we look at them; just as you say, they grow up as we do. They aren't static narratives; they fit themselves around us like our shoes."

He could feel the excitement in the room, made keen by a sense of helplessness: the whole well-oiled juggernaut of the seminar was hurtling out of control, and since there was nothing they could do about it, the people around the table had decided to enjoy the sensation of novelty. It was the first real thing that had happened all year.

"What if fairy tales bind us together in a kind of dissent?" he went on, as if he hadn't noticed how the room had changed around him. "What if they work outside the laws of society, and even against them? They speak for subversion as much as for order."

"Quite so," said the chairman, seeing his chance to rescue things. "The value of transgression. Saturnalia, the Lord of Misrule, all of that. We need ways to release, or express, our demons as much as to go about our business."

"Mardi Gras," said a small voice in the corner, and the chair, relieved, said, "Exactly so. Examples can be found in every field."

"But no, it's something more than that," the intruder said, and now the room was electric. The rumor had it that he'd been off ever since his trip to Damascus the year before—"under a foreign influence," as the person who knew him best, Alejandro Mazzini, said. It was said he'd stopped handing in chapters to Sefadhi, and was running off in search of manuscripts that didn't exist; he'd taken the Sufi madness all too seriously. "A story has as many secrets as a person does. Hidden implications, shadow meanings, layers that lead to other layers. And the most interesting part of a story is the part we don't see at first, where the clues are all hidden. The princess in the tower asks the gallant knight to save her, say. But maybe the real meaning of the story is that the knight is moved to the quest by pride, or stubbornness. Maybe he's only using the princess as a way of playing out some urge that has nothing to do with her at all. Maybe, as the Gnostics say, she's only a reflection of another part of him, a higher self that is imprisoned, and so his risking his life for her has nothing to do with her, but only him."

The room was silent; he'd plunged off a cliff, and no one else would follow.

"And maybe"—now there was no stopping him—"maybe, when he breaks in on her little room in the tower, he sees that he's really the captive, and she's the one who can release him. That he is carrying the castle with him everywhere he goes, while she, in her tiny chamber, is quite free. And maybe, further, when he carries her down the stairs and out into the world, she's terrified. She doesn't want to leave the castle, everything she knows. She's never been on a horse before. The knight has thrown himself into the story and made it his own. Without even noticing that it's not the story he had thought it was."

"A great burst of eloquence," the chairman noted dryly, not unhappy to be given the chance to exercise his power. "And, to go back to Kevin's thesis—our reason for being here, after all—what do we think of religion as a form of collective, even we might say collectivist, myth-making?"

And Kevin took the reins again, and spoke up for law and order.

By the time the presentation was over, there was very little time for questions, and the buzz that was running through the room clearly had to go outside with its news, to be released. Someone said something about Jung, and Vijay Mishra, from England, asked, as he always asked, about Northrop Frye. Elaine, who had almost completed her dissertation on female shamans in Korea, said, "Maybe we could say that fairy tales are our way—our only way—of privileging the ghosts that our official textbooks marginalize."

"A fine way to conclude a memorable session," said the chair, relieved to have brought the train safely back to its sidings. "We meet again three months from now with"—he discreetly consulted his notes—"Emma, on Hildegard of Bingen."

"Thank you," said Sefadhi, as he brushed past him to the corridor. "I think you've just made my job of telling the Department you need special treatment much easier."

.   .   .

By the time he got home, taking the long way round, she was gone. He looked for a note on the desk, guessing that there would be none. He tried to see if she had left something of hers lying about, but she'd cleaned up before she left. The plates were back in the cupboards, everything was back the way it had been before she'd ever arrived.

Opening the closet, on a sudden impulse, he found it stripped of all her clothes. Previously she'd always kept something there, as a way of laying her claim to the space, and reminding him of her presence; mostly as a way to ensure that she'd always have a reason to come back.

When someone dies—he thought suddenly of Rumi, and all the ecstatic poems that had been keeping him company for years—a part of her disappears, and everything else that is suffused with her, the invisible part, grows more intense than ever. He smelled the ylang-ylang she'd kept for weeks by his bed. He saw she'd forgotten to take away the tea she'd brought for her monthly pains. Under a pillow, a long golden hair as from a fairy tale curled out.

When he went to bed, she was closer to him than she had been for months. He talked and talked to her all night, and when it was light blew out the candle, the blue and gold of Isfahan, that was the ornament of a shared romance.

The next morning, he made a list of all the places he would not go because he had gone before with her: an anti-map of sorts. He even put away all the unread books he had by women, in case one of the novels' scenes had a woman casting an appraising eye on men, and he saw her in the character. Yet whatever in him was taking all the precautions was not the part that might have gained from them. He rode back from the library that evening—the library had always been the safe place for being all alone—and when he saw a light on in the house, he accelerated all the way home; and then remembered it was he who'd left it on, in case she might unexpectedly return. A fool, he thought—maybe this was what she'd really left with him: her bitterness—is someone who longs for the very person he's just banished.

She did come back, a few days later, in mid-afternoon, but it was as if it were someone else, an amateur actress, doing a poor job of impersonating her. She said "Cool!" when she saw the new cups he'd bought—she'd never used the word before—and the cross above her low-necked dress was new, or new to him. The not-so-sure, maybe former lover reads all the same texts as before, but in a different light. She was wearing her hair up, he decided, so she could take out the pins for someone else.

"The deadline's coming up," she said.

"Five or six weeks. More, if I get the extension."

"And if you don't?"

She wanted him to help her, he suspected, and to make it easier for her to leave.

"If I don't, I have to leave the country. Abandon the thesis, as likely as not, and make another life elsewhere."

"Leaving me where exactly?" She was looking for things that would hurt her, and this time he obliged.

"Leaving you anywhere you want to be. You've got time, money, you can do anything."

He slept on the sofa that night—as if, again, he'd picked up her habit of coming upon the right gesture only after the occasion for it had passed—and the next day, seeing her lying in bed, unsleeping, waiting for something that would spring the lock, he came and sat beside her on the bed. "That park you were always mentioning? Did you ever go there?"

"How could I? I've been away." Her sister had told her about a place at the foot of the hills which no one knew about; they'd resolved to go there, long ago, and make it part of the private map they were drawing up in their heads.

The sun had come up by the time they went outside, struggling through the early-morning fog, and by the time they reached the empty parking lot on the far side of town it was hot. A small trail, hardly kept up, led back through the trees; insects of some kind whirred and jittered all around. They took the narrow path up into the woods, and after a few minutes came to a stream, thin and silver, running up towards the mountains. Large boulders, logs, and branches damming and redirecting the flow.

It was a smudgy, sultry, listless afternoon, the day seeming to twitter and whine around them, and as they dandled their legs in the water, walked along the bank, the gnats, or whatever they were, buzzed and swooped. It was sticky and scratchy and hot; the day pricked at them, at their faces, the exposed parts of their skin. She put on a summer hat to protect her from the sun, and when he saw her walking down to the stream in front of him, in the long white dress and hat he'd last seen in New Mexico, he came up behind her, and kissed the back of her neck.

Hands caught hands, released; the day was hot and the water cool.

She'd brought a book of Indian love poems to read him—less to draw him in, he felt, than to shut him out in some way, to remind him of all he was closing the door on—and when she sat down on the rock, as if to read to him, he went off exploring in the woods, deeper and deeper towards their darkness. The day drowsed on, dawdling and slow, a twitter everywhere, as she paged through the gold volume with its green inscription, reading the love poems to herself.

He walked back, crackling, over twigs and leaves, and when he came back through the trees there was nothing on the rock but the book, turned over, and the fancy white pumps she'd brought. He looked along and saw her upstream, holding her dress in the way he remembered from the very first night on the beach; the water splashed against her legs, and wet spots appeared on the dress. Then, as she stumbled against a rock, her hat fell off and her hair was all loose, in her eyes, in her mouth, across her neck, a broken angel's nest.

She came back, walking slowly, to where he sat, occasionally jumping when she hit her foot against a jagged point, or when the water suddenly grew too deep or cold. When she got back to the rock, he could see abrasions on her legs, small red cuts here and there, and when she leaned forward to kiss him, he tasted salt, sweat, hair; her legs left wet shadows on the rocks.

Her feet, her legs were cool and bare; her mouth had all the collected warmth of the drowsy afternoon. The flies, the gnats, were chattering, and from the far side of the trees they heard a car starting up, a truck perhaps, idling, footfalls, a scuttling dog. The water where it came off her legs was cool on him, her face cool and warm at once where she rested on his chest. The rock against his back warm on the naked skin, and the sun high above the trees hot in the bright afternoon.

They didn't say anything as they lay against the rock, in the small sanctuary of the riverbed, but when she leaned over to kiss him again, loose hair, wet mouth, cool legs, warm lips, he felt her thigh urging at his in the way he recognized. Her eyes were closed; her pale face was open to the sun. She made room for him in what she called her home, and when he was there, she just said, "Whatever you do, just stay there. Don't move." And as he did, she began to cry again, silently, as if to force out the last vestiges of whatever remained.

She left of her own accord a little later, and as he walked her out to her car, he found a letter sticking out of his mailbox, a blue airmail envelope of the kind he knew from England. It was Hussein, of all people, thanking him fulsomely (and on an Indian time-scale) for his help of many months before, and "the authoritative insight of your scholarship." Someone had come over from Paris, he was writing to say, also to look at the manuscript, and he, too, was a good man who understood the value of such things; but all he had done was confirm him in the wisdom of what the "English pandit" had said.

The light that was flashing on the answering machine would be Sefadhi, he thought, with some oblique reminder of the deadline, or Alex, asking him to a movie that would only bring her back into their company again; and when, towards nightfall, he pushed it, sure enough he heard the Argentine polish. "I will be away for a few weeks," his friend announced, "I find I have a hunger for the old," though as the words came out his listener saw someone very young, Sophie, in the sun, throwing her arms around and seeing where she might fall. Someone else was calling, a "friend of a friend," she said, about information she had on a lost manuscript—California the home now of imported hopes—and then there was a surer voice, as from a former life: Nicki, back in West Hollywood, "rather at loose ends," as she put it, "and wondering if you might have time for a visitor." He remembered the last time she'd come up to look in on him and, dialing the number she'd left, said, "Why don't I come and visit you there? Save you the drive and get myself out of the house?"

He'd caught her off-balance—done a Nicki on her, in effect—and all she could say in her surprise was, "Brilliant. I'm sure there's room enough for two."

She was staying in one of those bright new metallic places designed to consecrate L.A.'s status as a postcard, a fashion statement for Europeans, and the room was all white, with a hot tub on a terrace and a view of the hills through the smog. He took her out for sushi in the Valley, and as they talked he saw she wasn't acting only on her sister's behalf: somewhere along the way, she'd stepped out of the costume drama that is English life, and now she couldn't find her way in again.

After dinner was over, he took her up to Mulholland, to see the lights—Los Angeles always most enticing from a distance—and then they went down to the coast and followed it around, distant shouts reaching them as they drove past the arcade, the distant Ferris wheel, in Santa Monica. "It's always most attractive if you treat it as a playground," he said, and she looked over at him as he drove, not sure of what was coming over him.

He took the long way back, giving her the Anglo tour of Angeleno curiosities—the graveyards, the pink mansions and baroque leather bars—and when they pulled into the underground garage again, a liveried bellboy nodded them in, and the desk clerks, deft with this kind of situation, said "Miss Chancellor," as if she were returning with a takeout meal. She yawned in the elevator, but it was a yawn that didn't say "Leave me alone" so much as "Look at what I'm trusting you with."

"I for one am not going to waste the tub," she said when they got back into her suite, and he started to make himself busy with something he didn't need to do. He heard her changing in the bathroom, and as she came out, "It'd be a crime not to use it. When I'm back in London, no one will believe . . ." and then the rest of it was lost as she stepped out onto the terrace.

He'd taken pains to say nothing about Camilla over dinner—Martine knew already, in any case, and it was too complex a story even for him to figure out—but now, as he saw she'd left the door open behind her, he thought of the small figure in her white dress somewhere in the city, asleep and at peace, hardly guessing that another woman, in her stoical way, was crying out for his company.

He went out onto the small deck—she smiled up at him, wide awake—and the warm night hit him after the artificial cool inside.

"Coming in?"

"I don't think I should."

"Really? Just for a minute?"

"I think I should be getting to sleep. I have to leave early in the morning."

"Don't be a spoilsport." She was on the verge of asking right out.

"Martine," he said, though it was another name he was thinking of. "I don't think your sister would approve."

She looked away—explanations were a worse blow to pride than the rejection, especially when they said, so flagrantly, that they were taking your pride into consideration. A little later, as he lay on the couch, he heard her coming in, bare feet walking heavily on the plush carpet, and the door to the bedroom closing with surprising force.

In the morning, she was quick to remind him that his presence was no longer required—"I ought to be calling Martine for her birthday," she said, as he kissed her goodbye—and to tell him that he wasn't what her sister wanted, either. As he walked out into the corridor, he saw himself, a year before, opening his address book and seeing the date written out in a boy's hopeful hand. It would be one year to the day this weekend.

.   .   .

Sitting at his desk, he thought again about what the poems said: Give up on hope and you might as well give up on life. Give up on hope—this their shadow meaning now—and you were betraying what you claimed to hold. Doing, in fact, what he had always found so saddening in her: accepting defeat as a fact of life.

He picked up the phone, the madness still alive in him, and said, "Camilla: there's a special occasion coming up and I wondered if you'd be interested in joining me for it. A first anniversary of sorts. An achievement. I'll be marking the historic moment at seven p.m. this Sunday: I'm inviting a lot of people, but all of them are you." A year ago he'd have thought this pure insanity: masochism, or stubborn blindness, a refusal to learn from the mistakes of the past. But why had he come to California if not to step out of the range of such a voice?

He spent the next day making up a map—their map, the one they'd superimposed upon the world—and he drew up a kind of treasure hunt, as if a personal version of the Sufi metaphor. If she followed the instructions, she would start at the CD player and activate the song of Zanzibar (the second drive in the hills, the mist coming in and out of the car as they drove past turns), then open the refrigerator to take out the mango juice akin to what she'd given him in her sister's kitchen. Step 3 would lead her to the bed, where Yeats lay beside the candle with the colors of Isfahan. Step 4 would lead to what lay beside the candle and the book, which was him. Step 5—or so his instructions put it—would lead to herself, and the better person she always longed to find.

In other circumstances he would have shuddered at the foolishness of this; not long ago, he'd have looked at it with Nigel's eyes, or Alex's. But part of the point of the whole exercise was to show how "foolishness" could be redeeming sometimes: "You know 'silly' comes from the Old English *sælig,* meaning 'blessed,' " she had said once, with her unfailing gift for surprise, and he had replied, "As 'idiot' comes from the Greek for 'private person.' "

He pinned the note on the door at six-forty-five, and though the wind was up, the piece of paper was secure. It was still light, as it had been on the early drives, and the new candles he'd bought would keep on burning for several hours. He hadn't rung her to confirm she was coming; this was about a leap of faith, after all, a venturing of something in spite of everything that had passed. Die to expectations, and abandon your petty pride.

He waited and waited, and at nine o'clock—the light had faded over the ocean now, and the night sounds had begun—he got up and took the note down from the door. He pushed the PAUSE button down on the CD player, he blew out all the candles. *Déjà-vu*, he thought, can sometimes mean "twice shy."

A little before dawn, though it seemed several lives had passed through his head as he lay in the bed, the sentiments of the poems blurring into the life that was actually unraveling, and the arguments in his head gaining force and persuasiveness, as if they could put disappointment in a box—he heard a tapping at the window. A soft tap, unmistakable—it brought back taps and taps of many months before. He buried himself deeper in the sheets, and then he realized he was turning into her again: inviting someone to come and hiding when she arrived.

"Hello? Anybody home?" It was, as ever, her sweetest and most hopeful voice, the one she knew he couldn't turn away from.

"Hello? Johno? Are you there? It's me; I'm sorry I'm late."

To close the door on her was, in a sense, to give in to her, and admit that all her "monsters," as she often called them, were right; he'd put himself in a position in which he had to open up.

"Johno—you must be here. I saw your car outside. I'm bringing a surprise."

The high, sweet voice kept calling and calling, the tapping went on against the screen door, and finally he went over and opened the door.

"Thank you. I've brought everything."

In one great leap she collapsed onto the sofa, and books, brochures, tapes, and packages spilled out. She'd even brought a bottle for the party of ten hours before.

"I hope you don't mind. I wanted to get everything just right."

What could he say?

"At first I was scared," she went on, "and then I thought, 'He doesn't like me to be scared. I'll give him a present he'll never forget.'"

"Why should you be scared? I invited you."

"I know. But"—she looked at him, as if surprised—"you're mad, aren't you?"

"Not mad. Just defeated. You win. I give up."

"What do you mean?" For the first time something else came out of her voice, from behind the cheer. "What are you saying?"

"Nothing. You're right. I was stupid to think otherwise. You win."

"I brought you this," she said, and pulled out, fumbling at the bag, what looked to be a coffee-table book, in wrapping the color of imagined stars.

"Thank you."

"You're not going to open it?"

"Later, perhaps. At some more propitious moment." He took it over to the bedroom closet, and put it away in a corner.

"I wanted everything to be perfect."

"I'm sure you did. I know." The fight was out of him, and his very lack of temper terrified her.

"I knew you'd be mad at me. It's what Greg said, too."

He handed over, without a word, the present he'd bought for her—a small dime-store ring in which two waves intertwined so you couldn't tell where one ended and the other began. "I'm really tired. I hope you'll excuse me." Politeness in him meant distance: it was the wall he put up that was more resistant than any locked door. If he didn't leave now, the thought came, they'd burn so many bridges they wouldn't even be able to say hello again.

Up in the hills, the sun was just rising over the farthest mountain, and by the time he'd reached the spot below "their house," there was nothing but a sea of clouds below. Truly one could feel a god here, dangerously far from everything that aged or died.

"Maybe you're late," he said to himself, more vocal alone than he could be with her, "because you're late. Not because of what your parents did to you twenty years ago. Not because of any elaborate psychological mechanisms and a fear of intimacy, and a stubborn determination to destroy what you love. Not even because you want at some level to make things go wrong so that you can hide inside the comfort of your fears. Maybe you're late just because you're not good with time. As people have been late for centuries."

What the absent spirit might have said, he could not hear. When he got back to the house, the early morning already feeling exhausted, she was seated in the bed, bent over, writing a message of some kind on a large paper towel (the letters already blearing on the rough surface). She'd let down her hair and changed into her white nightdress; he could see the gloss she'd applied with her thin pencil. The strand of pearls around the pale neck said this was a person he couldn't hurt.

"Are you coming to bed?" she said, as if the world had just begun.

"Sorry. That's the last place I want to be."

"Is there anything I can do to make you feel better?"

"I don't think so. The part you probably want to touch went into cold storage sometime late last night."

"I wrote you this." She presented the paper towel to him as a little girl might show her parents the text on which her teacher had written "A." Already the words were wavering, almost blotched beyond his comprehension.

"I can understand if you never want to see me again. I'd never want to see me again if I were you. I never want to see me again even though I'm not you. I bet it feels like you've gone to all this trouble for nothing. It's not for nothing, but there's nothing I can say to make you believe that. I think I've used up all my IOUs. You've tried so hard to get the better of my demons, and I don't think anyone could try harder. But they've been in there a long time, and they don't give up easily. I could get down on my knees and say, 'Please, please, please don't give up on me.' But I'd only disappoint you again before long, and then I'd have to watch your heart break over and over. I guess the only thing I can say is 'I'm here if you want me.' "

Someone crying out for help, and yet, if he extended a hand to help her, he'd be pulled into the dark swamp, too. The Sufis never dealt with someone from a culture that hasn't had a chance to grow up or lay down roots.

"I wish it were different," he said, "but I've only got a few weeks left, and the fellowship . . ."

"I know. If we go on like this, we won't even be friends any more."

"See you in a few weeks, maybe."

"Maybe," she said, and when she walked to the door a little later, in her scruffiest clothes, she took even the candle by the bedside.

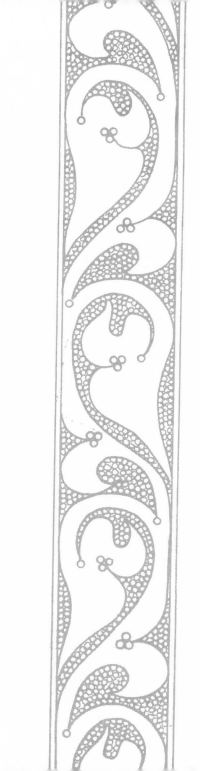

IV

Almost as soon as he heard the sound of the huge car turning the far corner, he threw himself into his poems with a cold fury, and though some of what he wanted to say, and what they said to him, sounded flat now, as remote as another man's prayer, some of it came to sudden life. The words came out in one impersonal rush, and he congratulated himself on having mistakenly destroyed the strange final chapter. "It's your way of being personal, I suppose," Martine had said in Paris, "returning to the impersonal. But it doesn't help much with the washing up."

The chapter he wrote now was on "Metaphor and Coincidence," and it was about how, if you live far enough away from the world, everything you do is a symbol, because the person who is doing it is not the person who will die. You enter a mythic space of sorts—a place where there aren't any clocks—and everything carries a resonance deeper than itself. You aren't yourself, but something more, and so everything you do, everywhere you go, takes on a different meaning. An abandoned house becomes an emblem of a future of which you can make anything you choose. The desert becomes the place where there are no props or signs or coordinates and the only protectors are wind and silence and space. The person you love becomes a hope.

The chapters came quickly now, and for a moment he felt himself back in the very space that Rumi had admitted him to: the rarefied, charged space where a door means an opening, and the city walls speak for the defenses you've built up. Metaphor was critical to the Sufis, he found himself thinking, because it was itself a metaphor: it said that behind the things we see, behind the people who speak, there lies another dimension, and that other person sees even the things of the world in the light of the eternal. "The nature of growth—of love or faith or anything—is that the person who thinks in terms of appointments and plans and dates gives way to the person who thinks of something deeper. The literal world cedes to the allegorical, and the geometric box from the marketplace becomes an emblem of God."

Occasionally, carried away by his chapter, he thought back to the first Persian poem he'd ever read—FitzGerald's *Omar Khayyám,* the most popular translation in the English language other than the Bible, so they said—and tried to imagine how some unknown Victorian might take the sentiments of the Persians and organize them into tidy quatrains.

> If, with the fire of love I burn,
> Away, away, I hope you'll turn,
> And yet, when all the earth is scorched,
> I'll leave you with a single torch
>
> A torch to light your slow, sad way,
> A torch to turn the night to day;
> A torch to guide you through the dark,
> Until, unknowing, you embark
>
> On boats that pass across the seas,
> Sudden as lightning, not by degrees,
> To a place you know as your deepest home,
> Next to me, and my love, in a gold-blue dome.

When he finished, though, he realized that his efforts were poorer by far than hers, as if he wanted to box up what he cared about into jokes or crossword puzzles. Precisely the habit that had made him saddest of all in her: to pretend to be a smaller person than she was.

The English word "symbol," he remembered, comes from the Greek *symbolon,* referring to one half of a knucklebone carried as a token of identity to someone who has the other half. Only when the two halves, the two people, are brought together does the whole have a meaning. "A metaphor is a species of symbol"—the words of Edward Hirsch jumped out at him from a book. "So is a lover."

That night, the next night, every night of the week, she kept him company as he'd feared she would. In the bed, hair falling about her face, soft hands reaching down, grey eyes losing focus, turning smoky. Years of reading Sufis, and he'd turned into an adolescent. When he got up to steady himself by reading the poems, he found, as he might have known had he been more conscious, that they were exactly what he didn't want to hear. He put them down as if he'd picked up burning metal.

Though he went to the library in the days—an uncontaminated space—she stole out towards him in the stacks, or suddenly appeared at the carrel where he'd been sitting the day after New Mexico, the morning of Kevin's seminar. He picked up a book called *Farsi Verse Forms,* and a piece of paper fell out from it: a picture of a tower, with a star above it, and a spiral staircase in its belly, going up and up to a figure with long hair falling to her waist. It looked like her—it looked like hers—but it might have been someone else, an accident playing on an overprepared mind. At the back of the book, he saw that it had been taken out from the library only two weeks before.

That night, "Johno" at his ears, her eyes fluttering as they did when her lips began to part. The feel of her mouth against his throat, her hair brushing his hips, and then the great gulps with which she'd cry, letting her face collapse into the vagueness that she feared.

A week or so later, the deadline still ticking away on his desk, everywhere he turned in the apartment, a letter arrived, the first one she'd ever sent him through the mail. The lettering was clear, as if she'd written it and written it beforehand; the postmark said "Los Angeles."

"Dear Johno," it began, and it was surprisingly free of crossings-out,

I won't say I'm missing you because you'd rather that I didn't. You don't like me to be negative or to talk about what I don't have when I do have so much to be thankful for. And I won't say, either, that I haven't thought of you—and thought of you and thought of you, till it all runs out in a wet mess. You said something about how what I called "love" was really "need." But at the level where I feel it, the words don't matter. It all hurts just the same.

I ask myself, when I'm feeling up to it, where did I go wrong? Did I make a mistake in loving you, or in not loving you enough? Was my mistake in admitting that I might miss you forever, or in acting as if I wouldn't? Now you'll say I'm sounding like a movie again, and maybe I am, because movies are about something real: much realer than those books you hide behind.

This is the part of the letter where I'm supposed to say something constructive. About everything I've learned, and how I've gained so much from loss. Just like your Sufis do. But I'm not you, and I don't have your spirit of sweet hopefulness. I'd love to share it but I can't. My experience doesn't bear it out.

So now I'm sounding senseless, and you can tell yourself you're well rid of someone so negative and self-pitying and crazy. And there's nothing I can say to that—I never could see why you had any time for me. Once you said I was full of false confidence, and another time you said I was scared, and I don't think you could see they came from the same place. Just different ways of making the same plea.

I sound like you, don't I? Everyone says I do—at least I sound different since we began spending time together. Your marks are all over me, inside and out. Everywhere I turn in me, I find the residue of you. I'll probably be in a new relationship by the time you get this, but you'll know it's not really me that's in it.

So here I am writing you a letter that sounds like an accusation. Which is my point, I guess. Even my love letters to you sound like accusations.

Oh well, I hope you're okay, and making up ground with your thesis. Maybe we can meet again when it's all over. Then you can tell me what you think of my present.

Is it sunny where you are? You always did love the light.

Love,
your faithful Camel
(or should I say, "Need, your faithful Camel"?)

The present! Absentmindedness is a sign of transport, the Sufis said; Rumi longed to be absentminded. But in his case, it felt only as if he'd caught the local attention span. He opened the closet door, and there it sat in the corner, in its shining paper of silver and gold, as sad as a Valentine at a funeral. He closed the closet door, and the package filled the room (as the unknown manuscripts of Rumi, once he heard about them, instantly effaced all the manuscripts he had). Every door you didn't open—he thought of their early nights together—becomes a potency, infused with magic.

That night, of course, he couldn't sleep. He walked through alleyways of argument, cul-de-sac leading to dead end, and then a small opening leading to another, and then a cul-de-sac. The "we" she'd mentioned that night—referring to him or to someone else? The gold necklace from an "old boyfriend"—meaning Alejandro, or someone he didn't know about? The package itself in the closet: had she meant it to be a farewell, or was it her last, desperate chance to try to start again? If it was something personal, it would only sting; and if it wasn't, it would sting more.

What if he couldn't sleep without her ever again?

As soon as it was light, he pulled back the closet door and picked up the package, as heavy as the book he was sure it contained. He bounced it up and down a few times, and then brought it to the light. He slipped the pink ribbons off as once he had slipped off other straps in just this light. On the gift card she had written, only, "From your shadow."

Then, no longer patient, he tore the gold-and-silver wrapping off and found, as he'd suspected, a box of the kind in which people keep photo albums or scrapbooks. Maybe she'd given him a register of their times together; maybe an accounting of her life.

It was neither. When he pulled the cover off the box he found a book, a thick book, its cover the color of night, with a heart, in gold, inscribed at its center. Here and there, across the dark-blue background, flecks of gold like desert stars.

Inside, on the first page, as if it were a formal volume from the Ottoman court, was an inscription, though not in Turkish or Arabic, but classic Farsi. "Be wise, be generous, keep secrets close." At the very bottom of the page, where in imperial documents there would be a title, another epigraph in Persian: "The love of fire, the fire of love."

Farther inside, as he carefully pulled back the pages, were poems: poems on every page, facing one another like mirrors on opposite sides of a long corridor. Nearly all the poems were of the same short length, and each was laid out at the center of the page, as if the text were from the Quran. Around them, as in a holy book again, avenues, tendrils of gold, containing the poems like a frame; but where in a Quran it would be the word for "Allah" that would be written in gold, here it was the word for "love."

Clearly the manuscript wasn't "authentic," in the sense of being old. Its pages weren't worn, and it honored the traditional conventions just enough to take liberties with them. Yet that in no way detracted from its value, material or otherwise. Someone had copied and copied the poems, as a copyist of old would laboriously inscribe the verses of a master poet, taking up residence in the poet's house over the months he reserved for the task. At the very end of the book, where again an imperial title would belong, this one read, in Farsi, "This Heart I give to the Beloved. All that goes in it, all that goes with it, belongs to the Eternal Friend. This is my only will and testament. All I have to give is everything."

He paged back and forth through the volume, careful about how he turned the pages. He thought of the Bibles he had seen at college, written out by candlelight in a cold dark cell, the very act of writing an act of worship, personal and impersonal. The calligraphy was of a kind no amateur could fake. At the very bottom of the last page, whoever had written the poems out had inscribed, "There is no god but God."

He thought back to the books like this he had seen in museums and at exhibitions; he thought back to Westwood and even to Hussein's musty library in Jaipur. To someone who hadn't worked with the texts, all these books would be similar. And yet the verses in this one were mysterious: they were not from the Quran, of course; nor did they all seem to come from Rumi, or some other classic poet.

He carried the whole book, wrapped in a towel, to his desk, and closed the curtains and lit a candle, as if daylight would damage the gold lettering. He tried to minimize the number of times he turned the pages, though he knew he had to rough out a translation before he could put the whole thing away.

He pulled his dictionary out of the desk, and, by the flickering candle, began to write.

> Woozy, we drain the glass.
> Again; then again; again.
> "We're not ourselves," you say.
> "We never were," I answer.

> Subject, object of this sentence:
> Does it matter?
> The drummer drums.
> We turn.

> A secret turning in us,
> And the world turns and turns.
> Head is unconscious of Foot,
> Foot of Head. Who cares?
> They turn and turn.

The last one, he knew, was Rumi, a verse known to every school-child in Iran. The others were like cousins of the same, outlines, though whether they were by disciples, taught to write in the same spirit, or whether they were poems by the master that he didn't know, he couldn't say.

Outside, a few tourists sat beside their hampers, and an occasional surfboard could be seen at the point. He started down the steps and then turned back. He could no more walk away from the poems than from his own shadow.

> Why fumble with your books, your candle,
> When something else has taken light inside you?

The translations muddied the issue, of course, placing a cloudy light over the poems, rendering them perishable, as it curiously seemed. And yet the meaning pressed through the syllables nonetheless. As when—why think of this?—her eyes suddenly filled with tears, on the rough road to the monastery, and he could imagine her a tent lit up in the fiery late-afternoon light.

Were they code, of some kind? A present, and if so, from whom? Were they a message, written in a hidden script, or just some souvenir she'd picked up in L.A.? The only person who could tell him was the person he'd asked to leave.

He ran through the map he kept in his head: Talmacz was too far away, and too closely implicated, in any case; Sefadhi was already "away on business," adding fuel to the rumors that he dealt in antiquities on the side—and, besides, he would hardly rejoice at a glittering new distraction one month before the deadline. He thought of Alex, Mowbray, Pauline, and found himself in a maze again: it wasn't even clear whether the book came from the Islamic world or the diaspora.

He turned back, in spite of himself, thirsty, half possessed, to the poems running in perfect lines, innocuously, through the pages. Thirty percent or so, he realized as he translated, came from Sufi's most famous master; the others were more like ghosts, or shadows, of Rumi's impulse. And, more strangely still, they were like weak imitations of the "health club" Rumi of current legend: all his talk of transport, and none of the grief, the ache of an inner jihad. He put the book in the bottom drawer of the desk, and thought himself a "taken" man again.

At night they went through his head, the lines in the foreign script, the words he'd translated: "Let me in, you cry at the door," "Love himself has made a space inside me that is light." A secret turning, a drummer drumming, figures seen only in outline. This one he'd first met many years ago, in Istanbul, with Martine; this one was like the pale sister of the famous couplet. He slept restlessly, bobbing on the surface of himself, and sometimes, when he descended deeper, he felt as if he were running through alleyways, the lines coming after him like footfalls. When it was daylight, he went straight to the desk, as straight as he'd gone to her in lieu of the desk for all these months. If she'd meant to release him to the other room, she'd succeeded beyond expectation.

> The crow caws and cackles.
> This bird is silent.
> Which of them has more to say?

> You come but I am nowhere.
> No when. No why. No you.
> You leave, and you are everywhere.
> No me.

He thought, for some reason, of the two bearded men who had visited so recently, the one so rapt, an arrow on fire, the other a boulder who never moved. These terms, even in translation, were the same as theirs, but then that was the point of Sufism: The spokesman is emptied of himself and all that comes out from him is universal. He speaks for everyone as the lover in his transport is every other lover.

And besides, much of this might be him. In bringing the words into English he felt at times as if he were carrying jewels, kept under a special light in a vault, out into a dirty kitchen, where they looked just like any other baubles. It became hard to tell what was him, and what was they.

> You the sky, and I the astonished earth.
> What makes you grow new again inside me?
> How should the earth know what you have sown with her,
> It is enough that you know: she is big with you.

Almost an insult again: another one of Rumi's best-known poems. It was as if the book (he now thought of it as an unknown person) were playing games with him, deliberately taunting him with things he knew, so that the mix of false and true grew more confounding. As if someone were to include a soliloquy from *Hamlet* inside a newly published play, not as reference or allusion, but as if it were being written for the first time. Or else—and this would be most fitting—someone was trying to explode all thought of identity and authorship, as if to say (most Sufically of all), "Who cares who wrote this? It is itself, like any child."

> Cause, effect; before, after.
> What need of terms?
> The moon is bright outside the city walls.
> Some men, far off, begin to turn.

To pull himself away from the labyrinth into which he was beginning to be drawn, he walked into the other room, and thought: this is California, at the end of the twentieth century. These are cryptic poems of the kind I might, in certain circumstances, mock. I am a graduate student on a fast-fading scholarship, with chapters to complete. What do these poems mean to me?

And then, back at his desk, he would be far away again, in Konya or Shiraz, and people were gathering under cover of dark outside the city walls. He was translating the loves, the longing, of someone he didn't quite know, but recognized (maybe himself, maybe the one who kept him company at night); and yet, really, what was translated was himself. He fell into a deep and sudden dream and saw a figure all in black jumping out at him; he woke up, shaking, with an overwhelming sense of evil. She'd passed on even her dreams to him.

> Before you, there were shadows, fears.
> After you the same.
> Why do I feel transformed?

> What is that knocking?
> Who goes there?
> Not you, or he, but I.
> I knock at my own door
> And no one answers.

Some of the poems—many of them, really—were like children's toys, flimsy, so fragile it felt as if they'd break off in his hand; others had a dissonance, as of some modern copies of an old chant. Others still might have been deliberate fakes, or reminders, in some way, of how he'd misread the poems before. The more obscure the verse, he remembered reading in a book, the more likely it was to be authentic: since which impostor wishes to create something that can't be understood?

At times now he felt as if he were on the long early nights when the darkness had led them on and on, as if they were explorers: so intimate, she'd said, they'd hardly needed to touch. Skins, selves, everything had seemed to dissolve; as if they had crossed a threshold and now whatever passed between them was light. It was the other Californian tragedy, he'd thought at the time: once you see a spark in someone, or think you've found a Golden Age, you can't settle to anything less. You become a wanderer for life.

Now he picked up the phone and wondered how he might approach her. He imagined Greg or Kristina or the male voice that said, "Talk!" The only thing he could say to any of them, "Please tell Camilla to call," was what she knew already: the point of the whole exercise (except, of course, she'd given him the book as a present for an anniversary: maybe she'd never expected it to be a goodbye present, too).

The light began to fade and darken in the sky, and the wind came up outside. He saw the pieces of bush that would skip past on the pavement outside the abandoned house, heard the doors rattling in the place where they'd slept on the floor. It was as if he'd stepped out of himself, into some alternative life that had been waiting for him all along, just as the streets around him were back to their summer selves now, a ghost town.

He lit the candle on the desk, his nightly ritual now, and as he looked over the running, skipping lines, their dots, their strokes, his eyes began to blur and he saw waves of sand running across the desert, and meaning nothing. The beautiful lettering became pure ornament, as when a Sufi, singing a ghazal, takes leave of meaning and flies off into a cry. Hundreds, thousands of bodies lined up in a great space, heads bowed as one, feet turned to the heavens, so many of them there was no individual body, just a mass, a great network of connected lines. And then he bent down more closely and thought he saw a hesitation here, a small amendment there. Perhaps a change in mood, a latter-day revision?

When the knock came in mid-morning, he jumped up and ran to the door to open up, preparing his face to meet her, and found himself looking at the startled face of the mailman. "You know it's a public hazard, not collecting your mail? People get the wrong kind of idea."

"I know," he said wearily, and signed for the special shipment, from Los Angeles: a photocopy—he knew before opening it—from Sefadhi, of the scholarship stipulation. The Iranian way was always to push mildly, insistently at the back window.

There was another letter, postmarked Bakersfield, and he recognized the writing almost without looking at it.

John,

Funny, isn't it, how well we communicate on the page? But in person we're always at one another's throats—in every sense, I guess. It's one of the things I miss. You told me you had to avert your eyes from my "official self" to see the self you cared for; but then, I think, you began to avert your eyes from everything, or the "official self" blotted everything else out, because you certainly weren't seeing me any longer.

Which meant, as you know, that I couldn't, either. You were the way I forgave myself. You were the way I told myself I could be better, or at least that I had better things inside of me. I didn't ask for that, it just came with the territory. You became the place where I put my better self.

So now I'm gifted with this sense of who I am, or could be, but there's no way I can get to it. You've shown me a better world and then walked off with the key. It's all right for you, you have your books, your desk, all the places you can be when you're alone. I have only you. That's my equivalent. You are my books, my private space, my chance for something better. Not because I think you're so great (God forbid!), but just because I find myself with you. What you found in New Mexico I find in your arms.

Plain and simple.

But not fair. Because you can go to New Mexico anytime you choose. But I can't take myself to you. And if I do, it takes me weeks—months—to recover from the devastation. Or recover from the missing you. So I'm screwed either way, if I have a good time or a bad one.

Which leaves me alone, with my heart in another town, in the safekeeping of someone who's off reading poems. It's unfair and unequal. What did I do to deserve this? Fall in love with you?

You know I wish you well. But I feel like I'm alone here, in the dark. You were the best thing that ever happened to me. Until it stopped happening.

Miss me lots—

Love (even if you don't want it),
Camilla

The next day, he took himself up into the hills. It wasn't what he'd expected to do, and he still had to be careful to drive along streets he'd never driven along with her. But this predated all that: the first place he'd discovered in Santa Barbara, out on the southern edge of town, in the hills, near a grove of oak trees, the sky always unnaturally blue above the thin, deserted road.

Off to one side was a seminary, and on the other a sign in elaborate calligraphy announcing the "Church of I AM." Farther up, the community of nuns, belonging to an Eastern order. The first time he had come up here, he'd been amused to find that all the choice real estate was in religious hands: as in some old story in which the king has everything but peace, and so stands ready to give all his wealth to any wise man who can put his heart at ease.

The congregation of sisters worshipped in a great temple set against the mountains, fragrant with sandalwood and incense, and all around it were flowerbeds and fruit trees. Down below, in the far distance, the misty outline of the coast, and the sea, usually deep blue, framed between the eucalyptus trees. On the steps of the temple, looking out at the great distances, he felt everything come into clarity.

He parked the car and walked up to the space beside the moss-green bell. She'd given him a present, which perhaps she'd planned to explain to him, but he'd sent her away, and so turned it into a mystery. It might have been a way to pull him back to her (in which case, somehow, it had done all she might have wished). It might have been her ultimate act of generosity—to hand him over to what had always seemed to tug him away from her. It might have just been an attempt to help him in his thesis: in the New World they still believed in giving people what they wanted.

He sat in the summer light, in the silent afternoon, and let the sun wash over him. One time, in Fez, he'd stolen out of the room while Martine was sleeping, and tried to go back to the Old City after dark. She'd admired a pair of amethyst earrings in the suq, and now he was determined to surprise her with them. But of course he'd got lost almost instantly—that's one way locals stay ahead of visitors in Fez—and the more he'd tried to find his way out, or back, or anywhere, the more he'd felt like someone chasing his own past. Even in daylight it would have been hard to find; at nighttime it was impossible. Wild music came out of the stalls, and urchins pulled at him, offering him this place, that one; men in hoods appeared suddenly around corners, and then vanished again into the dark.

It was like, he realized now, being lost inside a piece of music, but one in which there was no melody or rhythm he could make out. And the more he tried to escape, the more he was lost at its heart. "I help you, sir?" "You buy from me?" "Your wife, sir? You want for your wife?" "My sister, sir. My uncle. My friend."

"Quite a long excursion," she'd said when at last he'd found his way back, attaching himself to a pair of Germans who'd had the sense to bring a guide with them. "Got in deeper than you thought?"

Against her ancestral manner he was always helpless. Even the earrings he'd picked up from the Germans' expensive hotel looked hollow now.

"Very nice. Though you still haven't told me what you were doing all this time."

"Looking for these."

"Of course. What else would you be up to?"

Another of the moments to match, like a pendant, the early morning in Istanbul.

When he went back to his desk now, he knew where he was going. "Camilla," he said, after picking up the phone, dialing the number that led to her answering machine in Los Angeles. "I did open your present, and I'm astonished. I don't know what to say. Honestly, I'm speechless in every way. Can you tell me anything about it?"

It was useless waiting for her call—she might not get the message for weeks, and even if she did, she might rejoice in his discomfort. The person who responded to him might be in hiding, or (this was Camilla) might have become someone quite different. Wanting to feel he was doing something, he drew out a long piece of clean paper, and wrote.

Nigel:
Can you help me with something? Something stupid. I won't bore you with all the details, but I want to make contact with

someone, in Spain, and, for reasons that are complicated but not entirely dishonest, I don't want him to know I'm contacting him from California. I know it sounds utterly mad, but take it from me that it's what this mad field entails.

So could you please just sent the attached fax—a cover letter, and these four pages of poems—to him, as from yourself, and ask him to reply to you? If he sets the Revolutionary Council on you, I'll make it up in some way to Arabella.

Thank you, really and truly: whatever you want from California will be yours, and I'll still be in your debt.

Warmest wishes,
John

Then, lighting his candle again, and drawing out the book, he returned to the desert. It felt as if night winds were blowing around the flimsy house, perched so precariously at the edge of the cliff— "the far edge of the world," as he'd once called it to Nigel—that it was all he could do to keep himself upright. The nightly ritual under candlelight began to seem some private act of worship, performed each night for a God he couldn't name.

> The drunk in the street
> Sees two bottles where there is only one.
> This drunk in my house
> Sees one bottle where there are two.

> You say you are in love,
> But all I see is you.
> True lovers become flame,
> Become smoke, become ash.

These ones, if possible, seemed even more resistant than the earlier ones, more knotty; there was less and less of Rumi—or of obvious Rumi—as the book proceeded, and he thought of a ship passing through headlands and then moving out into the open sea. He was being drawn deeper and deeper into what he couldn't understand—as if someone was deliberately drawing him on, placing a familiar sign, a well-known quatrain, just at the place where he might be tempted to give up. And so leading him farther and farther into the light of what he didn't understand.

Had Rumi not written sixty-five thousand couplets in his intoxication, had concordances not all been in a Farsi that was still something of a stretch for him, perhaps he could have turned to a source in the library—or at least a foreign library—and quickly isolated the poems that were known to be by the master. But he didn't have the resources for that, or the time, and something else told him that to attempt to unriddle the meaning of the book in that way would be a kind of profanation—like making word counts of the Bible.

> Leave yourself at home,
> The Beloved has no need of you.
> Who does he want to see?
> No one.

The poems were growing more curdled, more obscure: farther and farther from the rounded clarity of Rumi, which made him think now of the richly painted low doors of Damascus in the near dark. The phone on his desk was the only silent thing in the room. "You're far away even when we're in the same room," she'd said once, on his sofa. "You remove yourself inwardly, I remove myself physically. It comes to the same thing."

In the morning, when he awoke—or pulled himself out of a crowded and confused sleep—he saw a piece of paper hanging out of his fax machine, and tore it out.

> Dear Mr. Nigel Carpenter,
> I thank you for your enquiry of this afternoon. I further thank you for thinking to solicit my opinion as what you so orientally call the "leading expert in this ancient field." I read the

poems you sent and feel obliged to tell you that the book you have discovered, if this is an indication of its contents, is worthless. These are pathetic falsehoods that mock the work they steal. You will notice, for example, in the third one, that the poet writes like a copy of the great Sufi, yet his "turning," his "drinking," and his "love" have the stink of the daily. They take what is sacred and make it cheap.

I regret this bluntness and hope you understand that honesty is better than politeness in such a matter. I hope you will not trouble anyone else with these copyist's works. They are foolish things that laugh at the originals.

I do not know your name and I do not know where or how you study. I have every reason not to answer your fax at all. If I do so, it is only to ask you please to desist from what you are doing. For us, these poems are holy works. They do not need your coquetry.

Sincerely,
René Guzmán Espinoza

You are the violation of my vows,
My apostasy, my faith.
I shatter myself and you,
I bend to pick up the pieces.

You move me
Out of stasis.
I see your reflection in the mirror.
I can't tell me from you.

No, no closer.
Stay away!
Already you are as close to me
As the fire to the flame.

He was getting sloppy, or tired, dead to the meanings and their echoes. "Out of stasis" meant almost nothing. And what was the difference between "fire" and "flame"? They were defeating him in some way, and he was losing hold: in the walls of a foreign city yet unknown.

> Asleep, and being comforted by a cool breeze,
> Suddenly, I saw a grey dove
> Soar above the trees and sob with longing;
> In her anguish, I heard my own.

As if to tease him again, just as he neared the end, the verse of the Andalusian poet that Rumi cites, as if to throw everything into question once again.

The poem should have been the last one in the book—it looked as if it had been deliberately placed on the final page, as both summary and final testament, the way, he thought, when he was very young, they played "God Save the Queen" at the end of the cartoons his father took him to on Saturday afternoons. So that, on heading out of the theater, people would be thinking of their majesty—the might of Empire—and not the alien myths of Hollywood.

In this case, though, on the final page, which was traditionally left blank, or inscribed only with a glyph of some kind, a coded indication of the calligrapher's identity, there was one final poem, and it was an odd one to put at the end of the collection, for it was one of the least suggestive. The words were thick and blunt—he thought of nails being hammered into a coffin—and were quite without the mystery, the aroma even, that gave the other poems their potency. There was no talk of "fire" or "wine" or "turning," none of the ambiguity that allowed the other poems to wear veils and be many things at once; these words were almost militantly prosaic. As if, perhaps, they were a challenge thrown out to the translator, to try to make something out of words that were entirely without shade and texture. Or maybe a reminder that he could only be a vessel, a transmission.

There was as little space for him as for a French translator of "The cat sat in the hat."

> My hand
> Your hand
> Connected
> Over
> His hand.
> No division in
> Our hearts.

He wrapped the book in its towel again, got up from his desk, and, walking down the few steps that led to the beach, felt more alone than in all his years in California.

He had never credited her with cunning: part of what was so refreshing about her, to someone from an older world, was her transparency, feelings passing across her face like clouds across a pond. Even her most elaborate devices—the heavy-handed mentioning of "Greg," the times she'd answer a question by hiding behind a pun—seemed as guileless as a little girl's. And yet now, somehow, she had performed a master stroke, made him captive to her, or passed on, by some curious osmosis, her sense of anxiety and guardedness: as if, through her gift, she'd made him feel as lost and without center as she sometimes seemed to be.

He took the book to the bank the next day, keeping the four pages of photocopies he'd sent to Cádiz, and when he took out a safety-deposit box for it, the woman asked him for a code word by which he could identify himself in future. "Camilla," he said without thinking, and she looked up surprised. "A friend's name?" "No," he said, "just my own name rearranged."

. . .

He had to get moving, though: the deadline was closer than ever now, and his thesis had been forgotten. If he didn't force his mind in another direction, the lines would keep going round and round indefinitely. You are the violation of all my vows. Beside you I'm beside myself. Leave yourself at home.

After his morning run, he showered quickly and got in the car, driving south. He went along the coast, as if something was pulling him back: he passed the bikers' bar from the night when she'd brought him back from the airport, and then he passed the line of beach houses, where they'd lain one night under the stilts. For days after, every time he took off his shoes or jeans, grains of sand would come trickling out.

At Santa Monica, he drove up to Wilshire and followed it all the way to Westwood, and when he turned onto the smaller street, it was as if he were back a year before: old men at little tables on the sidewalk, the same men as before, perhaps, their glasses of tea before them, with cubes of sugar at their side. "Happy Nowruz" on many of the shopwindows, though the Persian New Year was now many months behind them, and Farsi newspapers blowing across the sidewalks. L.A. was turning more and more into a desert city where tribes assembled with their exotic goods, converging from all directions, and traded their special keepsakes for those of other groups.

He parked on a side street and walked back along Ohio to the main boulevard. He walked down to where 9763 should have been—had been a year before—and couldn't find it. He walked up again, and back, here and there registering landmarks from his previous trip, and there was nothing. Where the bookshop had been—Islamic Arts—there seemed to be a mock-fifties diner, the New World Café. He went in and some Asian kids greeted him, looking blank when he said something about Iran.

On the same block, a few shops away, there was another bookstore, which he thought he remembered from before: the child's drawing books in the window, the flamenco guitar, the stack of Farsi dictionaries. When he went in, he was in a version of the place he'd been before, though some of the props had changed. As before, the man on duty, vigilant as a bouncer, came up and asked him what he wanted.

"Just looking," he said.

"Our books are all in Persian."

"*Midounam,*" he replied in the man's language, and enjoyed a temporary victory.

"Our books are for people from Iran," the shopkeeper pressed on, as if he had stepped into a mosque without the faith.

"I know that. That's why I came here. I have these"—he pulled out a page from his photocopies—"and thought someone might be interested."

"What is this?"

"It's something I've found. I was told this was the place where a master might be able to help me." He was bluffing, of course, but the man couldn't turn him away now.

"Come," he said, anxious to put the matter into other hands. "I show you my uncle."

At the back of the store—overlit aisles of magazines and knick-knacks, as before—was a small office, where a man with little hair and a generous belly was laboring over his accounts. He looked up when the cashier led him in.

"Yes?"

"I know you're very busy, but I wanted your advice." Foreigners play the supplicant in Iran. "I have these poems"—he passed over the page of photocopies—"that a friend, from Tehran, gave me, and I don't know what they mean. Can you help me?"

The man looked at the paper, ignoring everything he said, and looked closer: the level of craftsmanship clearly impressed him.

"This only?"

"No. These, too." Deliberately, he handed over the other three pages he'd brought. The man looked at them, went through them again, looked some more.

"This is Rumi," he said. "Only a book of Rumi."

"The first poem, I know, is his. But the others I cannot find in the collections."

The man was silenced. He looked at them again.

"So—you are wanting to sell?"

"At this point, only advice."

"Why do I give advice so you can get money? It doesn't help me."

He realized, abruptly that the positions were precisely reversed from the previous year. This man was saying to him what he had said to the man's neighbor.

"I only wanted an evaluation."

"Without the whole book, I value nothing." Except the man had already told him all he needed to know by not dismissing the poems instantly. Clearly, he was dealing with something of significance.

He went out again into the mid-morning sunlight, and, recalling where he'd gone from here the last time he visited, he drove across town again, to the house he'd seen from the Chandler novels. There was no sign of her anywhere inside, though—no sign of life of any kind; the weeds in the garden were taller than they'd been before, and when he peered in through the unclosed curtain, at the painting on the wall, it didn't seem to be a tiger this time, but a deer, perhaps an Islamic gazelle.

"It's like you're looking at a stained-glass window from the wrong side," she'd said once about his studies. "In broad daylight. You're seeing the same thing the people inside the church are seeing, but it's completely different."

Back in the car, he started driving back across the hills to Santa Barbara, and as he did so, he decided what he should do: he'd apply for an extension to the fellowship, leave it with Eileen in Sefadhi's absence, and then go off in search of someone who could identify with his predicament. Mysteriously, a friendly face came to mind, a slap on the back, a hearty greeting, and when he returned to the little house by the sea, he went straight to the desk and called India.

"Hello? Yes? Hello?" The immemorial confusion seeped into his room over the international phone lines, and then the sound of someone muttering, perplexed, and then slamming the phone down. He dialed again—"All circuits are busy"—and then again: the whine of a fax machine. He gave it five minutes, and on the fourth try he got what sounded like Hussein's private secretary, and then, suddenly, from another instrument, a boom that might have come from early Evelyn Waugh.

"Hello, Mr. Hussein. It's John Macmillan—yes, I'm sure you

remember—and the reason I'm calling is that I have a manuscript of my own now, at least something in my hands, and I remembered you told me about an evaluator . . ."

It hardly mattered what he said, since Hussein couldn't make out most of it in any case, and was now shouting back, "You are here in Jaipur? Now? Please, you must be my guest, I'll tell . . ."

At last he got his message across, and Hussein said, "Of course, I'd be honored to be of assistance. I'll ask Ahmed to fax you the details."

Next morning, when he awoke, there was a name and number in Paris.

One of his students had told him, years before, about the courier system—fly across the Atlantic for next to nothing—and on the fourth day of his vigil, he got an assignment, and boarded the United flight for Paris, armed with nothing but his small black carry-on and the parcel given him by the company. He felt curiously like a spy—Sefadhi's story now came back to him—and after he'd handed over his unknown booty to a man at the other end, he took a bus into the heart of the city. It was raining, as it always seemed to be here, and when he found the place he remembered from before, the man said, "I am so sorry. Without a reservation, there is only a room for two." Too perfectly, he found himself in the same room he'd once shared with Martine. High up, on the top floor, amidst the gulls on the grey rooftops, the windows of the garret across from him where now a woman sat applying her mascara, and a little girl tinkled away at a piano. A rooftop is a basement in reverse, he thought: an angel's place for hiding things.

At dusk, after a long sleep, he went out into the Jardin du Luxembourg, and stopped for coffee and pastries at the place where they'd gone for a final treat. She'd been blinking a lot, as if to pretend she wasn't upset. "It's almost as if you only trust what you can explain. It should be the other way round, shouldn't it?"

· · ·

The next morning, he arrived at the institute at nine-forty-five, hav-ing threaded his way through the industrial landscape with its slo-gans of hate and violent partisanship, the passions of the bazaar alive here along the Seine, around the corner from the Notre Dame, the university. The professor had suggested they meet at the top, and as he rose through floor after floor in the elevator, rising through Mit-terrand's folly, he felt as if he were a character in some inscription, ascending along the walls of what seemed one great passage from the Quran. Until, at the top, the message ran out, and there was nothing but the sky.

He looked out from the rooftop at the steeples and spires studded across the grey skyline, their crosses like headstones in some ceme-tery built above the clouds. Around him, the canvas umbrellas at the tables, white and folded, looked like nuns huddled in the rain, all the more so as bells began pealing hosannas from the nearby church.

Inside the spacy grey cafeteria where the man had told him to appear, the hexagons and stars from the patterned windows threw strange shadows across the floor, and he felt more than ever as if he were a cipher in some geometrical design, who had meaning only if put together with the coats lined up on the racks, the modular chairs, the woven shadows. "Sometimes you are inside a circle when you think you are outside it": the unsettling words of the stranger in Seville.

The room was not very crowded at this early hour, and he did not imagine it would be difficult to spot the itinerant scholar. An elegant Frenchwoman was sitting alone at one table, throwing her Eastern shawl across one shoulder as she paged through a fashion magazine, brown eyes stylishly lined with kohl (he saw Sophie in a future life). At another table, a group of men from the Middle East were huddled together in dark jackets and grey trousers, as if chatting about the latest threat in Jerusalem, or Homs. The professor, when he came in a few minutes later, belonged to another order: cream sweater, aviator glasses, and a worn leather book-bag over his shoulder. His well-coiffed hair was grey, and his jacket, light for summer, was obviously expensive.

"So—you have ordered already?"

"I waited. What can I get you?"

"*Café,* only." He put down his things and said, "Monsieur Hussein is your friend?"

"Acquaintance. I went to look at his manuscript—a little before you did, I think."

"Ah yes, the manuscript."

The mint tea, the *café au lait* arrived, and he felt the man waiting for a prompt.

"As I said over the phone, I've actually found myself changing places with Mr. Hussein. I'm now where he was."

"You have a manuscript?"

"I have something. Whether it's a manuscript or not—"

"Yes, of course," said the man. "Perhaps I cannot help, but I am interested."

He pulled out the four pages of photocopies and passed them over; if everyone he consulted saw the same pages, he could read each one's level of involvement.

The man took off his glasses, "YSL" on their sides, rubbed his eyes, and put them on again.

He sipped his tea, and waited for an answer.

"This is in confidence, no?"

"Of course. I'm grateful to you for even looking at them."

"Of course." A small, elegant bow. "What do you think they are?"

"I honestly don't know. Some, as you can see, are Rumi; the others, I don't know."

"I, too. They are interesting, certainly. They have the same flavor, the same spices, but the taste is different."

"Exactly."

"I would like to work with them. If you have the whole manuscript, perhaps you can give it to me and, three weeks, four weeks later, I send you an answer."

The book had been a gift; and perhaps, too, a treasure. It was a private act, which somehow he was dragging into the public arena.

"The whole manuscript is in California at the moment. I'm reluctant to carry it around."

"Of course. But for me, you understand, I cannot say anything with so little. You want my advice, but you cannot show me what you have. It is the *débâcle* of the times: Dzogchen sutras on the rue St.-Jacques."

He looked up at the unusual phrase, and remembered where he'd seen it before: the fiery article on global scatterings that Mowbray had given him from the scholarly journal. By someone, he remembered now, who taught art history in Paris, and so was unfamiliar to him.

"I think I've read something of yours," he said to the man. " 'Postmortems in the Postmodern Era,' something like that."

"Yes," said the professor, shrugging, "a favor for a friend. A friend in America."

"You wrote a whole article as a favor?"

"I let him use my name. The terms are his."

"You had an arrangement?"

"A private arrangement," said the man, as if that was the way to end the discussion.

"And in terms of my manuscript . . . ?"

"In terms of your manuscript, I wait till you give me everything, then I tell you what you have."

"I'll try to do that later. First I need to know if it's authentic."

The man stood up, his pride clearly bruised. "I thank you for the coffee," he said, with more formality than was called for. "I think you need to talk to somebody else. I will ask Aisha Crespelle if she has time to see you."

Wild Arabic music swirled out of the little shrine decorated in the shape of a peacock. Around him, once more, the kind of atmosphere he might have seen in the teahouse at the eastern entrance of the Umayyad Mosque: men in ancient jackets gathered over what seemed to be a perpetual argument; a grave old man alone, sipping at his tea as if wanting to stretch the cup out through a lifetime; a whirling, hypnotic melody that sang of love and desolation.

He thought of his adviser, planting articles in magazines, it seemed, much as he had planted Pauline in Arizona; getting professors in France to put their names on what he'd written, as he got small presses in Los Angeles to publish the pieces in English. For all he knew, Sefadhi was working through Camilla to give his prize student a manuscript that—nothing seemed impossible—his adviser had written himself.

Aisha Crespelle was dressed in a blue blazer and grey slacks and—what he hadn't expected from her first name—had a healthy blond ponytail that spoke of a house in the country, riding lessons at dawn. He ordered tea for them both, and she looked back at him across the table in the Parisian way: appraising him sexually as much as socially, and hardly bothering to conceal her surprise at his relative youth and lack of funds.

"I imagine Professor Richy explained why I am here?"

"Of course," she said. "He always does."

The "always" wasn't encouraging, but he pressed on: "My adviser, Javad Sefadhi, is second to none in his admiration of your work."

"I thank him," she said.

She pulled out a pack of cigarettes from her bag as the tea arrived, and a thin gold lighter. At the next table, a noisy group of young girls from Scandinavia were untethering old backpacks.

"I hear you have poems. But what do you want me to do with them? Do I look at them and then pretend I've never seen them? You show me something beautiful, and then I never see it again?"

"I was thinking we might come to terms."

"'Come to terms,'" she said. "And if the poems are fakes, then what?"

"That's a chance you have to take. If they're fakes, I've come all the way from California in vain."

"Why me? There are other people more eminent than myself. Maybe I will read your poems and then tell you they are worthless and make use of them myself?"

"That's a chance I have to take. Those doubts apply to anyone I might consult."

"Show me what you have," she said, tired of the fencing, and tipping her ash impatiently into the Cinzano tray. "Show me what you have so I can have some idea of it."

"These are the only poems I have with me."

"Yes," she said, taking them from him, and then going through them once, twice, returning again and again to the second page. "Yes. These are something."

"Something important?"

"Something different. What you should do with them, I can tell you without payment."

He looked at her encouragingly.

"You burn them. Now. Before you leave Paris. If you keep the others in California, as soon as you return to California." She took a long drag on her cigarette—smoking was how people in Paris punctuated their conversations. "The people to whom these poems belong have suffered already." He'd guessed from her first name that she came from somewhere in the Middle East, and her watchfulness, her briskness said something about what she'd lived through. He thought back to the Iranians he'd met in Los Angeles, and the shards of a former life among which they tiptoed.

"These poems are like a bomb in a crowded square."

"I realize that. I just wanted to know what they are exactly. For private reasons."

"For private reasons you do not come to me." She sat back and looked at him for a long moment.

"I have a friend," she said, "an old friend from Tehran. One month ago, he goes back to collect the things he left in his house when he left. It is all gone—taken by a friend, an enemy, the police, some criminals, he doesn't know. Then he goes to the airport to leave. 'Sorry,' they say as he's leaving. 'You are free to leave, but this little girl with you, she must stay.' 'But she is my daughter.' 'You say she is your daughter. How do we know she is not someone you are taking away from Iran?' 'I show you her passport, her papers. I give you the DNA.' 'We are sorry. You are free to go. But the girl, she must stay here.' "

She stubbed out her cigarette in the metal tray. "If you have a love letter, you do not take it to the government." If someone whispers in your ear, you don't ask a stranger what it means. Least of all in a country where whispers have repercussions.

Back in his little room, he picked up the postcard of the mosque he'd bought. He looked at it and looked out the window. Then, as if to renew an old hope he'd put away for a long time, he wrote on the back,

> *Wherever there is a ruin, there is a hope for*
> *treasure.*
>
> —JALALUDDIN RUMI

When he got back to Santa Barbara, the only message waiting for him was from Sefadhi, speaking as if through clenched teeth. "In light of your new discovery, I have effected an extension of the fellowship; a stay of execution, if you like. The papers will be with the IRS soon. I hope you can put this year of grace to happy use."

There were no letters in the mailbox, no faxes curling out of the machine. He put his carry-on back in the closet, and as he did so he saw, stacked in the corner, the letters from her he'd put where he wouldn't see them. He bent down to pick one up, saw a face smiling at him through a windshield, and put the envelope quickly back.

The autumn days passed smoothly, tonelessly, and he began at last to pick up the pieces of his life and put them into a kind of order again: on Thursday nights tennis with Dick, movies once a week, and the trek to the library every morning at seven-forty-five. With an extension of twelve months, he could go back to the glass of wine in the terrace in the evenings, the occasional consultation of poems he hadn't read for a long time. They'd run away from him when he looked at them again—as Sefadhi had, and Camilla; as he himself had, perhaps—but he was stirred by the same cadences he remembered from what seemed a previous lifetime.

Camilla sent no letters, and made no calls; no doubt she was hiding in someone else's apartment now, putting whatever concerned her where she would never have to see it. He stepped around the books, the places they'd seen together, and it felt sometimes as if he was living on the outskirts of himself, at a safe distance from the tumult of the inner city.

The new last chapter on calligraphy was easy enough to complete—writing itself as a kind of art, so just the transcribing of the holy words, the copying of them, became a prayer—and he devoted most of it to the master calligraphers who managed, in all their work, to leave some trace of themselves, some hidden signature, and yet to take everything else of themselves out of their creations, as if they'd had no part in them. A few days before Christmas, he completed the last sentence of the dissertation, and looked up to realize that, thanks to the extension, he was now six months ahead of schedule, instead of six months behind.

One chilly afternoon, just after the New Year, a card arrived from her—an image from a Persian manuscript, of course, now kept in Oxford—and inside it, in the familiar looping scrawl, she wrote, "I hope you're doing well. I'm not so great. I lost the best chance I ever had. I don't expect another one very soon. Your fond admirer, Camilla Jensen."

In the same mail, another card, in the antiquated blue-black script he remembered from his undergraduate days, made out to "John Macmillan, Esq."—and inside, a Renaissance picture of a Florentine Virgin, her ornate blue shawl, imported from Arabia, covered with Arabic characters that said, "There is no god but God" (his old professor's idea of a joke, no doubt).

I was very happy to receive news of your completed thesis; well done. I wonder whether you shouldn't go to Persia now you've met your obligations towards it. Not that you will necessarily find much there; but until you do go, you shall always think you might.

Gratuitous advice from a superannuated counsellor.

With warm regards,
Benedict Mowbray.

Christmas had been quiet, and over the New Year, celebrations had seemed inappropriate: one year before, he'd been in the Taj, slipping under the surface of the world to find the secret flame burning in the basement; a year from now, whatever happened, he'd be in another country—the fellowship stipulated that much—and the poems that had kept him company for all these years would be behind him. He thought sometimes of the book in the bank, and put the thought away.

Outside, the light had resumed its winter sharpness, as if someone were outlining every detail with a razor-point black pen, so the days were particular in a way they could never be in the broad-brush summer. Sharpness in the elements highlighting uncertainty everywhere else.

He'd set aside the whole of January for putting together his footnotes—tidying up the loose ends of the thesis—and after the early months of restlessness, he was beginning to recapture the gift of sleep. Sometimes whole weeks would go by without a night of sleeplessness. One night, when the phone began ringing in the dark, he got up as if still asleep and stumbled through the room.

"Hello," he said, and there was nothing.

"Hello," he said, and was about to put the phone down—a student prank, he assumed—when he heard something at the other end, not so much a voice as a sound, so distant it felt as if it were coming from the far side of the world. He had a vague image of bells in New Mexico, and waking up in the predawn quiet to look at the stars through the window, after a dream of Isfahan.

"Camilla," he said slowly. "Is that you?"

He heard only low breathing at the other end, and then what

sounded like choking, or someone laughing so hard she couldn't get the words out.

"Camilla, is that you? What's happening?"

She didn't say a thing, and he imagined someone shuddering, speechless, at the other end. He thought of the time once when they'd come so close to breaking one another that he'd gone out to take a walk before the damage would be irreversible. When he'd come back, he'd seen her through the window, in the long black dress she'd put on for a special occasion, sprawled across the bed, shaking convulsively, as if in a fit, her small hands fisted at her sides. As haunting a sight as he'd ever seen, of someone locked into a small space with the person she most feared (herself).

"I was hoping you would call," he said now, to try to draw her out. "I've been wanting to hear your voice."

"My father's dead."

"What's that?"

"My father's dead! Can't you hear anything? They found him in his study." She cackled in a wild way, and he realized that what he was hearing was the opposite of laughter. "It was the excitement of his birthday, the doctor said. Going out on a high note." And she shrieked again, as if it were the funniest thing she'd ever heard.

"I'll be right there. Are you at home?"

"Don't!" she said into the receiver. "Don't come any closer! Stay where you are."

He stopped for a moment, to let her retrieve herself.

"You need someone, Camilla," he said at last, when she said nothing. "Someone who cares for you."

"If I need someone who cares for me, I don't need you. Come any closer and I'll kill you."

He let her cry, or get out whatever was inside her, and then just said, "If there's anything you need, I'm here. If you want something, anything at all, just tell me."

"Whatever I need, it isn't you." And the phone came slamming down around him.

· · ·

There was no getting to sleep after that; he thought of her alone, in a city haunted by the person she saw as her tormentor, he imagined her putting on her long dress slowly. A few hours later, while it was still dark, there came a knock on the door and, half expecting it, he went to the side door and let her in. Her face was ash, and her white skin against the white dress gave the impression of someone who couldn't touch the ground.

He held her briefly, and she fumbled past him. "I didn't know where to go or what to do. I didn't know where to go."

"I'm glad you're here. You're safe. What can I get you?"

And then, realizing that what she needed most was a freedom from all choice, he led her into the bedroom and made a space for her.

"Is there anything you'd like?"

"A new father." Her voice was still strange, as over the telephone. "I think I need to sleep."

"Sleep; I'll be here beside you."

He sat beside her as she lay and saw her fall into another space. It had been a long time since he'd seen her in this position, smelled her face cream, watched the calm that stole over her face when she was resting. She stirred once, a few minutes after she'd nodded off, and he put a hand out to assure her he was there. Awake, it had seemed as if some aspirant Camilla was in his room, the amateur actress come once more; asleep, it was her again in his bed.

When she awoke, she pushed herself deeper into him, as if to shut out the light.

"Can I get you anything?"

"Nothing's going to bring him back."

He smoothed her hair, sang a soft song he remembered she liked. When she awoke more fully, she was a little more herself. "Here we go again. I come to you and leave all this garbage on your doorstep."

"I'm just happy to see you. I'd been thinking of how I'd get to see you."

"Like you get to see a sleepless night." The bitterness was the only part the actress had got right.

"Do you want to tell me about it?"

"No. I don't."

She slept most of the day, and when it was dark, the small new candle burning as before (he'd gone and bought a new one after she'd taken the old one away), she said, from where she lay, "There was this call in the middle of the night. I went over, and there was an ambulance parked outside. The Browns, the Gottliebs were there. My mother was in her bed crying. I didn't think I could ever feel sorry for her before."

"She must be devastated."

"She's got his will, his safety box. That's all she cares about."

"But she was crying."

"She was crying. She misses him. Now she doesn't have anyone to use."

"What do you feel like doing?"

"Running away, hiding. The same things I always do." The anger came out in every direction, and it didn't matter whom it stung; the world had done what it always did, which was to let her down.

"She wore at him and wore at him. Day after day for thirty years. Rubbing at him till there was no him left."

"But he stayed."

"Of course he stayed. He was too weak. She made him think she'd die if he left her on her own."

He went into the kitchen and brought her juice. Then, settling down beside her again, "There isn't anything you want?"

"Just take me away. Anywhere."

They got into his car, he wrapping her up in his coat and bringing along blankets, and they drove to the ledge just beneath the once-abandoned house. Planes hovered over the town below, red lights winking on their tails, and the grids of yellow lights shivered and blurred as if ready to be snuffed out. Occasionally a car would come around the bend, and crazed shouts would pass into the mountain silence, Californian revelers off to practice whatever forms of private worship they observe outside the city walls.

"Thank you," she said, taking long breaths and looking out the side window. "I needed this."

"L.A. is very far away."

"It never happened," she said. "It doesn't exist."

The next day, again, she spent all the daylight hours in bed, not coming to the phone when Kristina called, not stirring in response to anything he said. She woke towards nightfall, and he asked her the same question he always asked, so she would know she was at home.

"What would feel nice?"

"Do you have some juice?"

"Juice we can do."

She was coming back to shore at last; a little color had returned to her cheeks, and her voice had come up a few notches from the deep. But they were still walking over splintered ground; he was ready to see her wince and recoil at any moment.

"Is that all?"

"Do you have anything to read to me? I think that would feel nice."

"What kind of thing?"

"Something from your poems. Like a year ago."

She'd given him an opening to ask about the manuscript, and, as a kind of reassurance, he asked her nothing. Instead, he went over to the desk, where he kept the photocopies he'd made, and came back with the pieces of paper, as if they were just sheaves from the usual papers on his desk. He didn't know yet how much she even knew of the content of the poems. When she moved up to squeeze his hand, he noticed the ring he'd given her on the wedding finger.

"Here goes. These have never been heard by human ear before. Hot off the press."

She pressed herself into him and closed her eyes.

> All night aflame,
> I turn and turn.
> The wind shakes my trees.
> I shiver in my bed.

The world spins all around me.
Heavens fall, angels scramble at my feet.
I turn and turn,
The ground is rich with stars.

"They don't sound like the usual ones," she said, and he, looking down at her, couldn't tell if it was canniness speaking, or
innocence. "They don't even sound like they're from the same
culture."

"I can read you P. G. Wodehouse instead," he said, not taking the
bait. "S. J. Perelman or something, to make you relax."

"No. This is nice. Go on."

These words, my wounds, a homesickness.
A bird calls above the sea.
A light on the shore, a light.

He was trying to read her poems whose provenance he didn't
know—not the ones that were from the best-selling Rumi anthology—
but whatever her response to them, he couldn't tell: her eyes were
closed and her breathing was regular.

When you left, I did, too.
No I at home any more.
Only this candle, this quiet burning.

Her body was so still, he thought she might be sleeping.

"Are you there?"

"I'm here. I'm listening." He looked at her, and thought how the
poems would have sounded even to him, two or three years ago:
mystification, perhaps, empty portent.

We never move, the earth spins round.
The heavens come down, and the ground rises up.
Why talk, then, of your whirling?
It is the skies that turn, not we.

"They're all the same," she complained. "They all say the same thing. It's like watching the dervishes in L.A., turning and turning again and again."

"That's why I hoped they'd put you to sleep." And, for the first time in the new year, he heard her laugh. "One more, and then I'll leave you in peace."

> Down this street, down that one,
> To the center of the maze.
> Nothing waits for us but silence.

"'But silence'!" she announced, with what might almost seem delight. "That's a Johno phrase!"

When she awoke—night had become day again, day night—she was closer still to the person he knew, and he thought she might yet be herself, so long as she was far from Los Angeles. But the life she knew looked more like an empty house than ever, her only formal and practical protector gone, her sister always off on mysterious errands, and all of her, legally, in the hands of the person she regarded as a demon. He'd thought of her life before as a small hut on the edge of the abyss; now it was as if the roof was gone, and the wind had blown away one wall, so all she could see from where she lay was empty space. She needed fortification, he thought as he watched her sleep; and when she'd been in need of someone to hold, she hadn't gone to Greg's house, or Kristina's: she'd come to him.

"What would you like to do tonight?" he said as she stirred. Darkness everywhere outside and the beach was emptied out. Shouts, footsteps disappeared, and the silence took over around this time.

"Can we go somewhere?"

"Anywhere in particular?"

"You told me about your friend's house, downtown. With a tower."

It had been months ago, on one of their first drives, and he'd happened to mention Bill's Victorian house near the center of town, with its aerie at the top. "It's like a bird's nest," he'd said, and her face had lit up, and then he had forgotten all about it.

"Can we go there now?"

He rang up to see where Bill might be, and the answering machine was a blank: as a restorer of old sculptures, his friend was often gone for months at a time, and every now and then a call would come, from Oaxaca, or Florence, once from Siem Reap, asking him if he could use his spare key and go into the house to find something.

They drove through the dark to the center of town, the Moorish cinema lighted up just behind them, and went in the old Victorian house through the back door. It still had an old formality—doors and divisions marked out in a nineteenth-century way, and a parlor where a lady might play the piano, a back room where an Emily Dickinson might write her poems.

He led her through the building to the stairs and then up the red carpet to the landing, filled with nothing but books. "He's in Art History," he explained. "It's his idea of decoration." Then up a much narrower set of stairs, bare wood and turns, till they came to what might have been an attic.

It was a small hexagonal room, with windows on four of its six sides. The lights of the town came in through three of them, houses on the hills, sometimes cars from the road below. Through a fourth, the pier in the distance and the sea. He turned on a light, and they were in a universe of two. "No," she said, "it's better without." There was just enough light from the street to make sure they wouldn't fall.

"It's like a treehouse," she said, walking round it, while he sat back. "Except more comfortable."

"And this time you're not alone in it."

She stopped and sat in the middle of the room, and he left her to her thoughts, sitting against a wall. Then, after they had been silent in the dark room for some minutes, she stood up and came back to where he was sitting, and, kneeling down at his side, began kissing him all over, his lips, his neck, through the shirt she began unbuttoning.

"What is it? You don't have to . . ."

She pulled her white dress over her head and began pulling the pins out of her hair.

"It's all right, Camel. I'm happy to be quiet."

She shook her hair free and looked down at him. Her face was without color, and she looked more unprotected than he'd ever seen her. She began kissing his chest, his nipples, down his stomach. He felt the tears all over her face and the cheeks wet where they grazed him: someone pretending to be her again.

She shivered as she settled herself on top of him, and then, after many moments in the silence, in the dark, she got up and picked up her dress, put it on quickly without a sound.

When they were back home, she put her things together, as if to leave.

"Is there a funeral?"

"I don't know. I'm still in hiding." But if she were hiding, he thought, she would surely be anywhere other than Los Angeles, and the memory of her father, her waiting mother.

"Do you need company? A bodyguard? A semi-professional escort?"

"I need nothing, thank you." She'd already disappeared into the person she would be at the other end. "You've given me plenty, thank you."

The days went slowly now that they were empty. He didn't want to give Sefadhi more details about the new manuscript, and Alex was wary and cordial since their meeting over a common girlfriend. The book in the bank and the woman who'd come to visit were safe in their mysteries, and both of them, at some level, seemed to ask him not to ask too much.

One of the new habits he'd made in the new year was to go to the library every Monday to read the exile papers from Los Angeles: a way of keeping his Farsi up, he thought, and keeping in touch with the émigré community with which he'd begun to feel such sympathy. When he picked up the *Iran Daily News,* a few days after her unexpected visit, it was to see the usual black-and-white pictures of balding travel agents, and announcements of concerts featuring favorites from the old days. At the very bottom of the front page, though, there was something that caught his eyes, as if it was half familiar.

"ESTEEMED PROFESSOR DIES," the small headline said, and its short, formulaic text read:

Professor Ferdows Azadeh was born in Shiraz in 1938. Educated at the University of Tehran, he was a professor of astronomy at the same university until his migration to the United States in 1978. Here he was a much-loved and respected member of the Westwood community known for his solemn observation of ancient Islamic custom and serious commitment to the cause of a free and democratic Iran. "He was the soul and spirit of our circle," said Parviz Rastegar, a longtime friend and academic colleague, who worked with Professor Azadeh in many activities. "He knew the name of every star, in English, Arabic, and Persian. When he wrote poems, his friends would weep."

Azadeh is survived by his wife, Katrina Jensen, of Los Angeles, and two daughters, Kristina, of Santa Barbara, and Camilla, of Los Angeles.

"My father's from—somewhere else," she'd said, that first day in the kitchen; all the tales she told were of her mother's home, in Denmark. Physically, clearly, she was her mother's daughter, to a fault; for all he knew, the man who seemed to have come to the U.S. a few years after her birth might not even have been her father by blood. But Kristina, he remembered, had that rich dark hair, the splashes of color, you might expect to find in the northern suburbs of Tehran. Even the casual elegance.

He went back to the first time he'd knowingly been in the same room as she was, at McCarthy's lecture. He remembered, suddenly, her interest in the Iranian lecture, the fact she'd known how to find the dervishes. All the forgotten lore she'd sometimes pull out from her college days about Vita Sackville-West and Harold Nicolson. In the house, during the long, rainy interlude, her sudden rage when he'd spoken of Isfahan.

The white dress, he thought now: the Persian color of mourning. The body buried within twenty-four hours, as specified by the Quran, and then perhaps a eulogy at the mosque three days later, and a ceremony forty days after the death. The cards she'd brought, always from Persia; Sefadhi's passing reference (or had it been in Seville?) to someone called "Ferdows," connected with the poems in some way.

Even her silences became a little clearer now, all the things she couldn't tell him, lest to do so would be to give him another confused reason to be drawn to her. She'd told him how she wanted to flee everything associated with her parents; and yet another part of her, her blood, surely propelled her towards what she knew to be her birthright. He saw her sitting alone, now, in the city that was most frightening to her; he looked at his own calendar, with its long spaces of unclaimed openness; and then, picking out a piece of paper, he began to put down something he'd been thinking of for a very long time.

Dearest Camilla,

I wish I could do something or say something that would make it all better, take you out of whatever loneliness or sadness you must be feeling now. I wish I could wave some wand or say some spell that would make it all go away. But I don't think I can. I could tell you how it felt when my own parents went away, but every loss is particular, and I don't think any words can really be much help. That's one of the things I've learned from you.

All I can say is that I'm here if you need me, or if you're looking for somewhere to get better. And we've worked so hard to build something up outside ourselves, it would be a shame—more than a shame—to let it go uncared for. It would be like locking ourselves out of our abandoned house in the hills. I know I've done nothing to draw you out of hiding; probably, being me, I've only succeeded in pushing you even farther into hiding. And I haven't won your trust—I haven't even earned it. I'm only just beginning to see all the things I couldn't see before, running off in search of manuscripts when something much more valuable, more meaningful, was in my arms.

You'll expect me now to start bombarding you with questions, about your father and Iran and all the parts of your life I never knew about before. I want to know the answers to all that as much as you'd expect. But another part of me—maybe this is your influence, too—feels that none of that would really answer anything. It would only be just another kind of diversion, more information to keep me away from what matters.

So—all, I will say is, 'Come with me to Persia.' Not for a long time, and not with any itinerary that's going to sound too daunting. I can take care of the arrangements, the expenses (I've still got all that leftover money from the Fellowship); all you need do is bring yourself. It's a trip I've been wanting to take for a long time, for obvious reasons, and now I can see it's the trip you need to take, too. Now that one cycle's ending, it's the way to start a new one. A better one.

I know what you're going to say to this: that I've really lost it now. Iran is the last place you want to go—a country run by madmen who've destroyed every last civility of an ancient culture. A place dangerous emotionally and in every other way, especially for someone with her roots there.

But unless we do go there, I think, we'll always be stuck in some way; unable to move forward. If you stay where you are, you'll never break through the patterns that you know; at least coming to Iran will make all the other places that you dream of that much closer. And if you don't savor every moment, maybe you'll look on L.A. a little differently when you return.

I won't go on and on, especially at a time when you've got a million other things to consider, and must be feeling more vulnerable than ever. All I will say is that, if you can't bring yourself to try this now, maybe we can find another destination, closer to home—somewhere where we can find something outside ourselves and our small concerns, the way we did in New Mexico. And if even that sounds too much, I will, though reluctantly, retreat in silence.

You know, though, whatever happens, that all I want for you is a place where you can feel safe. Your happiness is the secret of my own.

Love, truly,
John

Five days later—no answer yet—he took a greater chance, and drew out from his suitcase the card he'd brought back from Granada, of the Alhambra under moonlight.

> *Mas, en este abandono de los dos*
> *en los dos, ¿qué nos dábamos?;*
> *el brazo de la cruz de nuestro cruce,*
> *¿qué flores y qué espinas*
> *del camino infinito recojía?*
> —Juan Ramón Jiménez

Behind it another card, picked up in Westwood, of a traditional wedding in Tehran, the bride and groom sitting before a mirror, each watching his own and the other's reflection, the only thing beside them on their platform—and in the mirror—a small Quran placed upon a prayer rug.

> *And yet, in this abandonment of both*
> *in both, what did we give each other?*
> *In the arms of the cross of our crossing,*
> *what flowers and what thorns*
> *did it gather on the road without end?*

You're the most persuasive person I've ever met," she said when, finally, she called, though she didn't make it sound like a compliment.

"I don't want to persuade you to do anything. Just offer up an opportunity."

"You see—you're smoother than a politician."

"Point taken. I'll shut up."

There was a pause on the other end, as if she was waiting for more persuasion from his end.

"It's a war zone over there."

"They're not fighting any longer. I wouldn't take you to a place that wasn't safe." He thought of her neighborhood in Los Angeles, the beaten-down bungalows, the broken stores, but let it go.

"And all that money?"

"I've got to spend it somehow, on something connected to my project. Once we get there, it's incredibly cheap."

"Why me?"

"You know the answer to that. I wanted to do it even before I heard about your father."

"You see what I mean? You could get me to jump off into the Grand Canyon."

"Only if I had a safety net at the other end." He kept silent about her mother, let her come slowly to the decision by herself.

"I don't expect you to say anything now. But if we do go, it'd be best to go soon, before the New Year there. The only condition is that we have one talk beforehand."

They met at the little Mexican cantina on the short road that led to the beach, where once they'd heard the German women, and Sting lying down in fields of gold. The same three men with their pomaded hair were strolling around the same six or seven tables, closing their eyes to the chorus of "La Cucaracha," while the same woman with tired yellow hair slapped orders on the carousel. A girl of eight or so walked from table to table, selling roses.

"The same table as before," she said, as they took their places in the garden. "Neutral ground."

She looked better than when last they had met, as if she'd gone down into the Underworld and now had come back up into the light. She had a solidity about her, even a self-possession, that she'd always tried to hide before.

He ordered Coronas for them both, and then, as she fell into an uncertain silence, said, "Can you tell me something about him now?"

"You sound like a shrink."

"Only a friend."

She didn't have much to tell, in any case. She'd never met any member of his family, she said, except a brother who'd always asked them to call him a "friend," and not an uncle: her father hadn't even wanted his daughters to take on his name, for a Persian male the ultimate act of sacrifice. The years of looking over one's shoulder did not go away quickly.

"And that's why you studied all those women travelers to Iran?"

"That's why I almost didn't. My parents didn't want me to have anything to do with all of that."

The little girl was at their table now, looking up at him with plaintive eyes, near-moist. He looked across at his companion, and then said no. The three men walked around in the small space, singing of doves and nightingales.

"And your mother?"

"What about her? She knew everything. But she kept it to herself. That's how she is. It's what she had on him. It's what she had with him. It's what she had that Krissie and I could never touch."

"Did you learn much Farsi?" It was a way of sidling towards the manuscript.

"None," she said, and he realized there was no way of ever knowing for sure. "My father freaked out even when I told him I was studying Isabelle Eberhardt and Freya Stark. 'Englishmen's Persia,' he said. 'All lies.'"

"And Kristina?"

Her face changed, and he saw what circumstances hadn't erased in her. "Oh, Kristina could do anything. She was their golden girl; their pride and glory. She knew how to play them like an oud." He felt the sting of all the words she'd taken pains not to use with him before.

"I got all the wayward genes," she went on, as he dug at his enchilada, "the scared, insecure ones; she got him."

He sipped his beer in silence, and waited to see if she'd go on.

"It's nice here. It never changes."

"It never will, so long as no one chic discovers it."

"The undeveloped world," she announced brightly. "That's what they should call it. Not the 'developing world,' but the 'undeveloped world,'" and when she said that, he knew she would come to Iran.

"Kristina's the one who handles his legacy, then?"

"I guess. She was always the one who did his errands for him, went back and forth."

"Khalil and so on?"

"I guess. They never told me much. But I know my father still had lots of friends over there, especially within the Shia community."

Suddenly the foreign words came out, which for all this time she'd been so eager to keep away from him.

"And Sefadhi, too, must have been one of your father's contacts?"

"Your adviser?" she said, and the pretense of innocence was so unconvincing, he realized it would be useless to ask more.

"I just felt"—he sipped at his beer—"or assumed, really, that that's how you got the manuscript."

"The manuscript's different."

Suddenly she seemed deeply interested in her rice.

"You've got to tell me something, Camel, if we're going to take a trip together."

"The manuscript belongs to me. That's all you need to know. My mother doesn't know about it, Kristina doesn't know about it. It's mine, and I gave it to you."

He sipped his beer so she'd go on, but she seemed to have said her piece. The three men came to the climax of "Guantanamera"—the day's last high note—and two teenagers in stained white shirts came out to begin stacking chairs.

"I don't have a clue what the manuscript means, or even what it is. It's beautiful, but I can't work out its context."

"You don't get it, do you?" she said, looking at him as if she could hardly believe he could be so slow. "You understand why I gave it to you, don't you?" Now that it was agreed she'd be coming, she didn't have to be careful with him any more.

"I think I do."

"It's not as if I can afford a wedding ring."

He looked down; somehow, with her, he'd always been worse than foolish.

"It's not as if I expect wedding bells, you know."

The place was closing around them, and they walked out into the dark.

V

There is a secret flight from Los Angeles to Tehran, across borders that are technically closed, to places that are officially unreachable. If you know how to work out the routings correctly, if you know how to read the papers in the right way, you can go to the Alitalia counter on a certain day, at a certain time, and there, above the check-in desk, is a small sign, no larger than a license plate, that says "TEHRAN, via Roma."

There were people all around them when they arrived, banging large bags against their legs, moving in a cloud of Guerlain and Dior. Head scarves and tight jeans and excited teenagers carrying televisions or generators back to their loved ones at home. Around the huge departure hall (a mosque in reverse, he thought, looking at its large empty spaces), the *mujahedin* in their pressed suits were going from one startled group to another, showing them photographs of what the Second Revolution had wrought: the battered faces of dissidents, medieval instruments of torture.

He looked quickly to see how she was taking it in, and he saw apprehension, confusion, wariness; but also, what he hadn't expected, hope. Her eyes were bright as she took her boarding pass from the woman behind the desk, and she moved more briskly than she ever did at home, as if on her way at last to one of the adventures she'd been reading of. When she asked him how Sefadhi had procured the visas so quickly—a "friend of a friend," of course, in the Interests Section in Washington—he took care not to tell her how his final meeting with his adviser had gone.

"Is there anything I can bring back for you?" he'd asked his teacher, coming to collect the documents from his office.

"From Iran?" said Sefadhi. "What is there to bring back from Iran?"

Their connecting flight, when they arrived at Rome, was delayed for two days—some unspecified problem at Mehrabad—so they went into the city and caught the train to Venice. When they came out on the quay beside the Grand Canal, in the bright winter sunshine, Death suddenly loomed before them, shouting something out, and then danced away. Satan was by his side, sticking out his tongue at a Frenchwoman in thick furs. On the water, groups of harlequins were racing by, jumping up and down and calling out to visitors, and a Pierrot in the prow of a boat reached his hand under the skirts of what looked to be a courtesan. They'd wandered, without meaning to, into Carnevale.

It was Kevin's thesis, and his own, all brought to vivid life (a woman in a gold gown sailed past, stately as a queen, a small gold mask held up to hide her eyes): the pagan, animist spirit that hides out inside even the most modern of places. But it was something else, too, more unsettling. Everything you know about us is wrong, the Lenten costumes said. Underneath what you see is another layer, and underneath that, still another.

They made their way to St. Mark's, turned down a small alleyway where he'd been told a Moslem building still hid out, and as they did, a skeleton lurched up to her, leered, and said something unintelligible before vanishing again. On every side of them, women in black and scarlet costumes, outlandish, and jesters, zanies, figures from a devil's medieval banquet. At Halloween, he thought, we play at being monsters for a night; here the characters seemed to suggest that we are in fact monsters who play at being human.

They walked along thin lanes, over arched bridges in the hesitant light, their breath coming up to greet them and halo them in the cold, and as they walked they passed groups of contemplative birds, a man whose face was chalky white. Dante was over here, talking to some ghost, and Casanova over there, arm in arm with what might have been Beatrice (or a secretary, in her waking hours). After dark, they went to a far corner of the city—someone had slipped a flyer into her hands, and when they'd opened it up, they'd found not the advertisement they'd expected, but directions to what seemed to be a private party. But when they got to the house marked with a scowling face, there was no number on the door, no sign. He knocked, and there was no answer.

She pushed at the door, and it gave, and they were inside a dark, narrow corridor—close and hot—with phantoms, clowns, and courtiers pushing in on them from every side, everyone turned inside out, as if they had become all that they dreamed of becoming—all that they feared to become—the other fifty-one weeks of the year. A demon was crouching in one corner, where a woman was laughing huskily, the larger woman above her dressed so you could see nothing of her but her breasts. The bodies pressed in on one another in the crowded space, intimate, suffocating, warm, and there was an overpowering smell of wine, perfume, something else.

They passed into another room and saw, at its far end, in the near dark, a skull above a door. "Follow the skull," whispered a voice who must have guessed they were foreign from their costumes. "Always follow the skull." They did so—she leading him now (strangely invulnerable in her cat-faced mask, and the long black cloak they'd rented from the sad man in the shop that afternoon)—and inside this farther space there was virtually no light. Men became women, became men again; a character who seemed to have stepped out of one of the Bosch canvases they'd seen at the Duomo came and planted a kiss on her cat's mouth, then reached for him. A man all in black handed her a card, and she said, "Come on. Let's go farther."

When they got to the next room, pitch-black, someone snatched her away from him, and he was alone in a crush of shapes and moans. From every side could be heard gasps of some kind (was that her?), and mutterings, unclaspings. A hand reached for his belt, began to untether it; someone else was breathing on his neck, and moving up towards his ear. He heard a sigh—it could have been her—and then the hands were creeping up under his shirt, reaching for his wallet, and he broke away (there was a curse), and flung himself back into the previous room, the one before that, out again into the corridor, where King Ludwig was peering down the dress of a woman whose face was deathly white.

Then out again, past the last few figures, into the dark, where he leaned down, hands on knees, to catch his breath in the cold. A cat was waiting for him in the dark, and she took his hand and led him back down the long silent lane, past the locked doors, towards the center of town.

"It's almost like we're walking through your poems," she said, softly, for they were lost, and they felt like intruders at a private show.

"I don't think so," he said, still rattled from the party. A couple was under lamplight, circling around each other in the brief light. There was the sound of heavy drapery falling away from somewhere, a sharply taken breath. "It's not higher selves, just different ones."

The dervishes in Los Angeles—he didn't need to remind her—hadn't needed costumes to make themselves something different.

When they got to St. Mark's again, they found a warm spot in one corner—the fellowship didn't extend to a hotel room in Venice—and sat amidst the debris. An hour or so later, the sun began at last to come up above the canal, and they saw figures emerging out of doorways, or stepping out from boats, like actors coming out to take their final bows at the end of an all-night performance. One or two were dressed as Moslem holy men, or Moors from centuries before.

They took a boat back to the station—the colonnades of St. Mark's echoing and empty—and as they went along the canal, saw figures in wigs, women with moles painted on their cheeks, laughing and kissing passionately, while a man in black sat at the back of a lonely boat as if being led across the Styx on the last journey he'd ever take. On the station platform again—tourists in thick sweaters hugging themselves against the chill—he looked back at the shivering reflections in the water, and wondered how it could ever become something different.

"What do you think it'll be like a week from now?"

"More confetti on the square."

. . .

"We move on and on, in search of mystery," he wrote on the plane, while she slept, "and then we come to see that the only mysteries we want are the ones we'll never solve. And all we can do is try to cage with reasons what we know to be beyond the scope of reason. Till at last we surrender to something beyond us, and become unknowable ourselves."

It was pure madness, a part of him knew, all the more so since his thesis had been not so much completed as abandoned.

As the pilot made his announcement of their imminent arrival, she stirred, and he followed her gaze out to what seemed to be utter darkness, broken by the great lights of a building they recognized as the Khomeini shrine. Beyond it, the fainter lights of the city going on and on till they ended in emptiness again, and darkness. "It really is a desert," she said, marveling, as if she'd never believed it until now. "Like L.A. Except the lights are all turned out in parts."

When they stepped out of the terminal—the scowling guards having waved them through—the winter cold slapped them in the face, and as they lurched towards the center of the city, and the mountains to the north, the taxi driver said that it was only truly Nowruz, New Year, when the snow had melted on the slopes. The hotel that was waiting for them was bare and cold—heating another of the luxuries apparently banned by the Revolution—and as soon as the door was locked behind them, he jumped into her bed for warmth. For superstition's sake, they'd taken two beds instead of one.

Out in the street the next day, the cars coughing on all sides—the Shah's most audible legacy—he had the sense of being lost inside a maze. Belching trucks and constant horns, and over everything a sense of grime, or chaos, as if the city itself were wearing old black clothes that hadn't been cleaned in years; and deeper than the disorder, a sense of constant apprehension. The people around them were all dressed in brown or black, as if to mock the comparisons with Los Angeles, and he thought of the men he'd seen in Damascus, their fraying shirts and moth-eaten jackets giving a poignancy to their talk of revolution.

"I don't think you're going to find what you're looking for," she said, and he realized she wasn't talking only of taxis; it was impossible to find anything in the town, and even the mountains by which they'd been told they could orient themselves were often hard to make out in the smog, brown over black over brown.

"Even not to find something might be something," he said, and she looked back at him strangely, though not without affection.

As they waited and waited for a car, a woman came up to them, and said something to her in a Farsi so colloquial he couldn't make it out. Then another woman, as if emboldened, came up and handed her an orange. A few children came over to inspect the aliens, and a third woman, eager perhaps to show off her English, came and started asking them questions, or translating the questions of the others. "How long have you been married? How many children do you have? Why do you come here?"

He gave them answers, as the official leader of the party, but the women were mostly looking at her, smiling or gesturing as if to make some contact. An old lady stopped and plucked at the fabric of her coat, as if to remark on its quality. Another one motioned at her scarf, as if to say they were all in this together.

She smiled at them, gestured back, and when they were back at last in the hotel, she said, "It's like the black-and-white Los Angeles." The perfect way to put it, he realized; and they like those beings who long to step into a black-and-white movie, as if that is the way to step into simplicity or purity, or something innocent they've lost.

The next day, a Friday, the day of prayer, they went up into the mountains, as did half Tehran, it seemed, and soon the downtown area was a brown smudge in the distance. It was sunny still—pale, thin winter sun—and the people around them streamed past the tea-houses as if to put behind them the imported chaos of the modern city: the coughing cars, the running gullies, the kids lighting fires in the streets. Here whole families were sharing food—Persia the country that had invented the picnic—and couples took themselves off into the shadows, or sipped shyly at orange Fantas under trees.

They stopped for tea, and he looked at her as she drank—her dark face-scarf, her black pants, the dark coat she wore over everything, for concealment—and realized that she'd neutered herself in a way, and covered up all that she usually showed in public. And yet, in the same breath, she'd recovered a kind of light. The winter brought color to her cheeks, and some layer of complication that she usually wore was gone. A part of her was the rosy-cheeked schoolgirl in Scandinavia she might have been years before.

"You look well," she said, as if reading his thoughts.

"You, too. This place agrees with you."

"I never thought . . ."

He said nothing, so she'd get the thought out.

"I guess"—she paused again—"I guess I never thought it would be so rich. The poverty I expected. The dirt and the chaos, all the bad stuff. But I didn't expect all this." In the streets, the previous day, it had been she who had pointed out to him, with a smile, the sign that said, "DEATH TO AMERICA": the only sign she'd admit to being able to read.

As they went back towards the hotel, they found themselves in one of the gracious, tree-lined streets which the regime had not yet managed to turn into high-rise buildings or mosques.

"He must have grown up somewhere like this," she said, and then said nothing more. The next morning, they were in the desert again—a great brown emptiness for as far as they could see, with nothing to relieve it, as they drove towards the south, but the glittering golden domes where the Ayatollah Ruhollah Khomeini—"the soul and voice of God," as his name meant—now slept.

He'd had the feeling, ever since he'd come back from Damascus, that whatever he would find in the context of his manuscripts, he would find in Isfahan; and the intuition had been strengthened when he had remembered that it was the city where Sefadhi had studied (and, he thought now, the city that had roused her to rage on the rainy night in the abandoned house). The imperial capital announced itself with a sudden blaze of blue, visible from far across the desert, after miles and miles of scrubby grass and blankness. Turquoise, lapis, aquamarine—a great shine of color in the winter sun that looked like an oasis of extravagance.

They took a room in a small travelers' inn near the river, and began to take the measure of a town that felt relaxed, itself, in a way that Tehran, the modern capital, could never be. Couples were drinking tea under the famous bridges, and groups of students were walking along the river, laughing and pushing one another as they did. The center of the city was not some grey building that changed name with every change in government; it was the great mosque made of holy verses, its blue impenitent. "It's more like Persia here," he said, and she began to say something and then held back. He looked at her and realized she was moved, in some part of herself; it wasn't anything like what she'd imagined.

"It's still Iran," she said, as they passed a group of boys who stood against the wall watching them as they passed; the city remained a Hizbollahi stronghold, and some of the boys who looked like college students were the same ones who, on ayatollahs' orders, picked off journalists on motorbikes, or placed bombs on the doorsteps of maverick professors. Yet here, too, as in the capital, women and children came up to them everywhere they went, offering small presents. "How many children do you have? What sport do you practice? What do you think of Iran?" An old woman stopped in front of her, eyes so moist it looked as if she would cry, and handed the strange woman from the far-off, rich country a bag of sunflower seeds.

They were going back to the hotel to rest when they passed a gang of small boys on a bridge, pretending, not very successfully, to look away from them. She stopped, and suddenly, impulsively, bent down and gestured towards one of the smallest boys. He looked away, not happy to be approached by a foreigner (and a foreign woman, at that, with a strange-looking instrument in her hands). But finally his curiosity got the better of him, and he stepped forward a little, to see what it was she was carrying.

She showed him with gestures how to push the pink button, and then they stood before him with a smile. The boy focused, clicked, and handed the camera back to her, delighted.

"You see?" she said. "They're just like children anywhere."

. . .

They hadn't come only for sightseeing, of course—or told themselves they hadn't—and when they stopped at a café for tea, he said, "I don't really expect to find anything." She smiled, as if she knew that his saying so meant he did. The poems that he carried round with him everywhere here, in spite of the risk they represented, were growing more creased every time he pulled them out, and soon, they both knew, they would be torn, and lost entirely (photocopying secret poems did not seem a good idea in Revolutionary Iran). He took them out now, and put them back again, as if not to hex the enterprise with his hopes.

Back in the hotel, she said she wanted to sleep; the desk clerk had nodded his greetings at them as if still impressed that this foreign woman, explaining why she had a different name from her husband, said she kept her mother's name as a gesture of respect. She was tired, he realized—all the years of waiting, the seasons of looking through catalogues, the stresses of the last few weeks accumulating. But she was also telling him silently to go off in search of what he needed without worrying about her.

He took off in the direction of the synagogue, and, once there, began to see if he could find somebody who could speak English (he would never get out what he had to in Farsi). But the Jews who lived in Iran had kept alive only by living quietly, among themselves; the last thing they needed was to jeopardize their security by tending to the trivial concerns of a foreigner. Nearby, at the Church of St. Luke, he couldn't even find a person to answer the bell. "Hello?" he called out. "Anybody home?" but there was nothing, no sign of movement.

He began walking back to the room, defeated, and then, passing a library, he had an idea. Years ago, at a conference, someone had told him that they kept lists of the Revolutionary faithful in the libraries, as a public gesture of gratitude (and, too often, as a secular reward for their martyrdom). He went into the place, nodded at the man behind the desk—he'd deliberately dressed down for the trip and not bothered to shave—and then went to the back, where they seemed to keep public records.

He found what looked to be the area for public listings, and, coming to the volume for 1359 (or 1981, as it would be in the West), he pulled it out. There was a long list of names of those who had "served the Truth," and among these there were three Sefaredis, though none of them began to look like the man he knew. Going quickly through the long rows of tiny pictures of men, solemn-faced and bearded, on page after page after page, felt eerily like looking along the rows of gravestones in the cemeteries, a young boy's picture on each one, and a photo of Khomeini on the other side. He put the book back—no "Javad Sefaredi" here—and began to walk out.

As he did so, something made him think of another library, across the world, and Pauline's mention of how their adviser, in his younger days, had sometimes chosen to go, for whatever reason, by his father's name. He went back to the same shelves and pulled out the volume for 1358, seeing if he could spot any sign of an "Ardeshir Sefaredi."

He went quickly through the pages, and then a boy looked back at him—a full head of hair, a virgin's eyes, and some quality of ardor and possibility that looked nothing like the man he knew. The boy's beard was young, unformed, and he looked as if he had never heard of cuff links or Italian suits, let alone of California; the strongest element in his eyes was fear. But just behind the fear was something else, a kind of pride almost, that he could give himself over to the Revolution. The look of someone who might write a fiery treatise on the desert of faith in a land of anarchy.

He put the book back, and began to walk along the road he'd come on before. Children came up now and then and shouted, *"Khareji, khareji!"* A couple of boys looked at him as he walked past: who else but a spy would leave a rich country behind and come to their more difficult land? There was the sound of ironworkers in the distance, the ceaseless honking of taxis.

He heard almost none of it, though. He was thinking of a man—a boy, really—who had given up everything he knew, or loved, to serve it far away, in a place where his sacred texts would be turned into greeting cards, and his prayers treated as if they were just love songs.

"You look better," she said, looking up when he came in. "You must have found what you were looking for."

"I think I did," he said, and started packing away his things.

In the evening, when she fell asleep again, he went out one final time, following whatever prompt it was that told him he'd find what he needed here. In the late afternoon they'd gone, as if magnetically pulled, out to the great mosque, and found themselves in what might have seemed a whole city made of words; the yellow-and-blue patterns on the columns and the walls took its visitors into a realm of pure worship. In one area, she'd pointed out the calligraphy so free that even a mullah couldn't read it; the point, she'd said (no longer shy about telling him what she knew), was that you had to give up your rational mind and stop even trying to understand it. All that mattered was the pattern.

Walking through the mosque, and the square that led up to it, he'd felt erased, as if they'd moved, in some way, from a place where they were monarchs of everything they surveyed into another order, where they were very small indeed. Not just in space but in time as well, the centuries around them stretching out like the grand expanse of the desert. They'd left a world of moments for one in which people were governed by, even buried under, the grievances of four centuries before, or the rivalries of a previous dynasty. And all the years of enmity and suspicion gave the city a somewhat melancholy air, the more pronounced for all its beauty; he thought of a man who got up in his Sunday best—coat and tie and polished shoes—though his wife had died ten years ago and now he was eating alone every night.

He went out towards the main square again—the bridges illuminated after nightfall, so they seemed more than ever like props from fairy tale—and as he walked through the riddle of streets around the hotel, he caught smells of cooking from some kitchen, saw men seated in a circle on the floor, heard the slap of backgammon tiles from the cafés where the old men crouched over heavy wooden boards. Children ran this way and that in the dark, playing hide-and-seek or tag; a radio crackled from some far-off alleyway.

There was almost no one in the main square at this hour; only, in the distance, a few dim figures, just visible, drifting into the mosque for the day's last prayers. He sat on a bench and thought how his life and hers were threaded together like overlapping skeins in a carpet, as she'd said long before: the lecture the first afternoon, Oxford before that, all the other unexpected convergences that culminated here, in the city they'd both been thinking of, for different reasons, for so long.

"Hello, sir."

He turned around to see a young man beside him. In tight blue jeans and a black leather jacket; of college age, perhaps, careful not to get too close.

"Hello, sir. Where do you come from?"

"From England," he said, so taken aback he forgot the cover story they'd agreed on in advance.

"England, number one!" said the boy. Green eyes and a faintly feminine air.

He looked around them and realized there was no way out; the boy had timed his approach for when no one else was around.

"You like Isfahan, sir?"

"Very much, thank you."

"You come to our country many times?"

"This is the first. But I'd like to come back."

"Thank you, sir," said the boy, with a small bow. Neither of them said anything for a while. Then the boy again: "You stay one days, two days, in Isfahan?"

"A few. I leave tomorrow. You?"

"I am Isfahani, sir. I am student of your English."

They fell quiet again—they were linked now, but neither of them could think of anything to say—and then the boy said, "You come to my house, sir." It wasn't quite a statement, but it wasn't a question, either. He looked more closely at the boy but couldn't tell what lay behind the offer: maybe it was just the fact that he was alone (since, so long as he was with a woman, no one would ever invite them home)?

"Is it far?"

"Not far, sir. Close."

He looked at the boy and thought: if not now, when? The answer to his questions would not come in the streets.

They got up and walked together, away from the center, he trying to follow the names so he could find his way back, if need be, and the boy asking him about Michael Jackson, the Dream Team in Barcelona. They passed through a maze of dusty lanes—a figure called out to the boy from one of them, there was a group of boys in the dark in another—and he thought of the boys they'd seen in the streets this afternoon, agents, they'd agreed, for the regime's dirty work. (What teenager in Iran would have a room of his own, unless he had a high-up sponsor?)

Finally, the boy stopped at a small black door, and ran up the steps inside it. He came after, smelling something rotting, fumbling against the wall in the dark.

At the top of the stairs was a square, empty room fit for an ascetic. On one wall, a torn calendar of Mecca; on another, wrapped in fine cloth on a shelf, what he took to be a Quran.

"You take tea," said the boy, and before he could embark on the three-part refusal—let alone say no—the boy was gone, leaving him alone with the signs of devotion. The massed crowds around the Qa'ba on the poster, the paint peeling from the walls. Then the boy returned with two muddy glasses and a torn old bag of Oreos (his cousin in Los Angeles, he explained with pride).

They talked in a desultory way of the World Cup, Madonna— "You know Michael Jordan?" the boy asked—and then, as if this had been the point of the whole meeting, the boy said, shyly, "You like poems, sir?"

"I do, as a matter of fact, yes."

"Please." His host rummaged through a sheaf of papers under his low table and then extended a scrap of notepaper, its edges torn. "I made into the English," he explained.

> I am made mad by the beauty spot above your lips, my love,
> I see your eye and fall sick.
> Open the cellar door to me, every day, every night,
> I do not like the mosque or the seminary.

"Like Hafez," he said, not knowing what else to say, and the boy, pleased he'd caught the allusion to the mole, smiled and put his hand to his heart.

"Our Imam," he said, and then opened a book he kept under

the table to reveal a picture of the poem's author, the Ayatollah Khomeini.

The effect of the poem, no doubt inadvertent, was to tell him all he wouldn't find in this small room—the folly, in fact, of even mentioning his own poems. They talked a little more about Hollywood, the cousin in Los Angeles, and then, saying something about "foreigners' security restrictions" (the boy looked impressed), he got up and made his escape. When he came into the room, she was standing at the window, as if she'd been trying to imprint something on her memory.

"You find anything?"

"Nothing much."

"I wish we could stay and stay," she said, and then, as if she'd gone too far, she hurried to cover it up. "I mean, it's nice here, safe."

Shiraz was only a few hours away, but all the planes were booked, and their funds would not last forever. As they took their seats on the bus, he thought back to the first time he'd heard the name mentioned in the context of manuscripts, in Damascus, and felt that something at last was being brought to a close. If the lines on the star map converged anywhere, it was surely in the place where her father had been born, and many of the country's most celebrated poets.

They were given the front seats, as before—the seats of honor, closest to the heater—and when he looked at her, by the window, he saw someone less encumbered than he'd ever seen in her before. It was as if the Camilla that he knew had been cleaned out in some way, purified; and he, too, perhaps, living simply in this alien place, and moving with more purpose. They couldn't touch in public, of course; it wasn't even wise to laugh or whisper together. But that meant they were back in a kind of innocence—the first nights, when they'd made love all night, she'd said once, without ever touching.

"It's not like what you expected, either, is it?" she said, following his thoughts.

"No. Completely different."

"Different better or different worse?"

"Better, I think. More friendly."

"And someone else is doing the driving."

He didn't say anything for a long while, and then, "We get to take everything seriously here except ourselves."

"You're not wishing you were alone?" But the way she said it told him that she knew the answer already.

Behind them, the other passengers leaned forwards at times, as if to catch the words of a foreign language they couldn't understand; they'd become celebrities of a kind here, or at least VIPs. More important, though, in this foreign place, they'd been brought together, as a couple. His interests were hers, her needs his.

The bus stopped at regular intervals, to let people off, to take new passengers on, and then they were in the desert again, no coordinates or signs for as far as they could see. Miles of emptiness and sand, and then the darkness began to fall, and they were in a place even farther from orientation or real life. The night outside unbroken by lights or trucks or dust storms. He looked out into the blackness till the night made her fall asleep, and then he, too, was asleep, woke up, fell asleep again, till suddenly there came a decisive jolt and the bus stopped moving altogether. He looked outside but could see nothing: the same night as before.

"What's happening?" she said, as she woke up, too.

"I don't know. We seem to have stopped."

"What's going on?"

From behind them came a great clattering, and then the other passengers began moving through the aisle and out into the dark. They stayed where they were, not knowing what was going on, and then, after a few minutes, they felt the bus being pushed on its side, almost as if it was about to be overturned.

"What's happening?" she said again, the panic rising as he felt them off-balance, and then the bus landed on all fours again.

"I don't know. It must be some kind of problem."

"I know it's a problem. But what's going on?"

Around them the bus began rocking again, back and forth, as if the passengers were going to push it over, with them inside it. Then silence again, and nothing but the dark.

They remained where they were—to go out, into the foreign cold, seemed even more dangerous than staying in their seats—and then, at last, a man came in and said, "Excuse me. Broken. Tomorrow, Shiraz."

He motioned for them to follow him, and they went out into the dark, their bags heavy in the night, to see the other passengers standing around or sitting in the emptiness while a couple of boys argued about something on the axle. It was cold, and there was nowhere to go in the dark.

A little later, as mysteriously as everything else here, a car arrived, and the man motioned for them to come with him, and they began juddering away from the bus. After twenty minutes or so, they arrived at a small, empty square, with houses (or huts, really) on every side. It was silent as a ghost town. The man—the designated English-speaker, they gathered—went up to a door and knocked, and then there was another face there, and they were being led into a narrow, unlit corridor. A door was opened, and the man pointed them into a room as empty as a cell. He made the universal gesture of sleeping, then disappeared.

It was a small space, with a pile of stones in one corner, and a rolled-up carpet in another. Through the window came the moon above the small houses, the sound of the wind from the desert, the cold.

"I don't like it," she said, walking around as if to find some piece of consolation.

"I know. But I don't think we've got much choice."

"I thought you spoke good Farsi."

"When I'm at home, perhaps, with my books."

They sat against a bare wall, and the wind rose up again outside. He put his arm around her, she tried to sleep. But every time she stirred, he started from his sleep. Every time he woke up from a brief dream, she did, too. The night went on and on, and the first light never seemed to come.

When he awoke, with a start, in the morning, it was to see the man from the night before bending over them, motioning urgently at his watch. She struggled up, face pale, and he saw, as he looked at her, that something had gone out of her in the night: she was the person she was in California, haunted, and more vulnerable than ever now that she was far from everything she knew.

"You're okay?" he said when they were ushered into the car. She nodded, but it was as if some guardian spirit in her had gone away; she'd seen the other side of her father's legacy. At the bus, a boy hurried up to them with two dirty glasses of tea and a handful of crumbling biscuits; they looked around and realized that their fellow passengers had spent the whole night here, sleeping in the sand if they slept at all. Everyone got back in now, and the bus started up, as if it were the beginning of a new journey. But she said almost nothing in answer to his questions, and looked out of the window dazed.

When they got to Shiraz, he got a room for them in the best hotel in town, and found a Buick to take them around, but at some level it was all too late; she hardly even smiled when the boys near the university, fluent in their English, chattered away, and one of them opened a book to show them a sentence translated into their own language: "Truth shows her face, her very beautiful face, in a veil. Only the travelers who go to other places can see her." The mystical sentiments of the coming man, Khatami.

"We'll go back tomorrow," he said, once they were back in the safety of the hotel. "Take the bus back to Tehran, find a room for the night in Qom, and take the next flight out."

The Revolution had given a kind of luster to romance, a secret charge, by pushing it underground, and in the hours before it was dark, when they went to Hafez's tomb, they found it was more full of courting couples than it might have been a generation before. The boys and girls sat here and there on the grass, eating rosewater ice cream, and now and then a pair would go up to the small, serene white pavilion and tell their futures there.

"You want to try?"

"I guess." She could never resist a game, he knew; and when he handed her one of the books behind the tomb of the mystical poet, she closed her eyes and flipped through the pages, then jammed a finger down.

"A little farther. You're between the lines."

She pushed her finger down, and he said, "There. You're on a sentence now."

She opened her eyes. "What does it say?"

"It says"—he paused, perhaps for effect, or because the Farsi was difficult—"it says, 'The adventure between me and my Beloved never ends. What has no beginning can have no end.'"

She looked at him. "How do I know you're not making it up?"

"You don't. You have to trust me."

The next morning, when he awoke, it was to see her, once again, at the window, as if she were tracing with her mind the streets her father might have gone down when young. And, in the process, putting away whatever had frightened her in the empty room.

"I'm still really glad we came," she said, not turning to look at him, as if that would break the spell. "I wouldn't have missed this for the world."

He'd expected bad dreams in the night, a sudden reappearance of the figure in black who'd terrified her before; he'd half expected something like the last night with Martine, in Athens, and the voice that wanted to destroy everything. But she'd slept without a sound all night, and now, as she turned back from the window, he had the sense (which he couldn't, wouldn't say to her) that she'd stepped through her fear, at some level, and come out on the other side.

The bus that took them back through the desert led them through a wasteland they thought they knew by now, a signless emptiness that hadn't changed, it was easy to imagine, since the flame was lit in Yazd, fifteen hundred years before; and as the sun began to fail, he could see no sign of habitation or relief. Soon it was dark and the bus was just snores, small stirrings in the dark. Outside, very occasionally, the lights of a small mosque, a passing truck.

He slept, she slept, each of them woke up at broken intervals, and then, when it was still dark, the bus suddenly stopped, and he looked outside to see nothing still.

"It's happening again," she said, fingers tightening around the wrist she'd been secretly holding under his cloak. He couldn't say it wasn't. The passengers behind them stirred and then, as before, proceeded down the aisle and went out into the dark.

"I'm scared."

"I know you are. It's okay."

"I'm really scared."

"They don't want to hurt us, I'm sure."

He got up and went out to see what was happening, and then, coming back, motioned for her to follow him. Outside, though the first light wasn't even visible above the mountains, the other passengers were stretched out in the sand, heads pointed in the same direction. The day's first call to prayer.

Her eyes were full.

"I've never seen anything like this," she said, and then went back to her seat alone.

Qom arrived in a great crackle of activity, men in black with white turbans moving this way, moving that, while others, whose black turbans marked them out as descendants of the Prophet, chatted away in groups, or hurried off towards their classes. Doves flew between the minarets, and they felt as if they'd stumbled into some medieval Oxford where the issues of the thirteenth century were debated as fiercely as if they were the issues of the day (as, perhaps, they were). The vultures, the blue jays of the desert, were far behind them now, in this old city of black gowns and earnest students, figures disappearing in the direction of the golden dome at its center, through an entrance that foreigners (a sign said in English) were not allowed to use.

They took a couple of seats at a café—she took out some coins and put them in a box with a dove on it (alms for the poor)—and a sullen waiter came and thrust down a plate of *sohun*, the saffron-flavored pistachio brittle for which the city has long been famous.

"How are you feeling?" he asked. She'd seemed better since their departure from Shiraz: the long drive through the desert, the unexpected stop, the prayers—and, especially, the tears—seemed to have cleared something out in her.

"Full. Exhausted. Spent."

"Different from before you ever came?"

"In some ways. This place doesn't have anything to do with me, the way I thought it did. But in another way, it has."

"It isn't a foreign country."

"It is. But not in the way I thought it would be."

"It's part of you, don't you think?"

She shook her head no. "I'll block it out when I'm home, the way I've always blocked it out. But at least I'll know it isn't black. It's . . ." She gave up the search for the perfect word.

Around them people were snatching up pictures of Khomeini, copies of the tapes of lectures he'd given years before.

"He used to live here," he said, telling her as ever what she was likely to know already.

"He still does," she said, and he was silent: she was right. The Ayatollah's furious stare met them everywhere they looked.

"Hello, my friends," said a voice nearby, and he turned away from the street to see a man dressed from head to toe in black, like a cleric. "You are from Germany, I think?"

"Denmark," he said, picking up the fiction they'd agreed upon before coming.

"Copenhagen, very good," said the boy (or man: it was hard to read his age). He followed their gaze out to where they'd been looking, at the figures disappearing into the narrow, flat-roofed maze around the mosque.

"You have your passports?" he said, with what could have been idle curiosity or something else.

"No. They have to keep them in the hotel."

"Of course." The stranger smiled. "You will join us for some tea?"

He looked across at her, and realized from her face that she, too, knew that they were trapped: whoever this unsought figure was, there was no way of getting away from him. If they left, he'd say he wanted to come, too; if they returned to the hotel, he'd ask to see their passports there.

"Why not?"

The "us," it soon became apparent, was only a courtesy: the boy had been trained, in issuing invitations, to avoid the impious "I." He was a star student, they guessed, who accompanied his elders to conferences abroad; he'd studied in Belgrade (hence the English), and now was savoring the chance to practice on some new victims (and to check up on them at the same time).

"We're actually leaving in the morning," she volunteered, playing up the Danish accent. The boy looked pointedly at her, as if to include her in the conversation.

"You don't trust me," he said suddenly.

They were taken aback; it was like being outmaneuvered at chess. Debating was still one of the skills they taught here; Khomeini was only the prize student among generations of such arguers.

"I take you to my house," the boy now volunteered, as if he'd come to some decision. "You would like to see it?"

"We're not allowed," he improvised quickly. "There's a sign."

"You are with me," said the boy. "I am—how do you call it?— Coordinator for the New Principles of Islam." The pride with which he recited the phrase was a small reassurance, but her face was pale again, and as soon as the boy disappeared, as if to prepare for their visit, she started talking to him under her breath.

"We don't know who he is."

"I realize that."

"He could be anyone. Why's he so interested in us?"

"He may just be courteous."

She looked at him as if he really were a child.

"I only think that . . ." He didn't need to finish. If they didn't take this chance, his silence said, something in them would never be put to rest. It had all come down to this one moment: the simple question of whether they trusted the boy in black.

"You'll look after me?"

"With my life."

The boy returned now, smiling, and they followed him out, tentatively, into the square. As he led them into the forbidden city, men in black passed on every side, sometimes stealing a glance at this foreigner in secular dress, or the figure beside him, pale, they could see, even with her headdress on. They moved like newspaper sentences in a holy book. "This is really okay?" she asked, but the boy was moving quickly, with a foreign air of purpose, down one lane, then another.

At last they came to a small black door. The boy opened it, and then climbed up a dark flight of stairs—Isfahan again—to what looked to be a small, dark cell. From outside came the sound of argument.

"You will drink some tea?"

"No, thank you."

"You would like some tea?"

"No. We're fine."

"You will join me in some tea?"

"Thank you," he said, registering the ritual of the three-part refusal, and the boy went out, returning very soon with three glasses of tea, a plate of figs.

"You are a teacher in your country?" the boy said as they sipped the tea.

"In Denmark," he said heavily, "my wife is a teacher. I am—well, actually, I am a student of Sufi poetry." It was clearly the most dangerous answer he could have given.

"You are interested in Islam?" said the boy, newly alert.

"A little. Saadi. Rumi. We went to Hafez's tomb yesterday."

"You are a good friend of Islam," said the boy, with what intention he couldn't tell; the town was old enough to entertain many levels of irony.

"And you?" To redirect the questioning.

"Shiraz," said the boy. "Mother, father in Shiraz."

"But you're here for good now?"

"God willing," said the boy.

They braved the figs, the bitter tea; there seemed no more to say.

"For what reason do you study Islam?" the boy tried again, his directness so sharp it could have been that of a spy (or of someone so guileless he didn't know he sounded like a spy).

"I like the ideas about surrender. Giving up." The boy looked confused. " 'Die before you die,' " he said, quoting the Prophet's reputed maxim in Farsi.

"You speak our language."

"Not really. Just a little."

Nobody said anything for a few moments, and he began to think that it was time to make an exit. He looked across at her to give a sign, and suddenly she spoke up.

"You should show our new friend what you've brought with you."

"He wouldn't be interested."

"Show him. He may be able to help you."

"What is this?" said the boy, curiosity aroused. "What do you have?"

"Nothing," he said, but she spoke up for him. "He has some poems he wants somebody to look at."

The boy looked at him expectantly.

He pulled the worn copies out of his pocket, the creased pages so crumpled and bent over that they were almost impossible to read. They'd been on his person so long they seemed to be a part of him. Then, very slowly, he handed them over.

The boy looked at the pages for a long time and said nothing. Finally, turning back to the first, the third, he said, "These are from Jalaluddin? *Mathnawi?*"

"I don't know, to be honest. Someone gave them to me in California. I don't know what they are."

The boy looked at them again, turning from page to page, careful not to tear the old pages. Then, at last, he handed them back again.

"Beautiful," he said. "Some. Some I don't like."

"Do you think they're authentic?"

The boy looked back at him, his English overtaxed.

"I mean, do you think they're real?"

"Of course they are real. They are here."

"Yes," he said. "You're right." He looked over to her to indicate they should take their leave of him, and saw a Camilla who looked new: transfigured, somehow, in this unfamiliar place, radiant and at peace.

"Do you think they're old?" he said, as they got up to leave.

The boy got up too and said, "The feeling is true. You cannot have an old feeling."

"You're right," he said again. "Thank you for the tea, for showing us your room."

"I show you only my room. You show me the light of God."

The answer was so genuine it shamed him, mocking his petty thoughts with its reference to what the poems meant, and the light that was their message.

Then, as they were walking to the door, the boy stopped again, as if he had been struck by something.

"I know who wrote those poems," he said.

"You do?"

"I know," said the boy, as they turned to him. "Your wife wrote them." He smiled. "You wrote them. I wrote them. In Qom we say, 'When we hear music, it is not coming from the radio.'"

"It all comes from God, you mean?"

"Thank you," said the boy, and then he was leading them down the steps, very fast, and back into the fallen world.

The next day, as they'd half expected, Iran fell away from them as if it had never happened. So far from everything they knew that even by the time they were in the airport, on the plane out, it seemed like a dream, or something they'd imagined. She fell asleep very soon, full up, no doubt, with all that she'd experienced, and he, paging through his notes for the last time, took out the crumbling pages as if to say goodbye to them.

The heart of their secret lay, he'd always felt, in the final two poems, the ones that seemed to have the least reason for being there. The well-known poem about the dove from Andalusia was a strange thing to put near the end, and the final one was so lacking in mystery, so clunky in its way, that at some level it seemed the most mysterious of all.

He looked down the long line of words trailing down in his translation.

> My hand
> Your hand
> Connected
> Over
> His hand.
> No division in
> Our hearts.

The "in" could be replaced by an "among," but that would not change very much at all. The only other word that could be different was that ungainly "connected" in the third line. He penned in "linked," but that hardly seemed to help at all. It could be "joined," too, and he wrote that in now to see if it would change anything.

He'd never know, years later, what moved him at that moment to look at the translation in that strange way, almost as if the words themselves were less important than the patterns they made on the page; almost as if they were glyphs or markings only, not carriers of meaning. But as he ran his eye quickly down the beginnings of the lines, he remembered something she'd told him once about the games she liked to play in school.

> M y hand
> Y our hand
> J oined
> O ver
> H is hand.
> N o division in
> O ur hearts.

He looked at her—closer than ever, perhaps, to a young man who had come from Tehran to Los Angeles, hope alight, and closer, even, perhaps, to a young woman who had come from Denmark to the

New World, with some hopes of her own, no doubt, and then he turned again to the last poem in the book but one.

> Asleep, and being comforted by a cool breeze,
> Suddenly, I saw a grey dove
> Soar above the trees and sob with longing;
> In her anguish, I heard my own.

The boy was right, he thought, putting the pages back in his pocket. Poems are what we make of them.

A Note of Thanks

As one who's never studied Islam or been close to Iran—and is of Hindu origin to boot—I was especially grateful, in pursuing this project, for whatever wisdom I could glean from others. To learn a little about Sufism and Rumi, I turned above all to the great Annemarie Schimmel and to Franklin Lewis; for a more general understanding of Islam and its place in the modern world, I was helped most by the writings of Akbar Ahmed, Malise Ruthven, and Seyyed Hossein Nasr; and for renderings of Sufi poetry, like many I was much inspired by Coleman Barks.

Among the many, many books on Iran that I consulted, I was most grateful for the fair-minded, open-eyed travel accounts of Christiane Bird, Robin Wright, V. S. Naipaul, Paul William Roberts, and the author of the heroic 1992 Lonely Planet guide to the country, David St. Vincent; for a more intimate sense of Iranian culture, I was especially helped by the novels of Shusha Guppy and Gina Nahai. One day in London, I picked up a new novel set in Isfahan, and found it to be written by an old schoolmate of mine, James Buchan; clearly, more than one student was dreaming of romantic Persia in our fifteenth-century Berkshire classroom. Most of all, I learned about the human side of Iran through the wise counsel of my new friend, Jasmin Saidi, my old friends Manou and Fariba Eskandari, Professor Abbas Amanat, and Sharon Rawlinson.

In bringing this book into print, I was buoyed beyond measure, as always, by the inspired wisdom and kindness of Lynn Nesbit—who, presented out of the blue with a manuscript about Sufism, was able to advise me on mysticism, tell me about her own trip to Rumi's tomb in Konya, and introduce me to an Iranian friend with whom she'd gone shopping for manuscripts in Damascus; and helped, too, by the legendary readers at Knopf, especially Sonny Mehta, Marty Asher, Robin Desser, and in particular my editor, Dan Frank, who threw himself into this book as passionately as if it were his own. Terry Zaroff-Evans copyedited the manuscript seamlessly, and Ayako Harvie and Rahel Lerner tended to my every need with grace. Nicholas Latimer, Pam Henstell, and Dave Hyde, among others, took wonderful care of me on the rare occasions when I emerged from my seclusion.

On a more private level, Peter MacLeod dug up fascinating background material in Toronto, and Mark Salzman and Steve Carlson read an early draft with responsive sympathy. Poor Michael Hofmann, my unpaid reader-in-chief, brought to every sentence his elegant, wise sense of when to speak and when to stay silent.

In certain invisible but essential ways this book is the product of the weeks and months I have spent at the New Camaldoli Hermitage in California for more than a dozen years now, and I owe the brothers and fathers of that Benedictine order more than I can ever say. Inspiration at home came from my mother, Nandini Iyer, a lifelong student and teacher of mysticism, and from my friend Patrick O'Donnell, who emptied his shelves to assist me. And in my tiny apartment in the middle of a Japanese nowhere, I was deeply grateful for such inspiration as came from far away, whether publicly, in the work of James Nachtwey, Peter Brook, U2, and Leonard Cohen, among others, or privately, in the warm and supportive messages of Tony Cohan, Mark Muro, and Susanna Kaysen. It seems only right to me that a book about love should be written in the company of my talisman, Hiroko Takeuchi, and of her equally radiant and thoughtful children Sachi and Takashi.

Permissions Acknowledgments

Grateful acknowledgment is made to the following for permission to reprint previously published material:

Coleman Barks: Excerpts adapted from *The Essential Rumi* translated by Coleman Barks. Copyright © by Coleman Barks. Reprinted by permission of the author.

Continuum Publishing Company: Excerpts adapted from *My Soul Is a Woman* by Annemarie Schimmel. English translation copyright © 1997 by The Continuum Publishing Company. Reprinted by permission of the Continuum Publishing Company.

University of Wisconsin Press: Excerpts adapted from *Debating Muslims: Cultural Dialogues in Postmodernity and Tradition* by Michael M. J. Fischer and Mehdi Abedi. Copyright © 1990. Reprinted by permission of the University of Wisconsin Press.

A Note About the Author

Pico Iyer is the author of several books
about the romance between cultures,
including *Video Night in Kathmandu,*
The Lady and the Monk, Cuba and
the Night, and, most recently, *The Global*
Soul. He lives in suburban Japan.

A Note on the Type

The text of this book was set in Sabon, a typeface
designed by Jan Tschichold (1902–1974), the
well-known German typographer. Based loosely
on the original designs by Claude Garamond
(c. 1480–1561), Sabon is unique in that it was
explicitly designed for hotmetal composition on
both the Monotype and the Linotype machines as
well as for filmsetting. Designed in 1966 in
Frankfurt, Sabon was named for the famous Lyon
punch cutter Jacques Sabon, who is thought to have
brought some of Garamond's matrices to Frankfurt.

Composed by Creative Graphics,
Allentown, Pennsylvania
Printed and bound by R. R. Donnelley & Sons,
Harrisonburg, Virginia
Designed by Anthea Lingeman